PRAISE FOR MARY-A

'The writing in this novel is vivid and
lifelike. Fans of historical romance will fall in love with this third novel from Mary-Anne O'Connor. *War Flower* is a roller-coaster of emotions. One minute it'll have you laughing; the next you'll be heartbroken. It's that good.'

— *Good Reading Magazine* on *War Flower*

'Mary-Anne O'Connor writes a great love story, and *War Flower* is no exception. It is a story of love, war, and forgiveness set against the political upheaval of the swinging sixties in Sydney and the killing fields of Vietnam.'

— *Better Reading* on *War Flower*

'O'Connor has written an insightful and well researched novel that explores the lives of the young men who were conscripted into service as well as what life was like in the sixties for those left behind.'

— *Beauty and Lace* on *War Flower*

'The story has multiple stories within that wove together in what is an attention grabbing story. Ms O'Connor's third book is heartfelt and full of controversial moments.'

— *Talking Books on War Flower*

'As we reflect on the lasting impact of a war that occurred a hundred years ago, Mary-Anne O'Connor brings us a story celebrating the good that can spring from war—love, hope and courage. In the heart-warming and heart-wrenching *Gallipoli Street*, the lives of three families will be irrevocably altered ... from one Great War to the next, family and faith provides the ultimate reminder of what it truly means to be human.'

— Meredith Jaffe, *The Hoopla*, on *Gallipoli Street*

'Through her sensitivity, beautiful writing and gift as a storyteller, O'Connor's readers come to know and love her characters.'

— *The Weekly Times* on *Gallipoli Street*

'In *Worth Fighting For*, author Mary-Anne O'Connor has drawn on her family history to create the characters of this wartime romance, set in country NSW, the big smoke of Sydney as well as Darwin and New Guinea as the war in the Pacific rages.'

— *The Weekly Times* on *Worth Fighting For*

'This book is a heartfelt tribute to the war experience, both on the front and the sacrifices made on home soil, featuring an enigmatic leading lady...O'Connor takes us on a journey to country Australia, to cities such as Sydney and Darwin, along with the battlefields of the Pacific, the harshness of Papua New Guinea and all the way to Pearl Harbour in her novel. As a result, *Worth Fighting For* is a book that is rich in historical detail.'

— *Mrs B's Book Reviews* on *Worth Fighting For*

'Ultimately *Worth Fighting For* is a tale of love, of hanging on and holding out hope when all seems lost. A tale of enduring through hardship and learning to live with the nightmares; a tale of hope, of loss, of friendship, betrayal and resilience.'

— *Beauty and Lace* on *Worth Fighting For*

About the Author

Mary-Anne O'Connor has a combined arts education degree with specialities in environment, music and literature. She works in marketing and co-wrote/edited *A Brush with Light* and *Secrets of the Brush* with Kevin Best.

Mary-Anne lives in a house overlooking her beloved bushland in northern Sydney with her husband Anthony, their two sons Jimmy and Jack, and their very spoilt dog Saxon. This is her third major novel. Her first, *Gallipoli Street*, was published in 2015, followed by *Worth Fighting For* in 2016. Both novels have become bestsellers.

Also by Mary-Anne O'Connor

Gallipoli Street
Worth Fighting For

WAR FLOWER

MARY-ANNE O'CONNOR

First Published 2017
Second Australian Paperback Edition 2019
ISBN 9781489263506

This is a work of fiction. Names, characters, places, and incidents are either the product of the author's imagination or are used fictitiously, and any resemblance to actual persons, living or dead, business establishments, events, or locales is entirely coincidental.

Published by
HQ Fiction
An imprint of Harlequin Enterprises (Australia) Pty Ltd.
Level 13, 201 Elizabeth St
SYDNEY NSW 2000
AUSTRALIA

Cataloguing-in-Publication details are available from the National Library of Australia
www.librariesaustralia.nla.gov.au

Printed and bound in Australia by McPherson's Printing Group

For my brother Matthew

There is nothing on earth more powerful than love,
no gentler bestowment than compassion,
no greater goal than peace.

Part One

Walls

One

Sydney, New South Wales, Australia, July 1965

'Might snow.'

Poppy Flannery gave him a nod, finding an expression that she hoped neither patronised nor encouraged the drunk as he huddled in his blanket on the ground, slurping from something in a brown paper bag.

She would have liked to inform him that she was studying geography as part of her leaving certificate and there was no evidence of it *ever* having snowed in Hornsby, at least as far as she was aware. Then she imagined what it might be like to spend the winter on a railway station and emptied her purse into his beggar's hat instead.

'Don't encourage 'im,' the station master warned her as he passed by, but he didn't try to evict the man and she was glad. Perhaps the company of constant, random strangers gave him comfort.

The drunk burst into a merry rendition of 'Let it Snow! Let it Snow! Let it Snow!' and the words followed her as she moved along. She half wished it would – at least they'd have something miraculous to cheer them up on this dreary day; it was so cold her fingers were icy little sausages that curled up inside her jumper sleeves. To make matters worse the train was late and now pulling in slowly, clanking and straining in crimson steel which had long earned these models the moniker of 'red rattlers'.

Poppy dragged her things on board, the smells of dank uniforms and forgotten lunches at the bottom of school cases filling her nostrils as she collapsed on the vinyl bench seat. It was wet but she was grateful for it, regardless. Most afternoons she was forced to stand, crowded as the carriages always were during the earlier school rush.

Pushing damp strands of blonde from her eyes and under her hat Poppy steadied her cello case as the train lurched forward, trying not to lose control of her other belongings lest they slide across the floor. That achieved, she relaxed somewhat, free now to take in the other passengers. Her eyes passed over the young boy picking at a scab on his hand and the elderly lady reading her book to keep scanning, spying familiar figures chatting beyond the doors: Barbara Rowntree, Judith Bentley and Raeleen Montgomery, three particularly vicious 'cool chicks' who were probably going home late due to detention. Poppy's twin sister Rosemary had dubbed them 'the Dogsquad' years ago when they first began to bully everyone outside the in-crowd.

The trio had taken off their hats and were now shaking their long, wet plaits free, a calculated risk considering Sister Ignatius often patrolled the trains to ensure uniform rules were being obeyed. Poppy suspected they did it mostly for the benefit of the boy who stood near the door and turned to investigate him herself.

He was quite attractive, tall and fair in his camouflage fatigues with a cadet beret thrown casually on his school bag. Watching him almost with the whites of her eyes lest he notice her stare, she observed that he was unwrapping something bound in milk bar paper. Something that smelt very, very good in the fetid air. This was what the police should use to torture the bad guys into talking, she thought to herself as the scent arrived in force. Then she couldn't think much further because her salivary glands exploded, flooding her mouth until she almost drooled onto her jumper.

Oh dear God, they've added vinegar.

Poppy forgot to hide her stare now as the boy lifted one fried, salty potato scallop in the air and took a big bite, ripping the crispy coating from its white, soft innards. The air around his mouth fogged from the sudden heat in the cold carriage air and his lips were shiny as he chewed, mouth half open, probably from burning his tongue, but he didn't seem to care. Suddenly she wanted to kiss that mouth even more than she wanted to eat those delicious golden discs, so sensual was his pleasure, so eager his hunger as his mouth devoured that flesh.

Then he did notice her and she felt herself blush as he paused mid-chew. A slightly teasing smile spread across his face, transforming him from 'quite attractive' to 'bloody gorgeous'.

Licking his fingers, he offered her the wafting pile. 'Want some?'

There was something so suggestive about it she could almost imagine he was asking her to share in carnal adventures rather than fried potatoes and her cheeks flamed as the old lady looked up with a disapproving frown, sliding her gaze from the boy to Poppy.

'I do,' said a voice heavy with flirtation.

The Dogsquad were on the prowl and Poppy could only watch as they approached, swinging their hair about and grabbing onto poles in predatory fashion. Rosemary predicted they would seduce the richest men they could find after graduation and have more money than any of the 'dags', the group she and Poppy were usually considered part of. Unless they got themselves pregnant over summer and stuffed up their North Shore housewife careers, Rosemary had added hopefully.

The train paused at Warrawee Station, sighing into inactivity, and the boy let them take a scallop which the prowlers divided and ate with exaggerated rapture.

'Mmm,' Barbara said, smiling at him as she licked her lips. The boy continued to eat, watching them almost expectantly, like he was used to this kind of attack. Then he shifted his gaze back towards Poppy and to her shock gave her a wink.

Contempt soured Barbara's otherwise pretty face and Poppy tensed, knowing retaliation would be swift and sharp.

'What are you doing coming home so late, *Ploppy*? Are you in an oompa loompa band or something?' she sneered, nodding at the cello. The other two girls laughed and all eyes in the carriage turned Poppy's way.

'Just the school band,' she mumbled, wishing she had the courage to tell Barbara such Bavarian groups were made up of brass musicians, not string, but of course that would just prolong the ridicule and scrutiny. Truth was she loved her cello and was majoring in music, hoping it would be her ticket to ride, as the Beatles would say, straight into university.

'Maybe she had to go to pirate class,' Raeleen suggested and Barbara let out a short laugh.

'Yes, where is that eye-patch these days, freak-show, or is Mummy changing the pattern?' Poppy felt every part of her body tense up at the mention of her most embarrassing teenage moment: the day her mother covered half her glasses with orange floral wallpaper to hide the gauze and bandaging beneath. Having an eye operation at thirteen was bad enough, having every person she passed stare and laugh at her mother's attempt to pretty the situation up was social suicide. The eye healed eventually, so well she no longer even had to wear glasses, but the stigma had long remained.

Fortunately the boy didn't ask any questions, seemingly more intent on finishing his feast, and Barbara moved closer, flirtatious facade back in place.

'And why are *you* home late? Or is this your normal time to catch the train?'

Poppy let out a relieved breath, glad to have the focus shifted from her, and listened to the answer. She had been wondering that herself; Poppy knew most of the boys on this train-line after six years of high school – by sight only, for the most part. Staring at his beret and fatigues she figured he probably had cadet training after school.

'Drills on Thursdays.' He shrugged. 'We moved recently. I used to live in Adelaide.'

'Lucky Adelaide,' Barbara observed.

The elderly lady made a noise of disgust and Poppy couldn't have agreed more. Looking at Judith and Raeleen she wondered how they felt about always being in Barbara's shadow while she did her thing as Queen Bee. Rosemary liked to say they all knew what the 'B' stood for.

The boy was starting to look uncomfortable and put on his beret to hide it, something that made Poppy like him even more.

'My station,' he said, moving towards the door as the train pulled into Wahroonga.

'What's your name?' Barbara called out as he alighted.

'Ben,' he called back, walking off with his back hunched against the rain.

Ben. The name echoed in Poppy's head as the Dogsquad ran back to their double seats, no doubt to dissect the whole scene and scheme about a way to run into him again. With their aptitude for earning detention, Poppy figured that wouldn't take long.

The train arrived at Waitara and she clutched both school case and umbrella in one hand, dragging her cello with the other, but the umbrella's fine material was flimsy defence against this particular afternoon. The wind whipped at her little arc, turning it inside out and flipping her about with it as the rain tapped at her face like a typewriter. Poppy struggled against it almost instinctively, her mind still reeling from the previous assault on her senses.

Ben. Each tiny shock of rain in her eyes reinforced the shock of his impact.

'Pass,' the ticket officer ordered and she wriggled to retrieve it from her bag and show it to him. She wished the dratted man would stop asking her every day – surely he recognised her by now. It was difficult to remain inconspicuous carrying a massive instrument. But she forgave him as music wafted from the little transistor he always carried, the sound of the Ronettes following her down the stairs in a freezing draught of winter. Their voices were filled with longing and she knew that song had just become the soundtrack to many hours of daydreaming about a boy on a train. A boy called Ben who wore camouflage fatigues and tempted her with salt and vinegar.

Then she lost her battle with the wind and watched her umbrella take flight and sail down the street, realising right at that moment that any attempt to ignore the force of that boy would be as futile as fighting the elements this day. The day that he became, to one rain-soaked girl clutching a cello case on the side of a road, her one and only baby.

'For what we are about to receive may the Lord make us truly thankful. Amen.'

It was quiet as they commenced eating. Robert Flannery didn't believe in having the radio on during dinner, let alone the television. He said it distracted them from appreciating how fortunate they were to have a good, solid meal in front of them every night. Besides, it was also an opportunity for everyone to share their news. The girls hated doing that. It was almost as bad as going to Confession, although Father John was far easier to appease than their parents. A few Hail Marys and all spots on the soul were dissolved in that little cubicle. Here in the Flannerys' kitchen nothing less than lives lived in perfect Catholic schoolgirl servitude would suffice and spots on the soul were considered grave stains.

'How was school today, Rosemary?' their mother, Lois, asked, looking at her expectantly.

'Very satisfying. I managed to get eighty-seven in that Chemistry exam which wasn't too bad considering the average was only seventy-two.'

It was a good pitch but Poppy knew her father wouldn't be satisfied.

'Thirteen marks short of what you're capable of though, isn't it, young lady?'

Rosemary sighed. 'Yes, sir,' she mumbled, picking at her peas.

'And what of you, Poppy?'

She raised her eyes heavenward, looking for inspiration. 'The recital went down well at practice although it kept me late and the train was –' filled with the aroma of delicious scallops and an even more delicious boy called Ben, '– delayed too.' Her father looked about to comment and she rushed to add something that would please him. 'I saw a homeless man drinking from a brown paper bag on the station. He looked so cold, he even said it was going to snow so I…er…gave him my pocket money.'

'Is that wise, considering what he will most likely spend it on?' her mother asked, fork pausing mid-air.

'No, well…perhaps not.'

'It's a better idea to give a man like that some food or clothing,' Robert advised between mouthfuls.

'Rosemary gave him her sandwich last week,' Poppy informed them, thinking that might put her sister in the good books.

'Did you? And why are you giving away my expensive ham?' her mother asked, unimpressed.

Rosemary's mouth dropped open as she looked from one parent to the other, like those clown heads at the Easter Show, Poppy observed, waiting for a ping pong ball. 'Well…he just…he looked hungrier than me.'

Their father sat back, observing the twins as they awaited his verdict. 'Matthew 25:40.'

Both girls quoted at once: 'Jesus said, "Whatever you did for one of the least of these brothers and sisters of mine, you did for me."'

'Quite so,' he said, nodding slowly. 'Charity should be your way of life, every day. But charity also begins at home. Is it charitable to give away your mother's ham after her hard work making your nutritious lunches each day?' He looked to them both and they knew he expected no answer. Robert Flannery enjoyed his dinner sermons far too much to tolerate interruption. 'Then again, if we walk past the least of our brothers without compassion we let the Lord down, do we not?' He tapped his knife thoughtfully on the tablecloth. 'You need to appreciate the hard work that comes with true charity as opposed to giving what you already easily have. Tomorrow you will both make your own lunches and this man's as well. To give truly is to put *all* others first.'

'And no messing up my kitchen,' Lois added, frowning, probably at the thought of a single starched tea towel out of place.

'Yes Mum,' they agreed.

Later that night Poppy stretched herself away from the table where she and Rosemary were studying and walked over to the window to see if the rain had eased.

'Well would you look at that…'

'What is it? Saints alive – Mum! Dad!' Rosemary called, rushing to open the front door, a sudden gust of ice invading the heated room.

The family joined her on the porch, each mesmerised by the sight of what appeared to be some kind of miracle. Snow had fallen on their Sydney yard, cloaking gum trees and sleeping hibiscus, transforming the lawn into a silver carpet in the moonlight. It was a wonderland. Like the pictures they'd seen in storybooks from Europe and America, where Santa arrived on a sleigh and children built snowmen that came to life.

The twins rushed out, picking up the powdery stuff and hurling snowballs across the drive, their laughter on the freezing air.

'Careful now,' Lois called, but their parents didn't try to stop them having fun for a change and the girls enjoyed that miracle too, pausing in their game to build their very own man of snow.

'What shall we call him?' Rosemary said breathlessly as they added two pebbles for eyes and a short stick for a nose.

'Ben,' Poppy replied, giggling at her sister's confused expression. 'I'll tell you later,' she promised.

It was quite late by the time Poppy shared her secret with her sister, in an excited whispering that had them looking forward to their dreams, and, as she clutched her pillow and gazed out at the beautiful night, she knew with certainty that her life had changed on this miraculous day.

Yes, let it snow, and let it be a sign that the beautiful night promised her the beautiful boy. That the magic wouldn't melt away, come tomorrow.

Two

'Come on, give us a look,' Graham 'Chappy' Chapman complained, trying to peer at the grainy faces over the rest of the group's shoulders. 'Is that Barbara Rowntree in the netball photo? Man, she is smoking.'

'One and the same. I remember she had a bra in sixth class,' Chris Plumpton said with authority. 'My mum plays tennis with hers. Nice family genes, if you know what I mean.'

'You're a sick puppy,' John Hawkens said with a shake of his head, but peered harder through his glasses just the same. They had gathered in the library with a few others to look through the convent school yearbook and research possible hook-ups at the school dance come Friday.

'Wait till you see her, Ben,' Chris said, pointing Barbara out. 'Bet you've got nothing like that in Adelaide.'

Ben studied the face and shrugged. 'Not in Adelaide but I think I met this girl on the train last week. Had some friends with her...a redhead and brunette?'

'Judith Bentley and Raeleen Montgomery.' Chris sighed. 'Divinity comes in threes.'

'Did you talk to her?' Chappy asked, half joking.

'Yeah, a bit. She came up and asked me for a scallop.'

'*She* came up to *you*?' The others were staring, impressed.

'Well, yeah. They were good scallops.'

'Let me explain something here,' Chris said, enunciating carefully, 'a girl like Barbara Rowntree doesn't approach *anyone,* even to get a free bit of potato. Guys approach *her.*'

'If they have the guts,' Chappy added, still slightly incredulous. 'What else did she say?'

'Just asked me why I was travelling home late and stuff.'

'Yep, she's definitely after him,' John said, looking to a thoughtful Chris for confirmation.

'Let me ask you something...did she swish her hair around like this?' Chris made quite a show of flicking his imaginary locks and the others laughed.

'She did do that a bit, actually,' Ben admitted.

'In like Flynn,' Chris declared. 'You have to make the most of this, my friend. An opportunity to score with Barbara is a rare and precious gift.'

'I don't know,' Ben said, shrugging. 'Maybe...'

'You're not thinking straight, man. Look at her!' Chris said, pointing back at the photo. 'There is no "maybe" here. You need to strike while the iron's hot.'

'...and the girl's hot,' Chappy agreed.

'We'll see,' Ben said, moving away as the bell sounded.

'*We'll see...*geez, you've got rocks in your head,' Chris told him as they made their way down the stairs. 'She obviously likes you.'

Guess she did make that obvious, Ben thought to himself as they lined up for assembly, wondering why that didn't excite him more. Then the national anthem began to play and he shut down any further thoughts of girls. There really wasn't that much point.

'It's hopeless,' Poppy said as she stared in dismay at the mirror. 'She won't let us wear anything that dates past nineteen-fifty. It's like she's trying to repel boys from us.'

'Of course she is,' Rosemary told her, frowning at the brown velvet and tugging at the hem. 'Maybe if we roll up the waistband...'

'Maybe if we just don't go...'

'Oh no you don't. You can't go telling me about some dreamy boy on the train then not go to his school dance.'

'Maybe he won't go.'

'Everyone goes. Try this,' Rosemary ordered, throwing a twin-set and skirt her way.

'Twins in twin-sets? We'll look stupid!'

'Pffi, guys don't know what they're called,' Rosemary said, turning up the radio. 'Ohh, maybe we could wear these.' Poppy had to laugh as her sister pulled out the fancy dress box, putting on their mother's long evening gloves and pointing dramatically as she sang along to the opening verse of 'My Guy'. Poppy sang back, giggling and dancing too. Clothes and costumes were held up and discarded in comical fashion now as both girls tried to outdo the other for bad taste; not a difficult challenge considering the contents of the box.

'Stop in the Name of Love' came next and well-practised routines took over as they mirrored each other, imitating Motown stars they'd seen on *The Ed Sullivan Show.*

'It's no use,' Poppy said finally, breathless with laughter as the song ended, and she fell on her bed. 'We'll have to be hideous.'

'Hmm,' Rosemary said thoughtfully, stroking the long gloves. 'You know, there may just be a way to make this work.'

'Unless you find a magic wand or a fairy godmother in that box I fail to see how.'

Rosemary turned to her and grinned. 'Not quite…but I think I may have just had the most magical idea of my entire life.'

Three nights later those words were reverberating in Poppy's frantic mind.

'So much for magical ideas,' she whispered in her sister's ear.

Rosemary didn't respond, but her eyes were very round as conversation in the room fell to hushed whispers and one by one people paused to stare. Poppy figured she'd pretty much give anything for a real wand right about now. Maybe then they could just disappear. But no, here they were, stuck at the doors of a boys' high school hall; the only (almost) identical twins, the only ones in exactly matching outfits and the only ones in full evening dresses that looked straight out the pages of a nineteen-fifties debutante ball.

And, as wretched, predictable fate would have it, the Dogsquad were making their smirking way towards them.

Barbara stood in front, model-like in a designer pencil skirt, expensive perfume wafting. She raked them from head to toe through thick black eyeliner, taking in every detail from their pale pink gloves to their heavily sprayed hair. 'And what the hell are you supposed to be?'

Poppy watched Rosemary's mouth open and close like a fish. Why couldn't her witty sister ever find words around these people?

'Some kind of experiment in bad taste, I'd say,' Judith said, copying Barbara's hostile stance in her blue and white shift dress. What Poppy wouldn't give to be wearing that number right now instead of her sister's misguided idea of a quirky twin fantasy theme.

'Why do the Flannery duo always look ridiculous?' Barbara said with a sarcastic, pitiful sigh.

'Because they arrrrrre,' Raeleen replied, pirate style, and Barbara and Judith laughed.

Poppy felt her face burn but it was too late to attempt a reply because the boy called Ben was walking towards them too, devastatingly good-looking in a black jumper and dark trousers and followed by a posse of his friends. Poppy felt her heart begin to hammer, and she clenched her purse hard.

'Well, hello Adelaide,' cooed Barbara, hand on perfect hip. 'Ready to hit the dancefloor? I've been practising all week, just for you.'

'Sure,' Ben replied, but surprisingly he barely glanced Barbara's way. He was too busy staring at Poppy and Rosemary instead.

'Twins?' he finally said, looking from one sister to the other. Then he locked in on Poppy and smiled that lightning bolt smile of his and her opinion of him went from 'bloody gorgeous' to 'beyond McCartney'.

But then the music started and her moment in his sun faded into the strains of the Beatles as Barbara reached over and grabbed Ben's hand, twisting him away. Then the other boys were grabbing other girls' hands and the twins were left to skirt the fringes of the hall and find the chairs where wallflowers such as themselves sat in discarded rows. To watch, to ache and to pray someone would come over and take their hands too.

'Well, you were right about one thing.' Rosemary sighed.

'What was I ever right about?'

'He actually *is* beautiful.'

And so he was. All the wallflowers were watching him, the boy with the golden hair dancing with the girl who no-one ever resisted; the girl who had any guy she wanted whenever she wanted them and who made sure every other girl in the room felt pathetic in comparison. Barbara had all the right moves, often bragging about her dancing awards, and she was using them to full advantage on that dance floor, seducing Ben with every sway of those perfect hips. Poppy could only watch from the wall, feeling insignificant now and overlooked.

'Rosemary! Poppy!' called a voice, and they were distracted by the sight of Peter Ryan approaching with his friend Ernie. They weren't the best looking guys around, in fact they were pretty much dags like themselves, but these two boys were always nice to the twins when they met in debating competitions and tonight it seemed they'd finally summoned up the courage to ask them to dance.

'Would you…can we…?'

Close enough, Poppy decided, jumping up with Rosemary. A ticket off the wall wasn't something to pass up.

Then they were in the throng, the bassline from the Yardbirds pumping in their ribcages and guiding their feet. Ernie and Peter were enthusiastic if nothing else and they soon had the girls laughing and twirling about in their bell skirts. They were even attempting the odd clumsy compliment that took some of the sting out of the terrible start to the evening.

'I think you look like a double dose of Doris Day!' declared Ernie and the girls giggled some more, allowing the boys to take them over to the refreshments table. Unfortunately, Barbara was nearby whispering god knows what in Ben's ear and Poppy couldn't help but watch them in pained fascination: the casual way her hand rested on his shoulder, the curve of his mouth as he smiled then blushed slightly at the messages being delivered.

'Want some punch in your punch?' Peter dared them, breaking Poppy out of her reverie and opening his jacket to reveal a hidden hipflask.

Poppy had never had alcohol before, except church wine of course. She probably would never have considered making her drinking debut at a school dance either, if not for Barbara deciding at that moment to kiss Ben square on the lips. That and the fact that Rosemary was already sticking out her glass and saying 'hit me' like a pro.

A few sly 'hits' later the night began to change. Suddenly the music was an irresistible force and they needed to share the feeling. The moves they practised privately in their bedroom were now on public display as they invited an ever-widening circle to join them in dancing to 'Stop in the Name of Love'. Twin left arms swam, twin right legs twisted, hands were on shaking hips and their audience was loving it, clapping in unison and urging them on.

Then Ernie was lifting them onto the stage and they were directing the room, pointing their fingers and encouraging five hundred teenagers to think it over.

It was a happy blur of influence, a rush of previously untasted feminine power. They shimmied to the left and the mob followed suit, they turned back to back and the crowd roared in approval. *We're a hit,* Poppy thought to herself with a giggle.

Then her gaze landed on a face in that crowd and all that strange new power the wallflower never knew she had flowed into one steady stream, straight into his eyes. *I'll be good to you*; she sent Ben the message and he mouthed the words back, like an actual promise, before Barbara moved in front and she was forced to break the link.

But as she stuffed breath mints in her mouth and waited for her father to collect them later that night Poppy clung to the residue the moment had left behind. They may have made a questionable fashion statement, they may even have made massive fools of themselves, dancing like intoxicated back-up singers on stage, but nothing could take away a third shift in their universe tonight:

Ben had felt her power in that moment too. She'd somehow delivered a brazen message, filled with possibilities she had no idea how to fulfil, and he'd accepted it, tasted it and held it for those few precious seconds.

Then he'd sent his own message straight on back.

Three

...and military experts say full protection from such attacks is impossible in this jungle war...

Ben watched the black and white images flicker on the television, glad he was at least spared the reality of colour, imagining the dark red of the bloodstains that marked the earth near the rubble. *You'll be seeing it first-hand soon enough,* his inner voice reminded him. He pushed it aside, turning off the news and making his way downstairs to where the colour could be controlled.

The smell of linseed oil, turpentine and paint greeted him and he breathed it in deeply, instantly comforted by the familiar world of art. After only a few short weeks of them moving in his new studio was a mess already and he was glad his parents seldom ventured into this private domain. They indulged his use of the space but wouldn't be impressed with the disarray that marred their otherwise stately and immaculate residence. Canvases were stacked haphazardly, brushes were clumped in tins and rags hung out of the drawers below rows of paint tubes, but it was an organised chaos to him.

Take a canvas, choose your brushes, fill the palette and tins.

The preparation process offered rhythmical comfort and he performed each step methodically, falling easily into the familiar routine, clearing his mind as he went.

Stare outside, relax. Deep breath. Begin.

The brush moved boldly, a swish of brilliant blue that danced to the left and found form. It was a bird, no, a woman. No, definitely a bird. Its wings were in flight, a blur of cerulean that ran now with the oil. He raised another brush and added green, watching the wings flutter before him, rapid in their movement. Their escape. Fly, fly, fly. He washed in a golden sky then a dark earth, stabbing at the muddy depths, then gliding above it.

'Fly,' he muttered out loud at the feathered tips of his subject.

'Wouldn't expect much else from a bird,' said a voice from the doorway.

Ben jumped with a start, almost dropping his brush before collecting himself and lowering his arm.

'True,' he acknowledged, nodding at his father and wiping his hands on a rag. 'Evening, sir.'

'Evening,' his father returned, quite jovially for him, but it was Sunday of course. Three scotches at the golf club then a gin and tonic tonight with his wife before dinner. The only drinks of the week, exactly according to routine.

Ben watched as Supreme Court Judge Thompson Charles Williamson, Charles to those who knew him, took a tour of the room.

'Quite a collection you have going on,' he said in vague surprise, probably at the sheer number of half-finished works on display. Ben briefly wondered if he should show him the few finished pieces he had in the corner but then dismissed the idea.

'What's this one then? Self-portrait?' He indicated a melancholy painting featuring a man staring into a mirror, one eye red, one brown, murky green pools in the basin before him.

'Not really,' Ben lied, unwilling to discuss the deeper messages in his work.

'Hmm,' said his father, seemingly amused at the concept. 'Bit way out for my taste but I suppose it's a break from all the study, eh?'

'Yes,' Ben said. 'It is.'

Charles picked up a smaller work, a painting of a cello case leaning against a train bench.

'I don't mind this…well, at least I understand what it actually is.' He smiled briefly and Ben tried to return it, still wondering why he was here. There would be an agenda. There always was.

'I spoke to the dean today – seems to think there won't be any issue in deferring your degree until you've finished service.'

Ben nodded. He'd expected that.

'Meanwhile…' Charles handed Ben a letter and something akin to pride crossed his face. Looking at the insignia on the top of the envelope Ben instantly understood why.

'Duntroon has accepted me?' A brief nod from his father and a scan of the contents confirmed that Thompson Benjamin Williamson would represent the third generation of men in his family to attend Australia's most prestigious officer training college.

He tried to look pleased, for his father's sake, but all he could really manage was a combination of resignation and compliance. No mean feat when a savage thrust of resentment sought to override it.

'Come upstairs when you're done here,' his father said, clapping him on the back before leaving. 'I think it's time you tasted your first real scotch.'

In truth he'd tasted it plenty of times before, siphoning small amounts from various bottles to take to parties in a single canteen of 'rocket fuel'. It always left a vile taste in his mouth.

He turned back to the bird on the canvas, staring at it for a moment before picking up a rag to wipe at it viciously, the brilliant blue bleeding into the brown, the gold glow smeared now with green. He rubbed until small particles began to pill on the board and his arms grew numb from exertion. Then he turned and walked away, not looking back in his usual way to cast one last view at his work of the day.

There wasn't much to see after all, just a vague, murky stain.

Four

The soft beauty of the string quartet floated down the corridor, brushing by the girl sitting on the steps before drifting out into the mist and rain. The stone was cold and it was making her backside numb but it was better than standing, Poppy figured, she just wished she could numb her brain as easily. Make it stop re-hashing the same thoughts over and over again. Was Ben really interested in Barbara or just going along for the ride? So to speak. She blushed at the unintended and unwanted pun. Would he be on the train this Thursday? Would he offer her a scallop? A lightning bolt smile? A secret message, just for her?

Would she ever be able to focus on anything else again in her life?

You'd better, she told herself, flipping open her Latin text with a frown and mouthing through the phrases. Exam trials were in three weeks and she was getting quite concerned that all-encompassing ruminations on a handsome boy were about to ruin her chances at a Pharmacy degree. It was bad enough she and Rosemary had turned into minor celebrities overnight and now had the admiration of the dags as well as the scorn of the cool chicks to deal with on a daily basis, especially Barbara's. She'd been less than impressed that the twins had taken the focus off her as the queen of the dancefloor the other night. The last thing Poppy needed was any more distracting thoughts to further clutter her already overladen mind.

But the lilting sound of Bach on Rosemary's violin was already plucking memories from her heart and planting them in the fertile soil of her imagination. Messages, messages. One face in the crowd. What if she had leapt off that stage, run over to him, shoved Barbara out of the way and…?

The sound of someone singing 'Stop! In the Name of Love' interrupted her thoughts and Poppy turned to see one of her classmates, Daniella Rossi, walking by, grinning as she went past in a swing of long brown plaits. It was a friend, not an enemy. The enemies swung weapons, not happy songs and innocent braids.

Stop in the name of your leaving certificate, Poppy told herself, flicking to a practice test to improve her focus.

1. *Dea <u>tantum invidiae</u> demonstravit.*
   a) of such jealousy
   b) which jealousy
   c) so much jealousy
   d) jealousy itself

Was she jealous of Barbara? Pluck, pluck, pluck. The memories pricked in time with the strings. Barbara's hand on his shoulder, her mouth covering his. Jealousy was growing in that mind-soil alright; it was coiling and thriving like a terrible vine, twisting through her body and strangling her soul.

She closed her eyes, forcing Barbara away, placing her own hand on Ben's shoulder, her own lips against the mouth that delivered those devastating smiles. Then the terrible vine morphed into something else; something longing to bloom, desperate to thrive. Each note was pulling it stronger, thicker in its yearning, and heavy buds clung to its branches, aching to unfold; to burst into colour and beauty.

To sway in delicious dance with the boy who shone like the sun.

Then she opened her eyes to the tears of rain instead and the wrenching music faded into it, leaving her alone, in reality. Just a girl sitting by herself on a numbing step.

Doors were flung open then and voices carried towards her as Rosemary arrived, excitement in her expression.

'See you tomorrow,' she called out and both twins waved to their classmates then gathered their things. 'Guess what?' Rosemary said, dropping her umbrella in her eagerness to tell.

'Oh no, whatever it is I don't want to know. I can't have any more stuff clouding my brain,' Poppy warned, shoving her book in her bag.

'Looks like you're going to have to. Guess who's been asked to try out for the Catholic Schools Orchestra?'

'You,' Poppy guessed, not terribly challenged.

'*Both of us*! And guess where the concert is being performed?' She didn't bother pausing this time. 'Surfers Paradise! That's in Queensland, Poppy. *Queens-land*.'

'Dad will never let us go,' Poppy told her sister.

'It's supervised. Sister Margaret and Sister Pauline are going.'

Poppy paused. 'Seriously?'

'Seriously.'

'Mr Roach says we're a dead cert.'

Mr Roach was their 'groovy' music teacher and liked to use expressions like 'dead cert' and 'happening thing'. The nuns didn't exactly approve of him and Poppy knew it was a 'dead cert' that he wouldn't be going to Brisbane.

'Poppy, it's *Queensland*. Beach parties and bikinis and…and surfies!'

'How are we supposed to do any of that when we're playing in an orchestra?' Poppy reasoned, amused at her sister's enthusiasm despite her scepticism. It had manifested into a little hopping routine.

'It's only two concerts over a whole week!'

'But it's supervised...' Poppy reminded her.

'Think about who by...'

She had a point there. Sister Margaret was getting on a bit and tended to doze off in class; she wouldn't be a likely candidate for late night surveillance. And Sister Pauline was the nicest nun at the school – everyone knew she was a big softie and hated discipline. The potential for adventure was certainly ripe.

'Queens-land,' Rosemary squealed, with perfectly timed hops.

Poppy felt a smile begin to spread across her face. 'When are these try-outs?'

It was Thursday, 'B-Day' as Rosemary had termed it: the day Ben caught the late train, but despite all the anticipation the carriage had proven sadly Ben-less. Poppy tried not to feel the horrible taste of disappointment settle in her mouth as the rattler click-clacked its way down the line.

At least it had stopped raining, finally, and the sun had returned. Imagine if he just appeared with it, she thought dreamily.

Then he did.

Like a magic trick she'd seen at the circus once when the magician made a girl in spangled shorts disappear in a black cupboard, then mysteriously re-materialise. Poppy had always wondered how he did that.

But this was an even better trick. She seemed to have made him appear out of sheer longing, the connection door between carriages swinging shut behind him. Dressed in fatigues, like a hero in a war movie. Devastating smile in place.

'Hey,' he said, sitting down opposite and throwing his hat on his bag casually, like he changed carriages and sat with her every day.

'Hey,' she returned, trying to sound cool but half swallowing the word. Her insides had turned into a bucket of eels and she wondered if he could actually see her pulse pumping at her temples.

'Hungry?' he asked, taking a paper-wrapped milk bar parcel out of his bag, the waft of potato scallops in vinegar filling the air.

'Starving,' she admitted. 'Although...no thanks.'

'Mmm,' he said, eating one with that unwittingly mesmerising sensual pleasure. 'Sure? They're really good,' he managed to get out.

'Trying to watch my uh...figure. You know, weight.'

'You?' he said, surprised. 'Why?'

Boys asked such pointed questions sometimes. 'I'm going to Queensland. I think. A week after the exams. Anyway...swimmers and...uh...all that.'

'That so?' he said, pausing mid-chew and grinning. She felt suddenly half-naked, like he was imagining her in a bikini, and pulled her already overly long hem down self-consciously. 'I'm going at the same time. Figured I should have a bit of fun before I go into the army.'

'I didn't know cadets were obliged to serve actual time.'

'They're not.'

'Oh.' Now she felt confused as well as naked.

'It's a family thing.' He shrugged. 'I'll represent the third generation of men in my family to go to Duntroon and become an officer, take a commission and see active service then come back and do law at Sydney Uni.'

He said it all lightly but she detected an underlying bitterness in his tone.

'Is that…is that what you want to do?'

'Can't see that I've got much choice.'

Poppy was taken aback. 'Well…it's your life.'

'Not really – I'm a Williamson. It's expected,' he told her, raising his eyebrows comically as he ate.

'Williamson,' she repeated absently, then blushed at the almost wondering sound of her tone; like knowing his last name was a cherished, revealing clue.

'Thompson Benjamin Williamson actually. The first name is a family tradition too but we all use our middle instead,' he explained, looking at her curiously. He probably thought she would go home now and dreamily practise writing her signature as his wife. *Mrs Poppy Williamson*. Worse thing was she probably would. 'Sorry, I should have introduced myself properly in the first place. What's your last name?'

She felt foolishly flattered he wanted to know. 'Flannery. Poppy Marie Flannery.'

'Poppy Marie Flannery. That's a nice name,' he said, smiling as he finished off his scallops. She felt the pleasure of that little compliment suffuse her.

'I was named after the war flower, you know, the one for the Anzacs; the red poppy? My sister Rosemary is the same, although that's technically a herb. My family were in the military too.'

'Ah,' he said, nodding thoughtfully. 'Guess we have something in common then.'

She was so pleased about that fact she began to babble. 'GP was in the trenches…that's my grandpa. He…er, likes the nickname. Anyway, he was in the Somme; you know, with the mud and everything. He was one of the men who played soccer with the Germans at Christmas and swapped things. Cigarettes, he said… he even got a nice case from one. Dad still has it in his drawer. It's silver, although I'm not sure it's real…seems a bit extreme that a stranger would give something so valuable to the enemy…'

'People do strange things during war, I suppose,' Ben said, and something flashed across his face that brought a halt to her babbling. War wasn't really a nice fact to have in common. Actually not at all.

Poppy searched for something to say, blurting out the first thing that came to mind. 'GP ate a rat once.'

'That so?' Ben said, looking startled, then he started to laugh.

'I'm sorry,' Poppy said, face flaming. 'I don't suppose you wanted to know that much detail.'

'No, no, I'm quite intrigued. What else did GP do?'

'He…er…well, he dressed up as a woman one time. To distract the Germans. I mean, it was from a distance, you understand…'

Ben laughed again. 'I think I need to meet this rodent-eating GP of yours. Sounds quite a fellow.'

'He is,' Poppy said. 'Although he doesn't see us much anymore. He lives up near Coffs Harbour.'

'Why so far?'

Poppy could hardly tell the truth there: because he wanted to get as far away from her father as possible. That he could never stand the Church and wasn't happy his only son had taken to being a 'bible basher'.

'The weather is…pleasant,' she improvised instead, calling on her knowledge of geography. 'Coffs Harbour is considered the world's most hospitable climate.'

Ben nodded thoughtfully although he still looked amused. Then he looked out and noticed Wahroonga approaching.

'My station,' he said, standing up and putting on his beret. 'See you soon, Poppy Marie Flannery.'

It wasn't until she was walking home some ten minutes later and got past the shock of the lovely way he'd said her name that another wondrous fact took precedence. A fact that made her almost run the rest of the way, take out her cello and practise like mad. She played and played until her fingers grew red and sore then sat to concentrate on her neglected Latin phrases.

But her pen had a mind of its own and it couldn't help but practise a beautiful new name instead.

Mrs Poppy Williamson…Mrs. P. Williamson…Mrs Poppy Marie Williamson…

Then the pen found another delicious word, just a single one, but it burst across the page in a thousand imaginings, tracing its way in swirls. It lifted her from a kitchen table on a cold winter's night in suburbia and transported her out the doors, along the long road north, far, far away and across the state line.

To a land so filled with sunshine it had been given a royal name.

Queensland.

It had been Rosemary's idea and seemed rather ingenious at the time. How were they supposed to know the Dogsquad would think of the same thing? It wasn't as if they were renowned for clever ideas, although this bordered more on a scheme. Walking to Wahroonga Station instead of Waitara Station may have added fifteen minutes of exertion to their morning but there were multiple benefits:

1. Ben caught the train from Wahroonga.
2. The sunshine had stayed. It was glorious in fact – cutting through the chill in brilliant defiance – and Wahroonga had a beautiful park and station gardens. (It won awards all the time, as their mother loved to tell relatives. She also liked to say they lived on the 'Wahroonga border' rather than

Waitara. Rosemary said it made them sound like desperate Mexicans.)

3. The exercise would do them good, especially with Queensland and bikinis beckoning.
4. Ben caught the train from Wahroonga.

Unfortunately, the glorious morning had taken an ugly turn and instead of having Ben all to herself to discuss eccentric family members and/or Queensland, Poppy was forced to watch Barbara in full flirtation instead. He was standing with his friends, ridiculously handsome in his blue blazer, and Poppy recognised Graham Chapman and Chris Plumpton from church. Church! Why hadn't she thought of *that* before? Maybe her parents would let them attend mass at the Wahroonga Parish this Sunday. Imagine that, a whole hour to stare at him, she thought dreamily, blinking the thought away as Judith caught her looking and whispered something to Raeleen. They nudged Barbara who cast the twins a look of cool dislike before turning her attention back to Ben, hair flicking now at maximum levels.

'You have to come along, Benny,' Poppy overheard her saying with a pout. 'Just wag the cadet thingy.'

'You don't wag cadets,' Ben told her, and Poppy wondered if she imagined a hint of annoyance in his voice. Perhaps Barbara heard it too because she instantly dropped the cutesy act and touched his sleeve, her tone now solemn with understanding.

'Then we'll go to a later session. It would be too unfair for you to miss out.' That earned her a small smile from Ben and Poppy swallowed against her envy.

'I'm not sure I want to watch a Beatles movie with you girls,' Chris protested. 'You'll all be swooning over McCartney and we'll be sitting there like mugs.'

Raeleen giggled and Chris looked pleased about that. Perhaps they're a new item, Poppy thought to herself.

The group went on to discuss what they knew about the first movie from the 'fab four' and Graham could be heard singing the title song, 'Help', rather badly, which made Raeleen giggle again. She seemed to giggle a lot around boys, something that both grated on and depressed the twins. Wallflowers didn't have the privilege of flicking their hair and exaggerating their amusement to impress the male species. They weren't privy to the art of flirtation and had little opportunity to practise (and of course when they did they were rather disastrous at it. Rat conversations a case in point).

Rosemary sighed and Poppy felt the longing within it matching her own. How must it feel to be a cool girl; to have a skirt at the knee rather than your ankles, to paint your perfect nails and bend every rule to attract boys like that who joked and flattered, however awkwardly. To be wanted. To belong.

The train arrived and they moved towards it in a sea of hats, letting the few adults go ahead and trying not to trip over bags and feet. So much for their ingenious idea, Poppy thought, disappointment welling. Isolating Ben looked to be a rare event, perhaps never to occur again. There were only so many B-Days left until graduation.

'Look out, freak-show,' Barbara whispered, almost knocking her over as she pushed past.

Then there was a hand, long brown fingers extending from a blue blazer, and it was steadying her then inviting her to go in front.

'After you, Poppy Marie.'

Gazing up from that hand and into those understanding eyes Poppy felt her determination to get to Queensland morph into obsession. It was time for this wallflower to bask in the sun.

Five

Sydney, September 1965

He wasn't ready. He hadn't even crammed the last of the quotes into his head let alone memorised character comparisons. He wasn't even quite sure if Hamlet's madness was real or feigned.

To be or not to be

That is the question

Oh God, what comes next? Ben felt the pressure closing in, suffocating and dark, and he struggled against it. But he was sleepy too. So sleepy he could barely raise his head to look at the question again. Compare and contrast. *Write some notes on a spare piece of paper. I don't have any paper. I don't have a pen. The teacher knows I don't know. Look at him. He knows. He's called in the principal and everyone is staring. Now my father is here and I'm not going to study law after all. I'm not even going to Duntroon. I'm going straight to Vietnam. Please, let me try to write something. Someone give me a pen! But they're giving me a gun instead…*

Ben awoke covered in sweat even though it was cool in his room. The clock ticked and the window rattled slightly and everything was as it should be at three in the morning. Everything save the fact that he was now wide awake. With shaking hands he opened the drawer and took out his cigarettes, then walked over to the window, lifting the latch. The bite of the cold night cooled his skin almost immediately and he lit one, the tobacco soothing. But the nightmare stayed, like a shadowed spectre; with only a month to go before final exams such dreams were becoming frequent. What if he didn't get the marks? What if the pressure got the better of him?

No, it was unacceptable, as his father would say. Williamsons studied law at Sydney University and Williamsons served their country as officers in the military. It was his duty and it was his honour. Any other ambitions would swiftly be wiped off the board.

Ben sat on the sill and let the fresh air invade and clear his senses as he looked out across the silvered night. It was an impressive view, he had to admit. The new house was more like a hotel than a home with the extensive gardens, the pool, the tennis court and the long drive. It even had servants' quarters, although no-one lived there. That was the price, Ben acknowledged as he dragged on his smoke. A privileged life had a cost and that cost was his capitulation.

He wondered what it must be like to be born in a normal family where people had regular jobs and lived regular lives. To be a teenager who practised shooting goals instead of guns. To have parents who viewed your artworks with pride rather than mild amusement. To come home late carrying a cello instead of wearing fatigues.

He smiled at that last thought. Poppy Marie Flannery. What a strange girl she was – clearly a bit nuts to go to a school dance dressed like his mother back in her debutante days. He grinned at the memory of her jumping on that stage and dancing like the

Supremes with her sister. So shy one minute, a total party animal the next. Tongue-tied on the train then blurting out outrageous facts about her grandpa. She knew less about flirting than any girl he'd ever met.

He thought about the light freckles across her nose, the blonde hair and those blue eyes that stared at him as though terrified. But there was something else too, something indefinable beneath the general prettiness that seemed to escape the attention of most. She was smart. And she was downright sexy when she forgot to hide it, chewing on her lip while she watched him eat. Sending him secrets with those eyes across the dark. He found himself wishing he could be the one to teach her how to turn that smoke into fire because he doubted she'd ever even kissed a boy. Then he wondered why most guys his age were so blind when it came to quality girls like Poppy and her sister. Why they idolised girls like Barbara instead.

He sighed as he thought about that one. She was gorgeous-looking, no doubt, but what he initially viewed as sexy and fun in her was starting to seem just plain controlling, in fact the more time he spent around her the less he liked her. No, that wasn't entirely true. He liked her legs, quite a lot actually, especially when they were bare and smooth to the touch under her skirt. Although she must have been freezing last Saturday night when she dragged him into the carpark behind Hornsby Cinema and kissed him against the cold bricks. Things got out of hand pretty quickly then and he regretted his own eagerness almost as soon as it was over. A quickie against the wall was the last thing he'd expected and he felt almost ashamed of it. There was nothing loving in it; nothing sweet. Just a root, as Chris would term it.

Not that he'd told any of the guys at school. He didn't want to tell anyone.

Ben flicked the ash, wondering why he felt unhappy about achieving every other guy at school's fantasy. But he did. Barbara may well be all the things a teenage boy dreams about, including him to begin with, but it was becoming more and more apparent that beauty didn't extend to the inside. He'd witnessed it clearly in her expression the other day when she'd 'just happened to be passing by' and dropped in to see him at home. To value his wealth, more like. Her ambition to marry well was barely concealed as she ran her hand across the drapes and tapped on the polished dining table with her long, manicured nails. There was a gleam in her eyes as she'd pressed against him at the door to kiss him goodbye and it wasn't desire or even flirtation. It was greed.

A memory came then of another pair of eyes, nervous and blue. They belonged to a stumbling girl trying to board a train, shrinking from the bully who'd tripped her. Barbara without the mask, watching with cruel amusement. Getting what she wanted the same way she did everything – with a push and a shove. Push the girl out of the way, shove the guy against the wall. Flick, flick, flick.

Suddenly Ben wanted nothing more to do with her – how the hell had he let himself get involved with a girl like that?

Because she's sexy as hell, the voice inside reasoned. Isn't she?

His body remembered the feel of that hot moment on the cool night in question, a reflexive desire flooding through him, but his mind was already halting it.

No, it isn't enough any more.

That's new, he thought to himself, surprised. Maybe he was developing a conscience about sex now that he'd turned eighteen. He'd certainly scored a lot more of it than most guys his age for some reason – girls seemed to like the whole cadet fatigues thing, strangely enough. Maybe they enjoyed the fantasy of the hunt.

Maybe he did, and now that he'd caught the prey he'd lost interest.

Ben frowned into the night, not liking that thought. Better to believe that other 'developing a conscience' idea, he decided. That made him less of a bastard.

Yawning, he returned to his warm bed and pulled the blankets close. Women weren't really that hard to figure out, he reflected, most of their true personalities were quite obvious. It was the sexual energy they sent out that always distorted the truth and stuffed a guy up. Well no more, he told himself as the drug of slumber began to pull. I'm developing a conscience…master of my own desires…

Then the thoughts became dreams and he was back in that exam hall again, only this time he turned into a bird and flew out the window. His feathers were green and blue and he was chasing a rat; into trenches, into gunfire and raining debris. But the rat turned around and he saw that now it had beautiful eyes and he tried to catch up to her but he was unable to move. A hot pair of thighs were wrapping around him, trapping him in their grip. Then a rag descended and began to wipe it all away, washing everything in oil, until all that was left of him was a smear.

Then he opened his eyes to a pale dawn and the empty canvas of a new day.

Six

Sydney, October 1965

Tick, tick, tick.

The clock was so loud, so final in its mechanical progression it felt like a bomb set to explode, scattering their futures far and wide as punishment for their lack of time management. Their insufficient studies; their general failings and ineptitude.

Tick, tick, tick.

You've no-one to blame but yourselves.

It was causing Poppy's mind to go blank, or worse, be distracted. Much like the hapless prey of the anglerfish she was writing about, a downright nasty-looking creature prone to dangling bioluminescent rods in front of impressive teeth to lure victims close.

Or like a girl watching a guy dangle scallops in front of his mouth on a train.

Concentrate Poppy. This is it – the last one!

She re-read the question once more and her recall capabilities clicked back in line, facts about marine life flowing now as she rushed through the final section of her Biology exam, trying not to panic as the clock hands moved towards the twelve.

'Ten minutes, ladies,' called Sister Margaret, who looked relieved to have stayed awake the whole time, blinking at her glasses as she took them off to rub them.

Poppy felt a rush of activity around her then as the students in the hall finished sentences and re-read their answers, crossing out and adding more in a frantic push to squeeze a few more marks onto that eventual number that would direct their fates.

'Time. Pens down and no speaking until all papers have been collected.'

Poppy put hers down slowly, stretching her aching fingers, barely registering the enormity of the moment now that it had finally arrived: the exams were finished – all the study, the angst, the pressure was gone. Rosemary looked over and they stared at each other in exhausted disbelief before exchanging grins.

It's over.

The last pieces of paper that confirmed their knowledge, or lack of it, were being taken from the twins' hands and now lived in piles up front awaiting judgement. Out of their control. Nothing more to be done.

Sister Aquinas, the vice-principal, entered the hall and strode over to whisper something to Sister Margaret before addressing them.

'Thank you ladies. I pray you've managed to excel today and we wish you the very best of luck.' There was sincerity there. She was a preferred leader to the cold fish that was Sister Pius, the principal. 'Before you go, a quick announcement: those of you who tried out for the Catholic Schools Orchestra will find your names on the noticeboard. I'm sure you will do the school very proud up there in Queensland and congratulations on this achievement. To all of you, please know that we will miss you,' she added, a little tearily as Sister Margaret dabbed her face with a hanky behind her. 'Safe travels…and may God bless you.'

There were murmurs of 'and may God bless you Sister' across the hall and a few sniffles here and there as well before they began to pile out. Then all tears were gone, especially for the twins, as they raced to the noticeboard, hearts pounding. Please, please, please.

'Charlton, Davidson, Eggles…' read Rosemary, scanning over heads. 'Flannery and Flannery!'

They turned to each other and began to squeal, hugging and jumping with the other fortunate contenders.

'Oh, I'm so sorry, Daniella,' Rosemary paused to console their friend whose look of disappointment said it all.

'Oh, it's alright. I'm sure I can swing my way north another way,' she said, shaking it off easily. Daniella Rossi had a wealth of relatives. She was sure to find an alternative somewhere on the coast.

The girls gave her a hug goodbye, promising to stay in touch before heading to the gates, joy and relief in abundance.

'Wait,' said Rosemary, and Poppy paused with her. 'On the count of three, ready?' She lifted her foot to make the final step to freedom and Poppy giggled, linking arms and doing the same. 'One, two, three!'

Then the Flannery twins stepped out of their convent high school together at last, joining in to sing with Daniella and other friends as they drove past out the gates, radios blaring with the sound of Martha and the Vandellas.

And right there, in the heartland of Sydney's conservative North Shore, two strictly raised Catholic schoolgirls took to identical dancing, right there in the street.

Seven

Broome, Western Australia, November 1965

'It'll never make it,' Angus Turner said, eyeing the Holden station wagon with doubt.

'Sure it will,' his brother Spike said cheerfully, banging the bonnet as he walked past and causing dust to shake free onto the floor. 'Turn the key for me again.'

He thought about commenting further but refrained, climbing in and doing as he was asked instead, then wincing as the tired engine knocked and rattled into unwilling life before dying once more.

Spike seemed to think nothing of this as he went about the business of searching for the right spanner in the metal toolbox under the bench, whistling along to radio as he did so. The Beach Boys were singing 'I Get Around' – Spike's favourite song right now. In fact, any song by the Beach Boys was his brother's instant favourite and he'd invested a fair amount of time learning the chords on his new guitar. That prized possession hung on the garage wall complete with an 'Endless Summer' sticker, right alongside their collection of surfboards and above the shelves that held an eclectic mix of wax, zinc and surf magazines.

Taking in his brother's overly long blonde hair and deeply tanned skin, Angus figured it would take more than a dodgy car to stop Spike now. The mecca that was Surfers Paradise in Queensland had become his obsession and he would be strumming that guitar around a bonfire there this summer no matter what stood in his way, including those pesky three thousand miles.

'What if we break down in the middle of the Territory?'

'She'll be right,' came the optimistic reply.

Angus tapped on the steering wheel as the grainy opening harmonies of 'Don't Worry Baby' floated from the speaker. It was double song Tuesday on the local station.

'Maybe we should wait until next year when we can afford a better car…'

'Angus,' said Spike, firmly now, 'I'm telling you: she'll be right! Live a little for godsakes mate.'

Angus frowned at himself, knowing he was the worry wart of the two, but with a brother like Spike it was impossible to be otherwise. For some reason Spike had inherited their mother's petite stature, the opposite of Angus who was tall like their dad. At five foot six and a half, Spencer 'Spike' Turner seem to spend most of his spare time making up for his diminutive height by living a life of reckless adventuring. Accordingly, Angus had spent most of *his* keeping his brother out of trouble and this trip was making him particularly nervous. Their father would say it had 'disaster written all over it', if either of them had bothered telling him.

'What are you so worried about anyway?' Spike said from somewhere under the bonnet.

'Breaking down, dying of thirst, getting robbed, getting killed, being buried in a desert and no-one ever knowing what happened to us…'

'You watch too many horror movies. No-one's gonna care about two harmless fellas from Broome.'

'Well, there's also the deadly snakes and spiders…'

'We get plenty of them 'round here,' came the muffled reply.

'Get plenty of surf 'round here too. Can't see why you're so obsessed with the Gold Coast.'

'Are you –' Spike hit his head on the bonnet in his haste to reply and paused momentarily to curse before continuing. 'Are you mad? Surfers *Paradise,* Angus. Beach parties, nightclubs, the Beergarden, hotels and swimming pools…'

'Seedy crooks in back streets…'

'Two words mate: *meter maids*; sizzling girls in gold bikinis who walk around and put coins in for you so you don't get fined. That's paradise for sure, come on.'

Angus paused in his worrying as Spike threw a magazine at him featuring one of the new maids under discussion, a gorgeous blonde called Annette Welch. She gazed at him from beneath her Meter Maid crown, beautiful smile in place above a gold bikini and a blue sash; so perfect-looking he momentarily forgot his arguments against going.

Just then 'She's So Fine' by the Easybeats started up on the radio and Spike's nod and grin was so contagious Angus started to laugh.

'Gold bikinis on the Gold Coast,' Spike confirmed. 'Sorry brother, we ain't got no other choice.'

It wasn't just dry, it was endlessly dry, and no amount of water seemed to quench their thirst. In fact Spike had given up trying and had opened a beer instead. It was resting between his legs as they drove towards a point on the horizon, one that never seemed to get closer at the end of the long ribbon of road.

'Oh for f…' Spike exploded, sticking his head out the window and spilling some of his beer. 'Holy hell, why'd you have to give him the prawn heads?'

'It's not Barrel's fault he gets hungry. You don't feed him enough.'

'Oh God, I'm going to die,' Spike choked, pulling his T-shirt over his face.

'Quit y'whinging. You right there, mate?' The nuggetty dog in the back seat gave a satisfied thump of his tail, mouth wide open as if he were laughing, and Angus grinned back at him. 'Wind must be flipping it back at you. I can't smell a thing.'

'You're enjoying this, y'sick bastard.'

'Little bit,' Angus admitted. Truth was, to his surprise he was enjoying himself in general – despite the heat and the flies and the horrific smells coming from their dog Barrel that he was pretending not to notice. Something about the wide, endless road was seeping into him and he was forgetting to be the sensible older brother for a change. Probably because he didn't have to go to work at Broome Mechanics, a job both brothers detested due to their tyrannical boss, or deal with their hopeless father and fusspot of a mother who had not cared and overly cared respectively that they were going.

Out here in the Never-Never there were no debts to be paid, no rules to be obeyed. Actually there was just nothing and that was suiting Angus just fine. For the first time in his life he felt worry-free as his usual preoccupations lifted off him one by one and fell behind on the endless red road.

Reaching down into the esky he took out a beer for himself, grinning at Spike's questioning look.

'When in Rome.'

'Who are you and what have you done with the worry wart?

'Killed him and buried him a few miles back. I'm his evil twin,' Angus returned.

'Gawd, imagine two of you.' Spike laughed, finishing his own beer and clicking his fingers for another. 'We never would have got out of WA.'

'Must be weird, being a twin,' Angus said, rummaging for a beer then holding the matching bottles side by side for emphasis, 'how they reckon they know each other's thoughts sometimes and stuff. Well, that's what some people say anyway.' He handed one over to Spike.

'The only interest I have in twins is purely physical. A matching pair with matching pairs if you know what I…oh no, not again…' He stuck his head out the window, pulling a disgusted face.

'God's punishing you,' Angus told him as Barrel gave a bark of seeming agreement. 'Pity we can't get the radio,' he said, ignoring Spike's groans and fiddling with the dial. 'Hold on, what's this?'

There was a scratchy sound and the word Vietnam could be made out in the monotone of a newsreader's voice.

'Get rid of that,' Spike said and Angus kept searching, in definite agreement. The government had recently introduced conscription, using a frightening lottery system for drafting based on a young man's birthdate. (Spike liked to say it was some rich polly bastard's idea of a joke to use the term 'lottery'.) Twenty-year-old Angus was of an eligible age and both brothers had been terrified he would get called up, halting this dream trip before it even began.

'Nothing doing,' Angus said after a while, giving up on the radio.

'Hey, who needs it? You forget I've got a whole bank of records stored right up here that I'm happy to play on Spike's turntable,' he said, poking his own forehead.

'Spike's tuneless turntable…' Angus began to object but it was too late.

The sun had begun to golden as his brother serenaded him with a rather ordinary rendition of 'The House of the Rising Sun' – but it was made more enjoyable by the beer and the welcome novelty of freedom as they rolled across the dusty miles. Just two guys and a flatulent dog on a red road filled with nothing, bound for gold bikinis, surf and paradise.

Eight

Hornsby Station, Sydney, November 1965

The trees at the centre of town were filled with hundreds of lorikeets making a loud racket and Poppy watched them flutter about while she waited impatiently for the bus. It really was very sweet the way they sat in pairs at times, nuzzling each other. 'Lovebirds' Rosemary called them.

'...and no matter how tempted you are, don't buy any of those tacky souvenirs,' their mother was saying, her instructions seeming endless that morning. 'You'll be wasting enough money on ice cream and goodness knows what.' She dusted an imaginary piece of fluff from Rosemary's short sleeve and made that little tsk-ing sound that appeared whenever her disapproval antennae were up.

'Yes Mum,' the twins said automatically.

Just then the bus arrived at last, filled with girls from Catholic schools across Sydney, and the sisters eyed the group within nervously. Along with half a dozen others from their school they were the last ones to be boarding, a consequence of being from the northern-most suburbs. Sister Margaret and Sister Pauline were already seated and Poppy supposed they'd been picked up from the convent. The former already looked half-asleep.

'Best manners mind, and don't forget to say three Hail Marys as soon as you hit Taree. More accidents there than I care to count –' Robert Flannery paused as his wife took a tissue from her handbag and he cleared his own throat, '– although I'm sure the good Lord will protect you. God speed now.' He patted their shoulders rather awkwardly and Lois hugged them in her uniquely stiff way. Affectionate the Flannery twins' parents were not, and strict certainly, but there was genuine concern underscoring their farewells and both girls felt its weight with a fair dose of guilt.

'Goodbye Mum. Goodbye Dad,' they called as they took their seats, pausing to wave out the windows.

'Be good,' their mother called, waving her tissue, and they nodded obediently, a little awed by their own audacity for they planned to be quite the opposite. Then at last the wheels began to turn and they pulled away from the kerb; past the noisy trees, past the cenotaph, the RSL Club, the Odeon Theatre and the pool. The twins watched it all pass by with a strange sense of disbelief.

'I can't believe they actually let us go,' Rosemary said and Poppy burst out laughing. 'I was so sure they'd change their minds at the last minute.'

'Me too!'

Neither had ever been on a trip without their parents before and it felt rather surreal, a feeling that seemed to be contagious throughout the bus. Cameras were clicking away and excited chatter filled the air. Rosemary made some kind of grunting sound from under her seat, searching through her bag, then straightened and patted her hair back in place. 'Right, smile!'

Poppy did, checking the fall of her flowered skirt first and patting her hair. It was exciting not being in uniform. Rosemary had been planning their new look for weeks, eager to make up for the school dance fiasco, and had styled both of them this morning in the latest Gidget fashion, something their mother begrudgingly allowed.

'Think I might ask the bus driver if we can turn the radio on,' said Jane Partridge, one of their friends who was sitting in front. 'Hey, want me to take one of both of you?' They nodded, handing over the camera, and posed together with self-conscious giggles.

'Beautiful,' Jane said, handing the camera back then moving off a little unsteadily.

Poppy wasn't sure about that. The twins' hemlines were still way too long to be considered fashionable and they had no make-up on, save a smear of cherry lip gloss, but Rosemary had done a good job on their hairstyles and she had to admit she did feel passable today. Perhaps even a little bit, well, pretty.

The miles began to pass on what would be a good fifteen-hour journey along the Pacific Highway and Rosemary settled in to read her magazine, looking quite comfortable already. Poppy wasn't, so she curled up with a pillow against the glass to gaze out at the scenery, half listening to the news that had come on with the radio.

In Saigon, Viet Cong terrorists have bombed a hotel today, one commonly frequented by US military personnel. Casualties are as yet unconfirmed but witnesses say at least six people have died and many more have been wounded...

Poppy frowned at the images that came to mind. US military...not Australian, she reassured herself. Besides, Ben hadn't even started training at Duntroon yet and it should all be over by the time he graduated, too late to be in harm's way. Then the bus driver blessedly turned the dial and, as fortune would have it, on came 'Be My Baby' by the Ronettes.

Touching the pane, Poppy watched the bushland roll by, letting go of images of war and falling into the part of her brain where Ben resided, safely in her world. The valleys were still hazy from a recent bushfire and she caught her own reflection against the misted grey; all round blue eyes beneath a thick blond fringe. She closed them to better daydream, the possibilities of what lay ahead assailing her.

Maybe the beautiful boy would think she was beautiful too, at the end of this long road to the north. Then maybe he'd forget about Barbara and fall for her instead, holding her hand as they walked along the shoreline, taking her in his arms and kissing her with those lips; welcoming her taste like salt and vinegar on a rainy day. The longing built as the bus rolled on, the lyrics of her Ben-song playing like a soundtrack to her very own Gidget movie, where for every kiss he gave her, she was giving him three. Warm in that glorious sun at last.

The song ended and she opened her eyes to watch the grey once more, the landscape as obscured as her fate, but one thing was certain: the boy on the train would be the boy at the beach, with Poppy right there with him.

And that was a beautiful thought, indeed.

Nine

Northern Territory, Australia, December 1965

'Sure thing mate. Hop in,' Spike called out as he opened the car door.

Angus was too preoccupied with studying the map and marking their progress with a pen to take much notice but as they took off down the highway once more he looked behind him with mild surprise.

'Jed,' he acknowledged, nodding at the Aboriginal fella they'd hung out with last night. He was lazily scratching Barrel's ears, an easy smile stretching across his face.

'Hey, big brudda.' Picking up the local blokes had become the norm for the Turners over the last few days, as had being referred to as 'big brudda' and 'little brudda'.

'You lookin' at them drawings again?'

Angus looked down at the map in his hand and shrugged. 'Need to know where we're going.'

Jed seemed to think that was rather funny. 'As long as we going somewhere.'

The miles stretched on through a long, typically hot morning, the sky so glaringly blue it hurt the brothers' eyes if they took off their sunglasses. Jed didn't seem to mind, his brown gaze watching the horizon with contentment as he sang to the morning. He had a rather good voice, as they'd discovered last night, when Spike played his guitar while they played cards and drank beer under the stars. They had been glaring too, so bright Angus felt he could almost pluck one from the black ink and take it home as a keepsake. Everything out here was extreme: the heat, the red colour of the earth, that brilliant sky. Jed's obsession with country music.

He was on his third Johnny Cash number and Spike was getting fidgety.

'How about some Beach Boys?' his brother suggested, cutting through Jed's extended version of 'Ring of Fire'. Just then there was a loud bang and Spike's attention was immediately on the road. It was a hairy few seconds as they slid and bounced about in a chaotic cloud of red dust, Barrel's paws slipping on the upholstery in a desperate bid for balance, the guitar clanging against the suitcases and surfboards in the back. Jed's whoops of laughter added to the general mayhem before they finally slid into the ditch at the roadside and lurched to a dead stop.

'That some crazy driving, little brudda,' Jed said, still laughing.

'Bugger me,' Spike declared, shaking his head clear before getting out to view the damage.

It wasn't good news. The tyre was well and truly blown with no more spares to replace it.

'Stuffed?' Angus asked.

'Royally,' Spike confirmed.

The three men sat on the side of the road and lit cigarettes, each thinking things through, the vast emptiness rendering them suddenly tiny, the isolation now overwhelming. There wasn't a sound to be heard nor a single sign of life in any direction, just that blue sky and red earth in continuous partnership, and the burning sun that watched them in an endless ring of fire.

'Could push it,' Angus suggested.

'Won't get somewhere like that,' Jed told him.

'Could sit here and drink beer till someone turns up,' Spike suggested.

'All out,' Angus said, sighing.

Jed leant over and reached into his rucksack, fiddling around for a minute before drawing out what he was looking for. 'Could smoke some yundi,' he suggested, holding up a bag of marijuana.

'Cool,' said Spike, instantly enthused.

'I don't think so,' said Angus.

'Whatcha got against yundi, big brudda?'

'Well, it's illegal, for a start.'

Jed laughed at him for the umpteenth time that morning. It was really starting to get on Angus's nerves.

'Who gonna care out here?'

'Not me,' Spike confirmed, watching Jed take out his cigarette papers and sprinkle the shredded leaves and tobacco with interest. Angus was pretty sure his brother had never tried marijuana before but you never knew with Spike. He had no filter when it came to what he deemed entertainment, including legality.

Jed lit the joint and drew deeply, handing it over to Spike who did the same, coughing a little but holding it as manfully as he could.

'Come on, big brudda,' Spike encouraged him, holding it out.

'None for me, thanks.'

'Stop being such a square, or has the worry wart made a return?'

Angus let out a humph. 'He's not too happy about being stranded, let me tell you.'

'Might as well do something then. Come on, we've been waiting all year for this road trip. Think of it as part of the adventure…live a little.'

Angus looked around him, figuring if he was ever going to try the stuff now probably was the best time. The only law enforcement out here was doled out by Mother Nature.

'You won't worry 'bout nuthin' after yundi,' Jed told him, enormous smile in place as he lit a second joint.

Angus envied that smile. Jed sure didn't seem to 'worry 'bout nuthin''. Might be nice to feel like that right about now.

'Go on,' Spike coaxed. 'We're only going to be young once.'

Angus gave in, taking it hesitantly, puffing just a little. It was surprisingly sweet.

'There you go. That ain't so bad, eh?' Spike said.

Angus drew a little harder then, emboldened, only to dissolve into a coughing fit so severe it almost drowned out Jed's laughter. 'Pass it back, big brudda. Boy, you sound like them bush pigs.' He made some imitative noises that were so realistic it made Angus chuckle a little too.

About five minutes later none of them seemed able to stop chuckling. Actually it was much more than that – they were doubled over, tears rolling. Maybe that was why Jed laughed so much, Angus realised. He was constantly stoned. The thought made him laugh so hard he had to lie on his back to cope with it.

It wasn't exactly the best position to be in when you realised you were surrounded by half a dozen tribesmen who didn't look like they wanted a lift, let alone a game of cards. They didn't look like they needed any help at all, as a matter of fact. And not one of them was laughing.

Ten

It was an unnerving thing to be scrutinised by a bunch of naked men. Unimpressed naked men at that. Angus was trying hard not to stare at their muscled torsos and assorted weapons but it was challenging to say the least. Being stoned seemed to be all about the amusement found in details, and what details these were: dark eyes glaring behind intricately applied paint, assorted articles that they carried over their shoulders or at their hip, some woven finely, others carved sharply for the hunt. Angus eyed the long spears they also carried warily. The Turner boys knew enough about Aboriginal fellas to know they had trespassed on the wrong day.

Even Jed had stopped laughing, Angus registered in sobering realisation. And Barrel hadn't barked once, sitting behind Spike's legs rather nervously, which was worryingly out of character. Angus hoped he hadn't been breathing in the yundi – who knew what level of noxious gases he might emit later if he had. The thought made him want to laugh again, which would really go down badly at this point. He focused on the eldest man instead, who had moved forward to speak.

'What you doin' here?' he grunted. The lines on his face were a fascination unto themselves; carved like clay. Stories were written there in their hundreds, the traces left behind of where he'd been and what he'd seen. And what had been taken away since white man came, Angus supposed, guilty now at their trespassing.

'We were travelling along the road but we blew a tyre.' Angus pointed at the car, glad he'd been able to string a coherent sentence together.

'This blackfella country. You can't stay,' the old man said and the others nodded.

'Sorry…we want to keep moving…but…'

The old man shifted his gaze to Jed, then said something in rapid native language. Fortunately Jed understood and said something back and an intense exchange took place until the man finally paused at something Jed said, frowning thoughtfully. Angus wanted to ask Jed what was going on but was too afraid of offending somehow. Besides, his tongue had turned into some kind of dry sponge that was too big for his mouth.

Angus watched as the tribesmen conversed together for a minute before making their decision.

'What are they doing?' Spike whispered to Jed as the men walked off the road.

'Fixing,' Jed whispered back.

He wanted to ask how on earth a bunch of native fellas would go about fixing a blown tyre in the middle of the desert but decided to just watch instead. What seemed to Angus a wasteland devoid of life had secrets these men understood; for instance it had spinifex, an endless supply of it in fact, and easy enough to gather when you had an impressively sharp weapon strapped to your hip. Apparently this seemingly useless, dry grass could then be twisted and bashed into a filling that could stuff the inner tube of a tyre quite satisfactorily.

All of this was done without fuss or explanation and once completed the native men stood back, obviously waiting for them to leave.

'Thank you so much,' Angus said, nodding at the row of blank faces.

'Really appreciate it,' Spike added, giving them the thumbs up, which widened the old man's eyes but was otherwise ignored.

There didn't seem much else to do then except get in and drive off, the wheel a little shaky but adequate for now. They waved at the men as they went and one or two raised a hand before they disappeared off into the red.

'Well, that was unexpected,' Spike said, breaking the stunned silence in the car. 'I didn't think I'd see two good uses for grass in one day.'

'Yeah well, lucky we smoke that yundi, otherwise that old fella woulda scared the shit outta me,' Jed confessed.

Angus turned to them both, bloodshot eyes round as a sudden idea occurred to him. 'Did...did that actually happen or was it just the yundi?'

'Course it happen,' Jed said, his grin returning. 'Didn't it?'

They all looked at each other and began to laugh so hard they had to pull over – which was just as well because they needed to check if the grass really *was* stuffed in the tyre tube now or if it was just the grass stuffed in their minds that had caused the whole strange tale to unfurl.

Then Jed took out the yundi again and they continued their journey under that hot sun towards the desert's edge, making up songs as they went along that grew more ridiculous and therefore more amusing with each passing mile, until finally the day began to fade.

Lights appeared and with them the relieving realisation that they'd made it to the next town, yet another outpost where they could stock up on supplies and stop for the night, but when they finally lay down sleep eluded Angus, despite the marijuana sedation. It was impossible to stop laughing and find slumber when Spike's voice filled the air with his favourite made-up song of the day.

'And it turns, turns, turns, grass in the tyre, grass in the tyre.'

Eleven

Surfers Paradise, Queensland, Australia, December 1965

She really sauntered rather than walked, Ben thought to himself lazily. Funny how he'd completely lost interest in watching her, although the others didn't seem quite so jaded, he noted. Apparently perving on Barbara Rowntree in a wet bikini was a sport John, Chris and Chappy never tired of, judging by the open-mouthed stares from under their umbrella that afternoon.

'You're one lucky son of a bitch, you know that?' Chappy muttered and Ben shrugged.

'I told you, it's over. We're just friends now,' Ben said, not that they really were of course. Barbara didn't collect male friends. What was the point?

'Don't think she's giving up that easily,' Chris observed as Barbara gave a customary shake of her hair before lying down, not twenty feet away.

'Good God,' said John.

'I think that show was for your benefit,' added Chris, dragging on his cigarette.

Ben stood up, ignoring the comment. 'I'm going for a swim.'

'Think I need one too,' John said, going with him. The sand was hot under their bare soles but cooled near the edge where the ocean lay waiting, the water refreshing on their sunburnt skin.

'Woohoo!' whooped John, diving in with enthusiasm and Ben laughed, following. God, he loved Queensland. Everything about it was truly like paradise: the sunshine, the perfect beaches, the pubs, the girls. It even had real surfers, beating their way out to catch the waves in constant worship of the swell. Lying on his back to float for a while he wished with his whole being he never had to leave this place and face the rest of his life. Even the idea of wearing a uniform seemed impossible in the freedom of the Gold Coast, let alone the heavy inevitability of everything else that came with it.

'Reckon they're going tonight?' John said nearby, interrupting his thoughts. He followed his friend's nod to a trio of girls jumping over the waves, their bodies glistening in the late morning sun, bikinis leaving little to the imagination.

'Maybe you should ask them.'

'Maybe *you* should. You're the one turning down a girl like Barbara.'

Ben considered. One of them looked quite a lot like Poppy Flannery which piqued his interest. Then the girl noticed him and waved, her friends giggling at her daring.

'I don't profess to know jack about women but I know one thing for sure: it's bloody handy having you around,' John told him, watching in awe as the girls bounced further away. 'You're a dead-set chick magnet.'

Ben said nothing but if he'd voiced what he was thinking he would have told his friend it meant nothing in the end. Whatever girls he met he'd ultimately have to walk away from, even someone like Poppy. It wasn't his body to give, nor his heart. Nor his life. All of that belonged to his family name, mortgaged for the honour of carrying it.

After a lazy swim they made their way back to the shore and were pausing to pick up their discarded towels when a loud commotion sounded across the beach – a combination of screeching brakes and blaring horns.

'Holy mackerel – check this guy out,' John said, laughing as a very battered-looking station wagon rolled straight off the road and clattered onto the south end of the beach in a spectacular cloud of sand. 'Park anywhere, why don't you.'

'One way to meet meter maids,' Ben observed, squinting his eyes at the two young men as they clambered out of the now-silent vehicle, scratching their heads at its apparent demise. Then one grabbed a board out of the back and ran straight for the water, uncaring of the stranded vehicle, the approaching lifesavers, the staring crowd or seemingly anything else.

'Now that's true dedication to the craft,' John said, amused.

But all Ben could feel was envy. For as long as he lived he knew he'd never have a moment like that; an instant of true, spontaneous abandon.

He would never own that kind of freedom.

'We made it!' Spike was yelling over his shoulder as he hightailed it towards the surf.

'What about the car?' Angus yelled after him.

'Who cares?'

Angus could see a few burly lifesavers who definitely cared, and a scandalised crowd of beachgoers to boot. They were moving towards him just as Spike was running away, leaving him to deal with the fallout as usual. He half wished Jed was still with them so he could smoke some yundi and not give a stuff too.

'You the driver of this vehicle?' asked one of the lifesavers as they arrived.

'No, he's uh…indisposed.'

At least the man had a sense of humour as Angus watched him look out towards the surf and grin. 'Can't say I blame him but you really need to get this thing off the beach.'

'Any suggestions as to how I do that exactly?'

'Grab some mates and haul it outta here.'

'My mates are all back in Broome.'

'That explains a few things,' said another lifesaver, peering at the old Holden that was caked in red dust as well as sand. 'How the hell did you make it here in that?'

'That's a very long story…'

'I'll bet,' he said, amused. 'Who wants to give this fella a hand?' he called out to the crowd and a fair few men came forward, joining Angus and the lifesavers in half pushing, half carrying the car back onto the road.

'Phew, that was thirsty work,' panted a young blond-haired man as they fell exhausted against it at last.

'Beers on me,' Angus said by way of thanks and quite a few took him up on it as they made their way across to the pub.

'What about your mate?'

'Brother, actually. He'll find his way here, believe me.'

The blond man nodded. 'He seems the adventurous type.'

'That's one word for it,' Angus muttered, ordering beers all round.

'Name's Ben. Ben Williamson,' said the man, sticking out his hand as the barmaid poured from the tap, lining up what you called 'pots' in Queensland, not 'middies' (a fact she tersely pointed out).

'Angus Turner, nice to meet you, all of you actually,' he extended his introduction, clinking glasses. 'Sorry to have polluted your paradise with our pathetic excuse for a car.'

'Hey, at least you made it. How far was it anyway?' another man asked.

'Three thousand miles across the desert, mostly,' he told them and they shook their heads as they drank, quite a few comments circulating about the 'mad West Aussie bastards'.

Spike arrived then and was told to put on a shirt before he shook the salt out of his hair and dove straight into the beer and the storytelling, which made it quite an afternoon. In fact, it was well past five when their new friends invited them to a toga beach party and they stumbled upstairs to get changed, having secured a room for the next few days from the begrudging barmaid.

Angus was ready first, his bedsheet pinned over his board shorts, and he stared out the window at the beach that was winding down from the bustling activity of the day, a calm pause before Saturday night on the Gold Coast began. Someone had painted graffiti on the toilet block wall and he read it with amusement. *Make love not war.* Not a bad idea at all, he had to agree. Cars still lined the road and carpark but most of the surfers had finished up. Boards were strapped onto roof racks and the ocean was empty, just rows and rows of curling blue. The beach was mostly empty too, now that the masses of sunbakers and families had retired home to make the swap-over into evening.

Angus stared out at the apricot-tinged horizon with the sudden, wondrous realisation that the sun was behind him: he was looking out at the east coast of Australia for the very first time. He'd have to make sure he watched the sun rise over it in the morning.

He hadn't expected it to feel quite so different from Broome but Surfers Paradise definitely had an atmosphere unto itself, almost like a heartbeat, and there was an air of excitement drumming up from below. It wafted through the window in a perfume of salt and pine, heavy with soap from people showering in the little units that lined the strip, and the scent of fish and chips mingled in – making him hungry for an early dinner.

Someone was busking on the footpath and 'Under the Boardwalk' reached him amid the click of women's heels and the pound of the surf.

Then something else beat at him, a different kind of hunger. It was the craving for the softness of a woman's body that hit him like a shot of whiskey, overtaking all his other senses. The sounds and the scents and the sights all drew it forth into one big dose of anticipation, because somewhere – out there tonight – was a girl, and she didn't know it yet but she was going to be in his arms down by that sea.

And he was going to drink it all in through her and funnel it into his entire being because suddenly it felt like some kind of destiny; as if he'd waited his whole life for the moment when he would find her here, a daughter of the east coast, welcoming him to paradise.

She fastened her bracelet, wishing Rosemary would hurry up and finish getting ready so they could go. It was only dinner with the other students, and the nuns of course, but they were still going out in Surfers Paradise at night for the first time and that was pretty exciting.

'Ready,' Rosemary proclaimed.

'Wow,' Poppy said as she turned and looked at her sister. The white shift really showed off the tan she'd been working on back home and the smudge of forbidden eyeliner was doing wonders for her eyes. Here's hoping the nuns didn't fuss over it. Poppy had done the same and was also quite pleased with the blue capri pants and matching top they'd bought at Tweed Heads this afternoon after a morning of sightseeing. It was covered by a thin cardigan for modesty's sake but maybe if they snuck off later she could conveniently leave it behind. Their friend Daniella had already been in contact, managing to stay up here with family as predicted, and if there was any way of meeting up with her Poppy was determined to find it.

The group was marshalled into the bus – a chatty, friendly lot, the twins were finding. They were mostly dags too and, as such, were straight-A types. The teacher's pets; 'wallflowers who played old-fashioned instruments in orchestras' being their common denominator. But they were also their kind of people – quirky, funny, a bit outside the box in general. Some of the outfits were questionable, even bordering on the eccentric, she noted, trying not to stare at Jane Patridge's bright yellow overalls, but there wasn't any bullying in this world. They all knew that pain too well. Dags were rarely bitchy.

These dags also loved to sing and the twins joined in an enthusiastic rendition of the Seekers' latest hit, 'I'll Never Find Another You', to the indulgent approval of the nuns. This was a musical trip, after all.

By the time they piled out of the bus and onto the crowded street excitement was high and Poppy observed Queensland nightlife with avid interest. School holidays had started and there were a large number of families – women dressed for dinner in crisp cotton skirts, holding hands with their husbands who'd swapped beach shirts for ties, noisy children in tow. They looked to consider their choices carefully as they read from the blackboards outside the rows of family restaurants.

Clothing shops were closed for the day but the mannequins in the windows boasted an array of surf wear that matched the atmosphere up here – casual shorts, Hawaiian shirts, straw hats and daring bikinis. They looked like frozen displays promoting decadence and the nuns ushered the girls along, pointing out various sights on the other side of the street for distraction. Then they arrived at their restaurant of choice, a conservative affair with its white picket fence and matching furniture, but it was outdoors which was exciting. Just right for people-watching and, after much fussing over what to order, the girls did just that, staring at the passing parade in fascination until the food arrived.

It was a pleasant evening, warmer than Sydney with the scent of frangipani in the air, and the company was pleasant too. Conversation centred around university courses and music, mostly, and the twins were enjoying themselves, although the people-watching was an ongoing distraction.

Families began to head for home and the crowds became increasingly younger as the party-seekers hit the streets. Young men in short-sleeved shirts had showered and shaved and were hunting down girls whose skirts were shorter than last season, many barely hitting the knee. Groups began to cluster within the throng. Meanwhile cars cruised up and down the strip, filled with grinning surfies who waved at their party with enthusiasm, honking their horns. Then a band started up at the Beergarden hotel on the corner.

'I love this song,' said a girl called Lizzie, her eyes shining.

'"Downtown",' Poppy said, recognising it too. She homed in on the singer's voice who was doing a fair impersonation of Petula Clark, feeling like she was inside the song itself. Like the whole world was here tonight, just waiting for her.

Unfortunately, the nuns had the opposite idea, deciding instead that it was definitely time to get their charges back behind the safe walls of the convent where they were billeted for their stay. Poppy went to the bus reluctantly, drinking in every detail to replay in her mind tonight, a perfect backdrop for teenage dreaming. Then they were halted by a voice.

'Poppy! Rosemary!' The twins paused on the bus stairs to wave at Daniella Rossi who was jumping up and down on the footpath in delight at having spotted them.

'Move on there, girls,' said Sister Margaret, who had looked ready for bed for the good part of an hour. The twins rushed on board then leant out the window, talking in hushed but excited tones as they made their arrangements.

Then the bus pulled from the kerb, away from the heart of the pulsing party, but two girls on board carried the rhythm with them, vowing to find a way to return somehow – to hold on to this night that would never pulse again.

To feel its every beat, right through till dawn.

Twelve

It had all been worth it – the lying awake in their clothes, the sneaking down the stairs then out the window into the rose bushes. The cut on Rosemary's ankle and the thorn prick on Poppy's bottom. Even being discovered by Jane Partridge who had insisted on coming along in her yellow overalls.

It had been worth it because the beach party Daniella took them to was the most intoxicating scene they had ever witnessed.

Girls shook their bodies doing the watusi in shorts and bikini tops and there must have been at least a dozen musicians playing guitars and drums near the massive bonfire. A makeshift bar had been set up by some enterprising individuals and beer bottles were in every hand. Poppy paid for three and they drank rather quickly, nervous about fitting in, but there were no walls on this beach, no seats to shrink over to and just observe.

'Grab on!' yelled a man in a toga as he passed by in a conga line and Poppy impulsively joined in, kicking off her sandals to better dance on the sand. Rosemary and Jane followed and just like that they were in – partying with the cool kids. Half-naked cool kids, Poppy noted, slightly scandalised as she touched the young man's bare waist.

'Why the toga?' Poppy found the courage to yell in his ear.

'Tonight we are gods!' he announced, gesturing at several others who were likewise clad in bedsheets and ivy.

'Gods of what?'

'Paradise!'

She laughed and held on as the line twisted through the crowd, craning her neck to see past him and perhaps find a tall blond figure among it all. There were plenty of fair heads to search through – the party was filled with surfies – and she noticed one had hair so long it touched his shoulders, just like the guys in the Rolling Stones. He was wearing dark sunglasses and dancing with Daniella who was doing quite a good job of matching his Jagger-like moves.

Poppy's eyes were drawn to a toga-draped man who carried a dog, also wearing sunglasses, and she giggled; he was staring at them and nudging a taller man next to him whose eyes widened as they passed. Poppy turned to see if Rosemary had noticed, and was surprised to find her sister staring straight back at the two men, with a rather flirtatious look. Five minutes into this party and any trace of awkwardness in her sister had vanished. Even Jane was chatting with the man behind her in the line. It made Poppy feel emboldened herself. The years of being dags seemed suddenly behind them now, the mystery of how to fit in solved in the simple act of just doing so.

Then she saw another man across the fire, hair gold above his sheet, ivy resting like a crown, and her new confidence deepened into resolve. He may look like some kind of god but Poppy would approach him anyway. She was done with worshipping Ben from afar.

'Ten, nine, eight…' yelled the toga-man in front.

'What are you doing?' Poppy said, stalled as the conga line stopped and he spun around, pulling her into his arms.

'Practising for New Year's Eve. Five, four, three...' he shouted, most of the crowd nearby joining in.

'...two, one! Happy Fake New Year!'

And then Poppy's lips were pressed against his at the precise moment her gaze collided with Ben's. Of all the ways she'd imagined the moment she would meet with Ben in Queensland *none of them* had involved her tasting her very first kiss with a half-naked man, barefoot in the sand still holding her beer. A very far cry from a girl with a cello case sitting on a cold city train. All traces of the wallflower gone.

It was like a slap, one that he totally deserved for not acting sooner. Of course it was only a matter of time until another guy discovered the woman in the girl, especially when she was dressed like that.

Poppy was barely recognisable with her make-up and hairdo, and that outfit may have covered everything modestly enough but it clung in all the right places, showing off everything her school uniform tried to hide. Ben had noticed that gorgeous figure first, unaware that it was Poppy's little waist that had caught his attention, Poppy's skin showing where her top rode up against the surfie who was holding her. It was only when the man had swooped in for a kiss and Ben had looked at her face that he'd realised with a shock who she was.

Then there was a moment of stunned connection followed by the mutual realisation that, once again, someone else was in the way. At least he hoped that was what she was thinking, then he might still have a chance.

'Benny?'

He recognised her perfume before he even turned to find Barbara standing behind him, hand on the hip of some undoubtedly expensive but still very short shorts that were causing people to stare as they passed.

'Hi,' he responded, already trying to invent an excuse to leave.

'Have you got a minute?'

Ben scratched his head while Chris made faces over her shoulder, drawing circles near his ear to emphasise Ben's descent into madness.

'Not right now actually, sorry.' He wove away fast but she followed, calling his name until he lost himself inside a bunch of people doing the stomp and made it to John and Chappy.

'Let me guess, running away from a woman?' Chappy said, offering him a beer.

'He's like a Beatle,' John observed, shaking his head.

Ben couldn't think of an answer so he just drank instead, giving himself a moment to consider his next move, but it was short-lived.

'Holy crap, is that one of the Flannery twins?' Chris said, staring as Rosemary went past in a conga line filled with togas.

'Rosemary,' Ben said, craning his neck and looking for Poppy.

'How the hell can you tell them apart?'

Ben wanted to say 'how the hell can you not?' but it was Chappy's turn to ask stunned questions.

'Since when do they have bodies like that?'

Ben would have answered that they'd been that way all along – if Chappy had only bothered paying more attention – but suddenly that was a waste of time. Sculling his beer for courage he strode off to find the matching sister before New Year was declared again.

1966 may well belong to his family, along with the rest of his life, but that dreaded countdown was some weeks away.

Right now it was 1965 and that still belonged to him.

'Barrel,' the man was saying, pointing at the dog with his beer, 'and I'm Spike from W.A.'

'Poppy.'

'Rosemary.'

'Nothing like a matching pair,' Poppy heard Spike say under his breath.

'We're, uh, brothers too. I mean siblings. Like you.' Angus attempted to explain, looking from one to the other nervously. 'Angus. Angus Turner. You're very…I mean, nice to meet you.'

'Nice to meet you too,' Rosemary said, staring as his toga fell off, revealing a naked torso above his shorts. He fumbled for the sheet, apologising.

'Drink?' asked Spike, nodding at the bar.

'Sure,' Rosemary said, but Poppy was too distracted to answer as she scanned the crowd for both Ben and the New Year kisser. She couldn't believe she'd finally kissed a boy and not only was it *not* Ben, it was in right in front of him. She hadn't even really got to enjoy it, as public and badly timed as it had been. Then Barbara had turned up and Ben had run off into the crowd, a fact that left Poppy wavering between bewilderment and hope.

'The ancient Greeks wore togas too although many associate them with the Romans. They tended to steal quite a bit of history actually…' Rosemary was saying to Angus and Poppy half-listened, registering with some amusement that her sister was about as good at flirting as she was.

'It's just a bedsheet. I used a pin but I've lost it,' Angus said, trying to loop it back in place.

'The ancients tended to use clasps.'

'I, uh…don't have one of those handy,' he said, red-faced and grinning. He was actually pretty good-looking, Poppy had to admit as she glanced over at him, and he seemed kind of endearing as he blushed and pulled at the sheet.

Rosemary stepped forward and began to tie it over his shoulder. 'This would probably work.'

Poppy was impressed now, and rather awed at her sister's audacity. Perhaps she was, in fact, the better flirt, drivel about ancient fashion aside. Mind you, Poppy was the one who had just kissed a boy within about a minute of meeting him – perhaps that put her in the lead. Or maybe that just meant she was 'easy'. A blush crept into her own cheeks now.

'Here you go,' announced Spike, returning with four beers. 'What should we drink to?'

'Don't say New Year's,' said a voice behind Poppy and she turned awkwardly, sloshing her drink onto Ben's partially naked body. Whoever suggested the togas tonight had a lot to answer for, she thought vaguely as he wiped some tanned chest muscles dry with his sheet. She forced her eyes upwards and swallowed hard against the butterflies that seemed to have taken flight from her stomach to her throat.

'Hi,' she managed.

'Poppy Marie,' he said and she felt ridiculously pleased that he used her whole first name. 'Hello Rosemary, you're looking well. See you've met some daredevil West Aussies already,' he said, shaking Spike and Angus's hands.

'I'm not really a daredevil,' Angus was quick to say.

'I don't know, you could tell them a pretty good tale about some spinifex…' Spike began and Angus blushed even redder than before.

'Dance?' Angus thought to ask in lieu of whatever response he could offer and Rosemary took his hand with a smile as they disappeared into the crowd.

A slightly awkward moment followed as Spike looked from Ben to Poppy, seeming to recognise he was in the way of something. 'Come on, Barrel. Let's see if we can talk any of these soft Easties into a night surf.'

Things were still uncomfortable after he left and Poppy racked her brain for something clever to say rather than one of her customary blurts.

'Want to take a walk?' Ben asked, and she breathed a sigh of relief. Plenty of time to think as they made their way towards the shoreline. Unfortunately there were plenty of things to imagine too – wonderful, longed-for things that made unexpected blurting a high probability.

They walked together slowly, the music fading into the pound and wash of the silvered ocean, and Poppy felt her heart strain and leap about with the movement.

'So have you been up here long?' she asked. There, that wasn't so bad.

'Just a few days. You?'

'Only arrived yesterday actually, but we've packed a lot in.'

'I can see that.'

That made her drink the rest of her beer in a gulp. 'Where are you staying?' she tried again.

'Unit on the beach. You?'

Damn. She walked right into that one. 'Convent...playing in the orchestra and...all that.'

He nodded thoughtfully. 'Sounds pretty cool.'

She looked at him in surprise and he laughed.

'You really have absolutely no control over that honesty of yours, do you?'

She flushed, laughing a little. 'I'm a blurter from way back,' she admitted. 'Anyway, there's not much point in lying about it.'

'Most girls would. They'd say they were staying at an aunt's or something.'

Poppy wished she'd thought of that. 'Sorry.'

'Hey,' he said, stopping and turning her around, taking both her hands in his. 'Never apologise for being honest about yourself. It's what I like about you the most.'

Unbelievably his long brown fingers were holding hers and she tried to form a logical sentence over the excited voice in her head replaying his last words. 'You seem pretty honest about who you are.'

His eyes lost a little of their confidence then, in fact she swore she could read doubt there in the grey-blue light. 'Not always.'

She wanted to ask a million questions, dive straight into those eyes and read more, but he chose that moment to kiss her instead and a million questions became a million answers as he poured himself into her.

This is who I really am. This is who I am and I want you.

The beautiful boy was kissing her in the beautiful night, devouring her like fried potatoes coated in salt and vinegar on a cold winter's day. But it was warm here in paradise and that warmth blended with the longing that flowed between them like the ocean itself, crashing and churning. He kissed her with more urgency and they fell to the sand, then Ben paused to stroke her face, his breathing short, his expression sweet with sincerity.

'You okay there, Poppy Marie?'

'Yes,' she said, heart hammering, barely believing she was lying next to him. 'I've liked you for such a long time.'

That made him smile. 'Nice blurt,' he said, before leaning over and kissing her again, slowly, rhythmically. It began to build, like a rolling set of waves, drawing her in closer with that delicious burning she'd felt whenever she imagined being with him before. Then he slid his hand under her top and she gasped.

'Sorry,' he said, immediately withdrawing it.

'No, it's fine. Really,' she told him, embarrassed.

'No, it's not. Not yet. We don't have to rush this, you know.' He sat back to watch her closely, grazing his knuckles against her cheek. 'I've kind of liked you for a long time too.'

It was so hard to believe he'd said it she couldn't help but blurt again. 'But what about Barbara?'

He paused, looking to consider carefully how to reply before simply saying, 'That's over.' Then he waited, searching her face. 'Believe me?'

'Yes.' She said it without any hesitation. She'd believe anything that came out of that beautiful mouth.

Then he grinned that lightning bolt grin and she could only stare, mesmerised, as he spread out the toga sheet then drew her close against his bare chest as they lay back down. 'Just let me hold you for a little while.'

Poppy wanted nothing more and she pressed her face against his skin, loving the silken feel of it. Loving him, she realised, desperate not to blurt that truth at least. Fortunately they talked of other things instead as the star-strewn sky drifted above: wonderful secrets and revelations that bound them ever closer with each passing hour; paintbrushes and canvases, orchestras and exams. Even wallflowers in wallpaper which made him chuckle, a delicious rumble against her cheek.

And all the while the drums beat and the firelight spun distant gold and the sound of some mad West Australian crowing and running into the surf carried from further down, but it meant little to the young couple on the sand.

They'd fallen into contented silence now, fighting sleep to stay in this moment. The stars began to mist in the salted air and Poppy watched them as she lay against Ben's heart, knowing her life was forever altered now. The wallflower would never return after this, not now that she'd tasted paradise.

Thirteen

She hadn't really considered there would be such a big crowd, the auditorium filled to standing room only, and she was more than a little nervous. Poppy had only managed two hours' sleep which didn't bode well for performing complex cello pieces. Rosemary was stifling a yawn and blinking at the music sheets in front, obviously not faring much better. It turned out she'd enjoyed a bit of time down by the shoreline herself, allowing Angus to kiss her a few times before the crimson of dawn gilded the ocean's edge and the twins were forced to find their things and make a hasty, if reluctant, exit.

The conductor raised his baton and they commenced, concentrating hard, allowing the hours of practice to take over as they performed automatically, the orchestra swelling to a rapturous crescendo as Mozart filled the room.

Poppy felt it fill her as well and she lost herself to the emotions: dark, intense, passionate then yearning, understanding at last how such intense feelings had driven the composer those many years ago. Sharing a timeless understanding across the ages. By the time they finished to tumultuous applause Poppy felt tears sting her eyes and raised them to find Rosemary watching her, witnessing the moment; acknowledging the journey that had led Poppy to the dawn of this day.

'Meet me again,' he'd whispered against her ear before her hands slid from his. 'I'll wait here, on the corner.'

'I'll come at midnight,' she'd promised, looking back for as long as she could until the taxi pulled away and broke their gaze.

Such a long time to wait, she sighed, looking at her watch which nudged on noon. Rosemary was meeting up with Angus too and Poppy wondered if they could figure out a way to get some sleep before dinner.

The crowd began to disperse and the students scattered in clumps to find their way towards their buses, a momentary chaos that allowed the twins to chat to Daniella who'd been waving from the crowd.

'Was that Ben Williamson I saw you with last night?' Daniella asked as soon as they were close enough to whisper.

'Uh-huh,' Poppy said, still scarcely believing it herself.

'Far out!' Daniella said, obviously impressed. 'You'd better stay out of Barbara's way – but I guess you can now we've left school,' she added, grinning.

'Hopefully, although I saw her up here last night too.'

'Wow, heavy,' Daniella said, nodding thoughtfully. 'Better lie low then. Who was your fella?' she asked, turning to Rosemary.

'A guy from Western Australia,' Rosemary shrugged, trying to look nonchalant.

'That's a long way to come for a beach party, mind you it was a total gas,' Daniella said, eyes shining. Poppy and Rosemary nodded, not quite sure what that meant but figuring it was something positive. 'Are you coming out again tonight? Rumour has it there's a party down at Tweed this time. Have to move scenes on account of the cops.' Poppy wondered where Daniella was picking up her new lingo. Probably that bohemian-looking man she'd seen her dancing with.

'We'll be out and about,' Rosemary said, still playing it cool, even adding a peace sign as they went, something Poppy had noticed a few of the kids doing last night.

'What was that all about?' said Poppy, giggling as they boarded the bus.

'When in Rome.'

'Wear a toga?'

'Sounds groovy, baby,' Rosemary said, putting on a pair of white-rimmed sunglasses that she'd purchased yesterday – her first ever pair.

'You know, you almost get away with that,' Poppy said, thinking her sister really was starting to seem kind of cool, despite the fact they were back in school uniforms today. The formality of them felt particularly strange after last night, like they were dressing up as their old selves. Back when they were insignificant and Barbara ruled their world. Poppy wondered at Daniella's words – would there be a moment of confrontation with her old nemesis? Chances were fairly high that there would be. The Dogsquad would prowl and bite wherever they were.

She turned to watch the ocean beyond the blur of grass that lined the road as the bus drove them home. Maybe Barbara's power didn't count as much up here, she figured, remembering the tenderness in Ben's expression, the urgency in his kiss. Perhaps beautiful boys didn't like man-hunters in Queensland. Maybe they really did prefer honest blurters instead.

'That was the longest day of my life, Poppy Marie,' he was saying and she clung to his words as she clung to his shoulders, so happy she could easily have cried. Ben kissed her and Poppy barely registered that people were whistling from across the street, nothing mattered but this sweet intensity that ran between them. Warm and intimate.

'What did you do all day?' she asked against his mouth.

'Actually I tried to learn to surf,' he admitted, chuckling. 'Never done it before.'

'And how did you go?'

'Wipeout city, I'm afraid,' he said, kissing her one more time then taking her hand to walk away from the streetlights and onto the beach. 'Angus and Spike were trying to teach me. They're really good.' He nodded over at Angus who was sitting next to Rosemary on the fence rail and laughing at something she said. They look happy, Poppy realised, the thought welcome.

There were no parties here tonight, just a few scattered fires with couples making out or small groups chatting and strumming guitars. The larger throng were probably down at Tweed Heads, as Daniella had predicted.

'Why haven't you ever surfed?'

Ben shrugged and that shadow passed over his face again, the one she'd glimpsed last night. 'I wasn't allowed to do anything much aside from cadets. Father terms such things "unnecessary distractions".' He said it in a silly, sombre imitation but it didn't quite hide the animosity in his tone.

'Rosemary and I weren't allowed to do much either. Guess that's why we turned out to be such dags.'

'Blurt alert,' he said, and she laughed. 'You're not a dag, well not to me. You're just…different.'

'That's not something a girl wants to be, trust me. We want to fit in and belong and…' She stopped herself then, wondering if she was admitting too much.

'Belonging to the cool crowd doesn't amount to much, believe me. It's mostly just competition – who has the best car, the latest gear. Who lands the hottest chick and all that rubbish.'

There was an uncomfortable pause which Poppy broke. 'Nice blurt.'

He grimaced comically. 'Good God, it's contagious.'

They walked along further and Poppy wondered if he was thinking about Barbara, wishing the subject of hot chicks hadn't come up. The moon had risen, the water catching its radiance in a brilliant, shimmering line, and Ben put his arm around her waist as they paused to watch it.

'I want to explain something to you but I'm not sure how to say it,' he admitted after a while.

Poppy felt her heart drop. This was it. Paradisiacal dream over. 'Go on.'

'Barbara was...well, an easier choice than you.'

'I'm sure she was,' Poppy said, moving away; trying not feel so suddenly, wretchedly hurt.

'No, no, I don't mean in that way,' he said, following her. 'She was an easier choice because I...well, I didn't take it seriously. I can't afford to take any girl seriously.'

'Well, I'm glad we cleared that up.' What a fool you are Poppy. A stupid, wall-leaning fool.

'God, I'm making a horrible mess of this. What I'm trying to say is I went with her because I couldn't get serious with someone then and I still can't now. I've got nothing to give for a long time ahead, Poppy. I'm going to Duntroon, then probably to Vietnam, then there's the law degree. I won't be free for years.' He took her hands and she saw that all shadows had been removed, vulnerability in their place. 'I'm serious about liking you but I...I've got nothing to give you except right now.'

His sincerity was evident but she found herself rebelling against his reasoning. 'One day you'll have more.'

'Not for a very long time.'

She pulled her hands away and walked to the water's edge to sort her thoughts. 'So what you're telling me is this is a holiday affair – don't expect anything else.'

He was silent for a moment before answering. 'I'm telling you I *can't* give you any more than that. I can't ask you to sacrifice all those years of your life waiting.'

She turned back towards him, the dark water eddying at her feet. 'What would you have happen in a perfect world?'

'This isn't a perfect world.'

'It's Surfers Paradise – let's just pretend for a minute. Pretend you can have anything you want.'

He watched her, the wind whipping at his shirt as a storm sounded far out to sea. 'I'd cheat time and jump past all that bloody duty…and come right back here to be with you.'

Poppy walked towards him slowly to stand close once more. 'Do you really mean that?'

'Yes, but I can't ask…'

'Perhaps not but I'm saying yes anyway,' she said in a rush, tears scratching her throat. 'I'll wait, Ben. I'll write and I'll…I'll only see you on leave and all those other things you don't want to ask me to do.'

He shook his head. 'No, you can't promise that. We hardly know each other really and you're too young to say…'

'I don't care,' she said, tears sliding now as she shook her head. 'You can't ask me to wait but you can't ask me *not* to either. I'll wait, Ben. I'll wait for you.'

He was still hesitating so she kissed him, unable to stop the desperation that drove the act, and she felt his resistance fall as he kissed her back. Lightning flashed closer, cool rain carrying on the salted wind, and she tasted her own tears as they clung together on the shore.

'What if I never make it home?' he whispered, fear there now as he rested his forehead against hers.

Her mind had no answer to that so her heart spoke instead. 'You have to come home. I...I love you.' She could no sooner have halted the words than halt the storm that was now pelting their skin.

He traced the rain off her face gently as she barely dared breathe. 'Blurting again eh?' Then he smiled that devastating smile and held her chin. 'Guess that's what I really love about you the most.'

Fourteen

Poppy hummed as she waited, her heart so light she simply had to kick off her shoes and walk along the wooden poles that lined the sand path. He was pretty late but she wasn't concerned. Ben loved her. *He loved her.* He'd said it three times now: once on the beach that second night and twice yesterday when she'd dared to fake the flu and wag a sightseeing outing with the orchestra group. How could a day driving around in a hired jeep with Ben possibly compare? How could it compare to anything? she thought dreamily, giggling at the memory of him bouncing along dirt tracks and hitchhiking for more petrol, shirt flung over his shoulder, his skin brown in the sun. He is so beautiful, she sighed, aching for him to arrive.

A sea eagle glided near the beach's end and she watched its serene surveillance restlessly. I know, I know, she told it silently, putting her shoes back on and sitting to wait. Patience is a virtue. Only it was pretty hard to hold onto it when a guy like that walked around without a shirt on half the day. Pretty hard to hold onto other virtues too.

'Girl here to see ya,' the landlord said with a knowing grin. Ben finished combing his hair then pushed past him to run down the stairs. Bloody Chappy talking him into one last ride in the jeep. Poppy must have got tired of waiting and tracked him down.

He rounded the corner with excitement, his smile fading as another girl stood and faced him, her expensive perfume filling the room.

'What are you doing here?' he asked, already looking to the door.

'I have to talk to you Benny – it can't wait. Can we go somewhere private?'

'Barbara, I'm just on my way out...'

'It's really important.'

'I just don't think it's good idea to...'

'Benny, I'm pregnant.'

She'd said it with a sense of triumph, he reflected later, and he'd known immediately that she'd hoped for this all along. Probably from the day she'd tapped her fingers on his mother's dining table. He supposed he should have seen through her but she was like a spider, her invisible webs woven strong, and he'd walked straight into her trap like the hapless prey he was. And now she was spinning more silken ties, binding him to her, and this time he was caught – no way to escape.

'You were the only one,' she'd insisted, and the damning words were like venom, piercing his skin and poisoning his veins.

Then that little piece of life he'd claimed for himself – the hope newly born that he could actually have something he chose – was ripped away.

She'd left not long after and he'd made his slow way back up the stairs, so different a man to the one who'd descended only moments before.

He sat for a long time before he packed his bags for home, but there was nothing else left to do. This was unalterable and unavoidable, just like everything else in his future. Better to leave Poppy to pace until she hated him, to learn to never again wait for a man. She deserved better than that, anyway. Better than what he could give.

Barbara had won after all, his canvas smeared by yet another duty. Just another cost to tag on to the honour of his name.

Part Two

Second Skin

Fifteen

Sydney, June 1966

Political activist James Meredith should make a full recovery after being shot during his 220 mile solo protest march in Memphis earlier this week. Martin Luther King has visited Meredith in hospital, praising his efforts and calling for action.

Angus leant over to turn up the radio, pausing in his work at the mention of the civil right leader's name.

It is predicted potentially thousands of protesters will now walk in support of Meredith's goal of encouraging black citizens to register to vote, in what is now being called the Meredith March Against Fear. His attacker, Aubrey James Norvell, remains in custody.

The rain pattered hard against the glass and Angus turned down the dial, preferring to listen to the wild weather than the political struggles of the world.

'Find some music at least,' Spike muttered from under the car he was working on and Angus obliged. It was the fourth wet day in a row, a fact that was depressing the hell out of his brother who began to sing along mournfully as Angus landed on a song. It was the Mamas and the Papas' 'California Dreamin'' and even Barrel looked dejected, his head on his paws as he lay next to Spike, following his movements with sad eyes. Angus would have felt the same way if not for the thought of his warm bed last night and Rosemary's soft skin under the blankets. As far as he was concerned the cold weather could stay as long as it liked.

'Smoko,' Spike declared, laying down his wrench and climbing out to fall onto the threadbare lounge in the corner. It fit his height perfectly and he propped his feet up on the arm at the end.

Angus walked over to fill the kettle, casting a glance at the dirty cups and plates near the sink. 'Waiting for the maid, are we?'

Spike ignored him, rolling his cigarette instead. He'd initially enjoyed the northern beaches surfing scene in Sydney but that was part of their endless summer. Now the spontaneous decision to follow Rosemary to Sydney with Angus was beginning to cool with each chilly day.

'Wish we had some yundi.'

'Not around the tools,' Angus reminded him as he filled both kettle and sink. It was hair-raising enough being around Spike as he wielded and welded his way about the workshop they were managing at Brookvale Automotive. Angus didn't like to imagine how he'd fare doing the job stoned. He lit a cigarette himself as the detergent formed a small snowscape and washed two cups with his spare hand. 'Cake?' he offered, wiping the suds away and taking a foil-wrapped package out of his bag.

'Mmm,' Spike said. 'What have we got today?'

'Banana,' Angus said, unwrapping the foil and sniffing the slab. 'Smells pretty nice.'

He finished his preparations and Spike accepted a slice with the cup of tea, propping himself up to better investigate the flecked brown cake with its creamy icing. 'She's getting better.'

'That she is,' Angus agreed, smiling at the thought of Rosemary in her apron last night, reading the ingredients out loud from her cookbook, flour on her nose.

'She could bake for you just as well in Queensland.'

'I'm sure she could.'

'She could study up there just as well too.'

Angus flashed him a look. 'Let's not do this today, okay?'

Spike shrugged, eating his cake sullenly.

'I told you, you're free to go anytime…'

'I just don't get it,' Spike said, exasperated. 'She's almost nineteen – who cares what her father says?'

'She says she can't leave Sydney and that's that.' Angus sipped on his tea, wishing she would reconsider himself. The occasional night that she could manage to swing behind her parents' backs wasn't nearly enough, not at the rate he was falling for her. 'She's trying to talk him into letting her board at uni which would change things.'

'Change things for you – won't change squat for me. I'll still be freezing my bum off and putting up with bloody wetsuits. We need to go back north – or west.'

Angus shook his head. 'I understand if you want to go but I'm staying put.'

Spike said nothing then, finishing his morning tea in silence before moving back over to the workbench and picking up the wrench. Angus knew his brother wouldn't leave. It wasn't something they ever discussed but being separated wasn't really an option for either of them. They were bound together by some kind of 'brotherly code', he supposed, a bind that stretched back as far as either of them could remember, stronger than most. Maybe because they'd both known the taste of too much cod-liver oil from their anxious mother. Maybe because they'd each spent years standing on the other's sidelines at football games in lieu of an absent, disinterested father.

They were empty words that suggested Spike would go anywhere without him, but they were easier words than the underlying truth. That was something Angus wasn't quite ready to articulate – not even to himself – because such an admission would buffet their world, much like the winds on this rainy winter's day. Words liked that changed lives, perhaps for good. Words like that may even break codes.

'Hello, beautiful,' Angus said, an instant smile on his lips as Rosemary kissed him lightly then met his green eyes with her own clear blue. She was standing on her toes to reach him, her knitted socks causing him to smile even more. 'Wearing the Nana booties again?'

'They're warm,' she said, wrapping her arms around him for a hug. She only ever gave long ones, like she couldn't get enough of that safe place that existed between them. 'How was your week?'

'Endless,' he said, breathing in that unique fragrance that clung to her hair, something both sweet and earthy. He'd asked her once what it was and she'd said it might be her shampoo but there was something else there beyond that store-bought, apple-scented stuff, something less definable. It held imprints of her daily life; university lawns and fallen leaves. Cake baking and wooden instruments. Either way he was intoxicated by it, to the point he'd bury his face in her pillow after she'd gone to keep those traces of her with him. He hadn't told her that of course. That would make him sound far too mushy.

'Do you want to grab some dinner?' he asked her. Aside from her booties she was dressed for going out in a woollen dress and tights, her shoes waiting by the door where she'd let herself in earlier.

'Uh-huh,' she said, but she didn't stop hugging and he soaked it in. The moment was interrupted by the sound of voices through the wall where Spike was welcoming his new surfing mate Reggie. That motivated Angus to get moving. Reggie was a major stoner and Angus was keen to leave before the waft of yundi filled the small side-by-side flats he and Spike shared above the workshop. Rosemary didn't need to have that much information about his world just yet.

'Come on,' he said, holding her coat, unable to resist kissing her cheek as she weaved her arms through.

They made their way down the wet and precarious stairs, umbrella low. It was bum-freezing weather, Spike was right. It bit straight through his jeans and flannel shirt and he pulled both his jacket and Rosemary tight.

'The usual?'

'Okay,' she said, gasping and giggling as they crossed the road and walked down to the little pizzeria on the corner. The aroma of garlic and roasting pepperoni drew them on and Angus swung the door open gratefully, straight into the warmth of pie ovens and a booming Italian welcome.

'Ah, Cowboy!' yelled Antonio, the proprietor. '*Benvenuto*!' Being from the 'west' promoted Angus to John Wayne stature according to this movie-mad Italian. Angus's penchant for checked shirts further confirmed the man's hopeful assumptions that there was a little more Hollywood western in Angus that he cared to admit.

'Howdy,' Angus said, grinning back, 'got room for me and the little lady?'

'*Si*, *si*, you come sit by the ovens, eh? You have the big Texan pizza tonight?' Antonio loved to make him his 'Texan Special' as part of their running joke, although the only thing that differentiated it from his usual special was the addition of hot red chillies. Despite some choking fits in the early days, Angus had now grown to rather like it, although it took plenty of wine and water to wash it down.

'I'm game, but no chilli on Rosemary's quarter.'

Antonio rubbed his hands together happily and called out to his daughter Maria to bring them the 'vino'. They were early so the place was yet to fill but it would, especially on a night like this.

'New poster,' Angus called to Antonio who was now flipping discs of floury dough high in the air.

'Jimmy Stewart and Maureen O'Hara. *Bella*!' he said, kissing his fingers in between flips. They looked at the large mounted image above them with interest. It was dramatic and colourful, like most of the movie posters that vied for space on the restaurant walls, with a scarlet-clad O'Hara clutching Jimmy Stewart against her breast underneath the title *Rancho Bravo*.

'Makes me want to go to the flicks. What do you think?'

Rosemary tilted her head at his question and toyed with her napkin. 'Well, there is a party that Daniella wants us to go to...but I think I'd rather just stay at the flat.' She was blushing and he took her hand. Angus knew she was trying to embrace this new part of herself – the woman she was becoming with him – but he also knew she was an innocent girl still, and Catholic to boot. She wasn't ready for the full experience quite yet and he was holding back until she was. All the same, the long hours spent discovering each new level of passion with her, inch by delectable inch, was pretty much the best way he could imagine spending Friday night too.

'I suppose I could just put a cowboy hat on,' he suggested, and she laughed, a slightly daring expression passing across her face. Angus grinned in response as the wine arrived and Maria delivered a basket of hot bread. Antonio baked his own crusty oval loaves then halved them before placing them under the grill, and the garlic butter oozed with each delicious mouthful.

'Still willing to kiss me after this?' Angus asked, crunching the bread and sipping his wine.

Rosemary tore a piece of bread and held it up. 'If you want to kiss them, join them, I guess,' she said, rather brazenly for her.

'Phew, they'd better hurry up with that there pizza, little filly. I need some chilli to take the edge off this darn heat,' he drawled. She giggled and the rest of the meal was spent flirting and laughing together until the restaurant was filled to busting and it was time to squeeze their way out.

'So long-a, partner,' called Antonio, throwing over a box of leftovers for Barrel, and they pushed their way out into the chilly evening, battling with the umbrella once more.

By the time they got home they were glued together, as much from seeking each other's warmth as wanting each other's touch, but as they made it back to the landing they heard an almighty din, drawing them to Spike's side instead.

'Better stay back,' Angus warned Rosemary as he opened the door to the sight of Spike playing his guitar and wailing a version of 'Wild Thing' into a microphone. A long pipe sat unashamedly on the coffee table and there were several empty beer cans lying about. Angus turned to shield Rosemary but she was already staring past his shoulder, her eyes wide as Reggie struggled to stuff green crumbs from a bowl into the smoking implement.

'Angus,' Spike sang, spying him with a wicked gleam and changing the lyrics, 'you make me freezing, you make everything chilly, brrr Angus…'

Angus turned and steered Rosemary firmly back to his flat, closing the door behind them and searching for a way to explain what they'd just seen.

'Was that a pot pipe?' she asked, straight out. That was one thing you could say for Rosemary, she never beat around the bush.

'No, no, that was…er…an asthma device. Spike's mate gets it…in the cold weather…'

'I'm not as green as you think I am, you know, and neither is asthma medication.' She could be downright funny sometimes too but he wasn't laughing right now.

'Alright, yes. Look I'm sorry. Spike is just a bit...well, wild. You know he likes the whole surfing scene and everything and...'

'...and he's homesick.' The 'Angus' version of 'Wild Thing' sounded through the wall as Spike continued to lament the cold weather in Sydney.

'Yes, he is.'

'And he blames me.'

'No, he blames me.'

Rosemary looked at Angus, digesting it all. 'Well, there's better ways to have fun in freezing Sydney than sitting at home wiping yourself out. Come on.'

'Where are we going?' he asked, surprised as she handed him his jacket and marched to the door.

'Somewhere a little wild.'

Sixteen

The blind was knocking ever so slightly on the kitchen door, the heavy sand-filled runner at the base unable to completely block out the draught. Poppy was half listening to it and half listening to her father discussing the pros and cons of running for council this year. It was something he'd long considered – too long. Her mother was as bored of the subject as she was, Poppy knew, focusing more on her embroidery and muttering the occasional 'you should do it then' and 'I'm sure they would have you'. Her father seemed to recognise her disinterest and turned on the TV, moving through each programme with a disapproving grunt, settling on a news story about Vietnam.

Poppy zoned out from it, trying not to think about war and soldiers and a fair-headed man training to join them. Yes, a man now, not a boy. The 'beautiful boy' was gone forever, dissolved and overtaken by 'the boy who never showed'. And now he was a man, married to a woman. The woman who always won.

She stood to walk up to her room, the drone of the newsreader's report too unbearable a sound for her to withstand. Far better to sit in her room and play sad pieces on her cello to further drench her soul.

Then the phone rang and her mother's voice halted her.

'Daniella for you,' she said, not entirely disapproving. The Rossis were well respected in their church – came from the right part of Italy apparently: Milan, not too far from France. That was practically Parisian, according to Lois.

'Hi,' Poppy said, pulling the cord around the corner into the hall.

'Hi yourself. That's the third time I've tried to call you this week. Are you or are you not coming to this happening party tonight?'

'I don't know. I think I'm getting a cold,' Poppy hedged. Truth was she hadn't really been anywhere much since Queensland, despite Daniella and Rosemary's constant pleadings. Their social lives were finally taking off, the wallflowers long gone now that they were university students and being brainy was the new 'cool', but Poppy was still trying to hide in the corner. It was a self-imposed exile; there were just too many happy couples out there in the world. It was bad enough noticing them at uni, holding hands in the corridor and kissing on the lawns; being around them in the close proximity of a party would be suffocating. 'Rosemary said she's going...'

'Ha. I'll believe that when I see it. She's too busy with her man and *you're* too busy being a square. Cold, my arse.'

'Sorry,' Poppy mumbled and there was a pause down the line.

'No, I'm sorry. That was a bit heavy...but I just really think you should get out, you know? Get your groove on.'

Poppy smiled into the receiver. 'I'm not sure I have one of those.'

'Everyone has a groove, baby, or so Cat reckons.' 'Cat' was the name of Daniella's bohemian boyfriend who she'd been dating since Queensland, although Poppy had it on good authority that his real name was Eugene Hawes and he was a part-time student and part-time shoe repair salesman from Carlingford. He obviously liked keeping that secret identity under wraps, preferring his alter ego, Cat: political activist and philosophical guru of the Arts Department. 'Come on, Pops,' she said, more gently now, 'you can't cry into your pillow over Ben forever.'

Poppy flinched at his name. 'I'm not crying into my pillow…'

'Yes you are.'

She was of course. Every day, in fact.

'I'm picking you up in half an hour and don't forget your grooving shoes,' Daniella ordered before hanging up.

Poppy made her slow way back to the living room, considering whether to actually go or not. Branches were being whipped about outside and the windows were misting against the dwindling light. It didn't look very inviting.

…casualties were high and authorities say the village was secured but at a cost…

The black and white images of the television flickered at her as Lois's voice interrupted the report.

'No later than eleven o'clock and make sure your sister comes home on time with you.' Poppy looked at her mother in surprise, realising she'd been eavesdropping. The usual firm set about Lois's mouth was there but something in her eyes betrayed a hint of understanding too. 'Wear your warm coat.'

Poppy nodded, slightly agog, then turned to mount the stairs. Sooner or later she had to take this first real step back into a social world, even her mother seemed aware of that much, despite being ignorant of the reason. Opening the wardrobe, she looked at the clothes hanging within, picking out one of Rosemary's new shift dresses and stroking the navy material thoughtfully. Put on the costume.

She dressed methodically and brushed her hair up into a twist, running as much kohl as Lois would allow across her lids. Fake it till you make it, Rosemary would say, and she touched her freckles lightly with powder, even smearing a teeny bit of lipstick on her lips then her cheekbones, rubbing it into a slight blush. Staring at her reflection she had to admit she looked the best she had in months. An actress ready to walk on stage.

The doorbell sounded and she took a deep breath.

'You're still you,' she told her reflection, 'you're still Poppy Flannery, just play the part.'

But she wasn't the same person, not really. Poppy Flannery was a different girl now, perhaps even a woman.

And never again would she truly be Poppy Marie.

The Young Rascals were blasting from the speakers as they shouldered their way through the crowd and Angus gaped at the scene, rather shocked that Rosemary was associated with what was, as promised, a pretty wild party. No wonder she was enjoying uni life so much, he thought, feeling rather jealous that she had a world separate from his. Especially a world like this.

'Dude,' yelled Spike to one long-haired man. 'Peace, brother!' he said to the next, giving the two fingered sign to anyone they passed. Rosemary had hit the nail straight on his brother's homesick head, encouraging him to leave his stoner mate and bringing him out to something like this. He'd be going to parties the rest of winter at the rate he was making friends.

'Woohoo!' Spike shouted to the crowd, throwing himself into a dancing throng that were congregated in the main room around the speakers. Someone had set up twirling, colourful lights and a bright red disc moved over Rosemary's face as she smiled up at Angus.

'I think he likes it.'

'Just how many of these have you gone to?'

She didn't say anything, just took his hands and danced instead and he laughed as 'Wild Thing' came on next. Rosemary had her mysteries, he realised, suddenly liking the fact. It was just another reason to add to the list as to why his brother would just have to put up with winter in Sydney. Watching Spike jump on the lounge to serenade cheering onlookers he figured maybe that was fast becoming a problem that may no longer exist.

Perhaps this wasn't such a bad idea, Poppy thought to herself as she drank her second champagne. The youthful noise and energy were infectious and the upbeat music was pulsating some life back into her numb senses, to the point that she could even appreciate the opposite sex. There were plenty of them to observe, nice-looking young men in an array of fitted suits with Beatles-esque hairstyles, and there was a good deal of facial hair on display, especially among the beatniks.

One tall man in stovepipe pants and a low-slung belt walked past, his black hair falling over his handsome face. 'Hey gorgeous,' he said, his grin loaded with suggestion.

'Hey,' she managed, drinking her champagne quickly and moving along the wall, happy to cling to it tonight. She was nowhere near ready for flirting just yet. Just then she spied Rosemary dancing with Angus and the amusing sight of Spike leading the crowd in the watusi as surf rock blared from the speakers. He'd worn a tie, it seemed, but somehow that had made its way to his head and was currently serving as a bandana.

Poppy thought about joining them but dancing seemed a bit too much of an undertaking so she went in search of Daniella and more champagne instead. That should prove rather easy, she figured. Daniella was bound to be with the more bohemian crowd which meant one thing: smoking. Sure enough they were in the next room where most people were puffing away, only the air was flavoured with something she'd smelt around uni a few times, something more pungent than tobacco.

'Hey baby, want to get turned on?' asked a man in black velvet, his tinted glasses not quite concealing his red-rimmed eyes.

Poppy stared at the proffered pipe trying not to appear too shocked. 'Not right now but er...thanks very much for asking,' she said, hoping that was the polite way to refuse illegal drugs. He stared at her then burst out laughing.

'You're most welcome, honey. Thanks very much for asking,' he muttered, still chuckling as he moved off and she squeezed her way over to Daniella who handed Poppy their shared champagne bottle automatically, busy as she was hanging on to Cat's every word.

'...and that's why the revolution has to start inside *individuals*. It's not up to the *politicians* or the *church leaders*, man, those dudes just want your conformity. They don't want your freedom...your passions. That fucks them up, don't you see?'

Poppy choked a little on her champagne at the use of the profanity but Daniella just nodded along with half a dozen or so others who seemed to emphatically agree.

'With the exception of Martin Luther King, of course,' said one serious-looking man with thick sideburns.

'All hail the king,' Cat conceded, 'but he empowers the powerless, don't you see? He wants individuals to have their own *personal* revolution. He dreams of a world without the chains of prejudice...'

'Where people aren't judged by their race but by their character,' Daniella added and he paused to point his pipe at her solemnly.

'King is a visionary,' Cat said, and Poppy swore he was adopting a deep southern accent as he warmed to the subject, 'but he talks of peace while our governments send us to war. We need anarchy, my friends. Revolution. This is a conspiracy against the common man, the subjugation of the masses…'

Poppy moved away, finding the subject too intense for her current mood, preferring to enjoy her champagne and listen to Bob Dylan wail from the radio instead. Daniella's cousin Maurice was renting this terrace house in North Sydney and, judging by the second-hand furniture and pop posters on the walls, his housemates seemed to be uni students too. The mismatched threadbare lounges and bedsheets over curtain rails somewhat gave it away.

Maurice was studying Medicine and was what Daniella herself termed a 'smooth operator'. Sure enough Poppy noticed him chatting up a curvy blonde near the milk-crate bookshelves while Poppy scanned the titles, noticing some thick tomes on Chemistry, the least favourite subject of her degree. Then her eyes rose up and collided with the dark-haired man from before and she vaguely registered that chemistry wasn't always a bad thing. His smile stretched into a grin once more and she swallowed the champagne that had pooled in her mouth in a gulp.

Maybe she should try talking to him – she had to start trying to move on from having her heart broken sooner or later. Perhaps it would do her good. He made up her mind for her by weaving his way through the hazy crowd, landing in front of her in sudden proximity.

'Hey again,' he said, holding her eyes with his as he took a sip of his drink. 'What's a nice girl like you doing at a party like this?'

Poppy drank some more champagne, searching for a something witty and flirtatious to say in response. 'How do you know I'm a nice girl?' Coming from someone sophisticated that would have been a perfect choice. Unfortunately, Poppy's nerves distorted her delivery, causing it to sound rather strangled. He looked at her questioningly.

'I'm not saying that's a bad thing. I like nice girls,' he swept his fringe back from his eyes and Poppy stared at the fluid movement, slightly mesmerised. Then he leant forward and whispered in her ear, 'I like teaching them how to be bad.'

Poppy couldn't even swallow now, barely managing to respond. 'Really?' she managed.

'Really,' he breathed, close and hot. Forget Maurice, this guy was the smoothest operator on the planet and she was falling straight for it. That thought sobered her enough to attempt a cool reply.

'How do you know I don't already know how?'

'What?' he said, losing the seductive tone momentarily, then he found it once more. 'Oh, how to be bad, I get it, yeah.' He leant forward to whisper again and Poppy noticed the pot on his breath. 'I'm sure there's plenty more you could learn…but maybe you could teach me a few things too.'

He leant his hand on the wall behind her and she felt dwarfed under his tall, tightly clothed physique. That's a lot of aftershave, she registered as he stared at her mouth. 'What say we blow the party and take this upstairs, give them all something to talk about.'

His seductive smile switched on in perfect timing, like a salesman well-used to closing the deal.

'I…uh…think I need to find the toilet. I mean the ladies. I mean excuse me.' Nice blurts, she admonished herself as she ducked under his arm and made her getaway, but she was glad she'd had enough wit to escape. Inexperienced she may well be but even Poppy Flannery could spot a player when she saw one.

Time to find Rosemary and the safety of Angus and Spike – guys she trusted.

She spied her sister still dancing with a smitten-looking Angus, his eyes glued to Rosemary's face, singing 'Eight Days a Week' like he wrote the song himself. Poppy couldn't help but feel a familiar grief pass through her but pushed it aside. It wasn't Rosemary's fault her relationship with Ben had ended before it had ever really begun. It wasn't anyone's fault. Ultimately, he just didn't want her – it was as simple as that sad little fact.

'Poppy, you made it!' Spike yelled, bouncing next to her, tie still wrapped around his head. 'Beer?' he asked, handing her one and drinking his own thirstily. He looked like some kind of crazed tennis player and Poppy smiled.

'Sure,' she said, putting down her now empty champagne glass.

'Rosemary said you might turn up. How awesome is this, eh? I didn't know Sydney had it in her.'

'Neither did I,' Poppy said, drinking her beer.

'Come on, let's dance,' he said, tossing his can and re-joining the throng as the brand new Rolling Stones hit 'Paint it Black' came on. Multi-coloured lights swam across the room, complementing the exotic, Indian-inspired guitar work. It was hypnotic, and both sight and sound flowed over her, sending her into some kind of strange musical ecstasy. She wasn't sure if she'd stayed in the smoking room too long or if it was the alcohol assisting her ascent into this delicious trance but it was consuming her entire being. She was moving with it, her arms swimming, her hips swaying, somehow free now to embrace the tragic laments of her soul. They were turning it into something beautiful, these Englishmen. Somehow they understood.

It was followed by the Supremes' 'You Keep Me Hangin' On', and Poppy almost cried as she sang along, drinking another beer, dancing with her eyes closed and feeling every word resonate. Had Ben used her? He must have. She felt used. She felt something else now too, something new.

She was angry.

Angry enough to have vengeance.

Angry enough to use someone too.

Poppy opened her eyes and walked swiftly through the crowd, stumbling a little but not caring, ignoring Rosemary's voice as she called after her, finally aware she'd turned up at last. But only one thing mattered right now: finding that tall player and making mad, passionate love with him. Getting some of that old feminine power back – the part of her she'd only ever tasted, never fully consumed.

He wasn't in the smoking room, nor was he in the hallway. Maybe he was upstairs. She climbed them at a run, clutching the rail before reaching the top and rounding the corner to the bedrooms. He was there alright, heading through a door and she went to call his name only she didn't know what it was.

'Hey,' she said instead, and he turned. But she was too late – he already had a sale. A woman in a short skirt with perfect legs. Long hair falling.

Flick, flick, flick.

Seventeen

The rain was forming in little beads that darted occasionally across the taxi window, the traffic lights causing them to look almost festive. They were becoming obscured now as Poppy's breath fogged the glass and she was tempted to write something there with her finger, like when she was a child.

'She definitely didn't see you?' Rosemary broke the silence.

'No.'

'Obviously had other priorities,' Rosemary scoffed. 'Who is he anyway?'

'Ivan Bentley – Judith's brother. Daniella told me while I was calling the taxi.' She said it matter-of-factly, as if cheating on your husband with your friend's brother was perfectly the norm.

'Probably been dangling him on the side for years,' Rosemary said, disgusted. 'Do you…do you think Ben knows?'

Poppy shrugged. 'If he doesn't he will, I suppose. Sooner or later.'

Rosemary tapped her purse on her knee. 'Well it's his own bloody fault, choosing that bitch over you.'

Poppy looked over at her. 'Using the B word now are we?'

'She's head of the Dogsquad. It fits.'

Rosemary sounded furious but Poppy just felt sad somehow.

'What's he going to do?' she wondered.

'Stay married to that cheating cow just like he deserves because he was too stupid not to see it coming. You know, I'm even angrier with him now than before. What a ridiculous waste of his life. I'll never understand why he did it.'

'It was an easier choice,' Poppy said, tracing a heart on the window.

'What do you mean "easier"? It's a million times harder! Now he has to go off to war with nothing to come home to – what kind of life is that? *Easier*,' Rosemary said, swiping at an angry tear. 'He could have been so happy with you. He *was* so happy with you.'

'Maybe Barbara just suits his world more,' Poppy said softly, tracing his initials in the heart.

'Well, you're well rid of him if that's what his world is like,' Rosemary declared. There was a pause as the obviously discomfited taxi driver turned on the radio and 'Barbara Ann' by the Beach Boys came on.

'Turn that off,' Rosemary barked.

Immediate silence followed.

'You should tell him you know.'

Poppy turned to stare at her. 'You're joking, surely.'

'No, I'm not. Maybe he'll get a divorce and choose you after all. Not that he deserves that but if he's the guy you want… I mean, who knows what she did to trick him into marrying anyway? It always seemed fishy to me.'

'She's always caught whoever she wanted.' Poppy shrugged. The rain pelted harder as she traced a zigzag through the heart, breaking it in half. 'Barbara always wins.'

'Yeah well, she won't be holding on to this prize for long. No man deserves to have to put up with that.'

The broken heart bled in watery tears now, running into the sill. 'Depends what he thinks he deserves.'

Eighteen

Royal Military College, Duntroon, Australian Capital Territory, Australia, June 1966

The pieces moved easily through his hands as he assembled the gun then dismantled it once more. He was the best in his company at that. Best in his company at shooting too.

Perhaps he'd be the best at killing.

Ben shook the thought away, trying to focus only on the routine, wishing he was holding paintbrushes instead but knowing the drill would have to suffice. Anything to stop his mind from running.

His hands were numb, despite the activity, but he was rarely warm down here in Canberra. It was a different kind of cold to Sydney or Adelaide, like the snowfields in the mountains were sending out icy invitations on the wind. Apparently it was tantalising to a skier but, unlike his two mates down here, Sam and Zach Hall, Ben had never tried the sport. The two cousins had been trying to talk him into going with them over the upcoming mid-year break but he'd been fobbing them off. Ben couldn't bring himself to tell them he had to go home to his wife. No-one here knew he had one.

He sighed, standing up to stretch his back. At least it wasn't raining today. The sun shone brilliantly through the windows, reflecting off the white walls of the college, and he imagined himself somewhere warm; somewhere far removed from military life. Golden sand and blue curling waves came to mind, a type of surf found only in paradise. Bonfires and bare skin. A girl with freckles on her nose, wrapping herself around him. Promising she would wait when the storm came.

He shook his head again, determined not to let himself think about her either. There was no point. Ben was living the life prescribed for him from birth, albeit with an earlier-than-expected marriage. She was suitable stock though, her blood blue enough to be considered acceptable by his parents. Their only real objection had been the lack of ceremony, disappointed that Ben had married quietly without guests. He'd lied and told them Barbara didn't want a fuss. Barbara had told them she couldn't bear to wait. Either way, the truth about the baby never needed to come out, if indeed it ever was that. The truth.

He supposed he'd never know.

The bell sounded for lunch and he put the gun away and straightened his uniform. Times were strictly adhered to here and he always followed the rules. They held him together like a second skin.

Rules kept soldiers alive.

Nineteen

Sydney, June 1966

Poppy read the letter again, wishing she could send it, before crumpling it into a tight ball and throwing it away. It felt good to pen the words on paper, like they were released to the world if not to him; a cathartic if painful little game she'd taken to playing after study. She started another, ignoring the dozen or so other drafts in the overflowing bin.

Dear Ben,
You're probably wondering why I'm writing to you. I know it isn't really appropriate considering I'm just the girl you rejected after professing your love to three times in two days.

Crumple, toss.

Dear Ben,
Barbara's cheating on you. She doesn't love you. She never did. I just thought you should know.

Re-read. Crumple. Toss.

Dear Ben,

This is probably a bit of a shock, I know. I promise I'll try to say what I have to say without being too blurty, although that may prove difficult, being me. Sorry to be the one delivering this news and I hope you don't think it's just sour grapes motivating me to write this but the truth is…

Poppy paused then. What truth mattered most?

…you deserve better than what Barbara can give you. Better than what she is doing behind your back too. She's hurting you and that hurts me.

I don't know why you couldn't see it coming. I don't even know why you married her except that, as you said, it was easier – choosing her instead of me.

She clutched the pen tighter, her vision blurring.

But I would have waited Ben. I would have given you my whole life. Fool that I am I'm waiting for you still – even though I know you don't want me.

The tears fell as she wrote the last.

Even if you never make it home.

Poppy's fingers splayed across the page as she slowly screwed it up like the others, laying her head on the desk, holding the letter in her palm for a moment.

She reached over to turn on the radio, wondering what song would play at such a moment and it was perfect really: 'Unchained Melody' by the Righteous Brothers.

But oh, how it made her ache. Worse, it seemed, than ever before.

She held the crumpled letter tight against her chest, owning those words now. They weren't sentences she could ever actually say or send, but at least they existed somewhere; they were real. They'd left her heart and found form in the world and somehow the concept made her feel just that tiny bit better.

Even if the paper was the only one who knew.

'You're going.'

Poppy watched her sister as she threw clothes about and searched for her shoes. 'No, I'm not.'

'Yes, you are,' Rosemary said, digging through the pile near the desk. 'What the hell have you been doing? You're turning into a bloody derro,' she said, gesturing towards the overflowing bin.

'Essay drafts,' Poppy mumbled, pulling the eiderdown up around her chin. 'It's too cold to go out.'

'It's just dinner at the pub, for godsakes. There's a band playing tonight too so it should be fun.'

'No more music…'

'Now I know you're becoming affected. Come on, put this on.' She held out a red jumper and Poppy frowned at it.

'Don't like it.'

'Well, get up and pick something you do like and stop being a brat!'

Just then Lois arrived at the door. 'Out of bed, Poppy – what's this sleeping in the afternoon nonsense? You're not a child.' Poppy sat up, immediately guilty. 'I don't know what's going on with you but I'll not have my house turned into a pigsty. Clean this up before you go out.'

'I'm not going anywhere,' Poppy said, shoving at her messed up bed-hair.

'Well, your father and I are going to the pictures so you can't stay home by yourself.'

'Since when?' Poppy muttered rebelliously.

'Since I've decided not to have my daughter turn into a derro,' Lois said firmly, flicking Rosemary an almost conspiratory glance. 'And watch your tone young lady. I'll give you forty-five minutes to clean this up and go,' she added before turning to leave. 'Be home by eleven.'

They stared at the door after her.

'I think I actually am becoming affected, unless our mother really did just agree with you.'

'More than that…she quoted me,' Rosemary said, tossing Poppy the jumper. 'Put this on and brush that hair. I'm think I'm scared.'

Poppy obliged and within the hour they were heading into the Greengate, all traces of Poppy's derro-state gone. In fact she looked great, as Spike pointed out on their arrival. Red turned out to be a complementary colour to her blonde hair and she'd lost weight over recent weeks, her waist petite in her black pencil skirt. Both twins were turning heads as they walked through the main bar and Poppy felt the eyes upon her self-consciously, hiding as best she could behind Spike and Angus until they reached the restaurant section.

It was busy but they managed to get a table and Poppy nodded at several people they knew, avoiding eye contact with Raeleen Montgomery who was there with her family. The last thing she needed was to deal with a member of the Dogsquad tonight.

Fortunately it didn't spoil her evening – Spike was too entertaining for that, regaling the girls with hilarious tales of their road trip from Western Australia last summer.

'I'm not kidding, Angus was as green as the yundi,' he was saying, much to Angus's embarrassment.

'It's the only time I've ever tried it, I swear.'

Rosemary gave him an amused look. 'Sure it is.'

'Honest.'

'Hey, I'm not judging you. I wouldn't mind trying it myself some time.'

'Seriously?'

They were interrupted by the sound of the band starting up next door and quickly finished their drinks to join the action.

'Just need to visit the ladies,' Poppy said and Rosemary followed but they were halted by the queue forming in the corridor. 'Should have thought of this sooner.'

Poppy wouldn't have minded, only Raeleen Montgomery was lining up too – directly behind them.

'Poppy, Rosemary,' Raeleen nodded, acknowledging their existence for a change.

'Raeleen,' they returned cautiously. It was awkward then and Poppy pretended to study the turn-of-the-century decor.

'How's uni?' Raeleen asked.

'Good thanks. We're doing Pharmacy at Sydney,' Rosemary told her.

'Yes, I know, Chris mentioned it.' They were surprised Chris Plumpton considered them a topic for conversation, unless to discuss Poppy's brief affair with Ben last summer. Poppy frowned, hating the thought. 'I'm at secretarial college.'

'That sounds…fun,' Rosemary said, nodding politely.

'It's alright. Just filling in time really.' Neither twin asked why but they assumed she meant marriage, probably to Chris. 'Have you seen anyone else from school?'

'We see Daniella Rossi quite a bit,' Poppy said, trying to contribute to the conversation as the line moved forward, painfully slow.

'I still see Judith but not that Barbara. Can't stand the sight of her.'

The twins stared at her, stunned.

'Barbara Rowntree?' Poppy said, realising immediately that was a rather stupid question.

'Well who else, Poppy Flannery? Of *course* Barbara Rowntree,' Judith said scornfully, then she dropped her voice to a whisper. 'Disgusting – what she did to Ben Williamson.'

'Terrible,' Rosemary agreed, nodding slowly as Poppy froze into stillness.

'Honestly if you have to trap a man into marriage...anyway, I'm sure you've heard the rumours.'

'Ha, rumours...of course we have,' Rosemary said, managing to sound quite unfazed. 'Where do you even start?'

'Well, with the baby, obviously, that's the worst part.' Raeleen gave a short laugh of derision. 'Fake baby, more like. That girl was no more pregnant than...well let's just say I went shopping with her a week before for certain *feminine* products. Need I say more?'

Rosemary managed to shake her head which was enough to prompt Raeleen to continue.

'Honestly, that girl has no conscience – never did. Chris and I want nothing more to do with her,' she said, spite lacing her words. It seemed the years in Barbara's shadow had taken their toll at last. 'You're up,' she told Poppy, gesturing at the door.

'Excuse me,' Poppy mumbled, pushing through and leaning against it heavily.

*She'd lied. Barbara had lied and that means Ben...*Poppy couldn't think the rest, she just knew she had to get out of this cubicle and find somewhere to digest it all.

'…still treating him like dirt. I heard she was seen out with Ivan Bentley only last week, getting it on at some uni party for everyone to see. Obviously Judith isn't speaking to her any more either and I can't say I blame her…'

Raeleen's character assassination of Barbara continued in the cubicle alongside but Poppy was barely listening now. She finished her ablutions automatically, rushing from the toilets to the front portico and drawing deep draughts of the frozen air into her tightened lungs.

Rosemary found her there, moments later, pale and shaking beneath the columned facade.

'She lied…she…said…' Poppy managed, her eyes pleading with her sister for confirmation.

'Fake pregnancy,' Rosemary said, fury lacing her words. 'I knew there was something weird about that marriage. I *knew* it.'

'He didn't choose her,' Poppy said, almost disbelieving, 'he did the right thing.'

'It was still the wrong choice.'

'I know…I know…but…'

Rosemary sighed, reaching out her arms. 'But now you love him even more?'

Poppy's face crumpled as she nodded and she fell forward to bury herself in her sister's embrace, giving in to the injustice of it all, the cruel heartlessness, no longer attributing it to the man who made the 'easier choice'. Now all blame lay at Barbara's door, she who always won, but Poppy now knew her victory was a hollow one. Because Barbara had never won, not really; she didn't have Ben's love.

The next day a young woman stood in the rain, debating with herself as to whether or not she was making the right decision.

The letter in her hands could impact several lives, so was she really justified in sending it?

But in the end she shoved it into the mailbox and strode away. It was time for more than one truth to come to light, she decided. Some words needed more than mere existence. Some words needed to be heard.

Twenty

He stood at the window, watching her walk to the post office and wondering yet again what it was that she was waiting for. It had to be something she was hiding from her family – undoubtedly a good thing. Maybe she was making moves to leave the nest at last. Angus felt excitement stir at the concept, figuring Rosemary could use his post office box to arrange that outcome as much as she liked.

'Ta-da!' announced Spike, walking across the room and placing an odd-shaped cake on the table.

'Wow,' Angus said, taking in the bright green icing and clumpy grated chocolate with amusement, 'that's rather...colourful.'

'Christmas in July,' he proclaimed happily, adding a bit of tinsel to the side. It stuck out at an angle awkwardly.

'But it's still June.'

'Close enough. Where'd my special guests get to?'

'Rosemary's gone to check the mail and Poppy's buying milk so they shouldn't be...' He was interrupted by the sound of the door as Poppy arrived, and Barrel let out a chorus of loud, happy barks.

'Hello baby,' she said, pausing to pat him before delivering the milk onto the bench. 'Wow, that smells wonderful.' Barrel followed her adoringly as she bent to investigate Spike's cake.

'I swear that dog has a crush on you,' Angus said, shaking his head as Barrel sat on her feet, his tongue lolling to the side.

'Just what I need: competition,' Spike said with a deep sigh but Angus wondered at the comment. His brother seemed a little more animated himself when she was around – if that was possible for someone like Spike.

'A work of art!' he was telling Poppy, turning the plate around and posing dramatically in Rosemary's apron. Poppy giggled, trying to extract herself gently from Barrel's weight as the door opened again and Rosemary returned.

'Anything interesting?' Angus asked, taking her coat and looking at the letters in her hand.

'All for you,' she shrugged. He looked at the shallow pile bound in a rubber band and decided to read them later. Spike's first attempt at throwing an afternoon tea party didn't need a stack of bills being read to spoil things. 'Goodness – all done?' Rosemary asked Spike, looking at the cake with amusement.

'I call it Christmas Surprise Cake!' he announced proudly.

'It's certainly…surprising,' Rosemary conceded.

'Sit, sit,' he instructed, pulling out chairs and pouring tea into mismatched cups. 'My finest cup. Almost has an entire handle,' he told Poppy, sliding it towards her.

'Thank you, kind sir,' she said, laughing. They made their tea and more laughter ensued as the cake had a minor catastrophe, avalanching onto the table and the floor as the lopsided arrangement lost its fight with gravity. Barrel gobbled up a good portion before anyone could stop him and Spike looked momentarily perplexed.

'Oh well, I suppose he'll be right,' he mumbled, serving up four generous portions for the humans. 'Dig in!'

'How the hell did you get it to be green on the inside too?' Angus asked, squinting at it.

'It's a bit murky...' Rosemary observed doubtfully.

'Just taste it and then judge me.'

They all began to eat and Poppy was the first to comment. 'Mmm,' she said. 'You know, it's actually pretty good.'

'Better than it looks,' Angus agreed. 'It's got a kind of funny taste though. What is that?'

'Nutmeg?' Rosemary guessed, taking a mouthful thoughtfully.

'Uh-uh,' Spike said, shaking his head. 'It's the surprise ingredient.'

'Is it some kind of vegetable?' Poppy frowned at her fork before eating a little more. 'Almost spicy, isn't it?'

'Sugary too. If a little, er...green,' Angus said, scooping some of the brilliant icing then shrugging and eating it.

Poppy began to hum The Searchers' song 'Sugar and Spice' and Spike immediately jumped up.

'Whoops, that's what I forgot,' he said, dashing downstairs and returning with the radio and his guitar. 'Thought I should bring both,' he said, tuning the strings. 'Any requests?'

'Well, if it really is Christmas...' Poppy said, giggling as Spike immediately began to play a medley of carols in parody, including 'Green Christmas', 'Oh Christmas Cake' and 'Jingle Smells', the latter a dedication to the constantly flatulent Barrel.

'Oh stop, stop!' begged Rosemary, wiping away tears of laughter as he launched into yet another: 'Silent Fart'.

'What, too offensive for the Catholics in the audience?' he said cupping an ear. 'Fine, fine, I'll make more tea.'

'That's it! It's tea – isn't it?' Poppy guessed, peering at the remnants of her cake.

'You're getting closer,' Spike said, returning to the table with a freshly filled teapot. 'It is a type of plant. Come on, round two – eat more,' he urged, cutting more slices and passing them along.

'How unusual,' Rosemary said. 'What kind of plant would you possibly put in a cake?'

Angus paused mid-fork, a terrible realisation occurring to him. 'You don't mean to tell me…?'

'What?' Rosemary said, taking another bite.

'I like it,' Poppy decided, sitting back contentedly. 'It's funny in a good way.'

'When is funny ever not good?' Rosemary said, giggling.

'When it's funny business,' Angus said, glaring at his brother now.

'Funny business. That's funny,' Poppy decided, giggling too. 'Because business isn't funny at all really, is it?'

Both girls began to really laugh now and Angus tried to think of a way to tell them the truth without freaking them out but Spike spoke up instead.

'It's a funny ingredient because it *makes* things funny. That's the surprise!'

Both girls were still giggling but Poppy managed to ask, 'How does it make things funny? Just by looking at it?' That produced another good minute of laughter.

'No, by eating it,' Spike finally said.

'But why would…' Rosemary paused then, her jaw dropping, obviously unaware she was sporting a large glob of icing on her cheek. 'Oh sweet Lord.'

'You said you wanted to try it. That night – at the Greengate,' Spike reminded her.

'The Greengate…?' Poppy said, sobering at the mention of that place.

'When they were talking about smoking…' Rosemary said, eyes wide at her sister. 'Only now we're…we're eating it.'

'*Green,*' Poppy muttered, comprehension dawning on her face.

'Surprise!' Both girls gaped at him, lost for words. 'So…what do you think of yundi? Do you like it?'

Silence ensued as they continued to stare. 'Say something, please,' Angus begged, scared of Rosemary's reaction.

'I don't think it's had any effect on me,' she told him dazedly. Just then the blob of icing on her cheek slid off and landed with a plop in her tea.

'Are you kidding?' Spike said. 'You're literally off your face.'

It was another ten minutes before they could all stop laughing because, as it turned out, Christmas Surprise Cake really was surprising. And the secret ingredient was, in fact, just plain funny.

Angus awoke at dawn the next day to a sudden downpour of rain which startled him out of a dreamless slumber and he looked at the clock as he sat up, feeling heavy and exhausted despite almost nine hours of sleep. Spike often said that 'stone-overs' made sleeping 'tiring', weirdly enough, and he was tempted to ring Rosemary and tell her that fact because it was actually pretty funny. Then he decided he was actually still stoned and got out of bed in search of more tea instead.

Barrel was snoring, exhausted from watching them all party on with glazed eyes and probably feeling the effects of a stone-over himself, Angus thought guiltily, but it didn't last too long. It had been too hilarious an afternoon for any remorse and it wasn't as if they gave the dog pot-cake on purpose. Barrel rolled onto his back and Angus couldn't help but smile at his fat little belly before sitting on the lounge next to him with his tea. The mail from yesterday was on the coffee table and he leant over to pick it up, figuring he may as well read the bills while he still had a nice buzz going on. Nothing was likely to bring him down right now.

Angus flicked through the pile: an electricity bill, a notice from council that they were digging up the road again this week, a letter from the government. That made him pause and he drew it out from the rest slowly, thinking it may be to do with changing electorates. He'd been wondering about that.

Then he opened it and read the words in disbelief, hoping somewhere in the back of his mind that he was actually still asleep. Or that the Christmas Surprise Cake was causing him to hallucinate. Or that this was surely a joke – just someone from the government's idea of funny business.

Only as the cold light of day crept across the floor that dawn he didn't wake up, nor did the letter dissolve into nothingness. No-one rang from the government to say they were only joking.

And there was no-one who was laughing, anymore.

'What is it?' Rosemary gasped, panting from exertion. She'd obviously run all the way from the bus stop.

Angus knew he was frightening her, telling to come urgently in the early morning without telling her why, but it just wasn't something you wanted to say over the phone. It wasn't something you wanted to say, full stop.

'I had a letter,' he said, deciding to come straight to the point. Angus handed it to her and Rosemary took it, confused.

'From who?'

'It's from the government,' he said, pushing past a lump in his throat as he articulated the news. 'Honey, I've been drafted.'

'Draft…drafted?' Her eyes looked enormous as she opened the letter. 'Oh God. Oh no, no…' She read the few lines then and dissolved into tears. 'Because…because of the date of your birthday they're making you go to Vietnam? No,' she said again, shaking her head, 'they can't do that. I won't let them.'

'Hush, now,' Angus said, pulling her close and she was trembling as she gave him one of those long, wonderful hugs. 'They don't send you straight to war. I'll have to be trained and everything – probably won't even see active service, I don't think.'

She was still crying and he pulled her back to face him. 'Rosemary, I need you to be strong, alright? And I need to ask you something.' He paused, waiting for her to calm down.

'Yes,' she said, nodding. 'The answer's yes. I will.'

'What?'

'Marry you, of course.'

He was momentarily taken aback but then he couldn't resist hugging her again. 'Oh my girl. I wasn't going to propose.' He rubbed his chin against her hair, half tempted to do so. 'Although I'm sure I will when we're a bit older. I mean I do love you, you know that, right?' He kissed her forehead and she nodded.

'Sorry,' she mumbled against him, sniffing loudly. 'I…I thought…'

'Shhh, it's okay.' He smiled at her then and she giggled a little.

'Wow, that's kind of embarrassing.'

'No, it isn't at all. In fact: Rosemary Flannery, will you promise to promise to marry me when I ask you in the not too far away future?'

She laughed then and nodded. 'I promise.'

'Good,' he said, stroking her cheek. 'And I promise that I promise to propose.'

She smiled up at him. 'Well, I'm glad that's all settled. Now, what were you really going to ask me?' She folded the letter with shaking hands, waiting.

'I want you to keep an eye on Spike for me. Make sure he doesn't get into too much mischief while I'm away.'

'I thought you said they wouldn't send you to war…'

'They won't, I mean, you know, when they send me to training camp, wherever that may be.'

'Alright,' she agreed uneasily, 'although I don't know if he'll really pay much attention to me.'

'He has to pay attention to his future sister-in-law. She'll make him an uncle one day, don't forget.'

Rosemary's eyes filled with tears once more. 'Promise?'

'I promise I promise,' he vowed, holding her against him once more. 'Marriage, kids, the whole shebang. This army thing is just a minor set-back for now, alright?'

'Alright – but no war. Promise me that too.'

'I…I can't exactly promise that…'

'Promise,' she repeated, a desperate edge to her voice.

'No war,' he said after a pause. 'I promise.'

She nodded again and they stood together in each other's arms for a long while, each knowing such a promise couldn't really be made but needing it nonetheless. At least they would face this conscription animal together, Angus figured, one shock at a time.

Twenty-One

Royal Military College, Duntroon, June 1966

His heart was hammering hard but he pushed on. Just one more mile. Ben knew this training route down to the last tree and rock, the familiar trail haunted his dreams now and with it this constant push to beat the clock, to beat everyone in his class. To win. It mattered not because he wanted the victory. It mattered because racing had rules and structure which made it part of that second skin – the thing that kept him alive.

Past the three black horses in the far paddock. Past the column of pines near the last marker. Through the gate. His lungs were exploding, heaving with painful pleas for him to quit but he pushed through, along the road, across to the red roofs and white walls near the parade ground, towards Sarge who held the stop-watch, surrounded by a crowd of onlookers from Kapyong Company who were cheering him on like mad. Twenty feet. Ten.

Finished.

It was a good result, he knew. His mate Zach was pumping the air with his fist and Sarge was looking over at him with the satisfaction of a man who had just won a sizeable bet.

'All hail the fighting Rats!' crowed Sam, as he and Zach led the company chant. It echoed across the college as others crossed the line and Ben managed to laugh through tortured lungs as his friends ran over to lift him up onto their shoulders.

'Put him down, put him down,' Sarge ordered, but he was smiling too. Everyone knew Ben was the tough old guy's favourite. The time was announced – a new record – to loud applause before the Rats moved off to their barracks to celebrate then pack for their mid-year break. The Queen's Birthday parade on the morrow would round off their first six months at Duntroon and the atmosphere was one of relief as they made their way along.

'You have to come to Jindabyne now,' Zach said, draping his arm across Ben's shoulder. 'You're a natural for cross-country skiing.'

Ben shrugged, not bothering to say no again.

'Two words for you my man: snow bunnies,' Sam informed him from alongside. 'Rich, married and bored. An ideal opportunity for a young man in uniform to uh…charm the pants off them.'

'I assume you mean literally.'

'I am both a budding officer and a gentleman and therefore literally obliged to be literal.'

'Sounds to me like you're planning to confuse the pants off them,' Zach said.

'If it's a means to a rear end…'

'You really are disgusting; you know that?' Sam told him, throwing his hat on the bunk as they arrived.

'Six months of men-only company will do that to a fella.'

Ben could relate to that much. His body was craving a certain woman's touch with increasing intensity but his only actual option for sex left him cold. Maybe he should go to Jindabyne tomorrow instead of home, have a meaningless affair with a stranger. Then the piece of paper folded into the back of his wallet silenced the thought.

'Hold your horses, look what Newman snuck in.' Zach nodded over to the sight of George Newman, the resident deviant, handing out bottles of beer in the corner and Sam walked over to shut the door. Newman whistled and tossed one over to Ben as a 'freebie' for breaking the college record and he took it gladly. Anything that numbed him was more than welcome.

'To Williamson!' Newman declared and the Rats toasted enthusiastically, Ben's surname repeated throughout the room. It was an unspoken rule that no-one in the Rats was ever referred to by their Christian name with the exception of Sam and Zach. Numerous nicknames had been tried out but the two larrikins of the group had somehow managed to hang on to their given names. Their constant ribbing of each other was amusement enough.

The cold ale was refreshing after such a long race and Ben drank it quickly, followed by another, then the numbing started to do its trick. Enough for him to ignore the dominant issue that had plagued these past weeks. Even enough for him to relax and laugh at the banter that accompanied such drinks with the boys.

'You'd think they'd give you a trophy or a medal or something,' Newman was saying.

'I can't remember the last time I got a trophy,' Zach lamented.

'For being the biggest wanker at St Pat's, wasn't it?' Sam said. '1963, as I recall.'

'Well, I couldn't let you take it out for the third year in a row.'

The evening rolled along with other such knocking to entertain him, but in the end Ben turned in earlier than most, the exhaustion of the day taking its toll. He fell into a deep sleep only to wake in the early hours as was his usual habit, instantly alert. Mind racing.

Ben tried to fight the impulse but in the end he opened his wallet, taking out a piece of paper that held the faint markings of tears and previous crumpling. He traced the creases thoughtfully, wondering yet again what drove her to send it. She'd obviously been in two minds. What if she'd left it in a discarded ball, unsent and unread? What then?

If she'd never sent it maybe he wouldn't be listening to his conscience right now. Maybe he'd be packing for the slopes and ignoring his sham marriage vows, a soulless man vindicated by the knowledge that his wife slept around too. Because it wasn't the news of Barbara's infidelity that made sleep impossible in the dark nights at Duntroon for Ben Williamson. He knew the woman he'd married. He knew she'd never stay true.

It was the news that the girl who'd promised she'd wait was waiting still that caused him to hang onto his soul; to ache for his freedom more than ever before. The rules that had held him together these past months were rewritten in those tear-stained blurts; fidelity and duty challenged.

Ben sighed, folding the letter and closing his eyes. The race he'd just run seemed insignificant now – it was nothing compared to one that awaited him – and there was no way to train for it. No record to break, no clock to beat.

Just the impossible task of going home.

Twenty-Two

Sydney, June 1966

It was warm in their little dining room. Lois had insisted they make rare use of the tiled fireplace, more to intimidate than welcome, Poppy suspected. It was the first time a 'suitor' had ever dared enter their home and Poppy knew her mother was sending him a very clear message of authority. *We are a respectable, comfortable family*, the fireplace said. *You'll have to prove to us you are worthy to court our well-brought-up daughter.*

'And what about you, er…Spike. Are you going to serve your country alongside your brother?' Her father's voice was Gospel-reading loud as he carved the lamb roast and he sent Spike a stern look above his glasses.

Spike was sitting alongside Angus in brotherly support but Poppy suspected he was regretting his loyalty around about now. 'I haven't received the draft as yet, sir,' Spike said, patting his wet, combed-down hair self-consciously. It looked overly long next to Angus's new crew cut.

'No need for a young man to be asked. I couldn't wait when I was your age – went straight down to the enlistment office on my birthday and donned the uniform with pride.' He glared at Spike as if daring him to comment, which he wisely refrained from doing. 'Spent two years in New Guinea and Borneo fighting those blood-crazed Japs and these commies seem even worse, if you ask me. It's God's work to protect a Christian way of life, isn't that right Angus?'

Angus tapped his fingers on the tablecloth nervously, very handsome in his new uniform, Poppy had to admit. 'Yes sir… only…'

'Only what?' Her father paused mid-carve and Poppy watched Angus swallow hard as he stared at the poised knife.

'I…um…I'm wondering about the rule. I mean Commandment. Thou shalt not kill.'

Poppy thought her father might counter-quote passages from the Bible, enraged, but he seemed to be taking an unexpected liking to Angus and waved the knife about quite casually as he replied. 'That doesn't apply to heathens such as these, young man. Evil must be stopped in its tracks so you'll be wielding the sword of angels when you fire your gun. Not an enjoyable task, I'll grant you, but a necessity, nonetheless.'

'Yes sir,' Angus mumbled, still staring at the sharp point of the meandering knife.

'He's not that likely to be deployed though. I mean, we're hoping he won't be,' Rosemary said.

'"We", is it?' Lois remarked shrewdly, switching her gaze between Rosemary and Angus.

'All of us, I mean,' Rosemary mumbled, blushing.

'Drafted soldiers still see active service a lot of the time. Wouldn't be much point otherwise, now would there?' her father said almost cheerfully as he added another slice of lamb to the growing pile. 'Where are you training, Angus?'

'Kapooka, down near Wagga Wagga,' Angus said, throwing Rosemary a reassuring look before continuing. 'It doesn't seem too hard so far. Just a lot of fitness mostly.'

'Sporting man, are you?'

'Not really. I do like to surf,' he cleared his throat self-consciously, 'but I guess that isn't much use to the army.'

Robert grunted, passing the meat down the table. 'I suppose you boys like that surf music…what are they called…the Beach Boys?'

That brought a sudden grin to Spike's face. 'Yes sir.'

'A bit too teeny-bopper for my taste, although they do have excellent harmonies.' The girls stared at their father in surprise. 'Why are you looking at me like that?'

'We just…well, we didn't think you'd approve of them,' Poppy said.

'Nothing wrong with music so long as it's appropriate and pleasing to the ear. Unlike those Bugs or Beatles or whatever they're called. That John Lennon should be jailed for what he said about our Lord. *Bigger than Jesus*. The gall of the man!'

'Robert,' Lois said quietly and her husband immediately composed himself, putting down the knife at last and taking a deep breath.

'Speaking of which,' he said, calmly now. He made the sign of the cross and Spike and Angus made a rather comical performance of following him which tempted Poppy to laugh. Fortunately the meal began and she was able to occupy her mouth with eating instead. The time passed without further incident and Poppy figured both boys did fairly well in the table manners department, although Spike made a bit of a mess with the gravy, sploshing it on the white cloth. Then he made matters worse by streaking it all over her mother's lace-hemmed napkin, muttering numerous apologies as he rubbed away.

'It's alright,' Lois said stiffly, 'just leave it be.'

'I'm so sorry,' he said again, 'such a waste of delicious gravy too.'

That melted her mother enough to offer him a second dessert later on.

By the time they walked down to the station together the twins agreed it had gone far better than they'd dare hope.

'Dad even shook your hand,' Rosemary said, looking at Angus in amazement.

'Is that unusual?'

'Very. Usually he just nods.'

'I think it's just the uniform. Not sure he would have been too keen on me otherwise,' he said, putting his arm around her.

'He may not be too keen if he found out we're going to be at the snow at the same time as you,' Poppy observed, flapping at Spike who was busy trying to put his arm around her too and making loud kissing sounds.

'The next five days can't go fast enough,' Angus said and Rosemary leant in to hold him closer. Daniella's parents had a chalet at Jindabyne in the High Country and the girls had been invited to go skiing – if there was any snow of course. Otherwise indoor activities would be on the agenda, which suited the girls just fine. Angus and Spike were renting a room at a hostel nearby and would undoubtedly find amusing ways to pass the time.

'Five days is yonks away. Who's up for some fun tonight?' Spike said, leaping about in front of them all.

'Think we might just head home,' Angus said, kissing Rosemary's hand and squeezing it tight. 'I have to catch the early train.'

'Bloody romantics. How about you, Poppy? I have it on good authority there's a get-together brewing at Cat's tonight.' Spike was a regular member of their party crowd by now and inciting Cat to blustering indignation was one of his favourite new pastimes. He seemed to take great pleasure in saying the most un-hip, right wing comments he could think of just to watch Cat lose his 'cool'.

'An evening of smoking and politics? I don't know…' Poppy hesitated.

'Oh come on. I've got a bottle of bubbly,' he said, then he paused, looking over at Angus and Rosemary who were now kissing a few feet away. 'And the thought of leaving you at home on a Saturday night, all by yourself in your room, lamenting about a handsome young surfer boy…'

'Lamenting is it?'

'Swooning, sobbing, performing some kind of Catholic rituals to bewitch the poor lad…'

'We don't use voodoo,' she giggled as the train arrived and they waved goodbye to Rosemary and Angus who were headed the opposite way.

'Hmmm. Well, you could always try the old Broome method of getting the person you fancy good and sloshed,' he suggested, investigating the contents of his bag and pulling out the bottle of champagne.

'Sure that's enough for both of us?' she asked.

'Probably not,' he said, rummaging further, 'not much of an offering for a party anyway. One really should bring cake.'

Twenty-Three

The streets were wet with recent rain and Ben supposed it was cold, although not Canberra-cold. But it was grey, as grey as his mind, which felt the familiar sensation of being wiped blank more brutally in Barbara's presence.

His wife sat next to him in a tight red dress, her black fur coat trailing below the hem. She was painting her nails and admiring her work, oblivious to the hostile stares the driver cast her in the rear-view mirror as polish fumes filled the air. It made Ben wonder momentarily if he actually hated her. Then he drank deeply from the flask he'd put in his pocket that afternoon, blanking away that thought with the rest.

'Bit early isn't it?' she said.

'It's Saturday night,' he said with a shrug. 'You want me to party, so I'll party.'

'You don't have to make it sound like such a chore, darling. Don't tell me the army's turned my new husband into a bore.' She blew lightly on her nails, not really interested in a response, he knew. If she was Ben could have told her he was always a bit of a bore – his grey mind had led a grey existence all those years. He was born to be boring. Born to be grey…or khaki anyway, he thought, half amused at the thought as he looked down at his every-day uniform. Barbara had wanted him to wear his fancy whites but he had that whole 'second skin rule' down pat after six months at military college. Dress uniform was only to be worn on special occasions – not to impress a bunch of Barbara's party friends.

'I still don't see why you have to wear those dreary things,' she said.

'It's part of my skin,' he said, taking another swig.

She looked at him properly then. 'Don't get too drunk, Benny. I want to show you off after going to parties all these months on my own.'

Ben almost laughed at that. As if Barbara could ever stand being alone. He half wondered if any of her lovers would be there tonight. Barbara continued on with her nails, red polish gleaming like blood. Maybe if he drank enough he would punch one of those men in the face; get into a proper blood-red fist fight. Feel something beyond this grey.

He stared back out the window, emptying the last of his flask, noticing the sky had cleared a small patch of blue. Then all thoughts of violence faded away, disappearing into that soft hue.

Poppy wasn't bored exactly, just restless as she wandered around Cat's parents' house in Carlingford, filled to the rafters with party-goers, pipes and politics, as expected. Still, Spike's antics had her amused.

'Having a prime minister *or* a president is an abomination on our existence,' Cat was saying.

'Couldn't agree more. Let's get the queen over here – we need a pure blood royal at the helm,' Spike said, poker-faced as he placed a saucepan on his head for a crown.

'The qu…' Cat spluttered so hard at that suggestion he had an instant coughing fit.

'You right there mate? Here, have some more yundi.'

Poppy giggled a little as she wandered through the crowd, drinking her champagne and scanning through the record collection near the turntable. Bob Dylan, the Beatles, the Yardbirds – it all looked textbook Cat until you dug a little further down and found the *Sound of Music* soundtrack and a good dose of lounge music in the mix. She drew one out, tempted to put it on, when a voice carried from the front corridor.

'We're practically newlyweds really but we just couldn't pass up an opportunity to pop in and say "hi".'

Poppy's hand froze as another person spoke.

'Ben Williamson. Nice to meet you.'

'Maurice Rossi, come on in and I'll see if I can find Cat. I didn't realise Barbara was married…'

Poppy didn't hear the rest of the sentence. Her blood was pumping too hard in her ears as the trio walked past and the sight of him filled her. Blonde, tall, handsome. A beautiful man with a beautiful woman, her ugly soul well hidden beneath the diamonds and fur. Poppy sank against the wall, seeking the comfort of invisibility instinctively in their presence, dazed with shock that he was in the room.

'What the hell is she doing here?' said Daniella, standing alongside with folded arms.

'She…she wasn't invited?'

'Of course not. Cat can't stand her – says she epitomises everything that's wrong with repressed democratic culture.'

'Then why…?'

'Probably to get revenge on Ivan, oh God, there he is,' Daniella said, nodding at Judith Bentley's brother who was lurking across the room. 'I'd say she wants to make him suffer for treating her like a one-night stand.' It seemed to be working. Ivan looked both jealous and stoned, eyeing the couple with sullen wariness.

'Barbara always wins…' Poppy said vaguely.

'Not tonight she won't. Come on, this should be good therapy for you.'

Daniella grabbed her arm to listen at the door of the lounge room where Barbara was commanding attention from the host and his friends.

'Just passing by. Can't have my lovely husband on leave and not introduce him around.'

'Ben, is that you? Good to uh…see you again,' Spike said, looking around for Poppy as the potential for awkwardness in the room seemed to dawn on him. She hid further behind Daniella. 'Um, this is my mate Ben. Ben, Cat, Cat, Ben.'

'Nice to meet you,' Ben said, offering his hand and looking uncomfortable. Poppy doubted he would have come if he'd known they weren't invited. Then she found herself staring at that hand and couldn't seem to focus on much else. Those long brown fingers that had held onto hers that first night on the beach; the moment she knew he wanted her after all. It made her feel slightly faint.

'Army man eh?' Cat said, looking at him with animosity and ignoring the proffered hand. 'Duntroon I see.'

'Yes, I've been in officer training. First leave in six months so I must thank you for your hospitality.' Ben said it clearly but there was reserve in his tone as he dropped his hand and eyed Cat's Che Guevara T-shirt and numerous political badges warily.

'Can't imagine the Vietnamese will be quite so welcoming. Looking forward to active service, are you? Bagging yourself a few commies?'

The room was very quiet as they all awaited Ben's response. 'Only a mad man would look forward to a fight.'

The air was thick with tension now and Poppy wondered if Ben was nervous as that hand clenched and unclenched at his side.

Barbara chose that moment to let out a trill of laughter, in her element at the centre of all the attention and drama, then it morphed slightly and sounded more like a whine. Then Poppy realised it actually was a whine and the party suddenly erupted.

'Cops!'

Joints and pipes and bags were being stuffed in cupboards and pot was flushed down toilets and sinks as people scrambled to hide the evidence before the police knocked on the door. When Poppy reflected on the scene later it seemed rather comical as someone had actually put *The Sound of Music* soundtrack on a few minutes before and the crisis played out to the tune of 'My Favourite Things'.

Then the knock finally came and people dove behind couches or ran out the back to jump the fence and all the while Ben simply stood there, the single soldier amid the chaos of this ongoing bohemian 'war' against authority.

'Answer it,' hissed Maurice from behind the curtain.

'You open it,' Cat hissed back.

'Do you think I should?' Spike whispered loudly, sitting openly on the couch, saucepan still in place.

'God no!' said several people at once.

The knock came again, more loudly this time. 'Open up. Police.'

Then the only man in uniform strode towards the front door, opening it abruptly to a blur of dark blue.

'Good evening sir,' Ben said, saluting the officer in front. From her vantage point next to the bookcase, Poppy couldn't see the man's expression but she imagined it would be one of surprise.

'Er, good evening. Sorry to disturb you but we've had complaints from the neighbours regarding the noise.' Julie Andrews' voice was, by now, crooning about a drop of golden sun. Spike looked over at the stereo in disgust, whispering, 'Who put that shit on?' which made quite a few people stifle chuckles.

'Turn that down, will you Spike?' Ben said, and the policeman craned to see past his big frame into the room as Spike jumped up gladly to switch the music off. 'I do apologise sir. Just a few of us enjoying a bit of a social gathering. I've got my first leave this weekend in six months and they were throwing a sort of welcome home get-together for me. Entirely my fault I'm afraid.'

'First leave, eh? I remember what that feels like,' the policeman could be heard saying. 'Where are you training?'

'Duntroon, sir. Officer in the making, God willing.'

'Good for you, good for you. Well…I suppose everything seems in order,' the policeman said. 'Just keep it down, alright son?'

'Certainly sir, thank you sir.'

'You're welcome, you're welcome. And er…best of luck in service to you. Come home safe alright?'

'Thank you sir. I will do my best.'

Ben stood at the door, saluting once more as they moved off, then closed it and walked back into the silent room. Then Cat peeled himself off the wall and moved over to stand in front.

'Thank you for that. You're…you're alright.' He extended his hand and Ben looked at it for a moment. Then he sighed deeply and shook it.

'So what's a man have to do around here to get a drink?'

'Forget the drink, give the man a spliff!' Spike declared, walking over and clapping him on the back. Ben laughed then and the sound of it was so familiar and so missed it brought tears to Poppy's eyes and she realised she'd barely dared to breathe these past few minutes, so overwhelming were the emotions pulsing through her body. Then Barbara walked over, calling him 'Benny' before kissing him on that smiling mouth, shattering any thrill Poppy might have been experiencing. Suddenly seeing him again was too unbearable a pain to be borne.

She had to escape it, now before he saw her. Before he read that pain for himself.

'Where are you going?' Daniella asked as she headed towards the kitchen and the back door.

'I have to go,' Poppy said, trying to move through the crowd that had begun to dance, Spike leading the way as usual.

'Don't you want to at least say hello to him?' Daniella asked, stilling her arm. 'It might be your only chance.'

'Doesn't seem to be much point,' Poppy replied, her voice breaking as she shrugged Daniella's hand away. 'It's really just goodbye isn't it?'

She made it to the kitchen, finding her coat and scarf and putting them on before skirting for the door, desperate now for escape. But then a different hand was on her arm, fingers long and brown, and she was forced to face the pain after all.

Ben didn't know why he'd stopped her when she so obviously wanted to leave but it wasn't as if he gave it any rational thought. There was certainly nothing rational about talking to Poppy Flannery, let alone touching her, but it was too late now. He'd done it reflexively, perhaps because of the emptied hip flask, perhaps because the stress of facing five cops to protect a party of pot-smoking hippies had left him full of adrenaline.

Perhaps purely because seeing her in the flesh had sent his senses into shock and he couldn't bring himself to let her just walk away after so many months of longing for that voice. That touch.

But her arm felt small beneath her coat and her face looked thinner too, like she'd been suffering. It made him ache, especially when her blue eyes finally collided with his and he could read the grief that lived there.

'Poppy Marie,' was what came out, and for some reason it made those eyes fill with tears. She opened her mouth to say something but nothing came so he searched for further words. Anything to stem that hurt. 'Don't leave on account of me. I'll…I'll go.'

'No,' she said, shaking her head, blonde hair falling from the twist of her scarf. 'It's not you…I just have to go somewhere to meet…to meet Rosemary.' She was lying and she was terrible at it, of course.

'Then let me order you a taxi.' There. That kept her here a little longer at least. 'I insist.' He led her over to the phone in the corner and she sat on the bench next to it, looking both shaken and wary as he closed the kitchen door against the music and dialled. 'Where are you going to?' She said the address softly and he strained to hear and relay it to the woman on the end of the line.

'What's Rosemary doing in Brookvale?' he said, hanging up.

'Angus,' she explained simply, avoiding his eyes as he sat next to her on the bench to wait. So Rosemary was still with that West Australian. He supposed he should have guessed that after seeing his brother Spike at a Sydney party.

'He moved all the way down here,' he said out loud, regretting the words immediately. Angus had done all the right things. Angus deserved a Flannery twin's love.

'Yes…but he's been drafted so they want to spend time…' Her voice faltered and he just nodded, sparing her the rest. They'd talked about that too once – making the most of their time together when he'd have leave between the long waits. Times like right now. Her hands were clutching the purse in her lap tight and the sight of it made him realise he knew exactly what he really wanted to say.

'I got your letter. Read it every day.'

She looked up at him, confusion clouding her features. 'What letter?'

Just then the kitchen door burst open and Barbara fell into the room, laughing at something Ivan Bentley was saying close behind her. 'Behave! My husband might…' She came to an abrupt stop, sobering at the sight of Ben sitting alone next to Poppy.

'Well, well, isn't this nice and cosy?' Barbara said, a sneer in her tone as she flicked her hair back over her shoulder. 'Haven't seen you for a while, *Ploppy*.' She stumbled slightly as she sauntered closer, steadying her balance against the back of a kitchen chair.

Ben felt Poppy immediately tense alongside him and decided his earlier thought that evening might actually be true: he really might hate his wife. She seemed to have gotten drunk very quickly, which wasn't a good sign – Barbara was even meaner when she was drinking. Ben stood up protectively and Barbara took the opportunity to slide her arm through his.

'Doesn't my husband look handsome in his uniform?' It was a declaration of ownership, not a question, and Poppy had no response. Ivan made a derisive grunt from behind and Ben looked over at him.

'Ivan Bentley,' he announced, in a belligerent sort of way. He stuck out his hand and Ben took it reluctantly.

'Ben Williamson.'

Ivan shook it in an overly firm, aggressive manner and Ben recognised there was more than alcohol driving the man's behaviour.

'You seem to have all the ladies' attentions tonight,' he said, a false smile stretching across his face. 'Mind if I steal this little one from you?' Poppy shrank against the wall as Ivan leered closer and leant on his arm above her. 'I think we have some unfinished business, you and I.'

'You're such a *tease,* Ivan,' Barbara said with the same trilling little laugh from earlier on. 'As if Poppy would have a clue how to take on a man like you.'

Ivan glanced over at Barbara before returning his focus once more towards Poppy, his tone suggestive as he replied. 'You know me – always up for a challenge.'

Poppy seemed to shrink away even further but had found some words at last. 'I'm actually going. We've called a taxi.'

'We?' Barbara's gaze switched back to Ben. 'Going somewhere?'

He wished nothing more than to say yes; to tell her to flush this marriage down the kitchen sink nearby, along with all that pot, and leave with Poppy right here and now but the silken ties Barbara had bound months ago were still in place. Part of those rules that lined that second skin. 'Poppy is,' he said instead, offering her his hand.

'Allow me,' Ivan said, pushing him aside with one arm and grabbing Poppy's with the other, hoisting her up.

'Let her go,' Ben warned, that adrenaline from before making a return and pumping hard.

'I'm…I'm fine,' Poppy said, but her face was pale and she recoiled from Ivan's touch.

'Come on, let's leave these two alone,' Barbara said as she pulled at Ben's shirt, but Ivan had his arm around Poppy now and she looked afraid.

'I said let her go.'

Ivan smirked, shoving Ben away as he started for the door. 'Tell it walking, commie-killer.'

Poppy struggled out from under Ivan's arm saying 'no' and Ben's instincts took over, outweighing further thought as his right fist landed on Ivan's chin, obliterating the smirk. Ivan reeled but managed to stay standing and swung back, punching Ben in the stomach and sending him sprawling into the bench.

'What's going on in here?' Cat said, walking in with Daniella and Maurice. 'Hey! *Hey!*' he yelled, running over too late to stop Ben swinging again, this time landing his fist on Ivan's nose which immediately began to bleed profusely.

'Break it up!' Poppy screamed but Barbara was laughing again, that strange trill bouncing off the walls as the two men crashed across the table, smashing the vase of flowers and sending roses, water and glass across the floor.

'Shit, my mum's kitchen,' Cat moaned as Spike entered the room. He seemed to take about a second to take things in before calling out to Ben who was squaring up to Ivan once more.

'Leave it mate – he's not worth it!'

Ben was breathing hard but he was far from done. Ivan, however, was a bloodied mess, shirt now soaked a deep red, nose obviously broken.

'Have you…' Ben panted, 'had enough then?'

Ivan paused, then dropped his fists, nodding, and Ben turned to walk away just as Ivan picked up a piece of broken glass and lunged at him. Spike moved so fast no-one saw it coming but a saucepan landed on Ivan's head just before the glass made contact and Ivan fell to the floor unconscious, blood pooling with the water.

'Ben,' Poppy said brokenly, agony in her voice, and he looked across at her as the room went still.

Then Barbara went to his side, wrapping her arms about him, crooning 'Are you okay, baby?' and Maurice bent to check on Ivan and Cat was calling an ambulance. Then the murmurs that follow such violence began, but none of it really registered to the soldier at the centre of it all. He was too preoccupied with the sight of blonde hair being wrapped in a scarf and the closing of a back door as Poppy made her quiet exit.

And all the while the blood ran, finding his feet, smearing across the white linoleum of a suburban kitchen floor.

Twenty-Four

Jindabyne, Kosciusko National Park, Australia, June 1966

The air was so cold she thought it might snow again but she was warm beneath the bundle of layers her mother had insisted she pack and the nearby forest walk was simply too invigorating to resist. The High Country had captured her imagination, a wonderland of snow-laden branches twisting beneath vistas of alps – craggy, ancient hillsides half-covered in snow. Like icing sugar on sponge cake, Poppy reflected, climbing onto a boulder to better see the view stretching in front.

A massive snow gum stood nearby, the colours wet with the melting snow and shining brilliantly in red, orange, green and silver, quite unlike anything she'd ever seen before. She wondered what it must be like to be an artist trying to capture such a beautiful and unusual subject then her mood quickly fell back to the melancholy of the past week. Better not to think of the beautiful man's artistic soul. Better to remember him in uniform, with blood on his hands.

She sat down, taking deep draughts of alpine air into her lungs, wondering how he'd been feeling since. Had seeing her torn him inside too? Was that what drove him to smash his fist into Ivan's face? Or was it just rage spurred on by insult and pride, like so many other men? She'd never seen that side of him before – a darker Ben. A human weapon. She supposed he'd need it if he went to war – that ability to cause harm – only that wasn't the man she knew. The man she knew was calm and intelligent. Kind.

Wasn't very kind of him to marry Barbara, her mind taunted, then again perhaps he thought it was. Ben's moral compass pointed duly towards duty when it came to matters of the heart. Poppy supposed he saw it as a form of kindness – to keep his parents happy and honour the family name. Only it wasn't kind to himself, and it certainly hadn't been kind to her.

His last words came back then and she closed her eyes against them. *I got your letter.* It seemed the truths she'd let exist on paper had grown and taken flight – all the way to Duntroon. Rosemary had defended her action in sending it by saying they needed to be heard, those honest sentences. Those raw, heartfelt blurts. Only written confessions have an especially terrible power. *I read it every day.*

She opened her eyes then and let out a small gasp. A wallaby had appeared nearby, his soft fur holding traces of snow, and she found herself actually smiling as she glimpsed a second, smaller one hop slowly towards him. They made gentle progress, finding long stalks in the thick, white blanket, leaving carved tracks behind. How magical nature can be when it simply exists, she observed. When nothing unnatural disturbs it; no duty, no rules. No man-made complications bringing violence. Causing wars.

When there was no reason to sit on a boulder with a broken heart, knowing those human rules were keeping the man you loved at war with himself.

With no way to find his way home.

The mountains were transforming again, for the fourth time that day by Poppy's count. What had started as a bitterly cold morning threatening more snow had turned into a sparkling day of cloudless blue skies, followed by an afternoon of racing white clouds on a stiff wind. But now it was about to turn very dark once more. Golden edges sat upon the slate-grey masses that moved slowly but steadily across the sea of mountain-tops, and it was time to find a place indoors and stay there.

Spike seemed to have other ideas. He was still outside, already drunk but comically so, building rather disastrous replicas of them all from snow and falling over quite a bit in the process. 'Angus' had an army shirt on over his amusingly fat torso and an enormous carrot in an inappropriate place. The girls were likewise 'endowed' but in the chest area – with large potatoes to be precise. It had made for an enjoyable show through the front window of the Rossi family's chalet but the sun was now falling behind that ominous cloud front and discussion began to turn towards dinner and more sophisticated entertainment.

'There's a band playing down at the pub – Spike said they're supposed to be pretty good,' Angus said.

'How does he know?' Daniella asked. 'Oh no, let me guess, the Swedes?'

Spike had spent the afternoon drinking schnapps with a bunch of Swedish instructors he'd befriended over the past few days while learning to ski. Apparently his reckless attempts to master the sport had turned him into an instant celebrity with the Europeans, especially after he crashed into an entire outdoor cafe, unable to find any 'bloody brakes'.

Angus confirmed her guess, then shook his head as Spike took a run towards his dilapidated menagerie of snow-people, failing an attempted hurdle. 'Mad as a cut snake,' he muttered while the girls laughed.

It took quite some time to dismantle the offensive sculptures in the Rossis' front yard before Daniella's parents came home, and even longer to coax Spike into going back to the hostel to shower and change, but they eventually succeeded. By the time the girls met them at the pub Cat had joined them for the weekend, fresh off the bus from Sydney and already being stirred up by the mischievous Spike.

'Compulsory bows and curtsies? Have you lost your mind?'

'The police are human too; might be nice to get a little bow from passers-by, or a curtsey, as I said. Actually that's got a nice ring to it doesn't it? "Curtsey a Copper". That's the way I'd roll.' He stood up to demonstrate and tripped over his feet, causing Angus to drag him back down onto the booth seat in the corner, looking around nervously for security.

'He's just teasing. Hey, handsome,' Daniella said, kissing Cat's cheek.

'Hmm,' Cat replied, still frowning but cracking slightly as Spike offered him a cigarette and batted his eyelashes. 'Oh piss off,' he said, taking one anyway.

'How was the trip?' Daniella asked.

'Long. When are they going to fix that bloody road coming in?'

'It'll be worth it when they're all done – lots of resorts opening, Dad says. Besides, the Hydro Scheme brought in migrants like me so it's not all bad now, is it?' Mr Rossi was an engineer and had spent years as an advisor on the massive alpine project, scoring the family chalet in the bargain.

'Not all of them fared as well as your dad though, did they? Without the unions…'

'Yes, yes, come on, let's start this weekend off with a smoko outside, eh? My treat,' interrupted Spike, winking and patting his pocket. That actually did the trick and Poppy was relieved to be spared a political debate so early in the evening as the boys went outside for a joint.

'Wait for me,' Rosemary said, rushing after Angus, but Poppy called her back.

'Don't forget your coat.' Watching her sister bustle off Poppy wondered just how often Rosemary had been smoking pot, uncomfortable at the realisation she wasn't privy to every small detail of her life these days. 'Hope she hasn't been making a habit of that,' she muttered.

'Well at least it will mellow Spike out and stop him from being such a monkey for five seconds. Cat falls straight for it every time,' Daniella said, giggling. 'Curtsey a Copper.'

It actually did seem to work somewhat; Spike was far less hyperactive on their return but still very funny. Or at least he found everything else funny, laughing until tears ran at the smallest things which was rather contagious and Poppy couldn't help but start enjoying herself, especially when the Swedes joined them.

All three were rather good-looking, sporting goggle-tans and flashing bright, white smiles. One of them, Oliver, was paying her rather a lot of attention and she wished she could summon some interest in him but so far the best she could manage was to let him buy her drinks and laugh at his jokes. They were delivered in a thick accent that was actually quite appealing and she felt some small victory that she could appreciate that much at least. It was progress, however tiny. A little hop in the snow.

The band eventually began and they were good, as promised, playing a mixture of the latest songs along with a bit of country that prompted Spike and Angus to sing along loudly, especially to Johnny Cash.

'Dance with me,' Spike implored Poppy, but he was having a hard time sitting straight and she doubted his ability to co-ordinate himself on a dance floor.

'Perhaps a little later.'

Oliver kept asking her to dance too, and she kept fobbing him off, but by the fourth time she was running out of excuses, especially with Spike now trying to cuddle up to her in the corner of the booth. Poppy disentangled herself to take Oliver's hand and be led away.

Unfortunately, the Johnny Cash song that had been playing ended as soon as they arrived and the band chose that moment to play the brand new Motown hit 'What Becomes of the Brokenhearted'. Poppy felt her mood deteriorate with each note, the words cutting so fresh and so deep she could almost feel she was still standing in that kitchen, watching the blood run. Haemorrhaging inside.

Poppy leant her face against Oliver's chest to hide her tears, allowing the pain to flow freely. To just exist, like the wallabies on the white blanket. Maybe it was better that way. Maybe it was the only way to find some kind of peace of mind. Oliver lifted her chin, puzzled to find her crying, then he kissed her, gently, and she allowed that too. Just exist, she told herself again. Exist until you take another hop, then another. Until the tracks behind you become filled with snow.

It was freezing, but Ben was used to that. The cold was just another assault to his senses, like the cruel words that fell from Barbara's mouth. Ivan's fist in his guts. Blood smeared on a white kitchen floor. His father's intractability, no matter what the cost.

'I want a divorce.'

He may as well have said he wanted the moon for all his father had taken him seriously.

'Don't be ridiculous – you've barely been married six months.'

'It wasn't...a choice. She told me...' He hadn't finished and hadn't needed to. His father had simply sent him a long, hard look over his glasses before holding up his hand to halt any further explanation. Men in their world understood the 'gentlemanly thing' that such situations required. He'd tapped his fingers briefly before delivering his verdict. Supreme Court Judge Thompson Charles Williamson was an expert at that. An expert at delivering sentences too.

'It's out of the question – the press would have a field day. Besides, you're back off to college, then service. If you really feel the same way in a few years we can discuss it further but you may find having children will,' he'd paused, clearing his throat, '...er, influence you somewhat.'

'I will never have children with that woman.' And he'd meant it. He hadn't slept with her since his return and knew then with sudden clarity he never would again.

'Be that as it may, you've a duty to perform right now and that's that. You've made your bed, so to speak, Benjamin. We'll speak no more of this until after you've served.'

'So I have your permission to divorce her then?'

'If that's what you still want we can discuss it at the time, but not before.'

Ben had said nothing, not even 'yes sir' which was a first. He'd simply left, his kit bag already packed, no goodbyes given. Just a short note for his parents to give to Barbara, telling her he'd gone. He hadn't even bothered to give a reason, too empty to make one up, but he suspected she wouldn't care much anyway.

She'd been distant since the party, dropping the wifely act as soon as they'd left that night, and Ben knew she was bored with him already. Barbara needed attention like a lion needs prey and he was done with feeding her ego. Not that she would welcome any talk of divorce when the time came – Barbara craved wealth almost as much as that attention and the luxurious family apartment his parents let her live in at Waverton wouldn't be something she'd let go of easily.

And so he was back down south with his Duntroon mates at the snow after all, and wondering why he was here, but there'd been nowhere else he could think of to go.

'Hurry up – the beer will be freezing over at this rate,' complained Zach as Sam finally came out and shut the door.

'Ready are we?' asked Sam, putting on his gloves for the short walk.

Ben nodded and they made their way down to the pub through a thick rain of white. Time to numb his senses once more.

Twenty-Five

She was trying to feel something, find that longing that ran like the ocean, but it had been left on the sand a summer ago. There was nothing Oliver could do differently, no blame to be laid, and as she drew away he seemed to recognise that, kissing her hand and leading her off the floor to the safety of the walls. But something was buzzing in her mind and she let that hand go, staring ahead as an old memory replayed across time.

Ten, nine, eight, seven...

He was holding her gaze; she'd just kissed someone else.

Six, five, four...

He was here, in the flesh, but people were still in their way.

Three, two, one...

'New Year's again?' Ben said.

'New Year's,' she echoed vaguely.

'Who was that?' The fireplace was finding the gold in his hair and it looked like a crown.

'Does it matter?' she said.

'Only if it matters to you.'

She shook her head dazedly and he led her away, across the crowd, around the corner to where the snow was falling hard against the panes. Poppy fell hard too, against the wall as he devoured her mouth like he'd starved for her these long months. She no longer cared that he was married; it didn't deserve that sacred term. He was hers, body and soul, and she could feel it sear through her as the longing found a tide of desire once more. This kiss was stronger than all the heartache and pain put together, almost unbearably sweet as he captured her mouth and kissed at her throat, his body tight and strained against hers. It was as if they were dissolving into one another; merging into a single being.

'Come home with me?' he begged and she nodded, no breath left for words.

Her only regret was that they had to run through a snow storm to get there, but she'd run through hell at that moment if that's what it took. There was a shock of cold, then a key in a door, then the comfort of heating. Then there was a bed and he was ripping off his clothes and she did the same until there was just warm, soft skin and bedsheets and the rhythmic pelt of the falling snow. His kisses were so urgent she almost couldn't stand to wait for more so she guided those long brown fingers down. Then he was kissing at everything he could find, drawing her into his being, worshipful yet hungry, and something more primal. She clung at his back and he seemed to understand as he covered her with his body and they become one at last.

It was like nothing she'd ever felt before, a moment of pain then something wondrous and almost desperate. Like she needed it to go somewhere further and further until it did, exploding like fireworks on New Year's Eve.

They lay for a long time afterwards, listening to that snow, no words needed until the dawn blushed and she rose to go. He watched her every movement as she held her jumper in front, suddenly shy as she picked up her shoes and searched for her jeans.

'I love you.'

Poppy stilled, letting that heart-stopping admission soak through her before putting her shoes down and coming back to sit on the bed. 'Nice blurt,' she said, fighting tears but managing to smile, her heart full. He was so beautiful in the pale morning light, his chest bare above the sheet, but his expression was serious as he started to talk.

'I spoke to my father…he wants me to wait until after I serve. To get a divorce.' He paused to gently push her hair from her face, his eyes locked on hers. 'I'll do it now if you want me to. He just thinks it will be less of a scandal for the family and I…' He paused, searching for words.

'It's that duty thing again, isn't it?'

He sighed, taking her fingers in his. 'Yes. It would be a big deal for them with the press and all.' Ben held her fingers a little tighter. 'I promise I am divorced from her in my heart already. We haven't even slept together for months…'

Poppy shook her head. 'Don't.'

So he paused for better words and found them. '*I will wait for you.* I know it's a lot to ask of you, to wait too, but when I come back I'll get that divorce, I promise. I want to be with you, Poppy Marie. Will you…will you still wait for me?'

As she watched the fear and the love in his face she knew then that Barbara had ceased to matter in their world. The laws of man had ceased to matter too.

Poppy let her jumper fall, no longer shy as she lifted the sheet to move back by his side.

Nature was magical when you simply let it exist.

Part Three

Dragon Fruit

Twenty-Six

Vung Tau, Vietnam, December 1967

The road was littered with fresh potholes that morning and Thuy Nguyen was having a hard time staying on her bike, especially with the water spinach in her basket constantly threatening to fall in the dirt. The sun burned down on her *non la*, the conical hat shielding her face well but heating her scalp. Not far now though, she reassured herself, lurching to one side as a giant rut appeared. Some American soldiers were mending it but they paused to watch her pass, nodding and grinning and saying 'watch out for the pretty lady' and 'morning there, miss'. She ignored them, lowering her chin so the *non la* concealed more of her face, giving them nothing.

Thuy reached the crossroads then and joined the morning traffic heading into Vung Tau. A chaotic sea of bicycles and mopeds cluttered the streets as vendors and shoppers alike headed for the markets and Thuy concentrated hard to navigate her way through, not keen to fall off like last week. Her mother had been less than impressed with the mud stains on her white dress. The port was thick with soldiers, mostly Australian, and she avoided them too. They were less forward than the Americans overall but when they drank beer they could be just as bad. One had called her a 'right sort' recently and, with her still-developing English, she wasn't entirely sure what he meant but she knew enough to understand it wasn't a gentlemanly compliment, despite the literal translation.

Both her parents had already set up the stand and she parked her bike behind it, unloading the spinach. They were arguing quietly in Vietnamese and she knew why without really listening. More troops had arrived that week and her father Bao was worried about Thuy's presence, in the public view of so many foreign men; 'they do not respect' had become his litany of late. Thuy's mother Anh was insistent she be here, however. Her own health hadn't been good of late and she needed Thuy to help load and unload. Besides, the money was good on a Saturday morning and the soldiers liked to snack on the sweet potato cakes Thuy cooked on the side of the road. It was becoming even more profitable than selling fruit and vegetables to the locals – although of course there were less of them these days. Thuy slammed the spinach down hard, earning a look from Anh.

A group of soldiers approached and she began to serve the cakes that were already hot on the smoky grill, forcing the resentment aside. Her father may not trust them to respect his daughter but he did agree with their presence here. They'd been sent to help, he often reminded Thuy. But it didn't feel much like help when your village was destroyed and you were forced to live a makeshift existence elsewhere, salvaging what life you could from new, less cultivated fields. When you were watched while you worked by foreign eyes of blue, brown and green; eyes that pierced the white material of your dress as if to see what lay beneath. Yes, resentment lurked and stirred within but she couldn't quite call it hatred. That was reserved for the Viet Cong.

The soldiers moved on as a second group arrived and Thuy lifted a steaming cake off the grill.

'Coconut-sweet-potato?' she said in the same sing-song way she always did.

'Are they as sweet as you?' one of the soldiers asked, his Australian accent strong. Thuy sighed inwardly. If only she had a thousand dong for every time one of them said that. Bao looked over, unimpressed, and she quickly moved on, taking the man's money and serving the next.

'Coconut-sweet-potato?'

This man was enormous and he held up his fingers indicating 'two', his blue eyes watching hungrily as she handed over the cakes. 'Thank you,' he mumbled, already eating as she moved on to the third man.

'Coconut-sweet-potato?'

'Sure,' this one replied, not really looking at her at all as he glanced over their table. He was tall, with brown hair and broad shoulders, and she imagined he was well used to women thinking him handsome. Thuy handed him the cake, relieved to be overlooked. She supposed.

'Put more cakes on the grill,' Anh instructed in Vietnamese. 'These men are too hungry today.'

'Yes, Ma,' Thuy said, obeying and resisting the temptation of giving the third man another glance as they left. Better to be invisible to foreign eyes.

Angus munched on the cake while he waited for his new mate Jimmy White to come back from the depot, enjoying it more than he expected. It was his first taste of street food since he'd arrived and he wondered at the ingredients, thinking he could send the recipe to Rosemary. Not that she baked that much anymore, unfortunately. She seemed more interested in hanging out with Sydney's 'Push', a throng of political types and university students mostly; anti-authoritarians who monopolised certain trendy pubs and cafes across the city.

It had only been a month since his deployment but it already felt like she was drifting away from him; drinking life in and tasting new adventures. Better adventures than he'd been having, Angus reflected, trying not to allow the shock of seeing a pile of bodies being buried after an ambush last week to re-enter his mind.

He took out the letter again, reading it for the fourth time since he'd gotten his mail last night. Angus had been desperate for contact after three gruelling weeks on patrol – needing it even more than a hot shower, denying himself that luxury until after he'd consumed her words.

Poppy sends her love but I almost don't want to tell you that. I want you all to myself in these pages like we are lying together in the sheets. Ha! See what I did there? Sexy metaphor girl – that's me!

Angus chuckled, scanning a few more precious lines.

I bought myself some black lacy underwear for when you get leave. Can you believe how debaucherous I've become? All your fault of course. Mum would DIE if she knew but she can't go through my drawers now that I'm on campus. I may start filling them up with all sorts of naughty things – just for you. Maybe make a private show. Is that the expression? Or is it 'give a private show'?

Oh, this is hopeless isn't it? Not exactly what you had in mind when you asked me to write you dirty letters, I'm sure. I don't think I'm cut out for the job – too many years as a wallflower.

She'd followed that line with a rather clever drawing of a woman in lingerie sitting against the wall with a flower for a face. Angus knew he must really be missing sex because it was kind of turning him on.

'Holy shit!' his new mate Jimmy in 3RAR exclaimed, walking slowly towards him and staring at the latest newspaper. 'Harold Holt's dead!'

'What?' Angus said, and their other mate Steven 'Body' Simpson moved over from where he'd been checking out some souvenirs.

'Went missing off the coast yesterday. They think he's drowned.'

'How'd that happen?' Body said, looking at the headlines. 'Don't prime ministers have bodyguards or somethin'?'

Jimmy rolled his eyes. 'Of course they do, ya big nong!'

'Then why…?'

Jimmy shrugged, lost for words as he handed the paper over to Angus who scanned the story in disbelief. The Australian leader's face stared out from the ink, a grey visage of the man who'd impacted so many lives, especially when it came to sending more and more troops here. 'All the way with LBJ,' he muttered to himself. 'So much power then just…'

'…gone,' Jimmy finished for him, clicking his fingers.

'What's it mean for us?' Body asked.

'It means a political shit-fight back home,' Jimmy told him, folding up the paper and shoving it under his arm as they walked back to the jeep.

Body looked worried as he tried to comprehend the impact of such news, not an easy thing for a man considered rather simple by his friends. 'Just what we bloody need,' he said, looking to Angus for confirmation.

'Hit the nail on the head there, mate,' Angus told him, patting his enormous back as they climbed on board. 'Right on the bloody head.'

The sun was low in the sky by the time Thuy arrived home and she took off her hat, lifting her hair off her neck as she watched it set. A breeze took some small amount of heat from the day and the sound of the creek soothed her, even if it was a stranger's water. A stranger's land. True, it wasn't far from where she had been raised in Long Tan, but it would never really be home for her here.

A late dragon fruit hung from the bushes near the giant tree at the water's edge and she wandered down to pick it, allowing the admission that it did hold its own beauty, Thanh Long Creek, so named for this sweet bounty that grew all along it. The fruit was popular at her parents' stall, although ripe pieces were rare right now.

The grass was thick and green along the shoreline and the sun burned a deep orange above the hills and through the trees. At least those craggy slopes were familiar, the same ones she'd watched her whole life; a gentle purple at this time of day, towering as if to offer protection from those who would bring harm to their world. But of course they never could. The French, the Japanese and now these Americans and Australians had all brought war here, each fighting for dominance and control of what had never been, and never would be, theirs.

Bao's voice could be heard from inside, still arguing with her mother. She knew what he would say if he could hear her thoughts, that these new foreigners were not invaders, they were allies, fighting the north and the Viet Cong, but she had her doubts. They would ultimately want control, just like the other armies before them. Vietnam was like that single piece of dragon fruit, something all men eventually wanted to pick and devour. Unusual and beautiful, vulnerable at its heart.

'Thuy,' Anh called and she looked at the fruit, deciding to leave it be before reluctantly returning to the hut. It was no use wishing the hardships of her life away. Wishing wasn't having, as ineffectual as her prayers.

The hut was still warm as they sat to eat their usual Saturday evening fare of leftover cakes and vegetables and Thuy tried not to notice that her mother had set the table for four again. She wondered if she would ever stop doing that; just give up once and for all.

Bao lit a candle, and they prayed together, mostly for gratitude, which Thuy struggled to feel. Then her father added the prayer Thuy hated most, the one for the owner of the empty plate.

With rituals now complete they began to eat in silence as the insect drone rose outside and the birds called out, gathering their offspring together too. It looked to be yet another uneventful night until Bao reached into his pocket and pushed a small tin box her way.

'What is this?'

'Open it,' he said and Thuy looked across to her mother, surprised to see rare tears in her eyes. Bao nodded at the box, insistent, and she picked it up slowly, tracing the cool metal before opening it at the clasp. Inside were papers, identity certificates and the like, and she lifted them to see there was something else hidden below. Thuy took it out carefully. It was a necklace, gold and fine, holding a deep red stone in an ornate setting and it glittered in the candlelight like wine, so exquisite it made her gasp. She looked to her parents, confused.

'It was my grandmother's,' Anh said, almost reluctantly. 'Now it is yours.' She'd heard her mother speak of it before but she'd never seen it until now.

'Take it somewhere and bury it,' Bao instructed. 'Tell no-one where – not even us. One day you may need it to buy your freedom.'

'Freedom…?'

'It is not something you will find here,' her father told her and Thuy knew that was true, but she'd never expected to be given the option of leaving.

'Where…where would I go?'

'Australia,' her father said in a tone that indicated he'd made this decision long ago. Thuy stared at him in shock. So far away. 'I have friend who has moved to Sydney and he has sons so you can still marry a Vietnamese man.'

'Marry…?' Thuy wondered briefly if she would ever be able to stop asking questions but every answer was leaving her reeling.

'Only if you go,' her mother said, seeming to waver as she looked over at the empty plate.

'She will go,' her father insisted. 'It is for the best.'

That night Thuy took the little box down to the creek, finding the tree near that single dragon fruit and she dug a hole beneath it, confident it was high enough to be away from the swell that would come with the monsoons. Then she picked the lone dragon fruit after all, turning it in her palms, admiring its unique beauty before peeling back its skin and claiming its flesh.

For Thuy Nguyen was tired of hardship; tired of denying herself any pleasure, any hope.

Perhaps one day she really could go to this home of foreign soldiers, this 'Australia', so far away. People said life there was easy for it was a rich country; a peaceful land without war.

Thuy stared out to the east, to where her old village lay scorched and abandoned, nothing but a moonscape of craters and rubble, and she tried to imagine a place where such things didn't occur. A life without hardship. A life that was free.

The dragonfruit was all gone and she tossed the skin, letting it fall into the creek to float away. Its flesh had been released and was now morphed into hers; life was strangely re-inventive in that way. You just needed opportunity and the wishing to return.

And to pick the perfect moment, when fortune was ripe.

Twenty-Seven

Sydney, December 1967

Someone had turned the stereo up loud in the dorms and Poppy strained to hear Ben's voice above it, pushing the phone hard against one ear and sticking her finger in the other.

'I said I'll be there about ten. Couldn't get the early train but I'm coming.'

'Why didn't you travel back with your parents?' She didn't add Barbara's name, hating the idea of her being there today, watching his graduation with that sickly sense of ownership Poppy had come to detest.

'Colonel wanted to see me.' He sounded evasive and she began to feel concerned.

'About your commission?' The music was even louder now and the Monkees echoed down the corridors, to the point that Poppy could barely hear above women's voices, laughing and singing along to 'Stepping Stone'. 'Ben? Are you still there?'

'I'll tell you when I get there,' came the voice down the line. 'Gotta run now but I...'

'What was that?' she said, missing his next words, but the line was dead and she hung up, disappointed. Then she looked at the clock and realised she'd see him in less than five hours after three long months apart and shrugged all other thoughts away, rushing to the room she now shared at Sydney University with Rosemary.

Daniella and her sister were both there, dancing around and laughing, clearly the culprits of the deafening music.

'Not again,' Poppy said, shaking her head as she turned down the volume and picked up the pipe and bowl, shoving them into the wardrobe.

'Hey, what'd you do that for?' Rosemary protested. 'Stepping stooooooonnneed,' she sang, stepping across the room in exaggerated fashion to retrieve it, causing Daniella to hold her stomach and fall onto the bed in stitches of laughter.

'God, you two. What are you doing smoking on a Friday afternoon anyway?' Poppy said tersely as she gathered her things for the shower.

'Having fun. Hey, stop being such a square,' Rosemary complained as Poppy took the retrieved pipe back out of her hands.

'Better a square than a stoner.'

'Not just a stoner, a *stepping* stoner,' Daniella pointed out and the two dissolved into laughter again. Poppy decided to leave them to it as she headed towards the bathroom.

It had been a sticky summer's day and she welcomed the pressure of the water, relaxing into it and allowing the warmth to soak through her tense muscles and dissolve her nerves. There were a few things playing on them. Ben's commission. Rosemary's behaviour.

Her sister had taken to smoking pot quite regularly now, especially since Angus went away. Her marks had been slipping too and Poppy knew the time was coming when she'd have to confront her about it – but not tonight.

Tonight belonged to a newly graduated officer with gold in his hair.

Poppy allowed herself delicious imaginings of what this night would bring as the soap glided across her skin. Long, brown fingers would soon take its place and she felt another kind of warmth flood her senses, the anticipation consuming her. She floated in that wonderful place a few minutes more before moving on to more practical activities: shampooing, conditioning, shaving. Then there were post-shower rituals to perform: hair drying, moisturising, applying make-up. It felt comforting, this age-old practice of feminine preparation; making ready to share the sweetest of rewards with the returning hero. Never mind that he legally belonged to another, he was hers in body and soul. Her lover, she realised, the word reverent to her now.

By the time she was dressed in a white shift and matching pumps it was almost six o'clock. Still an agonising four hours to wait, she realised with a sigh as she came back into the bedroom.

'Wow, you look good. Where are you meeting him?' Rosemary asked, glancing up at her as she ate a mango, her sister's favourite food. She was making quite a mess of it but Poppy supposed she had 'the munchies' now and refrained from comment. Both she and Daniella seemed to have sobered up and were getting ready to go out with Cat who, along with others in their set, were by now firmly entrenched in Sydney's Push scene. Poppy well knew what the night had in store for her twin; all political exchange, booze and heavy smoking – not exactly Poppy's cup of tea.

'Circular Quay,' she said, sitting on the bed to wait. 'He wasn't keen on me hanging around Central on my own.'

'What time?' Daniella said, yawning. She looked ready for bed, not socialising.

'Ten. Colonel wanted to see him after the ceremony.' Poppy frowned, worry over the terms of Ben's commission returning.

'Well, you can't just sit in here for hours on end. Come with us,' Rosemary said, finishing her mango. 'Mmm, food of the gods. So good.' She wiped her fingers on a towel and began to roll her hair up, pinning it a little lopsidedly. 'We're going to the Port Jackson.'

Poppy considered that, looking at the Beatles clock that ticked loudly on the wall. Four hours was a long while to stew.

'Spike's going,' Rosemary told her and that made up her mind. If you needed a distraction you may as well go with an expert on the subject.

Half an hour later they were walking into the rowdy Port Jackson Hotel on George Street, a popular spot among the bohemian set. The crowd was eclectic, ranging from serious intellectuals to peace-driven hippies, notable for their longer hair and shabbier 'threads', but they all held one thing in common: debate. The Push loved nothing more than to voice opinion, the focal point nowadays usually the war in Vietnam. However, the atmosphere tonight had a different undercurrent, charged by the headlines of the past few days.

'I'm telling you, it's a conspiracy,' she heard one man say as she passed, his beard almost touching his chest as he talked loudly above the din. 'Holt was a strong swimmer, there's no way he would have just up and drowned. It's an assassination, mark my words.'

'By who? The Americans? He just agreed to more troops, for godsakes,' another man argued. Poppy recognised him as a tutor from university; Boris or Horace or some such name.

'Not the Americans, Norris, the Chinese!'

The other man looked scornful. 'You can't be serious…'

'Two words for you my friend: Pine Gap.'

Poppy moved on, not needing to hear more about the proposed US base and what it meant for our 'national autonomy'.

Fortunately Spike was nearby and she managed to squeeze in next to him on the bench, welcoming the potential for humorous exchange between him and Cat instead. Spike looked pleased to see her, winking as Cat continued an address to the table.

'Any man who lies about his intentions to send thousands more conscripts to kill the yellow man deserved what he got.'

'Only the yellow ones, mind,' Spike said, 'the purple and green should strictly be left alone.'

'What about Vietnamese people's rights?' Cat said, ignoring him. 'They should be entitled to every freedom known to mankind...'

'And womankind,' Daniella put in as she arrived, sitting alongside him and kissing his cheek.

'And womankind,' Cat conceded, pausing to allow her a smile.

'He gave the Aborigines the vote,' one man in a paisley shirt pointed out.

'They were given the right to vote in '62,' Cat corrected him, 'Holt just allowed the referendum so we could vote for their civil rights, which I agree, yes, was a move in the right direction, but it's really just following in LBJ's steps, isn't it?'

'What's so wrong with that?' Rosemary asked, looking around cautiously before lighting a joint.

'What's *wrong* is that gradually diminishing the plight of our black brothers is irrelevant if the powers that be ultimately send them over to Vietnam to die. Or kill our Asian neighbours.'

'I just don't understand how they justify it. I mean, is communism really this big, evil monster they make it out to be?' one dark-haired girl asked.

'The short answer? No, it isn't. But it's a *threat* you see. It's all a big political game; it's all about power,' Cat said forcefully, meeting each person's gaze, 'and Holt was in bed with Johnson all the way along which means only one thing...'

'They were in love?' Spike guessed and several people laughed.

Cat pointed his pipe about. 'Oppression! *Control,* people, and there's only one way to fight it: anarchic protest. It's at the core of our very freedom! It was my *right* to lie down in front of a car carrying LBJ,' he said emphatically, referring to the protest he'd been arrested in during Johnson's visit to Sydney last month, his favourite new subject. 'I didn't do it because he's the president of the United States, I did it because he has too much *power.* That's my understanding of democratic rights: equality for all. These men are no more important than any one of us and if it takes anarchy to prove that point, so be it.'

'King says peaceful protest is the only true way,' the dark-haired girl said doubtfully.

'People like this don't understand peaceful protest; they don't respect it,' Cat spat. 'You know what that spineless arsehole Premier Askin said as we were lying there in front of the wheels? "Run over the bastards." Like I was a piece of *garbage…*' Cat thumped his fist on the table and silence ensued.

'You had *every* right to lie down and take a little nap,' Spike said, nodding solemnly. 'Political speeches can be very boring. Speaking of which, I think it's time for a drink.' It broke the tension and chuckles followed Poppy as she rose to go with him, glad to take a break from Cat's rhetoric.

They twisted their way through the crowd towards the line at the bar and Spike held an arm around her, making funny little asides as they went. 'Look out there, Rasputin,' he said to one long-haired, serious type; 'Jesus – it's Jesus!' to another.

'Spike,' she admonished, the Catholic in her scandalised, but she was giggling too. No-one seemed to take any offence as they moved on and he continued to make offhand, inappropriate comments. Somehow Spike always got away with being the court jester wherever he went, his affability acting like a protective shield. Even Cat tolerated him really, despite all the huffing and puffing.

'Now, what will it be? Rum, vodka, whiskey...?' he asked as they arrived at the bar and he dropped his arm.

'Just a white wine thanks,' she said, deciding to limit it to one or two tonight.

'Go on, have some of the hard stuff. You might get tiddly enough to let me have my fiendish way with you.' He wriggled his eyebrows comically as he said it but she detected something there that had been worrying her, especially of late. Something best avoided.

'Behave,' she said lightly, pretending to look for something in her purse.

A rare pause ensued between them and he seemed awkward as he asked, 'So...what's new with you then?'

'Nothing much,' Poppy lied. She couldn't exactly say 'oh, just continuing my affair with a married man around ten or so tonight. You remember Ben...' Daniella and Rosemary were the only ones who knew about it, although she suspected Angus had cottoned on. 'Just study and band and such.'

'That so?' Spike said, too knowingly for her liking. Perhaps he was more astute than she gave him credit for. 'One glass of white and a beer thanks,' he told the approaching barman before glancing her way again. 'No romantics from the Arts Department throwing pebbles at your windows yet?'

'Now why would they do that?' she said, attempting flippancy as the drinks arrived and they turned to go.

'Every Romeo needs a Juliet,' he muttered near her ear and she felt herself blush, stopping still to look at him. There was a moment then, when what had long been avoided looked set to explode, but the jukebox suddenly interrupted it, the funky beat of 'Soul Man' providing blessed reprieve. Spike's fleetingly intense expression melted into a grin. 'Come on, let's play pool,' he said, the court jester once more. 'I can't resist stirring the crap out of Cat and he looks set to thump me.'

'Sounds like a plan,' she agreed, relieved to have been spared a confrontation of feelings between them, but wary just the same. Something had shifted tonight along that fine line that runs between friendship and romance and, as much as she dreaded losing the first, there was no way to give him the other.

He was receiving plenty of stares and wished he'd thought to change out of his formal whites but Ben had been distracted when the Newman family dropped him off. Scoring a lift instead of taking the train had been a bonus, resulting in him arriving in Sydney over an hour earlier than anticipated, but he still hadn't claimed that longed-for moment of holding Poppy in his arms at last. Her dorm had turned out to be disappointingly empty and now he was simply wandering up and down George Street, in the faint hope she was here somewhere; possibly in one of the pubs that were filled to overflowing this warm summer night.

'Hey handsome,' said one girl, giggling as she passed with her friends, and he tipped his hat self-consciously, regretting his lack of forethought once more. Still, he was here now, and somewhere nearby was the woman he loved – that one who promised to wait. *Well no more bloody waiting tonight*, he promised her silently, marching through the doors of yet another hotel. *Not for even one single, stolen hour.*

They were pretty terrible, Poppy had to admit, but Spike seemed to think that more of an asset than a liability. It was certainly entertaining the other pool players in the room.

'Red ball, right pocket,' he announced, leaning over to take aim. The white ball flew, glancing the black instead, which ricocheted clean off the table, landing with a plop in his opponent's glass and sploshing the contents all over the man's chest.

'Sorry, left pocket,' Spike said, walking over to dab at the man's shirt, but he waved him away, laughing hard along with the others. Then he bowed to the room, claiming victory by default due to the man holding on to his ball (which he deemed 'a bit sick really') before leading a still-giggling Poppy to a table near the window.

'You're a disgrace,' she told him, wiping tears away from the corners of her eyes and sipping her wine.

'What do you mean? That was a beautiful shot. Not my fault he's a randy old perve.'

Poppy shook her head. 'What are we going to do with you?' He looked at her over the rim of his glass and that message from earlier in the night simmered once more so she spoke again, quickly. 'Aside from getting you some pool lessons...'

'I could *teach* pool lessons – teach the balls to swim anyway,' he replied and she had to laugh once more before he sobered a little. 'Actually I was thinking about doing something lately but you may not want to hear it...'

'Really?' Poppy said, a little nervously.

Spike sipped his beer. 'I was thinking about joining the army.' Poppy could only stare, incredulous, then he shrugged, looking away. 'Might not take me though.'

'Why not?' she said, still stunned at the outlandish concept of him being a soldier but addressing that first.

'Five foot six and a half,' he explained, 'I'm too short, apparently.' He was trying hard to sound nonchalant but Poppy could hear the frustration behind it. And the shame.

'But why...'

'I don't know why it matters, it just does. Wouldn't have said it to Napoleon, I'm betting, and he was a way bigger short-arse than me.'

Poppy waited for further explanation but he didn't offer any, so she asked another question instead. 'Why on earth would you want to go to war – I mean what are you even *thinking*...?'

Spike sighed, leaning back in his chair. 'I'm thinking Angus might need a hand, I suppose. That I'm bored working the cars on my own and that it might be a bit of an adventure. Good surf in Vietnam,' he added, finishing his beer.

'Surf?' she repeated, starting to feel annoyed now. 'It's not a goddamn beach party over there, you know. War isn't exactly *fun*, not even for someone like you.'

'Might have its moments; I hear Saigon's got some great bars.' He was spinning his glass around now and she knew the real reason hadn't come to the surface as yet, aside from joining Angus whom she knew he was missing terribly.

'Why else?'

'I don't know, anyway it doesn't matter, does it? They probably won't want me.'

Poppy nodded, still thoughtful. 'Yes. I suppose that's the end of it then. Fortunately.'

'A surfer's life for me,' he said with forced cheer as he went to stand.

'Spike,' Poppy said, stilling him with her hand on his arm, and that fine line blurred between them once more. 'Promise me you won't really pursue this...?'

He opened his mouth to answer, only the words never came; his gaze had lifted past her towards the door. Then Poppy turned to find the vision of a man in white uniform and the blurred line simply faded; burned away by the sun.

Twenty-Eight

It was raining in a hard, sudden pelt as the storm relieved the humid day and they lay listening in each other's arms as the window patterns made shadows on the wall. He was watching them intently and she knew he was tracing their shape and fall, the artist within aching to capture this moment. To hold it forever and defy the break of dawn.

'Time to tell,' she said gently, tracing her fingers across his chest.

Ben sighed and she knew already it was just as she'd feared: immediate overseas service. 'I ship out New Year's Day.'

Poppy felt tears threaten but swallowed them. 'I thought they usually gave graduates at least a few months.'

'They do.'

'Then why…?'

'I was awarded the Sword of Honour. Guess they see that as some kind of reason to fast-track me over there.'

'Congratulations,' she said after a pause.

'Thanks,' he said with a short half-laugh at the irony. Ben pulled Poppy closer, burying his face in her hair and kissing her on top of her head as she wrapped her naked form about him. 'I'm so sorry.'

'No,' she said, 'don't say that. You shouldn't be ashamed that you're talented and that you work hard.'

'Not just for the Sword, I mean for the whole bloody army-officer thing.'

'You value doing your duty. I'm proud of you for that.'

'I wish I didn't,' he admitted. 'I wish I was a hippie and we lived in a commune and made babies all day.'

She smiled against his skin. 'Don't mention that word just yet.' Poppy had gone on the pill after the snow trip, but she didn't want to tempt fate. Things could still go wrong, she knew, and the Catholic in her could never have an abortion. The pill was a big enough sin in itself.

'How long will you be away?'

'Twelve months, I'd say. I'm being sent to Nui Dat.'

Poppy remembered the name. 'Angus is there, isn't he?'

He nodded. 'Most Aussies are.'

'What will you be doing? I mean…' She stopped, not knowing how to phrase the next.

'I'll be fighting on the ground, Poppy. You have to accept that.' She nodded, not sure if she was quite able to.

'But will you have to…'

'Shh,' he said, placing his finger over her lips then kissing her with such longing and adoration it made her ache. 'There's no war right here and now. I don't want to waste this,' he whispered, shifting above her and kissing his way down.

The rain continued its rhythmic drumming and they made desperate love to the sound, each knowing many lonely nights lay ahead until he was free.

That the wait would be long, if indeed, he really could make it home.

Twenty-Nine

Phuoc Tuy Province, Vietnam, January 1968

The sweat was running into his eyes but Angus didn't bother wiping it away, intent on keeping movement to a minimum. Not so Jefferson, one of the two Americans on patrol with them, who couldn't seem to stop fidgeting to save his life – literally. The platoon was providing guard by taking the Milwaukeean and his friend Todd through unsecure territory north of Nui Dat. The Viet Cong didn't have tanks, at least not in this sector of the war, so Angus and his mates were often called upon to provide escort, one of many alternative roles in anti-tank platoon. They'd also been involved in infantry fire support, dog handling, long-range reconnaissance and night shifts on the machine guns. At least they wouldn't die of boredom, Jimmy often remarked.

They were a mixed bunch, mostly from South Australia, with various additional strengths: Jimmy was a trained medic, Body seemed to be able to handle a radio, and Hobbs, Stevo and Mitch were quite skilled on the guns. The only one who didn't seem to specialise in anything much was Derek, a used car salesman from

Adelaide, although he was rather adept at bartering with the locals and cheating at cards.

The two Americans had been a lot of fun to have around at base, swapping all sorts of colourful banter in broad accents and insisting the 'Ossies' drink whiskey and rye with them until the wee hours. They'd also brought with them some of the latest records from the US, including one woman named Janis Joplin who, for some reason, Body had taken a very strong liking to. He'd been found lying under the stars drunk a few times now, wailing about his heart.

Originally in artillery, Jefferson and Todd were now being trained in explosives, expertise of increasing value in a war moving underground. Tunnels enabled the Viet Cong to disappear and reappear almost phantom-like, making patrols like this one nerve-racking in the extreme. With an enemy potentially right under your feet stealth was everything; you didn't step on twigs, you didn't smoke, you didn't even sneeze let alone talk.

Unfortunately the usually cheerful Jefferson wasn't really coping with being on patrol in such heavily saturated enemy territory; from what he and Todd had told them of US forces over here this type of cat and mouse warfare wasn't their thing. Their army tended to strafe first, patrol last, relying heavily on artillery or air support to do its job.

'Can't see no point to this,' Angus heard him mutter uneasily. 'We're goddamn sitting ducks.'

Angus wanted to tell him he'd better get set to duck but then their leader, Colonel Franks, held up his arm, reminding them all to keep quiet. They were crossing another rubber plantation where large, waxy leaves cast dark shadows, providing endless opportunity for concealment. Each step of a boot was magnified in Angus's ears, each movement traced swiftly with his eyes.

'Bag more by blastin' like shit and cleanin' out after,' Jefferson murmured, and Angus could almost smell his fear.

'Shut it buddy,' Todd whispered back, but the nerves were getting the better of his friend now.

'Waste of fuckin'…'

The explosion shook the earth as Jefferson tripped the wire and there was a sudden rain of dirt and debris as the troop scattered behind trees, all senses now at full alert. Angus felt his heart thump painfully, holding his gun tight as she listened for any tell-tale sounds but the faint rustling and movement of men was drowned out by the agonised sobbing coming from where Jefferson had fallen.

'My leg, my leg…'

Angus squeezed his stinging eyes shut then swiftly opened them again, waiting for what would come next. Rapid fire cut the air somewhere to the left and he took out a grenade, estimating the location and distance of the source. It *tatted* again and Angus waited for a pause before standing to pull the pin and launch.

One, two…*bam*. Another earth shattering moment passed followed by staggered fire interspersed with Jefferson's now muted yet still pitiful cries. Angus looked over at Todd who was flat against the tree, eyes very white and wide in his dark face. He gestured to him for cover and Todd nodded as Angus readied himself to run at it. Then he was off, finding the next tree, then another, until he was near to a writhing Jefferson whose leg was almost dismembered. Angus tried not feel anything; there was no time for it.

Todd landed nearby, having badly exposed himself but obviously with the same goal: shut the noise down. His friend's audible pain was a death sentence here. Angus pointed at Body and a nod between the three was all that was needed. The big man took off at a run and Angus fired hard with Todd to give him cover as Body reached Jefferson, picked him up, dangling leg and all, and headed backwards as fast as he could go. It was deafening and intense but they'd somehow managed to get the American away from the action. Now to force the enemy to retreat so they could get him the hell out of here. A ferocious spate of close combat followed until suddenly, mysteriously, the Viet Cong withdrew; disappearing in that phantom way, like they'd never been there at all.

The Australians fell back and Todd rushed with them to check on Jefferson who was by now losing consciousness.

'Probably the best thing,' Jimmy said, opening his medical kit. Looking at what was left of Jefferson's leg Angus had to agree.

'That was some brave work, mate,' Angus told Todd.

'He's not used to this shit…oh man, he looks real bad,' Todd replied, ignoring the compliment and looking desperately from the soaking bandages to the thick foliage around them. 'How soon can we get him out?'

'Choppers will come. Eventually,' Jimmy said and Todd stared at him, his face reflecting what they all thought of that last word.

'Strap him tight Jim. Derek, watch the left,' Colonel Franks ordered with a nod, holding his own bloodstained arm.

'You're hurt,' Body pointed out.

'No shit Sherlock,' Jimmy said, looking over worriedly but Franks waved him away.

'I'm fine. Get on the horn.' Body did as ordered, radioing a call for support. The message got through but it would be some time before the helicopters came, or 'Huey' as they affectionately called them. Huey was the hand that pulled them out when they were hurt or stranded. Huey was every soldier's best friend.

They needed him more than ever now as they waited, taut with the knowledge the Viet Cong knew where they were, yet unable to move with a seriously injured man. It was one of the reasons they set so many booby traps of course – injuries needed tending and evacuation. Injuries took away whole troops. There was only one option available to them now and it was the one Angus hated the most. To sit tight.

And so they did, with the insects and the heat and the fear for company. Ten minutes. Twenty. The rubber trees swayed above them, allowing glimpses of a perfectly blue sky. Half an hour.

Then there were movements, almost undetectable, yet unmistakable to trained eyes and ears.

The colonel mimed instructions with his good arm and they positioned themselves to defend, warned to open fire only at his signal, desperate for the beat of Huey's blades as each further minute unfolded. Angus's heart hammered once more as the enemy materialised in a flash of black material here, a mutter of Vietnamese there. Then there was gunfire, splitting the air in rapid succession and Angus watched as the Viet Cong began to fall. Only the colonel hadn't given the signal. Then Huey could be heard at last, thudding overhead like a protective parent, machine guns peppering the earth.

And, as the Vietnamese disappeared once more, Angus could have sworn there was a sound of crowing. Last heard on a beach one night in paradise, a lifetime ago.

The big plane wasn't exactly comfortable but Ben had heard the troop ships were a far sight worse, hot and cramped and filled with the stench of sweat, or so Angus had written Rosemary in his letters. Ben had a Christmas package to deliver once he found him, somewhere on the sprawling Australian base below.

As he took in his first glimpse of Vietnam he figured it wasn't unlike Queensland from up here; turquoise water, golden sand, patches of tropical green, but as they came closer a completely different world came into focus. Makeshift, dilapidated and dominated by foreign armies, Vung Tau was anything but paradisiacal. He wondered how the people living there managed balancing both poverty and war. Not much of a life, he imagined, dreading some of the things he would see these coming months.

The plane prepared to land and Ben took a deep breath, reminding himself that this was a step forward, not back. Arriving in Vietnam ticked yet another box on the long list of duties he had to fulfil before he claimed a life of his own choosing. He had that to fight for now; no longer a blur of a man smeared on a canvas. There was something to hope for; someone he wanted to be. Every sacrifice, every challenge and every moment of fear and exertion would be offered up to that ultimate outcome. To live on his own terms. To be the man Poppy Flannery could love.

He was here again, ordering a cake, and he noticed her each time now; smiling. Asking what was new. How was her day? He didn't say it like the other soldiers, he had respect, although Bao would not agree. Thuy passed him the cake and took his money, wondering if she dared return his smile then deciding not to. But she did watch him walk away. She watched him whenever he was here now, as much as she could without her parents noticing.

His name was Angus, although it sounded strange on her tongue when she whispered it to the moon beneath the giant tree. He was tall and good-looking and his eyes were kind, the colours of the forest, or so she glimpsed when she dared meet them with her own. He was only a dream, a place to visit when she was alone, but when she did he gave life back to empty places in her heart. Even if she couldn't ever really trust a foreign man.

Angus was talking to a small child who was in line for the free dental clinic the Australians had set up and the child was smiling at him. She was free to. She was young. Thuy watched with a small smile herself as he gave her something from his pocket – a sweet, she supposed, judging by the look of happiness on the little girl's face. He began talking to the mother who allowed him to hold the baby in her arms while she unwrapped it. Yes, he wasn't like the other soldiers. This man took time. This man saw people, not victims.

Then she noticed his friends were engaging with the children too – the big man letting them ride on his shoulders, the other man showing them tricks with a coin. Perhaps these Australians were kinder than some of the other invaders. Perhaps she really could live in their country one day, like her parents wanted.

But after the war – there was no way she would leave now. Her parents needed her, even more so of late. The doctor had told her mother that her heart was sick, and would worsen, and Thuy was the only person left on whom they could rely.

'Ben!' she heard someone cry. It was Angus. He was greeting someone even taller than he was who was taking off his hat, revealing hair the colour of sunshine, and she blinked momentarily. The two men shook hands as she watched, envying their reunion. Wishing such things were possible in her world then remembering the futility of such a thought.

'Cakes,' her father ordered, following her line of vision, and she quickly obeyed.

'Coconut-sweet-potato?'

A soldier stepped forward. 'Are they as sweet as you?'

She flicked her eye but Angus was gone, at least he was until the end of the long day when she could find him again in her imaginings. Dreams weren't wishing, exactly. And even the war couldn't take those away.

'Gawd, what does she think I'm going to do with these?' Angus said, chuckling as he took out some knitting needles and wool from the pack.

'Maybe she thinks you can use them as weapons at close range?' Ben suggested, and the others laughed at the idea.

Mitch stood to head for the bar. 'Beer, sir?'

'Please,' Ben said, as Body pointed at another questionable item in the care package.

'What's that for?'

Angus picked up the large red handkerchief and grinned. 'I'm guessing she wants me to wear it like this.' He twisted it up and knotted it around his neck. 'It's a cowboy joke we've kinda got going…'

'Kinky,' Jimmy observed, arriving in the tent and passing the beers over from Mitch.

'What's the verdict?' Angus asked.

'He might hold on to his leg if they can keep the bloody infections this hell-hole breeds at bay,' Jimmy told them before noticing Ben. 'Oh sorry. Er…afternoon sir.'

'My friend from home, Lieutenant Ben Williamson,' Angus introduced him. 'Jimmy's our medic. He's been checking on an American guy we were escorting recently,' Angus explained. 'Met with a wire near Ba Ria before Body here carried him out.'

'He gave me his records,' Body said, tapping his bag with a wide grin. They hadn't left his side for days.

'Seems a fair exchange, some Janis for a leg,' Jimmy said, frowning at Angus's head as he arranged the bandana. 'What the hell are you doing with that now?'

'Might keep the sweat out of my eyes,' Angus figured, pushing it up higher. 'How do I look?'

'Not like that you idiot – you're not a bloody gypsy woman! Here, wear it like the bikies,' Jimmy said, shaking his head in feigned disgust as he took it off Angus's crown, folded it with the expertise of a true medic, and repositioned it, knot at the back.

'Well?'

'You know mate, I'm afraid you're just not cool enough to pull that off,' Jimmy told him, the crisp new cotton sitting up at a comical angle.

'Might not be an ideal camouflage choice anyway,' Angus conceded, tossing it back in the box. 'So what's the news from…'

'Can I have it?' Body interrupted, looking at the bandana hopefully, and Jimmy laughed.

'Now this I want to see.' He tied it around the big man's head then stood back to view his handiwork. 'You know something? That kind of works.' And for some reason it did.

'Keep your helmet on over it in the field though,' Ben advised and Body nodded, looking pleased as he viewed his reflection in the window before drawing his precious bag closer. It really was starting to feel a bit like Christmas, Angus reflected with a smile.

'Anyway, as I was saying, what's news?' Angus asked Ben, sitting back with a satisfied smile, having unwrapped every brightly papered gift in the pack. 'How's Spike?' He hadn't heard from his brother in several weeks. Spike was a terrible correspondent but Angus had at least expected a card from him at this time of year, or something.

'Actually Rosemary said she hasn't seen him for a while. He disappeared around the time I came home,' Ben told him. 'She thinks he may have taken off up the coast for a surf trip; said he'd asked a mate to look after Barrel and the shop.'

'He usually takes Barrel with him,' Angus said, and an eerie thought niggled at him, but he shook it away. Preposterous. 'Anyway, how's my girl looking? Did you catch up with Poppy too?' he asked, nodding at the care package.

'No, I er, saw her another time though,' Ben answered vaguely and Angus felt something akin to a snigger surfacing but squashed it.

'Who's Poppy? Is that the twin sister?' Jimmy said eagerly, picking up the photo of Rosemary that had come with the package.

Ben drained his beer as Angus answered. 'Sure is, almost identical actually. Hard to believe that God made two but just goes to show miracles can and do happen.'

'Single?' Jimmy asked and Body and Mitch leant over, checking out the photo as well.

'Last I heard,' Angus said, sending Ben a knowing look and receiving a frown in response.

'Any more beers hidden away back there, private?'

Thirty

Ba Ria, Vietnam, 1 February 1968

Ben had almost gotten used to the heat and the insects but the aerial insecticide spraying was another thing. It seemed the only way to make it solvent was to mix it with diesel fuel and the smell and greasy film had clung to his clothes and skin overnight. Although it was effective. Bugs littered the ground, along with alarmingly large spiders, and, as he'd witnessed a way back, even the occasional small bird fell victim to the stuff. He could only imagine what it did to his own lungs but that wasn't his biggest priority right now. The fact that the radio was down was a vast deal more disturbing, especially as the town they were heading towards to do their laundry and enjoy a bit of 'R and R' seemed to be exploding.

'I don't get it,' Angus said, crouching alongside, 'it's a national holiday. Surely Charlie isn't just going to ignore the ceasefire.'

'Might be a perfect plan,' Ben said thoughtfully, watching dark plumes mount into the morning sky. Colonel Franks was out of action for the time being, having received far more damage to his arm a few weeks ago than he'd let on, which had left the position open for a leader for this outfit. It hadn't taken much persuading from Angus for Ben to request the role to acclimatise himself to live combat. It was a shortcoming in his experience that had faded quickly after all those years of hard training and his long-honed skills as a soldier had won him the platoon's respect right from the start. The fact that he was a native South Australian didn't hurt too much either. But his gut instincts were telling him that the moment of real truth was arriving now.

The ground shook as another major explosion ignited and Ben turned to Body, his mind racing. 'Any luck?'

'No sir,' Body replied, checking again.

'Something's definitely off,' Angus said and Ben had to agree. If there was one thing he'd learnt so far about the Vietnamese it was that they were a traditional people. Ignoring the truce that usually applied over the Lunar New Year or 'Tet' period was highly unlikely, which was exactly what was making him nervous; no-one would have seen this coming.

'Where's the map?' he asked, and one of the men handed it over. 'Have you been down here before?' He pointed along the banks of the Song Dinh that led towards Ba Ria.

'Yes sir,' Angus added, always keeping the formality in front of the others. 'Bamboo as thick as your wrist. Not an easy way to go.' They were interrupted by the sound of armoured personnel carriers, the APCs, and Ben breathed a sigh of relief, moving to the side of the road.

'At ease,' the captain said as they drew alongside. Ben dropped his salute and moved forward.

'Radio's down sir. Trouble in town?'

'Two VC platoons running amok. We're heading in to secure HQ if you'd like to join in, although there's not a lot of room.'

'We'll manage,' Ben said, signalling for the platoon to grab onto whatever moved and they took off down the road towards the roiling black clouds.

'Don't figure it's patrol duty today,' Angus said above the rumble of engines.

'No,' Ben agreed grimly. Today the gates looked set to be open for out-and-out war.

Thuy made herself small, so small she could fit behind the pylon of the bridge and become invisible – not just to the foreigners today but to the greater enemy, the ones who had stolen what she loved, broken her heart, and now threatened to steal the rest of her. Blast her into the earth and leave her here to rot until her flesh fed the grass and the trees; the reeds and the lotus flower. The single dragon fruit.

The explosions of the morning continued but voices could be heard now too, close enough to hear her breathing, surely, and she tried to maintain it in a light, steady stream. The Viet Cong moved along the Song Dinh, whispering instructions, watching for signs of war, or lone Vietnamese girls. She'd seen what could happen to the non-VC; she knew what her fate could be. Her mind flitted to her parents, alone at the hut, and she wished fervently they had never allowed her to visit her friend at Ba Ria today, one of only a handful of days a year she ever had off. A holy day. Anger twisted at her insides. What was sacred before this war was no longer honoured; not even religion stopped their hatred. No respect.

'What was that?' called one soldier and she froze to perfect stillness.

'Bird,' grunted his friend and she let her breath-stream resume. It flowed shallowly until the river was empty once more, until she thought she might faint without deeper release. But finally they were gone and she let her chest fill with relief, unclenching her fingers, dark pink crescents lining her palms. The ground still shook with each bomb blast and she had to think fast; to wait it out here or flee became the agonising choice, but then the sound of vehicles made up her mind.

Thuy moved out from under the bridge to spy through the grass, ripping a small piece of her skirt away and wrapping it on a stick. They may not believe her, possibly shoot her on sight, but she moved forward anyway, the breath-stream now caught and still in her mouth.

'Hold it,' came the call as the armoured convoy paused and several Australian guns followed her as she moved out on the road, holding her little flag of peace tight. 'Keep both hands up,' the man yelled and she did as she was told, shaking but just able to do so. The man jumped down to run his hands over her form and she flinched at his touch. 'Clean,' he announced and she raised her eyes to the officer in charge.

'I am alone,' she said in English. 'I not VC.' Surely they would help, she reasoned, as the sound of explosions continued nearby, but so many others lie. Why believe her?

Then a man leapt from the back vehicle and ran down to the first, talking to the officer and pointing her way. Then he turned and she saw it was Angus and it wasn't a dream as he made his way over, forest eyes kind.

'Hey,' he said, 'any cakes stashed away? I'm starving.'

She shook her head, ashamed as a tear escaped and fell on her cheek. Then she remembered what she had to tell him, more important than this. 'VC down river. Thirty, maybe more. They just pass.'

'How long ago?'

'Five.'

'Minutes?'

She nodded and he rushed back to relay that information while she waited. The news split the group up and she saw Angus and his two friends were among the ones who would stay. And the tall man with the sun in his hair.

'You are to go with them,' Angus said, nodding at the trucks, but she shook her head.

'I come with you.'

He looked reluctant. 'That's not safe. They are going to Ba Ria…'

'That not safe too.'

The sun man came over. 'What are you waiting for? Put her in the APC.'

'She wants to come with us.'

He shook his head. 'Out of the question. Come on.'

Angus turned to her and his voice was gentle. 'Go in the truck to Ba Ria and I will come and get you and take you home after, okay?'

She wanted to say no, to say she'd rather be in danger with him, but the troop was already moving off and the trucks were rolling. And such words could only be spoken in a dream.

'Okay,' she said and he led her over to climb in. But as she rolled away her eyes stayed on his retreating back, watching him wherever he was.

They were in their sights but Ben was holding off, unwilling to let the opportunity presenting itself pass. This disappearing act of the Viet Cong was keeping the war at a stalemate and any knowledge of tunnel entrances in this region took priority over an ambush. Sure enough one VC went behind a tree and didn't come out, followed by another. Ben raised his hand, waiting for a third before giving the signal, but just then a sudden movement caught his eye. It was a man in Australian khaki, hurling himself across the clearing, gun in rapid fire.

'Ahhhh!' he yelled and Ben quickly let his arm fall as the platoon joined him in giving the man cover. He was running to the place behind the tree then just as quickly he was retreating from it, the explosion that followed him deafening; Ben could barely make out the effects through the dusty haze, only to realise the man was down, face first on the ground. The Australians fired into the smoke with as much ammunition as they could until they were sure the enemy were either dead, injured or had melted back into the jungle. Then Angus was up and running before Ben could say a word. He followed him in time to watch Angus turn the man on his back and check his vital signs.

'No, no, no,' he was moaning and Ben stopped still in his tracks, understanding dawning as he stared down at the reason for such terror. It was a familiar man alright, despite his face being blackened with charcoal; eyes closed and young body still.

'Spike,' Angus sobbed, his forehead falling against his brother's chest and Ben took off his hat, at a loss as to what to say. Then another voice spoke, quite strong and clear, and Ben knew those words would stick with him for the rest of his life.

'Stop bawling on m'pocket. You'll soak all the yundi.'

Thirty-One

Ba Ria was a sleepy town on any given day, even when soldiers came in droves to frequent the bar, buy souvenirs or get their washing taken care of, but today it had transformed into some kind of hell. Shopfronts crumbled to the earth, like tired old men sinking to their final demise, too exhausted to withstand the strain of standing upright any more. There was dust, broken glass, shattered doorways and splintered wood; crazed fowl ran and fluttered and people screamed in the constant roar of gunfire and artillery.

And all the while Thuy made herself small, behind a cart this time, next to a tree. The firm trunk felt safer than anything man-made, as if it could transport her to somewhere else where nature reigned in peaceful supremacy. Some foreign place where existence was a privilege neither questioned nor challenged; where people viewed a life of freedom through forest-coloured eyes. It was something she'd never known, having been raised in a country cursed by its own beauty and placement on the earth; the centre of the rope in Asia's constant tug of war.

Witnessing it all from behind her flimsy barricade she could only ache with the irony that these Australians came from that other place, yet here they were, in her homeland. Shooting the enemy who were once her kin, brainwashed sons and brothers diseased by this 'Communism'; this promise of a better life. But there was nothing better about this Vietnam.

A mother was crying, running into the street to pick up a bloodied child, perhaps dead, and Thuy blinked the image away. Great gaping holes now exposed the insides of buildings where people could be seen evacuating, running for survival with odd remnants against their breasts. A painting here, a clutch of papers there. Fire was burning the rest away now as what had been cultivated over generations fell to ash and scrap and rubble. And all the while the earth shook and guns blasted and now the sky began to thunder too as those metal beasts came to make more of this. To deliver further death and destruction to this once sleepy town. Unrecognisable now. Just like Long Tan.

Memories of her own village burning played over and again and Thuy wept without checking tears, each spate of gunfire shredding through her nerves, every explosion jarring further terror into her being. Soldiers fired from monsoon drains now and a young man ran from it, but it found him; red pocks down his back as he fell. Too cruel, too cruel. There were many bodies now, a girl no more than ten, a grandmother whom she recognised. She sold fish near her stall on Sundays. Flags celebrating the lunar year burned in the breeze and Thuy wondered if she should try to run too but her legs no longer had any feeling left. She was numb, shaking. Isolated.

Smoke obscured her vision and she was grateful for that much, at least. Let it fill her mind too. Let this day burn from her memory and cheat these men of war of that one small victory. It was her last thought as more APCs arrived nearby and the next wave began.

Then a soldier was there, almost upon her. Green eyes found hers. And Thuy was no longer alone.

Angus was reeling, not least of all from seeing his brother in Vietnam, thinking he was dead, then finding he was only winded and the same adventurous, irreverent daredevil as ever. It had been a quick catch up as they hitched with another convoy into town but Angus had the most important facts covered: Spike had made yet another reckless decision in life by up and joining the army. He wasn't even officially tall enough, according to authorities, but apparently that was an asset rather than a disadvantage in this war. Spike said they'd fast-tracked his 'short arse' over here and he'd been in and out of tunnels for weeks.

Then he'd gone on to tell Angus the extent of the underground network at play. Apparently there was a whole other Vietnam thriving beneath the jungle floor complete with sleeping quarters, hospitals, ammunition depots, even kitchens with extended stove pipes that carried the smoke sideways, hiding the room's location. No wonder they kept disappearing – far easier to live and traverse uncontested ten feet down.

But further conversation would have to wait because one look around had proved they'd just landed in a full-scale battle. The soldiers in the APC had told them the Viet Cong had attacked in the early hours that morning, securing important positions around HQ and other administration buildings. Even more disturbingly, rumours of hostages were going around and Angus knew Ben would make their rescue a priority. The more time he spent with him the more heroic Angus realised Ben was proving to be – but not in the mad way Spike operated, fortunately.

Angus had sought cover as his first priority, but he wasn't alone. Terrified brown eyes had collided with his and he'd felt a surge of relief to have found her so easily followed by a wave of protectiveness for 'Sweet-Cakes' as they all called her. She'd looked tiny and he'd taken up position next to her, covering her as best he could and firing back at the enemy. It was the first time he'd witnessed them fighting in large numbers, only having been involved in small jungle skirmishes so far. This house-to-house combat was a different ball game altogether and the number of Viet Cong holding position seemed sorely underestimated.

The VC were well armed with semi-automatic weapons and rocket-propelled grenades and Angus figured whoever had predicted a primitive foe over here had been badly mistaken. Most were small, many no more than teenagers, but they were vicious in attack and handled their sophisticated weaponry with skill. Ben signalled and Angus provided cover as he ran across the road to consult with another officer who was pointing towards the other side of town. A decision seemed to be reached and Ben gestured for the others from 3RAR to make their way over. Then Angus turned to Sweet-Cakes, making a decision of his own.

'You need to get out,' he shouted above the din. 'Take this,' he added, giving her a pistol he kept on his belt. 'Head back to the river and I'll come later.'

'I come with you,' she said, her eyes huge, and she flinched at yet another explosion.

Angus hesitated for the second time that day but he couldn't risk it. 'Not this time.' He turned to leave but she grabbed his arm and he looked down at it in surprise. 'I will find you, I promise.' Then she let go and he was off again.

'Poor little thing,' he mumbled to himself but then his survival instincts dominated all else as a grenade landed nearby and he crushed his body against a wall. Viet Cong were hurling them over a fence from someone's backyard and Angus watched Spike un-pin one of his own and throw it over. The explosion ignited and they seemed gone so the platoon moved onwards, watching for any movement, any glimpses of black. They were everywhere; in the trees, on rooftops, in ditches and dirt. Angus even shot one riding backwards on a motorbike, firing his machine gun behind. It sickened him, that death roll off the back, but there was no time to think about it. No room for fear, regret, shame or anger. He supposed that would come later.

There was a canopy up ahead, with fruit and vegetable counters still in place beneath, and Ben chose the spot for a quick briefing, the group squatting behind.

'Three Yanks are cut off and stranded in one of the occupied buildings. About twenty metres down there,' he said, checking a crude map the other officer had given him. 'I'll need all hands on deck – no separating. I'm looking at you, Spike,' he said directly, pausing. 'Actually, do you even take orders?'

'Not usually,' Spike said cheerfully and Ben looked wary.

'Well, just keep your head down, for godsakes. Angus, you'll come with me to grab these blokes; Spike and Jimmy, cover the flanks; Body and Derek, protect the rear. The rest of you just cover,' he added to Hobbs, Stevo and Mitch. 'Got it?'

They nodded, taking off once more and Angus stayed close to Ben as they made it to the building. Gunfire sounded from behind the courtyard walls and they rushed in, shooting the two Viet Cong responsible before bursting through to the Americans inside.

The three men were alive and well, in fact they'd obviously been enjoying the holiday before the mayhem began. Angus stared at the empty whiskey glasses and cigars in astonishment.

'You sure took your time,' said one and Angus let out a chortle of laughter, despite himself. Then he wondered how many other soldiers were already in party mode today and largely unaware just how serious these attacks had become.

'Sorry to break things up, gentlemen, but the war seems to have arrived,' Ben said briskly and they made their way out, their rather merry rescued party in tow.

'Holy shit,' said one as a shot whizzed over his head and the three men seemed to sober up rather quickly then. Spike took the culprit out then walked over, grabbing the still half-full bottle out of the man's hands.

'You're welcome,' he said, taking a swig.

'Drinks on me, but only when we get back to base,' Ben said, grabbing it and throwing it in the bushes. 'Move out.'

'Jeez, is he always this bossy during battle?' Spike muttered, following begrudgingly.

'Over here he has to be,' Angus told him, moving closer to his brother and watching for any more stray bullets. It was then that he realised Spike's presence in Vietnam wasn't the only new addition to their group this day. The worry wart had also arrived.

Thirty-Two

Sydney, 2 February 1968

The fan whirred in the corner as the American newsreader spoke, his voice a chilling accompaniment to the images flickering across televisions in Australia that day.

It is now clear that North Vietnam, along with their southern allies in the Viet Cong, had long planned what is now being termed the 'Tet Offensive', launching attacks across the country in hundreds of locations, despite a ceasefire being declared for the Lunar New Year. Casualties are estimated to be in the tens of thousands with many civilians among the dead.

'I can't believe they're putting this on TV,' Poppy whispered.

'I know. They're just … just children,' Rosemary said, tears falling down her cheeks as the ugly face of war told the western world far more than any words the commentator could intone.

'I thought we were winning,' Lois said, frowning at the screen, confused, and Robert grunted in agreement. Poppy frowned herself at that. Sometimes her parents were so naive, then again they didn't have people like Cat in their lives to balance out their conservative understanding of politics.

The broadcast then crossed to an NBC report in Saigon and images of soldiers lying dead in the street followed. Poppy searched for Australian uniforms but it too difficult to discern; probably a blessing, she supposed.

The nation's capital has seen terrible fighting these past two days with a suicide squad breaching the US embassy. Although now securely back under southern control the fighting in the city has been ferocious with one man executed by the chief of police right in front of our cameras.

Poppy gasped as they watched a man hold a gun to a Viet Cong soldier's head and pull the trigger.

'Dear God,' Robert breathed as the man fell to his death and Rosemary broke down into full tears.

The name General Nguyen Ngoc Loan flashed across the screen as the executor spoke.

These guys kill a lot of our people, and I think Buddha will forgive me.

Robert stood and crossed the room, turning off the television and facing his stunned wife and daughters.

'How can they do something like that?' Poppy exclaimed, beginning to cry herself, and her father came over to put his hand on her shoulder in a rare display of affection.

'It's not something for a young lady's eyes but we can only pray for the souls of such men, child. Pray for them all.'

Silence descended, save the hum of the fan and the choke of tears, as the shock of the report settled upon them. Then Lois rose from her chair, assuming her usual air of efficiency.

'Time to make dinner,' she announced, but then her tone softened. 'Not much of a visit home so far, is it? Come Rosemary, you can help with the potatoes.'

They went to the kitchen and Robert walked outside to smoke his pipe, leaving Poppy alone to deal with the inner turmoil the news stories had left behind. Music, she decided, reaching to turn on the radio, praying no more blunt words would fill the room. No more ugliness this day.

...the world is waking up to the truth about what we are asking our boys to do over there. Point is people, what are you going to do about it?

'Revolution' by the Beatles followed but Poppy changed the station, unable to stomach anarchy right now. She chose the soothing beauty of Aretha Franklin's voice instead, singing about saying a little prayer, as her father had advised.

Poppy turned her face to the sunset that was blazing behind the gauze curtains, aching with the gentle love and longing in the song. Somewhere in Vietnam Ben was holding a gun. He was being told to take other lives, to kill the Asian man and feel no remorse. But she knew the man she loved. His survival was still the number one fear that shadowed Poppy's every day, but it was increasingly being followed by fear number two: what he would have to live with if he did.

That night, as they walked from the bus stop towards the dorms, Rosemary opened up her large patchwork purse and took out a joint, offering it to Poppy, who refused.

'Might cheer you up.'

'I doubt it,' Poppy said, her heart still heavy.

'I need to get those images out of my head,' Rosemary admitted, lighting it then blowing on the end to make sure it was burning right. The action looked a bit too expert for Poppy's liking.

'There's other ways to do that.'

'Such as?'

'You could play your violin. You never practise anymore.'

Rosemary shrugged. 'Not much point.'

'Well...well, you could read a book or go to the movies...'

'Not quite the same though, is it? I don't want my brain to work. I just...I just want to find some peace for a little while. Blank it all out.'

Poppy considered that, trying to understand, then an idea struck her. 'You could try out those new yoga classes in the gym; find a meditative state without drugs. They were talking about that in tutorial last week, remember? "Alternatives to sedation"...'

'It's not the same. It wouldn't...wouldn't *comfort* you like pot.'

'So eat some ice cream or something!' Poppy said, growing exasperated.

'Well, I am rather partial to cake,' Rosemary said, grinning now and flicking ash her sister's way.

Poppy frowned. 'It isn't funny you know; I'm getting pretty worried about you...'

'Worry about our boys and the poor Vietnamese, not me smoking a little pot. Anyway, it's natural and harmless – people have been using it for centuries – and Cat says no-one's ever died from it,' Rosemary told her, pausing to inhale deeply. 'Relax,' she said in a tight voice as she held the smoke in her lungs.

'It's not just that.' Poppy stopped to face her. 'What were you doing in the back room with Cat and Daniella the other night?'

'What back room?'

'At that teacher's party – what's his name? Norris.'

'Nothing. Just chatting and smoking and whatever,' Rosemary said with a shrug, stubbing out the butt.

'You seemed strange.'

'I am strange,' Rosemary told her, stepping on to a low stone fence to walk it like a tightrope. 'Years on the wall can do that to a girl.'

'I'm serious,' Poppy said, following alongside. 'You had psychedelic music on – that Jim Morrison...'

'He was singing *people* are strange, not just me, *people*.' She began to sing the Doors song, giggling as she tripped off the fence then stepping onto it again.

'Are you taking LSD?'

Rosemary jumped off the end. 'Ta-da!'

'Are you?'

'No.'

'Let me rephrase that: *have* you taken any LSD? Ever?'

Rosemary ran her shoe along the fence a little unsteadily. 'A little bit. Just that night.'

'Rosemary! My God – you're...you're a *Pharmacy* student! What the hell were you thinking?'

'I told you – that maybe I don't want to think!' she said, throwing her arms wide.

'But what it can do to your body...'

'Yes, but you don't understand what it does to your mind! You abandon all thought and expand consciousness. Acid opens the doors to the third eye, Poppy,' she told her, tapping at her own forehead, 'Cat reckons that's why Morrison named the band that, actually. Clever, huh?'

'*Cat* says.' Poppy echoed, getting angry now. 'Are you his groupie or something? Are you all lying in the same bed and making that...that *free love*?'

'As if,' Rosemary said, amused.

'Well, how would I know? You never tell me anything any more. I feel like you're just...like you're turning into somebody else.'

'You're one to talk, moping about Ben and spending all your time in the *library*,' she said the word with comical exaggeration. 'At least I'm still living my life.'

'Ruining your life, more like, and we're coming into our final year – don't you even care about your degree anymore?' Rosemary was spinning again and Poppy grew impatient. 'You barely passed last term. What are you going to do with your life if you stuff this up?'

Rosemary stopped and bowed dramatically. 'Join the circus.'

Poppy scoffed, folding her arms. 'What would Angus say if he knew how you're behaving?'

'Don't talk to me about Angus,' Rosemary said, her flippant tone altering. 'You just worry about your own stupid love-life, if you can even call it that.'

That hurt and Poppy fell silent, not trusting what she might say.

'Look, I'm sorry,' Rosemary said after a pause. 'I just…I just can't talk about him after seeing those bodies on the TV today, fearing I might recognise one.' She sat down heavily on the grass. 'I can't deal with it like you can.'

It was like looking into a distorted mirror, watching a replica of your own face become stoned, but there was a terrible sadness underlying it that Poppy knew all too well.

'I'm not dealing with it,' Poppy told her with a sigh, sitting down beside her, 'I'm avoiding it, just like you, only I'm using study and playing cello and listening to music like I've always done. These drugs, Rosemary…they're dangerous.'

Her sister lay on her back and closed her eyes. 'I know what I'm doing,' she mumbled.

'Do you?'

Rosemary just nodded, humming the Doors song to herself, and Poppy let her be, knowing it was pointless trying to talk to her any further about the pitfalls of drugs while she was under their influence. Watching contentment overtake the grief in her twin's countenance Poppy was half inclined to ask if she had any more joints stashed away in that giant purse, but knew such pleasures were off limits for her now.

The eyes of the world had been opened today, the press bringing the raw viciousness of this war into homes on a global scale, and consciousness would expand in more ways than one. Some would weep, some would march, some would bury their fear in books, and some would find solace in the back rooms, where people were strange.

Thirty-Three

'AO Surfers', Bien Hoa Province, Vietnam, 12 May 1968

Smoke streams lined the sky, turning into smears of orange flame as twilight began, but Ben was too busy to really take much notice. They were digging pits as fast as they possibly could before they lost the light, shallow ones or 'shell scrapes' with no overhead cover. There wasn't any time for more.

He swore beneath his breath, wiping sweat away with the back of his hand and cursing the disastrous events of the day that would leave them so exposed tonight. The Hueys that were supposed to bring them over here from Nui Dat had been delayed due to US troops nearby needing urgent aerial support.

It wasn't that he begrudged the Americans that protection, it was that the army had so many goddamn rules but no understanding of when they should and shouldn't be reconsidered. How were they supposed to keep them all alive if they didn't bend in the most logical way? For surely it was purely illogical to land 3RAR here, directly in the pathway of the enemy's route to Saigon, hours late and waist-deep in grass. Not to mention the fact that they were also now facing the fiercest North Vietnamese troops known in this war: the 1st Division.

Artillery had arrived with them and soon found the sites chosen for the howitzers unusable, a situation that took all afternoon to remedy, and the departing American troops they'd encountered had done little to reassure them that more calamity wasn't headed their way.

'You're in tiger country now, buddy,' one had told him, a nerve-racking prospect. 'Tiger country' was a slang term for high enemy presence. Not a proposition you wanted to consider when you were in charge of a bunch of blokes about to defend an unfinished set-up in the middle of the night. In truth the area of operations had been termed AO Surfers and was divided into three sections: Newport, Bondi and Manly. Even the temporary Fire Support Bases, or FSBs, looked to be allocated beachy names, the first, Coral, being set up now. Not a bad omen for a surfer, Angus had commented when he heard, but he'd sobered when Ben told him what else the Americans had to say about the place. 'You won't have to go looking for Charlie here, buddy. He'll come looking for you.'

Finally they managed to settle in, despite the discovery of a nest of giant ants in the middle of their spot, but the atmosphere was badly strained. Even the newly transferred Spike was subdued, a first since he'd joined their platoon. Apparently his former officer was relieved to let the rule-breaking Spike go but Ben was happy to have him. Spike was reckless and foolhardy, certainly, but he knew more about Vietnamese tactics than anyone else they'd encountered so far. Angus attributed the fact to him being a natural deviant.

His bed finally finished, Ben lay down, exhausted, and looked up to watch the stars that were brilliant as always out in the Vietnamese countryside. This was the furthest inland he'd been and the landscape was altered, although he'd taken little notice of its aesthetics from the air, more interested in how the lay of the land affected their chances in battle. The long grass was bound to be of immense advantage to an army in attack and Ben was more worried about that than anything else. The 1st were notoriously well camouflaged and would use the natural ground cover to full effect. Like tigers.

It was slightly colder here, once the sun fell, and damp now that the wet season had arrived. Ben wrapped his arms around himself for warmth, allowing memories of Poppy doing the same to offer sweet respite from the frustrating day. It had been almost six months since he'd been away and she'd written long, loving letters every week – not that he received them that regularly, but it was worth the wait when batches arrived in fat little bundles. Barbara wrote too, although only occasionally; hers were barely a page long and so perfunctory he wondered why she bothered. Ticking the marriage box, he supposed.

He usually only read his mail in private but tonight he made an exception. Tonight it felt like the war was crawling up his skin and about to bite like one of those ants, so he took out Poppy's latest letter from inside his diary to draw comfort from it in the starlight.

I'm sending you this flower from my walk home today. It's only a gardenia but I love the scent. Hope it's not too brown by the time you get it but I suppose it will be. I read today that people who come through war unscathed are called 'warflowers' and I had the sudden urge to send you one for luck. Funny isn't it, the idea of the wallflower ending up with the warflower? We may have to wear matching wallpapered sunglasses this summer.

He smiled, smelling the faint scent that still lingered in the dried, pressed flower, reading on as best he could in the half-light.

Tell Spike if he doesn't write me a letter soon I'm throwing out all his surfboards! It's bad enough he's run off to war without telling anyone, let alone being some mad tunnel guy. I'm worried sick about him but I don't need to tell you that, I'm sure. Can't imagine he follows many orders.

'Got that right,' Ben muttered.

Hopefully it will all end soon anyway. We marched on Sunday, the biggest rally I've seen yet. You should have seen the streets! Packed with placards and people wearing signs and all singing and chanting. I was a little worried I'd get squashed at one point. I guess it's all working because the Paris peace talks seem to be going ahead and Cat says 'the days of oppression must fall now', or some such guff. All I know is we all want it to be over. Everyone wants you home but nobody more than me. I miss you so much, especially at night. I'm lying in bed now, your T-shirt over my pillow, pretending it's you. Breathing you in.

Ben tucked the letter back in the diary, his eyes too heavy to read further as sleep welcomed him into its drugged recesses. Then he breathed her in too, imagining he was holding her hand and walking her into his dreams. Into his arms, then his bed, feeling her soft flesh underneath. The sheets turned into a sea of gardenia petals, no, it was sand, and they were back at the true Surfers, the one without war. It was paradise and the sun was bright…too bright…

He awoke to deafening chaos and an exploding sky, the stars obliterated now by the hellfire of battle. The enemy must have watched their poor attempts at setting up this afternoon because they were attacking fiercely only hours later, hitting 1RAR who were in defensive positions nearby in a thick rain of fire, throwing mortar and launching grenades, machine guns pitting the air. Ben scrambled with the others, taking position, gauging priorities. They were too far away to provide support to 1RAR but close enough to watch the action unfold and it was an eerie, surreal experience to observe rather than engage.

The sky became thick with flashing lights and smoke and immense noise, so overpowering it jarred the ground along with the senses. Minutes of it that crept into hours.

'They've taken a gun post,' Spike panted, landing next to him after disappearing for some time. He'd also appointed himself platoon scout, something Ben had given up trying to supervise, especially as Spike was so incredibly good at it. 'Smart fella though – grabbed the firing pin before he took off so it's useless for now.'

'Quick thinking,' Ben acknowledged, but it was still bad news. Infiltration into Allied territory could hardly be considered anything else.

Hueys could be heard now and an evacuation seemed underway which meant only one thing: wounded. Ben wondered how many but knew the enemy would see far more casualties as splintex anti-personnel rounds ripped the air, savage weaponry that could take out dozens in a single launch.

Then an even more terrifying sight loomed overhead: a converted DC3 airplane, nicknamed Puff the Magic Dragon by troops. The iron beast floated through giant debris clouds that flashed with multiple explosions, banking slowly then dipping its head into a pylon turn to unload thousands of rounds of ammunition into the enemy zone. Ben watched, mesmerised by the red tracer bullets, unable to tear his eyes away from the macabre fireworks display.

It felt as if the battle would never end as it raged on in wave after terrifying wave, until finally the pale morning broke through, barely distinguishable in the haze, but with it came reprieve.

Word reached them that the enemy were in retreat, the gun post recaptured and the area secured, but as they moved out to collect the dead and wounded the sickly cost of the victory became visible. Bodies lay in their dozens, strewn in grim arrangements, bloodied, maimed. The beast and the splintex had certainly done their jobs. Ben looked at the still faces of this northern enemy, young mostly, like their southern counterparts, skilled soldiers in state-of-the-art combat gear. Each one somebody's son or brother or friend. Dead now. Being lined up in rows for a mass burial, the dirt falling over them like they were an unpleasant pile of garbage, quickly to be shoved out of sight.

He reached down and took out one young man's wallet. It held photos of family, possibly his mother, his grandparents. The boy's face was smiling in one image and Ben couldn't seem to stop staring at it, the pale visage in the dirt like a cruel mockery of that family portrait. Like someone was playing some terrible, sickening joke.

'Want me to check further pockets?' Angus said, watching beside him.

'No,' Ben said, clearing his head. 'No, just cover them over,' he instructed, walking off. But the photo ended up in his diary that night, next to the withered flower.

For some reason he just couldn't bring himself to throw it away.

Hobbs, Stevo, Body and Derek were playing cards and Derek was doing his best to cheat, especially picking on Body who was an easy target, but Spike was sending Body a few secret signals and Derek was losing, much to his confusion and annoyance. Ben was nearby, watching and smoking heavily, the pages open in his lap where he'd been sketching the scene. It was a good likeness – they all were – but Angus found it a bit odd that Ben chose to draw rather than write in his journal; seemed out of whack for a budding lawyer.

The 'sit tight' thing was back, what Spike deemed the 'crappiest of all military pastimes'. His brother was currently perched on a log nearby, perfectly positioned to see Derek's cards but pretending to be immersed in cleaning his gun. He was also in turns whistling then singing; 'Do You Wanna Know a Secret' by the Beatles and Angus knew he should tell him to stop – snipers were still around – but it was amusing him a little while he tried to write his letter to Rosemary.

He wasn't having much success. It was difficult to censor stark truths such as 'eight of our guys died the other night' or 'we don't know how many Vietnamese got killed but we buried forty or so in a crater'. Words like that didn't need to be written down. They didn't even need to be thought. Their impact was etched into all their skins like tattoos, a particular branding only the fellas who served over here would carry through life.

With every atrocity witnessed, every bullet fired and explosion felt, it was as if they were drifting ever further away from the average Australian; from a public that now screamed from the streets that they shouldn't even be here. Angus was conflicted by that. He hadn't asked to be conscripted – hadn't up and joined like Ben. Mind you, Ben was only following authority too. Whether it was family or government that placed them here, they were both just 'doing their duty'. Even Spike was here on some misguided mission of brotherly loyalty. Well, Angus supposed it was that.

Would people blame them for the acts of war they all had to perform?

Young legs covered over by dirt passed through his mind and he shut his eyes as if to erase it. It wasn't like they had any choice, he reminded himself again. Australia had demanded this of them and they were serving their country, like the two generations before them. This 'duty' word was sacred to their much revered forefathers; why should it be any different now?

Anyway, it was no use questioning the whys and wherefores and getting all philosophical out here in the jungle. The business of survival was still the priority at hand and the worry wart had more than one skin to protect.

His mind flicked to Thuy, as he now knew Sweet-Cakes' real name to be, wondering if she was still safe. Last week at the market she seemed different, edgy. He knew enough about the Vietnamese by now to sense when something was amiss, as subtle as the signs usually were. Not that she gave much away. Any girl that could hide near a river for six hours straight and not fire a single shot from her borrowed gun had nerves of steel, especially considering the number of Australians and Viet Cong that had been moving through that day.

He couldn't even say he didn't trust her, there was too much honesty swimming in that doll-like face for that. Vulnerability too. But she was hiding something important from him and, over here, that just didn't bode well.

'Sweetheart or Sweet-Cakes?' Spike teased, pausing with his whistling and nodding at the page.

'Don't be daft,' Angus said, rocked from his reverie and putting pen and paper away, but he felt a little guilty just the same. This over-protectiveness he felt for Thuy might be bordering on excessive and he didn't like the thought. Nor the implications written across Spike's annoyingly smug face.

Machine gun fire rattled not far off and they all paused in their activities, instantly alert. There'd been plenty of skirmishes over the past few days but, despite their sector being moved further west to an FSB named Coogee, no major conflicts had occurred since the first night. Silence ensued, long enough for them all to return to their individual distractions and Angus sighed, taking the pen and paper out once more. He decided to copy Ben's idea and simply describe the waiting to Rosemary; what they all did, what he thought about. Only he wouldn't be telling her what the worry wart had on his mind. He didn't imagine she'd want to hear about that.

Intense battle had returned, another long, viscous affair; six hours by Ben's watch and once again centred on 1RAR's defensive perimeter. The men in 3RAR were becoming frustrated now, keen to drive the enemy back and return to Nui Dat and familiar territory, although that didn't look likely to happen any time soon.

'Might happen a damn sight sooner if they let us get close enough to do something,' he muttered under his breath as the gunfire began to peter out, the endless night coming to a close.

'Talking to y'self is the first sign of madness, mate,' Spike said nearby.

'Sir,' Angus reminded him.

'Hey, I'm not even supposed to be in this platoon so pretend I'm not even here.'

'Bit hard when you won't stop jabbering. Do you mind, sir?' Jimmy asked, emphasising the last and holding up a cigarette.

Ben nodded. 'Light me one too, would you?' Most joined in, relaxing for the first time in hours, but Ben's eyes stayed firmly on the dying battlefront as he dragged on the smoke. Another gruesome clean-up lay ahead, and he briefly considered just sending the others and staying behind, however that would be breaking one of the cardinal rules of leadership: never send another man to do a job you'd be unwilling to do yourself.

But the truth was he was dreading it. Something had changed since he found that photograph, something he wasn't able to stop his mind from gnawing on. He finally understood the expression 'like a dog with a bone' because unfortunately there had been plenty of nervous lulls in the fighting over the past few days to give this new, inner mongrel space to chew.

He supposed that was what got to soldiers in the end, the ones who came back 'damaged' as the doctors say, not so much war itself but the length of the fight. Because the longer you were in it the more chances were that sooner or later you'd notice something, some stray little detail that instead of passing through decides to stay. Then it settles in with its bone, grinding away, until other details start fading. Important ones, like rules. And then the second skin keeping you alive starts shedding away.

'Fall out,' Ben said suddenly, forcing himself to start the search. If nothing else, he was obeying a rule: lead by example. He just hoped it would keep the dogs of war at bay.

Thirty-Four

'AO Surfers', Bien Hoa Province, 24 May 1968

They were digging again, this time in the pouring rain while laying wire and claymore mines and scraping out sleeping pits. Ben could barely remember that other, dry Vietnam in all this mud. The idea of landing on the floor of a rubber plantation and it feeling like concrete seemed impossible now as the thick red-brown muck slopped to the side. It would make an almighty mess of the tanks but they would get through okay, he figured, glad to have them making their way towards this new post, the currently under construction 'FSB Balmoral'.

He was relieved 3RAR had been moved again, hopefully closer to the major conflict, wanting this arm-wrestle to reach some kind of conclusion even if it did mean going out and finding the enemy in the morning. They'd been involved in plenty of ambush raids out here by now but Ben was ready for a full-scale battle. *Bring it on,* he told the mud as he worked. *Just get it over with then get me out of this place.*

The Animals song came to mind then and he began to hum it, Spike picking up the tune, and soon the others joined in until they were all singing along, like some half-demented chain gang, shirtless and muddy and digging in the rain. It felt good, Ben decided, thrusting his spade and thinking about home. The dogs couldn't chew when you were this engaged.

Soon the pits were dug, the overhead shelters were up and they were able to take a break while they waited for any news from HQ.

'Nothing doing,' Body said, checking the radio. 'Who's up for smoko?' He took off his helmet, red bandana in place, and Ben had to smile as the big fellow organised tea.

'I've got just the thing,' Spike said, patting his pocket.

'Not tonight,' Ben told him. He was pretty sure the enemy were close, even closer than HQ figured, and he wouldn't put it past them to wage a welcome attack like that first night at Coral. 'You won't be much use to me stoned.'

Spike shrugged, lighting a cigarette instead. He was actually getting pretty good at following orders – as long as he agreed – but he still refused to call him 'sir' and had taken to using a range of ridiculous titles instead. 'Highness', 'your worshipfulness' and the very annoying 'governor' had all been in circulation this week.

'What's the plan then, my lord?'

There was a general chuckling followed by a bit of throat clearing and Ben cast him a look before replying. 'Assuming we don't get hit tonight we'll go at it first thing. See what's out there…'

'…then blast the shit out of them so we can get the hell out of here,' Jimmy guessed.

'Pretty much.'

'Man, I sure could use a shower,' Angus said, flicking off a leech in disgust. 'When was I ever not covered in crap?'

'Not too sure but you've always been full of it,' Spike said, grinning. 'Tell you one thing, I'm definitely going for a surf when we get back to port.'

'Sounds good,' Angus said, lying back with a yawn and pulling his hat down. 'Wake me up when the war comes knocking, will you?'

Other such conversation continued and Ben stood up, only half listening as he stared out at the now torrential rain. Visibility was nil, which he supposed was in their favour; an early strike now seemed unlikely tonight, allowing time for the tanks to arrive on the morrow.

'Good thing or bad thing?' Body asked, handing him a cuppa and nodding out at the rain.

'If we can't see them they can't see us,' Ben said, shrugging.

'So we're both up shit creek without a paddle?'

Ben gave a wry smile, clapping him on his massive shoulder, but it was Angus who answered from beneath his hat.

'Hit the nail on the head there, Body. Right on the bloody head.'

Tracer lights and shots were all the warning they needed that the big fight was finally here and and 3RAR watched the sky with acute apprehension, their honed instincts on heightened alert. There had been activity that day, particularly directed at the travelling tanks, but they'd made short work of the enemy's attacks, convincing Ben that the tough old workhorses would work as well as artillery. Possibly better. Certainly they gave a sense of security to this platoon who were technically still referred to as 'anti-tank patrol', despite the multiple evolutions of their role.

Night had fallen hours ago but Ben guessed the North Vietnamese would wait till very early morning – it seemed to be their pattern. Sure enough it was almost four o'clock when the mortar bombs finally came and they knew straight away the enemy meant business. Rockets and machine guns joined the firepower and the night-hell they had only witnessed so far was now upon them. Whatever he'd expected Ben hadn't considered he could actually die, engrossed as he'd been with other contemplations, but when the sky illuminated and the full power of mass warfare was thrust their way it seemed inevitable. How could anyone survive this?

Some primal drive seemed to kick in because suddenly he was fighting back with everything he had, orders flying, hurling hell straight back in a rain of machine gun fire that shook his arms until they were numb. He didn't know if he was hitting anything; he didn't want to know. The time for thinking about such things would come later, he knew, but for now he just had one rational thought: to keep them all alive.

Almighty explosions sounded and Ben thought they might be torpedoes aimed at the wire but the tanks were blasting now, shaking the earth with their enormous power and sending any invaders to a sure death. Then the Hueys came and Puff sailed once more, strafing the jungle with dragon fire, and the orange clouds burned in an eerie pre-dawn as the enemy finally melted away.

Once he might have said they'd had a victory, that they'd won the day in the end. But Ben knew better than that after five months of war. No-one won anything in Vietnam.

Thirty-Five

Two days later Ben laid down his gun, exhausted by yet another night of nightmarish battle, wondering how much more 3RAR would be expected to withstand. It seemed endless, the foray into this perverse, other-world Surfers. Like the gods had gone mad and were seeing what it would take for him to join them.

Lights had been streaming from Coral for a while now, illuminating the area in front; preventing the enemy from rescuing their wounded, to try to bring the death toll up. The more enemy fatalities the sooner they could get out of here, Ben reminded himself, but it was a sickening prospect. The radio was silent but he decided not to wait or call through to command, giving the order to fall out and collect the dead once more.

There were so many of them. Later someone called it the Killing Field and so it was, a littered, open expanse filled with bodies, most only sixteen or so. Ben had heard the North Vietnamese had lowered the age of enlistment to fifteen, so perhaps younger. 'Forty-two' came the call, and prisoners were marched past the pile as a bulldozer pushed the corpses into yet another mass grave.

'Any casualties on our side?' he heard Angus ask.

'Only one,' someone said. 'A big fella, they say. Just up there.'

He pointed to Balmoral and something inside Ben's stomach began to roil as he turned, looking at the faces around him. Missing one.

Later Ben would wonder why he hadn't called out for Body to check the radio; why he hadn't done the usual thing of counting his own men first. He'd been too busy knowing they'd be counting the enemy's dead soon, never considering the unthinkable. That they'd be counting one of their own.

He began to run, throwing his gun away to get there faster. Surely it couldn't be him. Surely those mad gods weren't capable of this.

But as he reached the base Jimmy was already there, crying uncontrollably as he covered the giant body over. It didn't quite reach, that military blanket. You could still see a red bandana, now stained with blood.

Thirty-Six

Vung Tau, 1 June 1968

They'd been a ragged bunch when they'd finally returned to base, covered in red mud, exhausted; devastation masking every face, but the other Australian soldiers had come out to watch their return with some kind of silent salute of respect. Word had got back about the bloody battles and each man's expression told a story. The muddied ones spoke of the horror, the shock and the impact. The clean ones spoke of fear and sympathy for their countrymen. But every face shared the one truth that they all had in common: human cost was heavy, and it weighed down hard on them all.

It felt strange to be clean and wearing a fresh uniform a day later but far stranger to be saluting a coffin in the middle of the tarmac. They were all there, even Spike looked respectable, and the Australian flag rippled in the strong breeze but Ben folded it with precision, those years of training showing through. Angus knew he blamed himself, even though he shouldn't. A leader can't guarantee every man's survival, no matter how skilled he is, but Ben wouldn't see it that way.

Angus was starting to think Ben was really just too good a man for all this, then again maybe they all were. Surely none of them deserved to be here. And none of them deserved to die.

'Wait,' Jimmy said. He'd managed to borrow a record player and was putting on a song before they carried Body away. It was Janis Joplin singing 'Piece of My Heart' and Angus felt his own heart swell with grief, the tears running unchecked at the memory of Body, lying with his eyes closed singing that tune for all he was worth. Never to open them again, now. Every word was like a protest against this war that was stripping everything away, piece by piece; their ability to sleep, their right to a normal life, their choice to kill or not kill, and now this: their right to live.

Yeah, take it, Angus yelled in his mind, but it was in anger, not surrender. This war wasn't going to beat him yet, he decided, the defiance and passion that was pouring out of Janis fuelling his resolve. I'm not going to lose it, I'm not going to let it ruin my life and I'm bloody well going to survive. Looking across at Spike he read the same emotions in his brother's face. We're not leaving here in a box, he told him silently, and Spike nodded back. If he'd come here for him then they were going home together. Just let anyone try to take that piece of his heart away.

The song ended and they were watching in silence as the coffin was loaded and the plane prepared for take-off when a messenger came up to them.

'Turner?'

'Yes?' Angus and Spike both answered together.

The messenger looked slightly confused, adding 'Private A. Turner?' and Angus held up his hand. 'Uh, that would be me.'

'Here,' the man said, handing him an official-looking envelope.

'What is it?' Spike asked as Angus ripped it open and scanned the contents.

'Well bugger me,' Angus said, slightly stunned as he re-read the words out loud, '*six months of active service has now been completed and you are allocated two weeks home leave, effective 4 June 1968.*'

'But that's only three days away,' Jimmy said and Spike grabbed the letter, scanning the few lines.

'Three more days,' Angus muttered, raising his eyes as the plane took to the skies, 'and I'll be going home too.'

They all looked set to get good and drunk and Spike was already strumming his guitar and lighting a joint when Angus rose to leave.

'Where the hell do you think you're going?'

'Won't be long,' Angus told his brother. 'Just got to see a man about a dog.'

'Or a girl about a cake,' Spike guessed, teasing grin in place.

Angus didn't reply but he did flick his hat across Spike's head as he left. Truth was that was exactly what he was doing. He couldn't just leave after weeks away without checking on Thuy and making sure she was all right.

He walked down to the market where she usually worked but the stall wasn't there today. Looking around it didn't seem to be anywhere else either so he asked a man who usually worked alongside if he'd seen her. The man pretended he didn't speak English which worried him, especially as Angus had heard him chat to soldiers before and knew full well he was lying.

He tried another woman who sold eggs on the other side but she looked uneasy, saying only 'they gone'.

'Gone where?' Angus asked but she bustled away through the crowd. He followed her, getting more concerned now. 'Hey! Gone where?' he tried again, turning her around.

'Let go,' she said, pushing him off her arm. A few military police were looking their way now and she stared at them nervously.

'Tell me or I'll call them over,' he warned.

The woman seemed afraid of that so she answered him now in a low tone. 'They gone home. To farm near creek.'

'Which creek?'

'Thanh Long. That way,' she pointed, wrenching her arm away.

'How far?'

But she had really taken off into the throng now and Angus gave up on her, walking over to the man who hired motorbikes instead. 'How far to Thanh Long Creek?' he asked, pointing in the direction the woman had indicated.

'Twenty minute on bike. Take turn at pig farm.' Angus handed him some cash and jumped on the bike, hoping he remembered how to ride the thing from years ago.

But something told him there wasn't time for questions as he spluttered off down the road.

Thuy could hear everything from the secret place her father had made in the giant tree. Bao often panicked and ordered her to hide in here of late. Telling her to make herself small. They were searching again, knocking over chairs, lifting up floorboards, every sound a jar to her tightly stretched nerves.

'Where is he?' the sergeant shouted. He was Vietnamese. They usually were, these soldiers they used for raids.

'Not here,' Bao asserted, the same words he'd been saying for the past ten minutes.

'We know you're hiding him. Tell us where or we'll burn you down.'

'No,' Anh said, and Thuy could see her through the doorway, clutching at her heart.

Bao tried again to convince them. 'We haven't heard from him for over a year.'

'You're lying,' the man said, holding up the gun they had found in the garden.

'We don't know where it came from...'

'I'll give you one more chance,' the sergeant said, enunciating each word. 'Tell us where your son is. Give us Giap Nguyen.'

There was a terrible silence followed by sudden crashes and the pound of boots on the hard floor. 'Take them out!'

'No, no...' Anh wept as they led her and Bao out into the sun. Thuy could see them all clearly now. The swarm of men in uniform. Her parents' pitiful forms. They looked old and afraid and she longed to run to them but they'd sacrificed everything in life so far for her safety. The sergeant gave the order and the couple were forced to lie face down while soldiers poured gasoline on the hut.

'Last chance,' the sergeant said, but her parents didn't move and the signal was given for the fire to be lit. It went up fast, cracking and burning, taking away what was left of their meagre possessions, memories of Long Tan returning on the smoking wind. Then a machine gun *tatted* and there was much commotion and Thuy's eyes flew to see a young man dead in the grass. Then her parents stood up and her father began to run and even as she went to scream gunfire sounded and he fell to the earth too.

And all the while the fire burned and the sky turned black, but it couldn't block the sight of Anh grasping at her chest. Thuy watched in shock as her mother collapsed, somehow just knowing Anh was dying with the others. A heart that broken could never stay beating.

Then they left, those soldiers, just as they'd come; without permission, without compassion, no understanding or pause.

The sound of the engine faded, leaving only the hiss of angry fire.

And Thuy Nguyen knew, this time, she was truly alone.

He saw the smoke before anything else, moving to the side as a truck of soldiers rumbled by, then he made his way down to find its source; it was a hut, burning to the ground.

'Dear God,' he muttered, seeing bodies strewn about, his fear mounting each second as he ran towards them. It was Thuy's father, lifeless and pale, red stains spreading across his white shirt, and there was another man, young and dressed in black. Viet Cong. Realisation dawned as he turned to see a third figure. It was Thuy's mother but she was barely breathing. He ran over to her and grasped her hand.

'Thuy?' Anh whispered and Angus looked across to see her standing there, like a lost little girl, her face a mask of grief and shock.

'Ma,' Thuy said. It was as though she spoke from a great distance, so soft was her tone. She came closer and knelt down, taking her mother's other hand, large tears trailing her cheeks.

Anh said something in Vietnamese and Thuy nodded in response.

'*Tốt*,' Anh said, her hand losing strength.

'*Đừng đi*,' Thuy cried, breaking down, 'don't leave me.'

But her mother's eyes were closing now, only a single word escaping. '*Sự-tự-do*.'

The fire crackled and the wind stirred the grass as Anh Nguyen drew her last breath, and Angus felt Thuy's sorrow like an arrow as she took shaking fingers from her mother's still hand to lower eyelids. Then she said some kind of prayer, too faint for him to hear even if he could understand it, before lying her head against

Anh's breast and crying in racking, terrible sobs. Angus had heard people cry before but not like this; this was a pain so deep and so cruel he knew he'd never forget the sound. Yet all he could do was sit there and wait until she'd let it all out and eventually, she did.

Thuy rose shakily to her feet and he helped her up.

'What do you need me to do?' Looking at her stricken face he figured he'd pretty much say yes to anything she asked of him. 'Do you…do you want me to bury them?'

'Not yet,' she said, 'I need you un-bury.'

He stared at her, confused, but didn't say anything more as she led him over to a large tree near some dragon fruit bushes. It had a hiding hole dug into the base – the explanation for her survival today, no doubt. She looked around for something to use for digging and he spied a small axe nearby, going over to retrieve it.

'Here,' she said, pointing at the earth, 'but very careful.'

He dug slowly and gently and she waited in silence, her face still stricken but with some of that strength he knew she possessed resurfacing.

'That,' she said, hearing the soft clink of metal on metal and Angus carefully extracted a small tin box. She didn't open it, holding it close before choosing her words. 'I need you help me. I need meet with right person to go away.'

'Where do you want to go?'

'Australia.' She said that one word in perfectly unaccented English and he stared in disbelief.

'Why…how…?'

'I can pay.' She opened the box then, taking out a very beautiful gold and ruby necklace. 'It val…valubul.'

'Valuable.'

'Yes. Very much.'

Angus scratched his head, trying to think of ways to explain how impossible getting her to Australia would prove to be. 'Even if I could get you a ticket you'd need a passport and a place to stay and…'

'Yes. I have papers,' she said, lifting out some documents from the tin.

He tried to again. 'Look, I was actually trying to find you today to tell you I'm going away in a few days. I have leave – back home in Australia. Maybe I can make a few enquiries…'

Her eyes had widened at that news and she touched his arm. It felt as light as a butterfly. 'I come too.'

'What? No, no. Thuy, I can't take you with me. I wouldn't be allowed and anyway, I…I have a girlfriend. We promised marriage to each other,' he said, explaining as best he could, 'she might not understand if I turn up with you.' Thuy looked very hurt then and he wished he hadn't told her like that. 'I just can't do it,' he said, hating to let her down.

She turned away and walked slowly towards the hut that was all but gone; a smouldering mess. Nothing left worth salvaging. So she made her way over to the bodies in the field instead.

'I lose mother, father and brother, all in one day. I lose home,' she told him, her eyes more desolate than any he'd ever seen as she began to cry once more.

'They give everything for me. They make sacrifice. Brother turn bad, turn VC, but I good daughter. Mother – her last word. *Sự-tự-do.* I make promise.'

'What does it mean?'

'Freedom,' she said, almost collapsing now, then somehow he was holding her and she was curled up against his chest. 'Please, let me keep promise. Please Ang-gus, I come too?'

Perhaps it was those eyes, or perhaps it was the way she first said his name, but the words were out before he could stop them, words he had no idea how to fulfil.

'Alright Thuy, you come too.'

Part Four

Liquid Fire

Thirty-Seven

Sydney, 5 June 1968

It was very cold but brilliantly sunny and Angus would have laughed at Thuy's reaction to the freezing air on the tarmac if he hadn't been so worried about the person waiting at the terminal to meet them. Not that Rosemary knew he was bringing a young Vietnamese woman home with him from war. It wasn't something you could really explain over the phone. He was still trying to come to terms with the concept himself.

Aside from that complication he was extremely nervous and excited. Six months without seeing Rosemary had been torturous at times and he couldn't wait to round the doors at customs and lift her into his arms. Be on the receiving end of one of those endless hugs and smell that sweet-scented hair. But first to get Thuy through without any headaches.

As it turned out he needn't have worried about that. Derek, ever the con-artist, had managed to get her a passport almost overnight and Ben knew enough important people to get a visa fast-tracked. As Jimmy surmised, the old adage 'it's not what you know, it's who you know' tended to hold especial power in a poor country. Thuy watched with wide eyes as they stamped and processed her passport, standing close to Angus the whole time.

'Welcome to Sydney, love,' the man said, giving her a wink, and she gaped at him then nodded.

'Come on,' Angus said, taking her arm. He walked her to the doors then turned to explain the situation at hand.

'My girlfriend, the one I told you about, will be here, waiting.'

She looked upset momentarily but quickly hid it away. 'You want me follow a bit after?'

'Yes,' Angus said, relieved she understood.

Thuy put down her bag that in fact had very little in it and stood still to wait while he went on ahead.

'Just give me a minute,' he said, feeling bad, but going anyway. Then he rounded the corner and walked out, searching around until suddenly he spied her and she was running and he held her at last.

'Oh God, oh God, oh God,' she said. 'Oh my darling.' Then she was kissing him and Angus felt so joyful at the moment he completely forgot about anything else. He even forgot they were in public as he kissed her back with more passion than was probably appropriate.

'Hello beautiful,' he finally managed to say, burying his face in her unbound golden hair and breathing deeply as she gave him a long hug. 'I've missed you,' he said simply.

'I've missed you too.' She was crying a little and he kissed her tears away before she looked over his shoulder, whispering in his ear.

'Don't tell me you brought back a Vietnamese wife,' she said with a giggle.

'What…?'

'Someone's staring at you.'

Angus paused momentarily, cursing himself for not telling Thuy to wait a few minutes instead of one, then turned to handle what was, potentially, a very sticky situation.

'Um, actually this is a friend of mine who is emigrating to Australia. Thuy Nguyen meet Rosemary Flannery, Rosemary, Thuy.'

Thuy nodded politely. 'Hello, how are you? My name is Thuy.' It sounded rehearsed, like she'd practised that one a few times in her English class.

'Seriously?' Rosemary said, looking at Angus. He swallowed heavily, not sure what to say. 'You left the poor girl waiting around the corner all on her own? Hello Thuy, I'm Rosemary. Don't mind his dreadful manners.' She gave Angus a little slap on the sleeve before holding out her hand. 'Nice to meet you.' Thuy stared at Rosemary's hand before slowly stretching out her own, looking surprised when Rosemary shook it briefly. 'Where are you staying? Can we give you a lift?'

Thuy looked to Angus and he cleared his throat. 'Well, the thing is, she hasn't had the chance to line anything up as yet so I thought perhaps...'

Rosemary took a moment to comprehend what he was suggesting. 'She's...staying with you?'

'In Spike's room, obviously. He said it was fine.' That was quick thinking, he congratulated himself, but Rosemary still seemed a bit disappointed.

'Of course, why not? I mean it's just sitting there, empty.' Then she offered an overly bright smile to Thuy who was looking nervously at her. 'Let's say we go and collect your luggage, eh?'

'Lug-gage?'

'Your bags or suitcases or whatever. Goodness, you must have a ton of stuff if you're moving countries. I hope we can fit it in the taxi.'

'She um, doesn't actually. She lost everything...in a fire,' Angus told her.

'Oh my God, oh you poor girl,' Rosemary exclaimed, her sense of compassion taking over now. 'You must let me help you. I've lots of clothes and things, and my twin sister does too, although you're so tiny. I wonder if we have any nice coats that might fit – this cold must be a bit of a shock...'

She put her arm around her, still prattling as they made their way to the doors and Angus wondered what he'd ever been worried about. His Rosemary was the kindest woman in the world.

'Why don't we just take you clothes shopping tomorrow?' Poppy suggested gently. Thuy liked her. She liked both of them actually, although Rosemary was overpowering. And she kept touching Angus, even in public. It was hard to watch, but she'd known it would be. Thuy was here on 'terms' – poor until they sold her necklace or she got a job, beholden until she found her own place to live and her own people to befriend, heart-sick until she got over being in love with someone else's man. An orphan, a war victim. A refugee.

People were staring at her as she walked down these wide, clean streets, the only Asian in a sea of Caucasians.

'She has to have something else to wear,' Rosemary insisted, taking her hand and leading her into a glaringly lit shop. There were mirrors on the walls and the clothes sat in matching, perfect rows, every colour of the rainbow in many fabrics she'd never seen. 'How about something like this?' She held up a skirt that wouldn't even pass the knee and Thuy shook her head quickly. A dress followed but it had no sleeves and Thuy blushed at the idea of strange men seeing her bare arms.

She ran her hands down her own self-consciously and Poppy seemed to understand. 'It's a winter tunic. You wear this underneath.' She showed her what seemed an impossibly tight top, something called a 'skivvy', and Thuy blanched at the thought of how revealing it would be.

'I not need anything.'

'Nonsense. Come on, it's my shout,' Rosemary said, moving along the rows. It was only her second day in Australia and already she was wondering if she would ever be able to cope with such an alien world. It was so lavish and pristine. So privileged it made her head spin that Vietnam was so far behind, even without the war.

Water poured from shiny taps in kitchens and bathrooms; houses had six, seven rooms, even a separate one for a personal laundry. They all ate whatever they liked from a huge variety of foods but they rarely finished a meal. So much waste but why not? No-one was hungry. No-one was scared. In fact, no-one seemed to care very much about anything, saying 'no worries' to whatever she asked. She supposed she should be finding it comforting and wonderful but all she could feel was overwhelmed.

'How about some jeans?' Rosemary said, flicking through piles. Thuy shook her head. 'Why not?'

'They for cowboys.'

Rosemary laughed and winked at Angus which made Thuy blush again. Who were these Australian women? Why did they dare do such brazen things?

Poppy lifted a more reasonable dress out, navy and long-sleeved. 'This would look nice on you.' It was still too short but Thuy was so diminutive it would probably fall to a respectable length so she agreed to it. 'Size 6?' she asked. Thuy had no idea. All her clothes had been home-made in Vietnam, mostly by her mother. Her heart fell at the thought of those tired hands, endlessly working, now stilled forever in a grave beneath a giant tree, near the dragon fruit.

'Try these on too,' Rosemary insisted, putting a pair of jeans, a yellow jumper and a patterned skirt in her arms.

'Try?'

'The change rooms are over there,' Rosemary said, pointing as she continued her search.

Thuy felt shocked at the concept of actually taking her clothes off behind a curtain with people around, especially Angus, but didn't know how to say no so she walked over to it slowly, placing the pile on a seat in the cubicle and pulling the curtain shut.

'Come here, cowboy,' she heard Rosemary say to Angus and the sound of kissing followed. Thuy tried not to listen, still coming to terms with the fact that such things were commonplace here. The couple had slept in the same bedroom last night so she could only guess what transpired. Maybe Australians even had sex before marriage. The thought made her feel depressed and she took off her dress slowly, holding it against her chest lest anyone see through the curtain and pulling on the jumper awkwardly.

'How's the fit?' Rosemary called.

'I not ready,' she said back, quickly taking off the long white pants she always wore beneath her dress and putting on the jeans. Facing the mirror, she gasped at her reflection. The outfit was far too revealing, the jeans showing the outline of her backside and the jumper clinging to her chest.

'Any good?' Rosemary said, drawing back the curtain in a sudden swoosh. 'Wow – you look great!'

Angus was staring and Thuy was beyond blushing now. She actually felt faint. 'It not…for me.'

'Why not? I think you look groovy, baby,' Rosemary said, clicking her fingers. 'Wait, that's it.' She reached over to the counter and picked out a pair of sunglasses, handing them to Thuy who put them on doubtfully. 'Too cool for school.'

Thuy stared at her reflection through the shaded lenses deciding they were the only thing she liked so far. At least they gave her something to hide behind.

'Leave her alone now, come on,' Poppy said, pulling the curtain and leaning in to whisper. 'Don't choose anything you're not comfortable with Thuy. It's okay.'

Only it wasn't okay at all. She was an imposter, an interloper; ridiculous in a costume as she tried to play the part. But nothing could disguise the fact that she was still a foreign girl in a foreign land, trying to adapt to what was most foreign of all: her freedom.

She was dragging on a joint and the smoke drifted in swirls, catching the light that was silvered from morning rain. She was also brushing her hair in long, languid strokes and it was turning into silk that fell in a golden cascade. It was longer than when he left, almost to her waist, which he found sexy as hell, especially considering she was naked. Oh, the female form, he sighed contentedly to himself as she passed him the joint, breasts exposed, smiling knowingly as she continued to brush. Then the Rolling Stones came on the radio, 'She's a Rainbow', and she rose slowly, unashamedly, to crawl across the bed on all fours like a cat and sit astride him.

It was intensely erotic and he strained against her as she took control, riding him like a beautiful Godiva, all creamy flesh and long gold hair, leading him to a place of sweet passion and a shuddering release.

'Wow,' he said afterwards as they lay spent and contented.

'Mmm,' said Rosemary. 'More glow in the afterglow?' She rolled over and lit another joint, offering it to him.

'You're doing this rather a lot, aren't you?' he said, declining this time.

She shrugged. 'It helps me sleep.'

'It doesn't seem to be helping me sleep, although it is keeping me in bed,' he said, running his hands through her hair and watching it fall against her skin.

'I might just have to keep you here forever; tie you to it in chains,' she said, placing the joint against his lips. He drew the smoke in, mesmerised as she kissed him before he could release. 'My prisoner.'

'God, I'm never going to be able to leave now.'

'That's the general plan.'

She laid her head against his chest, singing softly along with the radio where the Beatles were lending advice to someone called Jude and he realised that going to war would be far worse the second time around. 'Duty' seemed an increasingly poor reason to leave heaven to go back to hell.

Thirty-Eight

Thuy wasn't sure where to look but she was especially avoiding eye contact with any of the young men. Her old wariness of foreign eyes had returned with force and she felt naked in her new navy dress even though it was very conservative compared to what other women at the party wore. Rosemary had a crown of flowers in her hair and her crocheted dress was short above knee-length white boots. She looked very beautiful, impossible competition for Angus's affections, Thuy well knew. Poppy had twisted her hair up with some kind of pins and her black skivvy and checked skirt were the height of sophistication, or so it seemed to a girl from the Vietnamese countryside.

The twins had wanted to put make-up on her but she'd refused, thinking her mother would roll over in her grave if she even contemplated painting her face like those ladies of the street. She was happy just to comb her fringe low and try to be invisible behind it but the crowd at this party held another agenda. Apparently 'Vietnam' was the most popular word in the room which made her the most popular person in it – despite her complete reluctance to perform the role.

'So what's it like in the cities over there? Are people protesting too?'

'I not been…'

'Do you live in a peaceful section or are you near the battles?'

'It everywhere…it not…'

'Why don't you just tell the soldiers to piss off home? I would.'

'I cannot say this.'

'Why not?'

Because I'm no-one there. Because soldiers have guns. Because I am a Vietnamese girl. 'Because they not go.'

'Do you want a drink?'

'No thank you.'

'Don't you drink?'

'No.'

'Why not?'

Because I am a Vietnamese girl.

'Smoke?'

'No thank you.'

'Don't you smoke either?'

'No.'

'Why not?'

'Because I…'

'Have you ever seen someone shot?'

'I…I can't…'

'Want to get some fresh air?'

'Yes,' she told him. I come with you.

Angus took her arm and helped her through a crowd that towered above her; she'd never thought herself short until she came to Australia. 'Fresh air' turned out to be cold but Thuy didn't care. She was away from those impossible questions.

'Sorry about that.'

'You not do anything wrong.'

'I guess,' he said, lighting a cigarette then gesturing with it. 'Do you mind?'

He seemed to be apologising for smoking and she gave him a small, shy smile, shaking her head. Maybe that was why she loved him so much. Always protecting. Always considerate and kind.

'I'm afraid you're going to come across a bit of that. People here don't understand.' The backyard of this house afforded a good view of the northern suburbs and they stared out at it together. 'They think this is the only version of reality.'

Thuy took in her new home, sitting peacefully in rolling valleys; solid brick houses shaded by eucalypt and jacaranda trees, two new words Angus had taught her that she couldn't get quite right. Most had beautiful gardens, carefully tended roses and carpeted lawns. Thuy didn't know anyone who worried about planting anything except food back in Vietnam.

'I not belong,' she said, the realisation cutting at her heart. How hopeful she'd been about coming to this place, never considering that it would be hard to adapt to paradise.

'You will, in time,' he assured her. 'It will just take some getting used to, like anything else in life. That's what my mother used to say anyway; time heals all pain.'

'You still have mother?' she asked. He'd never mentioned her before.

'Yes, both my parents live in Western Australia. It's a very long way from here, across the red centre; the big desert.'

'Why you not…' She paused, not sure how to express the rest.

'Live there? I guess it isn't really home anymore.' He looked pensive as he dragged on the smoke. 'Mind you Sydney feels strange too now. I think I'm suffering a little culture shock as well.'

Culture shock. That sounded about right. 'It all so big, and clean, and…and too much of things.'

He smiled. 'That's a pretty good summation. Too much of things. We see too much and they have too much – kind of hard to put the "too" and "too" together, isn't it?'

She didn't really understand what he was saying but she enjoyed sunning herself in that smile just the same.

'There you are!' Rosemary exclaimed, stumbling a little as she came through the back door and breaking the spell. 'What are you two talking about out here in the cold?' She shivered in her short dress, cuddling up to Angus.

'Vietnam,' Angus said with a shrug, dragging on his smoke, putting one arm around Rosemary.

'Well come inside and join the chat. Cat's planning a big march to support the Paris riots and he wants your input.'

'Why our input?' Angus said as Rosemary looked from one to the other.

'Because you both know first-hand what we're protesting against, of course! Come on,' she insisted, dragging on both their hands.

It was warmer inside but Thuy would have far preferred the garden. All eyes were on her again, and those terrible questions were back, but at least Angus was there to help this time.

Their friend Daniella was leading the discussion, pen and pad in hand. She was dressed in black from head to toe and Rosemary had told her it was because someone had killed a king last month. Someone called 'Martin Luther'. It wasn't hard to remember the name: a massive poster quoting him sat on the wall. He'd been a holy man, apparently, and his face was dark, like some of those American soldiers. Thuy wondered why anyone would murder him.

'What would you write on a sign if you had to choose your own words?' Daniella asked, and it was Angus who answered.

'End it,' he said, taking a beer out of the esky nearby and handing Thuy a cola. This stuff she would drink, having tried it before and finding it rather delicious.

Daniella nodded solemnly, writing it down. 'End it. Cool. What else? How about you, Thuy?'

She looked at Angus for help and he gave a perfect prompt. '*Sự-tự-do*?'

'Yes,' she said gratefully, '*sự-tự-do*. It mean "freedom".'

'Wow, that's really far out, Thuy. Thanks,' the man called Cat said, nodding at her thoughtfully while others around the lounge room murmured in agreement. She felt encouraged then and dared say a little more.

'My parents give everything for me have *sự-tự-do*. Australia is…paradis?' She looked at Angus.

'Paradise,' he corrected gently.

'I've heard Vietnam is very beautiful too,' Poppy said, listening nearby.

'Sometimes it is,' Angus said. 'Although it's pretty hard to appreciate it when people are busy blowing it all to hell or burning it down.'

Thuy flinched, recent memories surfacing, and he took her hand, giving it a little squeeze. 'Thuy's home was burned to the ground only a week ago,' he explained. He didn't look to say any more so she braved the rest herself.

'Whole family die,' she said softly and there was a general, horrified gasp.

'Oh honey,' Rosemary said, taking her other hand, tears in her eyes. 'Why didn't you tell me?'

Thuy didn't answer, carefully pulling both hands away. Sinking back in the couch, making herself small.

But Rosemary was like a lion now, strong and protective, finding better English words to fling on the streets. 'War murders families', 'Vietnam leaves orphans', 'Don't ask our boys to make hell on this earth'. And all the while Thuy sat between them, this woman and her lover, wishing she wasn't too good to hate.

Jefferson Airplane blared from the stereo, the swirling vocals floating in the hazy air of the small room at the back of the house, and Rosemary was nodding along to it, sporting rose-coloured sunglasses even though it was well past dark.

'Time to go home,' Angus said, hands on hips. It was the third time he'd tried to get her to leave but she wouldn't budge off the armchair, mumbling objections each time and promising 'soon.' He'd had enough now. Thuy looked exhausted, even though she wouldn't complain, and he was feeling a bit sleepy himself after downing quite a few beers. Besides, he was pretty keen to make love to his girl again – it would be a long time waiting back in the jungle and he needed as much of her as he could get over these precious two weeks. As it was he only had eleven days left, each sunrise arriving far too soon as the clock ticked down to the dreaded day of his departure.

'After this song,' Rosemary said, playing air guitar now in dramatic swirls. She was very stoned and he was getting a bit sick of it.

'No, now,' he said firmly, walking over and taking her arm to help her up.

'Hey, no, I need to hear this bit…'

'You need to go to bed. Give me a hand, will you Poppy?' he asked her sister as she walked in the room. 'God, how much has she had anyway?'

'You mean *what* has she had,' Poppy said, looking meaningfully at him as she took Rosemary's other arm. Angus stopped, holding the very unsteady form of his girlfriend upright as his concern intensified.

'What would she have had?'

'I think you'd better ask her that yourself.'

But Rosemary wasn't making much sense now and he decided the best course of action was just to get her home without incident and deal with it in the morning. He was angry though. What the hell did she think she was playing at?

Many hours later, as he watched her sleep, the anger had died away and he was studying her pretty face with more sadness than anything else. She stirred, opening her eyes to smile at him.

'Hey lover,' she said.

'Hey.'

'Hmmm, how did I get here?'

'I carried you.'

'Oh?' She stretched her arms, yawning, not seeming overly worried.

'Blacking out a lot these days, are we?'

'No, not really,' she hedged.

'Rosemary, what's going on?'

'What do you mean?'

'What are you taking?'

She rolled away, sitting on the edge of the bed and reaching for the bowl of mulled marijuana crumbs.

'No,' he said, walking around and pushing it away. 'Not now, for chrissakes. Tell me what's going on. Are you…are you on pills? Acid?'

She shrugged. 'A bit.'

'*A bit?* How could you possibly *do that?* Don't you know how addictive those can be?'

'Other people take them. Cat and Daniella and…'

'That's it,' he said, his anger returning. 'You're not allowed to hang out with those people anymore, you hear me? And no more of this.' He grabbed the bag of pot off the shelf and threw it in the bin.

'Hey...*hey*. Don't tell me what to do. You're not my parent,' she complained, standing up and facing him, but then she looked set to faint and sat back down.

'Look at you – you can't even stand,' he said in disgust.

'Stop yelling at me,' she replied, beginning to cry, but he was too enraged to care and flung on his coat.

'I'm going for a walk.'

'Angus,' she called after him, but the door had slammed and he was assailed by a bitterly cold dawn, the rain drizzling in a thick fog as he made his way to the beach to sort his feelings out.

The ocean was turbulent and wild, crashing in silver and grey in the pale light and the wind ripped at him as he went, flapping at his coat and freezing his legs. 'Unbelievable,' he muttered, raging internally at yet another cross to bear in his life. This couldn't be happening – home was perfect. Rosemary was perfect. Vietnam was the place where everything was impossibly wrong. Was he going to be forced to nurse his girl through drug addiction? Would he have to deal with heroin? Overdoses? Possibly her death?

The last thought stopped him in his tracks and he picked up a stick, throwing it as hard as he could into the sea.

'Ang-gus?' He turned to find Thuy a few feet away, tiny in one of Poppy's overcoats, her face pale with worry. 'What wrong?'

He picked up whatever else he could find, a rock this time, and sent it as far as he could towards the waves. 'Nothing.' How could she possibly understand this? A girl who'd never had a drug in her life – probably didn't even know what they were.

'Rosemary sick?'

Maybe she saw more than he realised, he thought, pausing, another stick in hand.

'She not look too good,' Thuy said, coming closer, the salty wind causing her hair to stick to her cheeks in wet strands. 'I worried for her.'

Angus sighed, chucking the stick away. 'She's...taking medicine. Too much of it.'

'Why?'

He shrugged. 'I don't know. To feel better, I suppose.'

'Maybe she scared for you. Her heart sad,' she suggested, and he looked at her, the truth shining through those few words.

'Maybe.'

'I understand.'

The emotion in her lovely face was transparent as she looked to vacillate between her compassion for Rosemary and her feelings for him. Angus couldn't just ignore it anymore. 'Thuy...'

'I understand,' she said again, stopping him, and he realised no more words were necessary. 'I look after her. When you gone.'

'I thought you wanted to find a Vietnamese community; people you can relate to better than we lot.'

She shook her head. 'No. I stay. Vietnamese girl no more.'

He smiled at her resolve and reached out to move her hair off her cheek before he even realised he was doing it. 'Thank you,' he said and saw her eyes fill with tears before she walked away.

Angus followed, slowly, digesting her words.

The wind kept him company all the way home, sweeping the anger away with it as he closed the door, and Rosemary ran to him, flinging her body into his arms.

'I'm sorry,' she wept, wrapping him in a long hug and he held her close, breathing in the scent of her hair.

But as they lay down together and promises were made, he saw the bowl had been emptied. And when he thought to look the next day, so had the bin.

Thirty-Nine

Nui Dat, Vietnam, 19 June 1968

I love you, I love you, I love you…

Ben couldn't even count how many times she'd written it on the page, in doodles and scrawls with little hearts intermingled with smiling sunflowers. 'I love you too,' he muttered back, kissing the paper because no-one could see. The others had all gone to watch an outdoor concert but he'd preferred some alone time with his newly arrived mail.

He was in his bunk in the officers' tent, enjoying the third read-through of Poppy's letters before scanning the rest. One from Barbara which he figured could wait. One from his mother, likewise. The newspaper garnered more interest, although it was a few days old, and he took in the images of Robert Kennedy's funeral, still disgusted that yet another leader had been shot and killed. Another man losing his life at the end of a bullet that had been fired far away from the war. How was the west supposed to help the Vietnamese find peace when they continually fought among themselves?

Student protests filled other pages, carrying signs that demanded an end to it all, and he knew in his heart it would come eventually. Public opinion had swayed since the Tet Offensive. He just didn't know if he would still be alive when it did. Or sane, if he was. Every day was a struggle now as his mind started to smear once more, the weight of death on his shoulders, too much blood on his hands.

They'd been on patrol again this week, witnessing napalm for the first time; 'liquid fire' people called it, running across the ground in great plumes of flame that melted clothes right off the skin, then the flesh from the bones. He'd been standing on a hillside with a clear view of the valley the Americans were striking from the air and it swept across like an angry, living thing, chasing all life, mowing everything down that stood in its terrible path, burning people alive. Ben knew the sight would play over and again in his dreams, yet another nightmare he'd have to somehow learn to block out.

Angus was due back today and he wondered what news he would have of home, more recent than the letters in his hand; envying how it must have felt to sleep in a bed with clean sheets and awake to a woman's touch after so many months of war. Ben doubted he would ever take such things for granted again.

The sound of a jeep reached him and he stood to look outside, surprised to see Angus arrive with Spike.

'I thought you were at the concert?' he said to Spike, clasping Angus's hand. 'How are you, mate?'

'Good, buddy, just give me a sec.'

'I saw the plane and figured he might want to join in,' Spike explained as Angus ran to throw his kit down. 'Why don't you come too, your majesty?'

'Come on. I can fill you in on the way,' Angus said, running back and jumping in the jeep.

'Why not,' Ben decided, having savoured Poppy's letters long enough. First-hand news was more of a temptation.

By the time they arrived the concert was well underway and Ben knew three new things about home: people asked a lot of dumb questions about the war, Sweet-Cakes seemed to be settling in somehow and something was seriously up with Rosemary. Angus hadn't articulated the last but Ben knew him too well by now for him to hide very much. It was there in the way he didn't make eye contact when he said her name, in the set of his mouth as he stared out at the countryside. In the demeanour of a man who should be completely chilled out after two weeks of sex and relaxation but seemed more on edge than ever.

The crowd could be heard even before the music, cheering and clapping enthusiastically. The sight of western women in tight dresses would have that effect on a thousand or so lonely soldiers, Ben figured, enjoying the view himself. They were twisting and shouting in spangles and lace, a pretty sight in the muddy amphitheatre. You could almost believe you were home.

'Beer?' Spike said, passing one over from a crate in the back.

'Sure.'

It was comfortable in the jeep and it afforded a good view so they watched the rest from their 'private box', as Spike termed it, drinking quite a bit and enjoying the show.

'Want to head into port?' Spike suggested after the final encore and there didn't seem to be any reason not to go so they took their little party onwards, meeting up with the rest of the crew at their favourite bar, The Black Orchid. After an hour or so a few of the performers began to turn up there too and the place was soon packed out, music blaring and standing room only.

Ben was starting to feel fairly drunk and the haze of pot smoke seemed to be affecting him too because he could have sworn he recognised one of the dancing girls laughing at the bar. She had long tanned legs and her hair kept swishing about. Flick, flick, flick.

'Barbara?' he said out loud, incredulous as he made his way over.

'Benny?'

She laughed then, high and shrill, before rushing to throw her arms around him and kiss him on the mouth, prompting jeers and applause from those nearby.

'Come on,' he said, taking her hand to lead her outside, before turning her to face him and dropping it. 'What the hell are you doing here?'

'Show biz!' she exclaimed, doing a little swirl. She was drunk, of course, and something else he guessed. She was also thinner and her skin looked sallow beneath the make-up. 'Made up my mind to use all those years of dancing to support the troops. Got myself an agent now and everything.'

Ben hadn't noticed her on stage but then again they'd been a fair way back. 'Which one were you?'

'I'm the main dancer,' she said, offended, 'the one in the leopard skin, didn't you see me?'

'No,' he said. He did actually remember which one she was now but he wasn't about to stand here and feed her ravenous ego.

'I would have thought you'd recognise this,' Barbara simpered, taking his hands and running them down her newly slim waist and hips. 'I've missed you, baby. I just hoped and hoped I'd be able to find you.' Her arms were around him then and she was holding him tight, or just holding herself upright, Ben surmised.

'You could have just written…'

'I did,' she said, frowning then pouting. 'Didn't you read my letter?'

Ben thought about her latest letter still lying unopened on his bunk and felt slightly guilty. 'We've been on patrol…'

'You're not on patrol today,' she said, walking her fingers up his chest.

'Where are you staying?' he stalled, unwilling to let this go any further and wondering what she was playing at. He'd thought she was pretty much over pretending this marriage was anything more than a piece of paper.

'Over there,' she said, pointing unsteadily towards one of the cheap hotels along the beach. 'Want to see my room?' She leant towards him and her mouth was close enough for him to smell the beer and cigarette smoke.

'I'm, uh…with my men…'

'They won't care; they'll probably be jealous.' She laughed that laugh again and he felt a surge of dislike. 'I want to check you out properly. Make sure you haven't got any holes in you yet.' She ran her hands over his chest and stomach and he grabbed them.

'I'm fine,' he said, 'but I think you've had a bit much, Barbara. Probably best to go sleep it off.'

'Nuhhh, let's keep partying.'

She was back inside before he could stop her, ordering another drink and flirting with the throng, and he sighed, knowing he would have to look after her now. Yet another complication in this endless tour of 'duty'. Ben headed back to his table and grabbed his beer, drinking it down fast to numb the reality of what had just transpired.

'Who's that?' Angus asked, and the others waited with interest.

'His wife,' Spike told them all casually before lighting a cigarette. Ben wished he could deny it.

'*Wife?* Wow, you kept that quiet, sir!' Jimmy exclaimed.

Spike dragged on his smoke. 'Funny that.'

'*That's* Barbara?' Angus said.

'She's a good sort, if you don't mind my saying,' Derek observed, staring across, and Ben supposed she still was, but the mask was slipping these days, that ugliness on the inside finding its way to the surface. And now she was finding her way back over to him, in the middle of a war, across a crowded room, and he could no more hide from her than hide her existence from his men. Barbara was a fact, pure and simple, and no amount of beer was about to change that.

'Benny boy,' she crooned, causing him to cringe and a few of the guys to snigger. 'My, my, are these your troops?' She ran a hand across Angus's biceps and Ben cringed even further.

'Uh, fellas, this is Barbara, Barbara, this is Spike, Angus, Jimmy and Derek.' He couldn't see any of the others so he supposed that would do.

'I'm the missus,' she told them, swaying as she toasted the air.

'So we're told,' Derek said, still staring.

'The good old cheese and kisses,' Jimmy remarked, toasting the air too, and she laughed.

'Cheese and kisses,' she repeated, kissing Ben on the cheek, her arm around his shoulders. 'That's me!'

'So this is who you've had hidden away,' Angus said, raising his eyebrows at Ben over his beer.

'He does hide me away,' she complained, 'but not anymore. I'm here, baby! I'm in Vietnaammm.' She said it loudly and too close to his ear before adding 'woohoo!' to the rest of the room. There was a fair bit of cheering from the next table and she wandered over to chat to them, flicking her hair as she went.

'Nice girl, isn't she?' Spike said and Ben gave him a glare.

'Knock it off,' Angus told him under his breath. 'Another beer, mate?'

'Thanks,' Ben said, but he was waiting for more from Spike. Angus wasn't the only one he had got to know better in the jungle.

'Must be hard on a woman, waiting all those long months while her man's away fighting. Probably gets pretty lonely, I'd imagine,' he said casually, and they both knew it wasn't Barbara he was talking about.

'I think you should take your brother's advice,' Ben warned, but Spike ignored him.

'Awful lot to ask of someone really, but I suppose if they figure you're worth it. A fine, upstanding type…'

'Watch your mouth, private.'

'Sure thing, your royal asshole.'

Ben swung before he really knew he'd done it, the frustration and anger more than he could withstand and it took Jimmy and the returning Angus to pull him off Spike who was now sitting on the floor, lip bleeding.

He regretted it immediately, but the damage had been done and he couldn't take it back. Still, he tried.

'I'm sorry, really I am…'

Spike stood unsteadily, wiping the blood away and looking at him with disgust. 'That's the second time I've watched you lose it over her, mate. You might want to think about that.'

And as he walked off a spot of blood fell on the floor until the tread of an army boot smeared it away.

Forty

Phuoc Thuy Province, Vietnam, October 1968

'Three, two, one...'

There was nothing, just silence, the same as the other thousands of time he had repeated it. Ben wished he'd never been told that land mines detonate three seconds after they are tripped, having become obsessed with counting ever since. Bullets he could handle – he was trained how to avoid getting shot, but these hidden death traps were another thing altogether.

He took another careful step, their progress arduous today as they crossed yet another open field.

'Three, two, one...'

Spike was checking up ahead for tunnels, disappearing and reappearing sporadically, and leaving markers for the safest way to traverse. Not that it guaranteed anything. No-one really knew where a stray mine could lie. A foot to the left, a foot to the right, any could be your last. Vietnam was covered with them and Ben couldn't imagine how the sappers would ever clear them all away. Maiming and death would be sure to curse this land for many years to come, yet another legacy to hand over to this decimated nation after years of oppression and war.

'Three, two, one…'

A pity really, that this was the particular way he handled it. Countdowns should be for exams ending. For kissing girls on New Year's Eve, he thought fondly. That was the last time he'd kissed Poppy, on the night before he left. Not another man this time. No-one in his way.

Well, Barbara still is, technically, he reminded himself, then he pushed the complication away. He'd already discussed all that with Spike, having forced himself to have it out with him the day after the brawl when truths had been laid bare, the time for secrets long past. There was no room for them here.

Spike had confessed he had strong feelings for Poppy and in turn Ben decided to come clean. He'd told Spike the whole story about Barbara and how he felt about Poppy, his intention of divorcing and remarrying, his family's position and the duties he had to fulfil. Spike seemed to understand although one comment still rang in Ben's mind, words that sat uneasily on an already pricked conscience.

'I know she said she'll wait, but how long could that turn out to be? I may know diddly squat about women, mate, but even I can see that wife of yours won't go down without a fight.'

The way Barbara constantly tried to get him into bed over the two days she was in town was proof enough that Spike was probably right. She'd obviously been thinking things over and come to the conclusion that this marriage mattered after all; that his family name and wealth were things she didn't want to relinquish easily. Not that she'd been too clever with her scheming. Even if he had been lonely and desperate enough to be seduced by her over here, it was hardly the actions of a respectable North Shore housewife to run off to become a drunken showgirl in Vietnam. Such behaviour was unlikely to impress most husbands or in-laws, but then again Barbara was too blinded by egotism to ever consider how 'most' people would react or feel.

She probably hadn't even considered the idea of actual divorce which was a growing concern now that Spike's words rang true. Things were likely to get very ugly when the time came. It was a lot to ask of Poppy, to wait through the war then wait through what could potentially be a prolonged and nasty legal process but she loved him, that much Ben knew. As long as those letters kept coming and the fire between them burned strong he was still holding that dream of a life of his own in his heart. And all the Barbaras and warfare and land mines in the world couldn't smear that much away.

Spike interrupted his thoughts then, whistling as he reappeared up ahead and pointed over to a farm where some palm trees were swaying lightly in the breeze above a woman selling fruit from a stand. Ben signalled back and they all made their careful way towards them for smoko.

It would have been quite idyllic if their nerves weren't so frayed. The day was clear and blue and the fruit that the woman gave them was sweet, mangoes and lychees and small mandarins. It was refreshing after such thirsty work and the men ate hungrily, conversation sparse after the intensity of crossing this deadly landscape for nearly four weeks now. It was getting to all of them, this constant threat of instant death, and Ben wasn't sure just how much longer they could sustain it.

'Check this out,' Spike said, calling them over, and they moved to a spot behind the trees where a tunnel entrance lay open.

'Holy shit,' Jimmy said, squatting down to investigate the deadly spikes covered in what appeared to be faeces.

'Unholy, more like,' Spike said.

'Why the poo?' Angus asked, wrinkling his nose.

'Infection kills too,' Jimmy said, walking away and shaking his head. 'Goddamn bastards.'

Derek looked like he was going to be sick and Ben watched him, worried. Of all of them, the conman from Adelaide seemed to be coping least well with these hard few weeks. Derek was a man who liked to be in control and there was nothing more uncertain than a Vietnamese minefield.

Ben checked his map, looking for somewhere to set up camp that night and found a town about five miles west. 'Come on, fellas, I've got a nice little village planned for camp tonight. Might even challenge you to a poker game,' he told Derek. 'See if we can't scrabble together a few beers.'

'Sure,' Derek said, but he still didn't look right, and Ben glanced over at Angus who was watching them both. He nodded back and Ben felt some relief that Angus always shared some of the heavy responsibility he carried each day. It would have been a far different war without him.

Ben stretched his back before putting on his pack, thinking five miles wasn't so bad. But then the counting returned and the afternoon became an endless, slow ticking clock.

'Three, two, one…'

Rat-a-tat-tat.

He supposed he could have seen it coming if he hadn't been concentrating so hard on the counting but that was a moot point now as they lay face down in the minefield. The Viet Cong seemed everywhere, crawling out of the ground like insects and firing through the long grass.

'Argh,' Derek moaned and the others all looked over, helpless to get to him where he lay – on the other side of an open section of earth. He was badly isolated with his left shoulder covered in blood, and he was writhing in pain.

'We need to get to him,' Ben said.

'I'll do it, governor,' Spike said, and he was off before anyone could stop him.

'Shit,' said Ben, firing madly to cover him.

'Ahhhhh!' yelled Jimmy, doing the same.

'What the hell is he doing,' moaned Angus, ramming ammo into his gun. 'Spike!'

Spike landed next to Derek who was still twisting about, but seemed alright as Spike gave the thumbs up.

'Stay down,' Angus yelled desperately, firing hard at the enemy.

Then the sound of Huey could be heard in the distance and the gunfire melted away and Spike stood with a relieved grin and took a step back towards his brother. And for some reason Ben counted.

'Three, two, one...'

The explosion was sudden and cracked the air in an angry cloud of debris, throwing Spike high in the air and landing him several feet away. And then Angus was running and Jimmy was screaming and Ben wasn't counting. Not any more.

'No, no, no...' came the terrible sound of a broken man. 'Come back, please, come back...'

Then the pitiful cries were drowned out by Huey's faithful drum, but he'd come too late this time. Angus stood, Spike's bloodied body limp in his arms, and he stumbled slowly forward, careless of his steps now, his face ravaged by a grief too inconceivable to hold. It was written clearly there, in the blood and the dirt and the tears, and it was being carved into every man's soul.

They clambered on board but Angus refused to let Spike go, holding his lifeless form close against his heart, wrapping a blanket tenderly and weeping in a helpless, desperate way as he rocked him to and fro.

Ben tore his eyes back to the field as Huey lifted them up, but each man knew that minefield went with them, forever, despite the liquid fire now spreading across it, obliterating it from the earth.

Life could be that easily annihilated, in a matter of mere seconds, in this land where brothers lost brothers. Where the tick of the clock tripped the cruel hand of fate.

Three, two, one.

Forty-One

Thanh Long Creek, Vietnam, November 1968

The Beach Boys' sweet harmonies lifted through the trees, 'God Only Knows' squeezing even more pain from Angus's broken heart. A huge piece was missing, now that the worry wart had lost.

Spike was gone.

He shouldn't have even been in Vietnam and now he'd never be going home. His body would return, the coffin already on its way back to Broome, but his life...his life would always end here. Just a collection of memories now, echoing in a foreign land where beauty and horror reigned incongruously side by side. That was the reason Angus decided to hold this little ceremony today, keeping some of that life physically in this place by burying Spike's guitar under the giant tree. The one near the dragon fruit and the burnt-out hut overgrown with grass and little flowers. The irony of it lying next to the grave of a VC wasn't lost on him, but somehow Angus found it comforting that a piece of Spike was now with Thuy's family. Like he wasn't leaving his brother here all alone.

Ben stood by his side and Angus knew his guilt was at the surface once more. He'd told Angus he'd be recommending Spike for a posthumous bravery award but in the end Angus supposed it didn't matter. Nothing seemed to matter anymore. Not even the fact he was going home tomorrow, tour of duty done.

Actually that did matter, he admitted to himself, ashamed he could feel something aside from his grief, but he'd never missed Rosemary more. And, if he admitted something deeper, he was needing Thuy. She'd lost a brother too, right here in fact. He needed someone who understood.

The beautiful song overlapped in those clever layers only Brian Wilson seemed able to devise and for some reason they made perfect sense today. They sounded like Spike. They encapsulated him somehow. Free, happy, chasing life for every precious second he lived in it, like an overgrown puppy, high on existence. Or yundi, Angus thought with a slight inner smile.

They sat now, at the creek, those who were left from their platoon, to have one last session in Spike's honour. Even Ben.

But as the smoke filled his lungs and clouded his mind one thought stubbornly refused to fade. It was a question really; a problem he just couldn't solve. He wished he was a holy man then, someone who could talk to God, because only He knew where Spike was now.

And only He knew what Angus would be, without him.

Forty-Two

Sydney, Christmas Day 1968

Bing Crosby was crooning 'White Christmas' and Poppy was helping her mother by setting the table when the doorbell rang. She went to open it but Rosemary beat her to it.

'Woohoo!' her sister cried, running down the stairs and flinging it open. Rosemary launched herself into Angus's arms to kiss him quickly before her parents could see and Poppy saw him try to smile, but not quite succeed. It made her ache for him, so strongly she wanted to cry.

'Come in, come in,' Rosemary said, grabbing his hand and dragging him through the doorway. 'Hi Thuy,' she said, kissing their friend on the cheek as she followed behind. 'Merry Christmas!'

Thuy looked uncomfortable and Poppy knew she felt like she was imposing so she went to her aid, rescuing her from the demonstrative attentions of her sister and asking if she'd like to help her with the napkins.

'Yes, thank you,' Thuy said, always keen to help out. 'I fold?' she asked, picking up the expensive linen doubtfully. 'Very nice.'

'Mum loves them,' Poppy whispered, smiling at her. 'Just don't splosh any gravy on them.' Her face fell then, remembering the time Spike did just that and how he redeemed himself by complimenting the taste. *No tears,* she admonished herself, especially for Angus's sake. This would be an impossible Christmas for all of them but she was determined to do her best not to make it worse for him, at least. Poppy snuck a look at his face, drawn and holding the weight of grief as he stood by the tree with Rosemary deep in conversation. It hurt to look at him now, finding traces of his brother's features that she'd never noticed before.

'Like this?' Thuy asked, showing her a folded napkin that was rather expertly done.

'Perfect,' Poppy told her, resuming her task.

Soon the wine was poured and the twins were included for the first time, having celebrated their twenty-first birthdays recently, an age their parents finally deemed responsible enough to be served alcohol. Little did they know how much she and Rosemary had actually consumed these past few years, Poppy reflected guiltily, let alone everything else Rosemary had indulged in of late.

Her sister didn't look well at all and her mother had remarked on it, asking 'Why are you wearing so much muck on your face? Are you ill?' as soon as they'd arrived. It didn't quite conceal the dark smudges under her eyes and she was far too skinny, her legs almost stick-like below her skirt, but she looked happy as she approached the table now, unusually so.

'Have the girls taught you how to say grace as yet?' Robert asked Thuy as they sat down. Her parents saw her as a charity case, a poor 'heathen' girl, rescued from the clutches of would-be communist overlords, delivered here by the Lord.

Poppy nodded slightly at her, urging her to say yes, and Thuy concurred.

'Perhaps you'd like to lead us tonight then.'

Poppy clasped her hands together meaningfully and Thuy seemed to understand.

'I Buddhist,' she said, looking at him nervously. 'It okay?'

'It's the birthday of Our Saviour; I'm sure He will understand. In the name of the Father...'

Thuy simply bowed, not trying to make the sign of the cross, and said her prayer quietly in Vietnamese before attempting a translation.

'We grateful, we thank cook, we give to poor ones, we use mind and have compa...com...we be kind,' she finished.

'Amen,' said Robert and the others followed suit. 'That's a very nice prayer, Thuy. I'd be interested in hearing more about...'

Ding, ding, ding. Everyone turned to Rosemary who was holding Angus's hand tight and looking desperate to say something.

'We have something to announce,' she said.

'Rosemary, I told you I want to speak to your father...'

'Well go on then!' she spluttered, gesturing towards Robert.

Angus looked at her, exasperated, then turned to her father, his expression altering to nervous. 'Excuse me sir, if it isn't too much to ask, may I have a moment of your time?'

Robert slowly lowered the carving knife he'd picked up and Angus swallowed hard.

'Now?'

'Er...yes please.'

Robert paused, then said, 'If you must,' before walking briskly into the lounge room. Rosemary giggled excitedly and Poppy hoped she wasn't high. She'd stopped admitting when she was, which was a big concern, but she'd promised to try to quit, for poor Angus's sake.

'More wine?' Lois asked, pouring smoothly as if nothing was at all untoward. Poppy drank hers quickly, earning a frown from her mother.

'Really Poppy, I...'

But the men were walking back into the room, just as quickly as they'd left, and Angus cleared his throat and kneeled down in front of Rosemary.

'May as well do this properly,' he explained, blushing slightly but continuing on regardless. 'I have asked your father's permission for your hand in marriage and he has kindly agreed so...' he paused, taking a ring out of his pocket and opening the box, 'Rosemary Flannery, I've loved you from the first moment we met. Will you...will you marry me?'

Rosemary squealed, nodding yes as he put the ring on her finger, then flung her arms around him while Lois tutted and Poppy found herself getting teary. Angus looked so earnest beneath that terrible sorrow that it tore at her heart.

'Yes, yes, well, let's eat,' Robert said, although he seemed happy enough. Angus had done the right thing, yet again. Poppy wondered how her father would react when she brought home a divorced man and he asked the same question, worrying about that for the first time.

Then she noticed someone else affected by the news and all other thoughts fell to the side.

Lying in bed that night she wondered how she could have been so blind for so long. It seemed so obvious now. Thuy was in love with Angus – desperately so – and Rosemary had absolutely no idea. Poppy knew that look, she'd lived it for a long time herself, and it was a wretched way to be. Poor Thuy, she sighed, living in the room next door all this time; trying to fit in to his world and befriend his girlfriend, now soon-to-be wife. As if being an orphan and a refugee wasn't hardship enough.

Someone downstairs was still listening to carols, probably her parents, and as she listened to the words of 'Away in a Manger' an overwhelming longing for Ben overtook her. She wondered where he was spending Christmas; where he rested his sweet head.

'The stars in the bright sky looked down where he lay,' she sang softly to the night. Then she closed her eyes, making her Christmas wish as she'd done since she was a small child. *Give me the beautiful man, Jesus,* she prayed. *Bring him home safe and deliver him into my arms. Such miracles have happened before,* she reminded Him, remembering a day on a train long ago when she'd longed for Ben so much he had somehow just appeared, like it was magic. And the first time she ever met him, so momentous a day it ended with the miracle of snow. And then another time, in other snow, when he'd simply appeared once more.

We are meant to be, Jesus, she told the Christ-child, *you've made something too precious to destroy. Give me one more miracle, I beg of you. Bring my Ben home.*

Mass had been long but she hadn't minded so much today. She was still full of Christmas prayer, the only defence she had against her grief and loneliness. It could be worse, she told herself, you could be Thuy.

No, at least Thuy knew her man was safe, even if he wasn't actually 'her man'.

She'd gone home after dinner last night and Poppy hated to think of her alone on Christmas Day, but understood too. Rosemary and Angus would be there later which was company for her, however torturous.

She was alone now herself, having caught the train back to university, lugging a bag of presents and Christmas cake. She supposed she'd study, or play the cello. Anything to stem the sad flow of her heart that moved in a constant teeter from angst to yearning. Missing Spike, missing Ben. Tired now of the endless waiting.

There was no sign of life at the dorms, just a door and a stairwell and an empty room filled with clutter and dust. And an envelope.

Poppy dropped her bag and picked it up off her pillow. It was red and had a Christmas sticker on it and she ripped it open to scan the lines of her own words, written long ago when she promised this wait. Then she turned it over and on the back were new words in bright green ink. *I made it.*

Poppy turned slowly as a noise sounded behind her, the step of an army boot. And he was simply there, like a miracle once more, hair catching the sun.

'Ben,' she whispered, rushing into his arms and he held her tight. He felt like Ben, he smelt like Ben, he tasted like Ben. 'You're real,' she sobbed.

'It's okay, it's okay,' he soothed, stroking her hair, kissing her deeply, drinking her in. 'I'm home, Poppy Marie. The wait is over.'

Then she laughed with joy so great she felt as if she would burst and he lifted her in his arms, carrying her to the bed to bare their bodies, to taste each other's skin in that glorious afternoon light. Passion and love combining.

Lying together afterwards both knew the hardest part of the wait was over. Whatever came after this was nothing compared to what they'd already endured. It was their turn for happiness; their turn for a life of their own choosing.

Now that duty was done.

Forty-Three

Coffs Harbour, New South Wales, Australia, 21 July 1969

The beach house was really just a heavily extended shack that the twin's grandpa GP had left to them in his will but it held a special place in Poppy's heart – which made it special to Ben too. The twins had been devastated at the old guy's passing a few months back, and Ben regretted he'd never got to meet him. But now that they were here he could feel GP's eccentric personality surround him. The place was a bit lopsided, to be sure, and there was nothing artistic about the wonky stairs and patched up walls. But what it lacked in style it made up for in location, sitting smack on the beach at Sawtell, just south of the main town of Coffs Harbour. Barrel couldn't seem to believe his luck, running and rolling with delight down on the sand in front, making passers-by laugh.

'Want some?' Cat offered, gesturing to a bong on the table that he'd just finished smoking.

'Better not,' Ben said. He'd been getting into it a bit too much lately and didn't want to do anything stupid now that he only had a year and a half of service left. Fortunately, he didn't look likely to see any more action, spending most of his time in logistics, his first-hand knowledge considered quite an asset to the pen-pushers downtown. It wasn't harming his future legal career either and he knew his father had a lot to do with the cushy, advantageous posting.

Pity he couldn't speed things up with his divorce, which was proving to be not only nasty, as predicted, but incredibly slow. Barbara wanted everything she could squeeze out of him, unsurprisingly, trying to tag all sorts such of terms like 'wife basher' and 'violent aggressor' onto his name. He'd never laid a hand on her, of course, but the latter label didn't sit well on his conscience, memories of crimson blood on white floors coming to mind. His parents were barely talking to him as result of the accusations, not because they believed her; they were just furious at the damage to the family reputation.

Ben didn't really care about that – he'd paid far too much as it was to be a Williamson, but he did care that it was delaying his ability to marry Poppy. She shared the bed in his new apartment a lot of the time, and her heart without restraint, but he wanted her to share his entire life. It was too hard trying to cope with normalcy after war alone. He needed more. He needed all of her.

'I've got something lined up for tonight; something special,' Cat was saying and Ben hesitated again. He guessed it was acid, something he'd tried once before, unbeknownst to Poppy, and it was far better than he'd expected. Like a beautiful dream that you walked through, unlike the night terrors that plagued him, no fears or memories to find.

The dogs of war couldn't chew when you simply packed your mind up and took it on a trip.

Unfortunately life wasn't so kind. At least the other guys were out of uniform most of the time now, although they all had army reserve commitments one weekend a month. Ben had to put up with dirty stares on the street on a regular basis and he found that hard to fathom – why were the public blaming the soldiers for doing their job? Did they think they enjoyed it, watching men fall to their deaths? The crawl of liquid fire? For all they'd been through the only thanks they'd got was a half-arsed parade and a few bars on their pockets that acknowledged they'd been to war. Angus said he didn't even tell anyone any more. These days no-one wanted to admit they'd been involved in Vietnam.

Personally, he blamed the media who'd televised stuff the public shouldn't have to see. It was bad enough the soldiers had to live with it – why give everyone else the nightmares? Unless it brought an end to it all, he supposed. Maybe if there'd been television in 1914 there wouldn't have been any modern warfare; no Anzacs, no diggers, no Rats of Tobruk or Kokoda heroes. No Vietnam vets who hid their faces and melted away, ashamed they ever wore the same uniform.

Ben hated it what it did to them and what it was doing to him, too. Outsiders in their own country, ostracised and made to feel guilty for facing death every day and doing what their country had asked of them; knowing it was unlikely anyone thought about Spike and Body sacrificing their lives at the going down of the sun.

Sometimes it felt as if they were still at war, watching each other's backs, keeping each man going. It had certainly followed them home, and only other veterans could possibly understand how alien that made you feel, to still have battles raging internally as you walked down peaceful, if hostile, streets. To think you'll at least be accepted back, if not honoured or revered, only to find out you're the new scapegoat. The enemy.

'I'll think about it,' he told Cat. Maybe it wouldn't hurt, just one more hit. He could use a fearless dream.

It's one small step for man…one giant leap for mankind.

Ben watched the astronaut take a slow step onto the moon's surface and saw Angus flinch. Three, two, one. He shook it away, trying to concentrate on images of the moon and the man up there, right now, making history for his species. Another story coming through that too-real television screen, only this was a pretty one. This step would be popular. It would be remembered with respect.

'How incredible that we can see it,' Poppy said softly. Her expression was filled with wonder and Ben took her hand, kissing her fingers.

'Imagine their view of us.' Poppy's eyes were round as she considered it, taking in the astronaut's second step.

'Reckon they flipped it for going first?' Jimmy said.

'Nuh, I reckon he just said "look over there" and legged it,' Zach Hall said and the others laughed. It was good to have his old mate from Duntroon on this holiday, although the knowledge that his cousin Sam was doing active service weighed heavily upon the vets in the room. Zach had been spared thus far, having broken his arm badly when skiing then undergoing two operations since. He was worried about Sam, of course, but he held an aura of naivety and good cheer about him that made it obvious he was yet to face live warfare himself. He reminded Ben of Spike in the early days – a little too much at times.

'Well, it won't hurt Nixon's popularity; space race punters – we have a winner,' Jimmy declared, toasting the television.

Cat mumbled something about capitalism but even the greatest of cynics couldn't help but be impressed by this moment. Neil

Armstrong bounced his way across the moon's surface and Ben squeezed Poppy's hand as she wiped a tear away.

Of all the aspects of the fight between east and west for political domination of earth right now this, at least, was a peaceful win as Buzz Aldrin joined Armstrong in placing an American flag. It barely moved in the lunar atmosphere and Ben had a moment of surrealistic wonder himself, imagining what it must feel like, to walk upon the sphere that had watched over mankind since their time began; illuminating the sky to keep them safe at night. Guiding the tides and lulling them to sleep. Like a gentle brother to the sun as it rose and set over a more mysterious, darkened world.

And now here it was in their lounge rooms, those distant craters beneath human feet; holding men at last on that silvered surface, which looked to be covered in some kind of powdery, ancient dust.

'It's beautiful,' Rosemary whispered and the room hushed to silence as the American president himself spoke to the astronauts via telephone.

'…as you talk to us from a sea of tranquillity, it inspires us to bring peace and tranquillity to earth.'

Ben's mind went out to Sam Hall, somewhere in a Vietnamese jungle no doubt, probably unaware that men walked on the moon above him. Facing the darkest depths of man's greed for control of the fragile blue marble they all sailed upon. Peace and tranquillity mere words, just floating in space.

'Well, who's up for tea?' Poppy asked after a while and Thuy went with her to put the kettle on. It was only early afternoon – too soon for drinking beer – although not for bongs, apparently. Cat was mulling some grass in the bowl as Angus looked warily on. Rosemary didn't seem too bad to Ben but Poppy said she hid it well, especially from her fiancé. Sure enough she declined a smoke now and Cat shrugged, passing it to Daniella.

'Happy birthday to you,' Poppy sang, walking in with a cake and candles, Thuy following with the tea.

Ben laughed, shaking his head as they all joined in and Barrel barked with excitement. 'You already gave me a party on the day.'

'I know but I have another big present to give you that I was saving for up here. Hurry up and blow the candles out!' Poppy said, dragging out a large gift from behind the couch.

Ben did as he was instructed and scratched his head at the package. 'What have you been up to now?' He began to peel off the sticky tape carefully and Poppy gave him a look. 'Oh, all right,' he said, laughing and tearing away now. Then he stood back, genuinely stunned. It was an easel, with canvases, paint and brushes and even some turpentine and linseed oil.

'Did I miss anything?' Poppy asked.

Ben could barely speak he was so touched. 'Only this,' he said, drawing her over for a hug and a kiss.

'Aww,' Daniella and Rosemary said and Zach picked up a brush.

'So it's to be a depraved art-fest up here is it? Bags being first nude model.'

'I don't think she bought enough white,' Jimmy said, picking up a tube and laying it alongside Zach's pale winter skin.

'Hey, don't pick on a poor country bloke. It's cold enough to freeze the balls off a brass monkey back in Echuca.'

'You didn't tell me he had monkey balls,' Jimmy said to Ben.

'That's it, I'm going for a sunbake and a one-armed swim,' Zach declared. 'Who's with me?'

'No thanks,' Cat said, shuddering, 'way too cold.'

'Should be alright for old monkey balls here,' Jimmy said and Zach swatted him with a towel.

'Sixty-eight Fahrenheit on average during winter,' Poppy said. 'That's twenty degrees Celsius.'

'That so, professor?' Ben said.

'Oh hush,' she said. 'You knew I was a dag when you met me.'

'And yet here I am, four years later, and standing in the house of your rodent-eating grandpa,' he said, pulling her back into his arms as the others clambered down the stairs, Barrel in tow.

'Yes you are,' she said, kissing him lightly and smiling. 'Now come on, let's set this up somewhere. I was thinking on the back verandah.'

Ben picked up the easel, following her, suddenly keen to get started. Maybe he didn't need any drugs to keep the fears away after all. Maybe a brushstroke was the first small step for this man towards that giant leap back into mankind.

'You're very quiet,' Rosemary said as they walked along the beach, sea spray misting in her long hair as it whipped about in the breeze.

'Am I?' Angus knew he was, of course. It was hard to keep excusing it away but he tried. 'Just a bit tired. Anyway, you're one to talk – where's my crazy girl got to today?'

'I'm still here. Just a bit tired too.'

That worried him but he refrained from comment.

'You jumped, when Armstrong took his first step.'

'Did I?'

She nodded and he attempted to explain in a way she could understand. 'My nerves are still a bit raw, I suppose. Slow, careful steps bring back bad memories.'

She held his hand. 'I can only imagine.'

'Sometimes it just comes out of nowhere. A car backfired the other day and…' He stopped himself, too ashamed to admit the rest.

'…and what?'

'It doesn't matter.' Finding himself face down in the gutter with his hands over his head had been one of the most humiliating moments of his life, but she didn't need to know that. Truth was he felt like an imposter everywhere he went, pretending to live a normal life – fixing cars in the workshop and buying milk at the corner store. But it was as if he walked in a false landscape and wore false clothes, for a soldier lived inside this civilian now. Angus feared he always would.

In fact, for some strange, disconcerting reason, it was only when he did his army reserve service that he felt like himself, perhaps because re-assimilation was just too much of a shock to the system. Perhaps because he couldn't return to being the innocent man he was, nor could he get used to this new version of himself, this 'veteran', but he did know how to be a soldier. Yes, he knew that role all too well.

'Angus,' she said, stopping to take both hands now. 'You have to open up a bit to me. I can handle it, you know.'

'You've got enough to deal with, getting through your final year and staying...focused.'

'Oh God, not this again.'

'You're still so vague and you don't answer the phone sometimes and I...'

'I told you, I've stopped,' she said dropping his hands and walking on.

'Everything?'

She nodded and he tried to believe her but she wouldn't meet his eyes.

'You're still so tired all the time...'

'It's the study. Anyway, I thought we were talking about you.'

Angus sighed, sitting down in the sand with Barrel and lighting a cigarette. Rosemary stood nearby, arms folded.

'You talk to Thuy...'

'That's different, she was there. She knows.'

Rosemary stared out to sea and the blue of her eyes reflected the waves, revealing a hurt that he saw too plainly now.

'Come here,' he said and she came over slowly, sitting beside him. 'I've told you before, I don't want you to know. It's just... it's too ugly, and cruel and...and brutal. You haven't had to go through that and I don't want you to see it here.' He brushed the hair from her forehead. 'I don't want to give you my memories, Rosemary, I want you to be happy. That's the best thing you can do for me now.'

'Spike would want that for you, too.' She said it softly, stroking Barrel's ears, and meeting his gaze with those aggrieved blue eyes.

'I know baby, I know.' He pulled her into his arms and they lay down together, watching the clouds run across the sky as light raindrops began to find the wind. 'I'm trying.'

She held him close for a long hug. 'Me too.'

It was technically good but there was more to it than that. The composition drew the eye from Angus and Rosemary sitting on the sand to the horizon and there was real emotion in the grey and blue brushstrokes that captured the winter sky, so skilfully you could almost smell the oncoming rain.

'What will you call it?' Jimmy asked.

'Not sure,' Ben said, shrugging.

'Something about the weather, I suppose.'

'Petrichor,' Poppy said. 'Er...that's the word they use to describe the scent of rain hitting the earth. It's Greek.'

'*Petra* means stone and *ichor* is the fluid that runs through the veins of the gods,' Rosemary added. 'See? I know more about the Greeks than just togas,' she told Angus and he smiled in memory.

'It feels like the scene's filled with anticipation, which works,' Jimmy said. 'What?' he added, looking around at the surprised, half-amused faces of the group. 'Aren't I allowed to have an appreciation of the arts?'

Ben raised his eyebrows. 'Both allowed and appreciated in return. You're right, it does work; *Petrichor* it is.'

He began cleaning his brushes and Thuy looked at one of the sketches he'd left scattered on the table. 'You do these in Vietnam?'

'Yeah, I kept a journal too. It helped pass the time.'

'He might even get around to showing me one day,' Poppy said, helping him clean up.

'One day,' he said, and she rolled her eyes.

'You very good,' Thuy told him, picking one up. 'What this called?'

'"Liquid Fire",' he told her.

'Napalm?' she asked and he nodded. Thuy dropped it quickly, like it actually burned, and hesitantly picked up another.

'This Vung Tau?'

Ben nodded again, rubbing each brush with a rag.

'Is this where you are from?' Rosemary asked her, looking at the detailed drawing of a girl selling food at a market.

'Yes,' Thuy said, a pained expression crossing her features.

'It looks like a busy place; did you work there?'

Thuy nodded, her eyes full now.

'Are you missing it?' Rosemary said gently, touching her arm.

'No.' The answer was swift and Thuy turned and walked away in a rush, embarrassed by her tears, Poppy supposed.

'Sorry,' Rosemary said to no-one in particular and a strained silence followed, then Angus put his arm around her.

'That's Thuy in the drawing. She had a pretty rough life over there – harder than you can imagine. Don't feel bad, you weren't to know.'

'What did she sell?' Rosemary asked, picking up the image and peering closer.

'Sweet-Cakes,' Ben, Angus and Jimmy all said in unison and a few grins were exchanged.

Rosemary looked at Angus questioningly. 'Nickname, was it?'

'Kind of,' he hedged. 'She made them right there on the street. They were pretty yum, let me tell you.'

'Maybe she could make some for us.'

'I don't think we should ask that of her,' he said, shaking his head. 'Might bring back too many memories.'

'God forbid we delve into any of those around here,' Rosemary said, sarcasm lacing her tone as she put the picture down.

Angus frowned at her. 'You just don't understand.'

'No, that's the whole problem, isn't it?'

'Hey...' Angus said as she began to walk away.

'You know something,' she flung at them all as she turned back around, 'it's like a private little boys club with you guys, with Thuy the only girl allowed in.'

'I keep telling you, I don't want you to know...' Angus said.

'Maybe that shouldn't be up to you,' she retorted angrily.

'You want to know? *Really?*' Angus returned, his normally calm demeanour vanishing. 'That woman next to her, here –' he pointed at the drawing, '– that's her mother who she watched die after her father and brother were shot. And there's the farm where it happened,' he said, picking up another sketch of a tree and tossing it across towards her. 'That's where my brother's guitar lies in the ground next to her dead family. We buried it there while they flew his body home to my parents who didn't even *know* he was bloody well there...who didn't know...' His voice broke and Poppy's heart ached for him as he fought against tears. Then he turned to run down the stairs and onto the beach, back hunched against the rain.

'No,' Ben stilled Rosemary's arm as she looked set to follow, 'he needs this. Let him cry it out for a while.'

'He never told me that,' she said sadly, 'about his mum and dad.'

'Angus saw himself as a third parent to Spike a lot of the time,' Ben said. 'I'd say he feels guilty.'

'Maybe that's why he won't go home to Broome to see them,' Rosemary said, watching his retreating figure as he walked along the shore.

'Probably. Anyway, at least you know that much now. Might help you to understand what he's going through a little more.'

Rosemary's expression was pained. 'How am I supposed to understand any of it when I wasn't there and he won't tell me anything? How can I help him…?'

'Let the boys club look after that,' Ben advised and Jimmy nodded too.

'We understand, lucky bastards that we are,' Jimmy said bitterly.

'You don't have to help him on your own, we'll all get him through this – together,' Poppy told her, noticing her shiver now. 'Come on, let's go inside for a nice cup of tea and maybe a bit of a chat.'

But as the rain settled in and the man in the distance began to fade Rosemary seemed to be fading too.

'Did you hear me, Rosemary?' Poppy said, her concern building.

'Yes,' Rosemary sighed, looking suddenly exhausted. 'Might just have a lie down instead.'

'That sounds like a good idea,' Poppy said, watching her walk inside and stumble slightly before Jimmy took her arm.

'Careful,' he said, before going inside too, leaving Poppy and Ben alone.

'She's on something, I can tell.'

He didn't disagree, putting the brushes down. 'Watch her tonight,' he advised. 'Don't leave her alone with Cat and Daniella.'

'They promised they wouldn't give her anything anymore.'

'People promise a lot of things when they're sober.'

They packed the artwork away in silence then, stacking canvases and sheets.

'*Petrichor*,' Ben said, taking one last look at his painting. 'Fluid from the gods' veins meeting stone. That's really very clever, Poppy.'

'It's the Greeks,' she said vaguely, staring at her sister's image in paint. 'They usually got things about right.' But it was Rosemary's veins she was thinking about and the fluids they might find. Drugs that could turn her sister to stone.

Forty-Four

Led Zepplin was belting out 'Communication Breakdown' from the stereo and Thuy was listening, trying not to be shocked by the sexual innuendo of the lyrics. It was a primal, lust-fuelled sound and she couldn't say she quite understood it, although it did make her feel restless for some reason, wishing Angus hadn't gone to bed. Sneaking looks at him when she felt like this were the only pleasures she allowed herself when it came to the opposite sex. And even that much made her feel guilty – after all he was an engaged man.

Robert Plant continued his open assault on Thuy's senses and she wondered what was going on behind the bedroom door in front. It was very late – almost one by her watch. She'd have been long asleep by now only Rosemary had emerged just as Thuy was about to go to bed, disappearing with Daniella and Cat into that room. They were 'druggies', Thuy knew, and not just the smoking kind.

Everyone else was sound asleep, including Barrel who was snoring on the couch, leaving her alone with the music and her worries. She took the vow seriously that she'd made last year; Thuy would take care of Rosemary whenever it was necessary. Hearing a thud through the wall she hoped this wasn't one of those times.

Thuy stood up and turned down the music, supposing one of them would come out to complain, but no-one did. Then there was another thud and she waited. Suddenly Rosemary staggered out the door, her face pale and covered in sweat, and she was hardly even upright as she fell into the room.

'Ang-gus!' Thuy screamed, grabbing her. 'Ang-gus, come now!'

Footsteps sounded and someone was shouting 'What the fuck did he give her?'

Then someone else was speaking urgently into the phone, saying the words 'heroin' and 'overdose' but Thuy didn't register who it was. She saw nothing but Angus's anguish as he held his fiancée close, stroking her face, begging her to breathe. Then the music was drowned out by the wail of a siren and Barrel was barking as they strapped Rosemary on a stretcher and wheeled her away.

'Please God, no, please no,' she heard Angus say, following close, and Poppy wept alongside, terror on her face.

Thuy loved Rosemary, like a sister too, she supposed, but that night it felt more like hate. How could she inject such a drug into her veins, let it burn through her like that liquid fire? How could she do this to her twin? To the kind man with the broken heart and the forest in his eyes?

How could anyone call that love?

She went outside to the ocean, to stare at the moon and ask Buddha to give her strength, remembering there were people on that magic pearl tonight for the very first time. Perhaps staring back, thinking about the choices of man. Creatures so smart they can build rocket ships and dance across lunar holes, but so foolish they've also made holes in their own planet. Holes in their arms to poison their blood. Holes in each other's hearts.

Thuy made her peace then, with Rosemary, remembering she was sick. That it was her worry over Angus that drove her to numb her pain. But whatever happened now he would need better than that; more than someone else's fear and self-destruction. He would need the best traits of humanity to shine in those he loved, like those first ever dreamers who reached for the moon. People who would tell him anything was achievable if you believed hard enough. That strong hearts could conquer all – even this war.

That *sự-tự-do* was possible on the inside too.

And to give that to someone else was, truly, love.

Part Five

The White Room

Forty-Five

Sydney, May 1970

'What do we want?'

'No more war!'

'When do we want it?

'Now!'

Hippies, businessmen, housewives. People. They filled the streets to overflowing, moving along in a united sea of humankind, calling in one voice for peace.

They marched in rows, holding signs and each other's hands, carrying flowers and many wearing badges with slogans like 'ban the bomb' and 'give peace a chance'. Then they began to sing the John Lennon/Yoko Ono song and Poppy joined in, squeezing Rosemary's hand and looking over at her twin with an enormous sense of gratitude. It was mostly for Rosemary's life, of course, but the fact that her sister's release from rehab had coincided with the moratorium seemed like some kind of divine justice. After all, it was her fear for Angus that had caused her to choose drugs in the first place.

All over the country people were rallying in their hundreds of thousands in support of troop withdrawal and an end to the war, sending one loud collective message. They were calling it 'people power' and Poppy could feel it today more than ever, flowing like a river down Pitt Street as well as every other capital city in Australia this weekend. It was coinciding with other protests around the world and she knew it would have an impact on the powers that be. They just couldn't possibly ignore this.

One Australian battalion had already been withdrawn as part of the 'Vietnamisation' process, as the American president termed it, essentially the gradual bolstering of the South Vietnamese army to allow them to fend for themselves and the slow withdrawal of foreign troops. Not good enough, according to the public.

Cat had turned up with Daniella, clean too, after six months in jail. He'd been a 'conscientious objector', as termed by activists, 'draft dodger' according to people like her parents, one of many who chose to sit in prison rather than go to war. He'd told Poppy he would never forgive himself for what happened to Rosemary and she'd believed him, but she still couldn't really look at the man. Daniella was off all drugs as well these days, no longer 'chasing the dragon' as people termed it. It not only terrified Poppy, it saddened her to think that this new generation were embracing this old poison, an abomination of the gentle poppy flower that symbolised the Anzacs. Poppy wondered how her namesake would be remembered now – as an icon of respect or an icon of addiction. A war flower in more ways than one.

The mounted police were out in force today but there had been no violence so far, just a few cheeky girls running up to put flowers on saddles, which met with smiles more than anything else. Not so in some American rallies, she'd heard, although the flowers there were placed in soldiers' rifles and tensions ran high when such marches were attended by millions.

Neither Ben nor Angus were here. Ben said he wasn't about to turn up in uniform after work to be spat on and called a 'baby-killer' again, like at the last rally, and Angus tended to avoid anything to do with the war these days. However the two couples were meeting up later and Poppy felt elated by the fact. It had been a long time coming waiting to be reunited as a foursome.

Rosemary had spent last night with Angus and seemed happy again, wearing a ring of flowers in her long hair like she used to do and giving the peace symbol to anyone who looked their way. No-one would think she'd been a 'junkie' only last year, her skin now glowing, her legs no longer resembling sticks. It seemed their parents' money had been well spent at the expensive clinic they'd sent Rosemary to in the mountains, not that anyone knew that's where she'd been of course. 'On extended holiday' had been the official Flannery line.

Someone began beating a drum and people began to clap as well as sing. The joyful sound floated down the city streets, bringing tears to Poppy's eyes as she thought of Spike, stepping across a field that fateful day. Lying forever in a grave over in Broome. Then she thought about Thuy, seeing her family killed, imagining how many orphans this war would leave. How much cost. Someone had told her recently there were more craters in Vietnam than on the moon, a terrible irony when you considered man's potential for greatness against his potential for destruction.

Boom, boom, boom. Yes, end it all now, God; bring them home. Let the politicians fight their own wars in boardrooms and parliament. Keep the youths of the world out of such folly.

Rosemary nudged her then pointed and they watched as some young men stood in a circle and burned their draft papers, wishing with all her heart Angus had done the same. If he'd never gone Spike surely wouldn't have followed. Still, at least these men would be spared now. Even jail was better than war.

Looking around her she had that feeling again, the gratitude returning, and with it an enormous sense of love for her fellow man. This was the best of her generation, the best of the cultural revolution the war had accelerated. And there was a shift in the world, happening today. It was time for peace to have a fighting chance.

He was smearing again, first his mind, with pot, then the canvas, with paint, running his brush across the white in a film of oil, finding memories in the darkest corners of his heart. It was Poppy's idea, to hold an exhibition, not that she knew he got high most times he painted. That wasn't something you told your partner when drugs had almost taken her sister's life.

Truth was he loved the feeling. Breathing it in was like placing a soothing bandage across his mind, allowing him to freely express whatever it was his soul had to say without thought getting in the way. The brush was gliding in orange and black today, sailing with Puff in a smoke-filled sky. Ben let it go, releasing the memory. Giving it to the canvas.

He only had six months to go in service and it seemed fitting to spend his spare time doing this; collating the experiences he'd endured in the army into a collection of works and putting them on display. There were things that needed to be said, truths that shouldn't be left buried somewhere, in foreign soil. His father didn't exactly approve, of course, but Ben was learning to follow his own rules now and this was another part of his life he was claiming as his own.

His parents were still distant but had thawed towards him somewhat now that the divorce was closer to being finalised. Enough to offer him the servants quarters of their home to be near his old studio, a logical choice now that Barbara looked likely to win the Waverton apartment. Poppy had made it quite homey but he longed for a place of their own. Yet another wait to endure. Still, there were far, far worse things in life, he reflected, glancing at the canvases around him.

The phone rang and he put the brush down, lifting the receiver.

'Hey,' came Angus's voice.

'Hey mate. How are you?'

'Not too bad, not too bad,' he said. 'Rosemary's home.'

'I heard. How good is that?'

'Very,' Angus said. 'You coming tonight?'

'Sure.' Ben waited for him to say something more, wondering what was really up this time.

'See you then,' Angus said abruptly and Ben listened to the dial tone, considering whether or not to call him back. It wasn't the first time he'd received calls from him like that, brief and seemingly pointless, more like a handshake than a conversation. Maybe that's all it was. Maybe he was just reaching out, needing reassurance that he wasn't the only one, Ben figured, looking back at the half-finished artwork. Chasing other dragons away.

Angus placed the phone down, staring at it for a long moment before crossing the room and lighting a cigarette. It had helped, a little. Hearing Ben's voice always did. But it wasn't the voice he really needed to hear and it never would be.

There was a knock at the door, even though they never locked it, and Thuy poked her head in, timid as always about disturbing him.

'Hello?'

'Hi,' he said, taking a beer out of the fridge and sitting down. 'What's up?'

'Nothing,' she said, coming in and watching him closely. She often looked at him like that, almost fearfully these days. 'You okay?'

'Yep,' he lied. He would be soon anyway, when Rosemary got home.

Thuy's eyes flew to the drawer and back again. 'Sure?'

'I'm sure,' Angus said. 'Stop worrying, alright?'

Thuy nodded, still standing and he knew what she wanted to do. 'Have a seat,' he offered and she did so, gratefully.

'Watch football?' she asked.

'Yeah, why not,' he said, turning it on. She couldn't care less about the game of course; she just couldn't bear to leave him alone.

The time passed more easily then, the beer flowing smoothly, the game a good distraction, and Thuy sat quietly throughout, keeping him company until the click of the door came.

'I'm home!' Rosemary exclaimed, running in and launching herself at the couch, throwing her arms around him. 'Ah, it feels *so* good to say that. Oh, hi Thuy, sorry. Didn't see you there.' Rosemary disentangled herself from his lap, looking a bit embarrassed. Seeing the person who found you overdosed for the first time since it happened could make you feel that way, he imagined.

'Hello Rosemary, you look well,' Thuy said quietly, although she seemed relieved.

'Good as new,' Rosemary told her, coming over to kiss her on the cheek. 'I haven't thanked you...you know, for what you did. Poppy told me.'

'It okay,' Thuy said, shaking her head. 'I leave now.'

'See you later,' Angus said, not meeting her eye as she crossed the room and the door closed.

'Got any more of those?' Rosemary opened the fridge, tossing Barrel some leftover pizza and taking out a beer.

'Do you think you should...?'

She turned and gave him a look. 'I was a drug addict not an alco.'

'I know, I know, of course.' Rosemary opened the beer and sipped it, quieter now, and Angus regretted making her feel self-conscious, like the girl he first met. It didn't suit her any more. 'I'm sorry honey, come over here,' he said and she did, gladly, leaning her body against him, her legs up on the couch.

'My favourite place,' she told him, taking his arm around her waist and cuddling close.

'My favourite person,' he returned, leaning over to kiss her mouth. 'Mmm, you taste like beer.'

'Well I must be a man's dream come true then,' she said, laughing.

Angus kissed her again, figuring that much was true. Then again she always had been, to him. She put the beer down and took his hand, leading him to the bed and he followed along, hungry for her now. With Rosemary back maybe he wouldn't need Ben's voice or Thuy's worried eyes. The drawer might stay shut on its own.

Forty-Six

Great Ocean Road, Victoria, Australia, December 1970

Angus was right, this felt bloody great. The rumble of the Harleys was a powerful sound and they were thundering along with the wind in their hair, beautiful women pressed up behind them. It felt incredible to be so free, to embrace that *sự-tự-do*, as Thuy called it. Not soldiers anymore, not even just mere men. Today they felt like kings on thrones; the nature before them their kingdom.

And what nature it was. The towering cliffs that fell below the Great Ocean Road were brilliant in the midday sun; a kaleidoscope of orange, brown and gold, gigantic sets hurling against them in forty feet waves. Ben couldn't wait to paint them. The ocean itself was a wild, churning beast, carried by winds that hailed from the South Pole itself, warmed by a Victorian summer but with traces of chill somewhere therein. It was a brilliant shade of blue that glistened silver where the sun danced and Ben laughed out loud at the sheer beauty of it all.

'Woohoo!' he yelled and Angus let out his Western Australian crow, bringing Spike with them in spirit, at least. Ben looked over at him and they exchanged grins. The dogs of war had been left behind for today; it was too exhilarating for them to come along. Jimmy was here and even Derek had made the trip, his one good arm holding the front of the side-car fast, but he was smiling too. The men from 3RAR were together once more, well four of them anyway, and it felt good to be reunited. Good to be alive.

Jimmy began to sing 'Born to Be Wild' by Steppenwolf and they all joined in; the thrill of the moment needed expressing. Poppy sang along in his ear and he managed to sneak a little kiss, loving the feel of her form through their jackets. The sparkle of the diamond on the hand that lay against his chest. His soon-to-be wife at last.

The sun-drenched miles rolled on and Ben never wanted the time to end but it did, eventually, and they pulled into a pub in search of burgers and beers. Ben would have loved a joint too but that would have to wait.

'Phew, how amazing was that?' Rosemary said, taking off her jacket and loosening her hair. It had whipped into quite a tangle and Angus laughed as she tried to unknot it with her fingers.

'Here,' Poppy said, tossing her a brush, and they went to freshen up.

'How the hell did two jokers like you end up with chicks like that?' Derek asked.

'I told you I'd end up marrying her in Nam,' Angus reminded him.

'Yeah, but you didn't tell me this one had his eye on the twin. Whatever happened to that wife of yours?'

'Divorced,' Ben told him, enjoying that wonderful fact but changing the subject. 'How's the used car business?'

'Good,' Derek said, 'although I'm thinking about buying one of those Harleys now.'

Ben wanted to ask how he'd go about driving one of the bikes but refrained. It was a taboo subject, Derek's missing arm. It had been more badly damaged that day in the minefield than any of them had realised and a full amputation had taken place about a year ago, Jimmy had told them. They were still in touch back in Adelaide occasionally. Derek hadn't mentioned anything about it as yet so no-one else was about to either.

'What are we drinking?' Jimmy asked the table, taking requests and going off to order.

'God, I'm as dry as a bull's bum going up a hill backwards,' Zach Hall declared. He and Sam were home at their adjoining family farms in Echuca for the holidays, only four hours away, so they'd joined up with them all today. Ben had been enjoying their company, although Sam had that look in his eyes now. The same one any vet carried. It seemed Zach was going to get away with not seeing active service at all, what with more and more troops being withdrawn. Ben envied him but was glad too, of course. It made one less of his mates afflicted by war.

Thuy hadn't joined them. She was working in a restaurant now and taking English classes, hoping to become promoted, eventually. Ben was glad for her. She needed her own life. She was far too dependent on Angus and that just wasn't going to end well once the double wedding went ahead in just over a year's time.

'We're back,' Poppy said, looking fresh and lovely as always, and he took her hand, kissing it softly.

'Bloody lovebirds, what's for lunch?' Zach said.

'Oh there are, look,' Rosemary said, going over to take a photo of the lorikeets that sat along the pub wall, the sea glistening behind. Angus's eyes followed her every move and Ben smiled, happy things were working out these days.

He picked up the menu and they ordered seafood, mostly, which seemed a bit more exciting than a burger. It came in baskets, golden mounds of deep-fried fish on a bed of hot chips, and they washed it down with quite a lot of beer. It was a pleasant afternoon after that as they slowly got tipsy and the Hall brothers entertained them.

'He was always a cheating bastard,' Jimmy was saying, laughing as Zach stared at the playing card in his hand, confused by Derek's trick.

'But it was a seven last time,' Zach said. 'Oh, you cheeky son of a…'

Everyone laughed as Derek dropped some of the deck, revealing several more sevens, and he shrugged. 'Deal's a deal.'

Zach handed the ten dollars over muttering something unflattering about used car salesmen and Sam leant over to address the group. 'In fairness, Zach is the king of gullibility. Ask him about Delilah.'

'Who's Delilah?' Jimmy asked immediately.

'She was the love of my life,' Zach said with a sigh. 'Pen pals for years at boarding school, wrote my soul out to that girl, quoting sonnets, confessions of the heart.'

'Whatever happened to her?' Rosemary asked.

'You're looking at her. She was me,' Sam said, to much laughter.

Zach paused dramatically, hand on his chest. 'Toyed with my teenage emotions like a cat with a mouse, cruel bastard.'

'But how did you know what she looked like?' Poppy said, still giggling.

'I stuck a photo of a girl from a magazine in a frame. He's still got it, I think,' Sam told her. 'What was that poem you wrote again?'

'Oh please God, let there be a poem,' Jimmy said.

'My heart, it goes boom, boom, when I think about you in my room,' Sam began, 'I can't wait to kiss your lips, I just hope I do not miss…' He paused. 'What was the next bit?'

Zach grimaced, continuing it for him. 'For my love for you makes me blind, please do not be unkind.'

They finished the rest together. 'I just think you're really swell, you're the turtle in my shell.'

The girls were crying laughing now. 'Why a turtle?' they said in unison.

'A turtle's a perfectly reasonable romantic metaphor,' Zach told them, drinking his beer in feigned offence.

'Ah, God, too much, too much,' Ben told him, shaking his head and wiping his own tears of amusement away. 'Say, where are we staying tonight, by the way?' he asked Jimmy who'd organised this trip.

'Farmhouse down the road. Come on, we'd better go before we get any more sloshed.'

'Bit late for that,' Derek said, swaying as they stood.

They got back on their bikes, driving slowly if unsteadily, and the Hall brothers led them in a rowdy version of 'Delilah' as they went. Ben thought he might fall off from laughter at one point but fortunately it was only a short way off. The 'farmhouse' turned out to be more of a barn than anything, with layered lofts and a lot of hay which Ben found a bit surreal, but in a good way.

'Be back in a minute,' he told Poppy, deciding getting even more surreal would increase the fun and going outside for a smoke. Derek had beaten him to it and they sat together in the dwindling light, swapping stories for a while.

'Watch out for snakes,' Derek yelled and Ben saw Rosemary walk past to the outdoor toilet, too late, but he put the joint out anyway.

'What are you naughty boys up to?' she called but didn't stop.

Derek peered in the dark after her. 'Should we offer her a smoke?'

'Definitely not,' Ben said, 'she, er...had a bit of a problem a while back. Don't mention it to anyone actually, if you don't mind.'

'Yes, sir,' Derek said, saluting like in the war days, and Ben went back inside. He doubted Rosemary would say anything to Poppy; drugs weren't exactly something she ever liked to discuss.

Poppy wasn't sure what woke her but she went down to the barn door anyway, trying to see out into the inky night. There were figures in the paddock and now someone was yelling.

'You're a low-life bastard, Derek, and you always were!'

'She was asking for it.'

'You should have said no.'

'Angus, stop, please...'

'I can't believe my brother died because of you. It should have been the other way around.'

Then there was the sound of a fist on flesh and Rosemary screamed and Ben came running out. Then Poppy ran too, to find Rosemary crouched on the ground where Angus lay, panting hard and lip bleeding.

'Where is he?' Ben demanded.

'He's run off that way...just leave it,' Angus said. 'Let him go.'

Poppy looked at Rosemary, shocked to see her dress was torn and there seemed to be a scratch on her face. And even the pale moonlight was enough to show that her eyes seemed unfocused and she looked to be very stoned.

'What did you have?' Poppy said.

'Just pot...'

'I don't believe you.'

'I swear, ask Ben...'

'Why should we do that?' Angus said, turning to stare at Ben.

'Yes, why?' Poppy said, staring too.

Then he lowered his chin and confessed. 'I had some as well.'

'With Rosemary?' Poppy said, incredulous.

'Of course not.'

'We'll deal with this later. Come on, let's get her into bed,' Poppy said, too angry with him to discuss it further now. Once she couldn't have cared less if he'd smoked marijuana but that was back when it was something harmless; a mystery ingredient. A Christmas surprise in June. Now it was a drop of poison in her sister's veins that were parched for drugs' venomous flow. To know it was near her, to have it yourself, was like throwing a match near petrol hoping they wouldn't make fire.

She'd forgive him tomorrow, Poppy supposed, somewhere on that ocean road, but right now she needed to watch over her twin. And pray the chemicals running through her now were like one-off spots of rain. A false petrichor with no storm to follow; no danger of finding stone.

Forty-Seven

Sydney, February 1971

The photo sat taped to the easel as Ben worked, tracing the young man's face in oil, immortalising him because it was the only thing he could do for him now. He might be just a body in a mass grave in a Vietnamese killing field but Ben imagined him alive as he painted, giving him forgiveness, like Poppy, giving him strength, like Thuy. Giving him a gun, like Angus.

He'd found him a few days ago, sitting there and holding it before shoving it back in the drawer.

'What the hell are you doing?' Ben had asked him.

'Nothing,' Angus had said. 'Just, you know, cleaning it.'

Ben had promptly gone home and thrown all his own guns away, advising Angus to do the same. Now he called his mate every day. Little wonder Thuy visited so often, sitting in that chair. Ben understood it now – she was watching Angus for a reason.

He'd told Poppy what he saw and she said she'd talk to Rosemary only he was pretty sure she hadn't, probably not wanting to give her any more things to worry about. Rosemary didn't handle problems very well, they all knew. Poppy said she was pretty sure Rosemary was clean at the moment but it was hard to tell. She wore a lot of make-up these days and the hippy threads she got around in hid her frame.

Ben sighed, putting the brush down. He found it hard to paint without the pot so he was hardly one to point fingers. Poppy had made him promise not to smoke it anymore and he could hardly refuse, all things considered. He poured himself a scotch instead, the nasty liquid burning, but it helped him relax after a while and he picked up the brush once more.

It was the last of the paintings he'd been finalising over summer for the big exhibition, an event he'd entitled 'Warflower'. He'd never forgotten the term from Poppy's letter. It seemed appropriate to use it, he was a survivor after all, and immortalising people who had died in oil kind of made them survivors too. Spike was there in a few, and Body, and now this nameless North Vietnamese man. It kept them all alive somehow for Ben. Kept him alive too. Without his art he wouldn't be doing nearly as well, that much he knew, and he was grateful for Poppy's thoughtfulness. And her understanding. For everything about her, really.

He looked over at her portrait, one he'd made with the actual letters she'd written to him in Vietnam imbedded in a glossy gel medium, raining down around her as she stood in the middle of a war zone, pristine in white. He hadn't shown it to her yet – it was his masterwork. It would be unveiled the night of the opening this weekend.

Ben poured himself another drink, thinking about the press that would be there along with a bunch of arty types the twins knew from university. It was turning out to be quite a big deal – even his parents were coming. Of course he was still expected to commence his law degree next month, it went without saying, but art was his true passion. He knew he'd never let it go now.

Ben picked up a tube of paint, adding to the palette, filling more tins with turpentine and oil. Then he dipped his brush, coating it finely, the old routine a comfort beyond measure each time he performed it. It made the other rules fade, another precious condition he'd managed to win in this newly negotiated life, and that fit just fine. Like a second skin.

Thuy was tired but she couldn't relax until she looked in on next door, equally worried about both of late. It broke her heart to watch them, like a slowly crumbling wall, each failing to hold up the sides. Angus was sad and Rosemary couldn't reach him – it was really as simple as that – but they struggled along alone, missing each other even when they were in the same room and Thuy could only sit and watch, futile to help. The three of them together, stuck on that wall. Trying to keep it intact.

'Hello,' she said, knocking as usual before entering, hoping they were home and safe. He wasn't, maybe still downstairs in the workshop, but Rosemary was, asleep in their bed, and Thuy checked on her before putting the restaurant leftovers in the fridge. Then she wrote a note that said 'dinner' with an arrow and left it on the bench, quietly making her way back out.

She returned to her own side, surprised to see her door wide open and Angus sitting within.

'Hey,' he said. He didn't usually just make himself at home like that. Then she realised he was very drunk and Thuy hung up her jacket, watching him.

'You drink today?' she asked and he nodded, looking tireder than even she felt, and his kind, forest eyes were bloodshot as he raised them towards her.

'Spike's birthday,' he told her. 'Woulda been twenty-five today. Two, five,' he said, holding up the same number of fingers.

Thuy sat down on the couch in the neat little room, waiting for more.

'You know what pisses me off…sorry, what annoys me the most? He didn't even get to go surfing over there. Kept talking 'bout it, never went.' Barrel waddled through the door and he leant over unsteadily to pat him. 'Hey, Barrel, hey little mate.'

'You want cup of tea?' Thuy offered.

'No…you know what I want? I want a question answered. Jus' one little question,' he declared. 'Why'd he haveta go over there? *Why*?' He held his hands up in the air helplessly then shook his head. 'Wasn't even 'sposed to be there but he came for me. You know? For me. Then he goes and gets killed…'

'Ang-gus…'

His face twisted in pain. 'It's my fault Thuy…shouldn't have been him that died…shoulda been *me*…'

'Don't say this,' Thuy said, wincing against the hurt of the words.

Angus looked at her and reached out his hand. 'Shoulda been me, Thuy,' he said, starting to cry. She came over and sat down, taking it, and he leant over to rest his head on her shoulder. 'Shoulda been me.'

'No, please Ang-gus. Please not be so sad.' She dared to stroke his head and he let out a shuddering sigh.

'I love you,' he mumbled before passing out. Thuy froze, barely daring to move as he rolled his head onto the couch, sound asleep, then she found her feet, standing in a daze. He'd never said anything like that before, nothing even close. Barely even touching her until right now.

Then she heard a sound and turned towards the still open door where Rosemary stood, staring at his face. Then her gaze met hers and Thuy felt that wall crumble, just a little bit more.

It was beautiful in every possible way. Poppy had filled the place with flowers and plates of expensive cheeses and the wine and beer flowed around the crowded room. Ben had been nervous at first, especially when he unveiled the major work, but the crowd response had been extremely enthusiastic. Already words like 'genius' and 'Archibald' were being thrown about and Ben noticed his mother looking at his paintings with actual interest. Even his father had said something positive, calling the painting of the dragon 'rather intriguing'. Ben really couldn't have been happier with the entire evening – even Rosemary seemed okay after a shaky incident last week when Poppy had found her stoned again, this time in the park. But she seemed fine tonight and Angus seemed to be engrossed in the artworks, which was important to Ben so, in all, it was a pretty massive relief after all the tension and build up.

'You did it,' Poppy whispered in his ear, kissing his cheek. 'I'm so proud, beautiful man.'

'You're the beautiful one,' he said, and he meant it. She looked stunning in a backless halter-neck gown, the silver and white material making her look like a queen. Her parents had looked a bit scandalised but kept any comments to themselves. After all the drama surrounding Rosemary he supposed they were growing more tolerant in some ways. They'd even accepted him into the family, despite the terrible tag of 'divorce' to his name, although he was starting to suspect that was because Lois was more than a little impressed by his family's wealth. This whole art gig didn't seem to be doing him any harm either.

'It reminds me of Cezanne,' he overheard Lois say to his mother who nodded in agreement. Ben had to smile, knowing his style had nothing at all in common with the great master's work.

Angus had been staring at one of the paintings for some time and Ben looked over, wondering if he should speak to him about it.

'Go,' Poppy said, following his gaze, and he kissed her once more before moving off.

It was a medium-sized piece portraying a woman selling fruit beneath palm trees and a very blue sky but there were cages underneath the ground, filled with men with terrified eyes.

'*Surface Dweller*,' Angus said. 'Clever.'

'Thanks.'

Angus took a sip of his beer. 'I sometimes wonder about her. Imagine what she says to her husband before she trots off to work: "Just off to the stall near the poo hole. Hope no-one falls in today".'

'Hope no soldiers run out from behind the tree and kill anyone. Terrible for business when they do that,' Ben added.

Angus made an amused noise, lighting a cigarette and offering one to Ben. 'Smoke?'

'Cheers.'

He lit it for him then drew heavily himself before continuing. 'It's weird to think of it, isn't it? That they're still over there, these people. That they actually live in Nam and probably will do, forever.'

'Assuming they're still alive.'

'Exactly.'

Ben nodded. 'It is weird. Still, at least our guys are getting pulled out, although I can't understand why it's taking so bloody long.'

'Politicians,' Angus said, shrugging, 'Spike always said they could use some yundi and a surf – the whole lot of them, with the exception of Harold Holt.'

Ben laughed. 'That sounds like him.'

'Yeah. He sure was a funny bugger,' Angus said with a sad smile.

'Bloody crazy sometimes too. Did you see that one sold?' Ben pointed his cigarette at a picture of Spike running across a rubber plantation, throwing a grenade in a hole.

Angus nodded. 'I figured I should buy something; after all we did go through all this bullshit together.'

Ben looked at him, touched. 'Wow – that's...well that's just perfect actually, but there's no way you're paying for it.'

'We're always paying for it, that's the whole point isn't it?' Angus said quietly, then he forced another smile. 'Forget about the money. He's my brother and I bloody want it and that's that. Another drink?' he added.

'Sure.'

Ben watched Angus melt into the crowd, thinking about the truth in his words. They would always be paying for it, it was true, till the end of their days, but you could choose the price; that was an amendment to the rule. Looking around the room Ben knew he'd found a means, now, to meet that end. A way to release those chewing dogs and keep this soldier alive.

His eyes landed on Poppy, laughing at something someone was saying on the other side of the room, more precious to him than any being on earth, and he knew her love for him was what had really brought him this far. Given colour to the grey man.

She wasn't just the woman he loved any more, she was the person giving him life.

Angus nodded. "I figured I should buy something after all we did. [illegible] all this building [illegible]."

Ben looked at him [illegible]. "Wow [illegible] well that's just perfect actually. But there's no way [illegible] paying for it."

"We're [illegible] paying for it. That's the whole point [illegible] and [illegible] other [illegible]. Forget about [illegible]. [illegible]"

[illegible]

[illegible] the end of [illegible] around the price that [illegible] looking around the room [illegible] to make sure that [illegible] and keep [illegible].

[illegible]

[illegible] on the other side [illegible] to turn [illegible] and the [illegible] what [illegible] [illegible] turn [illegible].

She knew it was the [illegible] was the [illegible] [illegible].

Forty-Eight

Sunbury Festival, Victoria, Australia, January 1972

It was really only supposed to be a last hurrah, a celebration of their wild days of youth before the double wedding next month but this was proving to be more than just a shared bucks/hens adventure. The two couples were bearing witness to a seismic cultural shift and Poppy was loving every second of this festival at Sunbury, just thirty kilometres out of Melbourne.

The radio stations were calling it the 'rock happening thing of 1972' and so it was, with an impressive line-up including Billy Thorpe and the Aztecs, Spectrum and Wild Cherries. But like Woodstock in America and Glastonbury in England, Sunbury was more than just a large-scale outdoor music festival, it was a statement of the power of youth culture.

It was an election year and already the Labor government looked set to win after twenty-three years of Liberal rule. Gough Whitlam was promising the immediate release of imprisoned conscientious objectors and the withdrawal of all remaining troops from Vietnam, and there was a groundswell building across a country that was tired of Liberal conservatism. It was the seventies. It was time for change.

And you could feel it everywhere here.

Hippies were evolving into even hairier beings with men sporting ponytails and wearing flared jeans with open shirts, or no shirts at all. Thongs seemed the only footwear of choice and there was rubbish everywhere, which didn't seem very planet-friendly to Poppy but she didn't care about that too much right now.

An estimated thirty-five thousand people were singing along to Billy, agreeing that most people they knew thought they were crazy too, and Rosemary laughed with Poppy, clapping with the crowd.

'This is so amazing,' her sister said and Poppy was glad to see that her eyes were clear and that she seemed high on just life tonight. She'd been trying very hard lately, Poppy knew, but this place was packed full of temptation and Poppy was sticking to her sister like glue. Thuy had stayed home and Poppy wondered if that was part of the reason Rosemary was so relaxed. There was tension over at their place these days. Two's company, three's a crowd, she guessed. But Thuy hadn't moved out for reasons perhaps Angus and Rosemary didn't pick up on. Or perhaps they did, which would be worse.

Poppy pushed that thought out of her mind, losing herself back in the music until the end of the song, everyone screaming for more. This is just what they all needed, Poppy decided. A sense of impending victory at last in the form of some good old Aussie rock and roll.

'We'd better go back and find the girls,' Angus yelled over the music and the chanting crowd. Ben nodded, the concert seemed to be ending anyway, so they navigated their way back from up front where they'd been standing. Someone had been selling watermelons all day and they were now being thrown in the air as the throng demanded another encore.

'Look out.' Ben laughed, ducking.

'They look good,' Angus yelled back.

'I'll go see if I can find some,' Ben said. 'Meet you back at the tent.'

Angus nodded and Ben moved left, finding his way to the edge eventually and looking around for some fruit vendors.

'Do you know where I can get some watermelon?' he asked one scraggly-looking man as he passed.

'Nuh, man, you don't want the melons, you want the mangoes. The golden goodness.'

'Sounds even better. Where from?'

'Where *to* brother, where *to*.'

'Er, yeah,' Ben said, wishing he hadn't picked him as the man began to give long, confusing instructions. Basically he was being told to head to the 'White Room', which was, apparently, a big tent on the edge of the festival that looked like it came from Roman times. Ben wondered if it even existed. It sounded like a bit of a hike regardless so he decided to go back to their own tents first.

It was quite a long walk across the garbage littered fields and busy festival campsite and by the time he arrived Poppy was already lying down, sleepy and yawning.

'Hey beautiful,' he said, kissing her. 'Want to come mango hunting?'

'No,' she said, giggling and hugging her pillow.

'I do!' Rosemary yelled from the tent alongside.

'You go,' he heard Angus say. 'I think I'll crash out in a minute.'

'Are you sure?'

'Yeah.' He sounded like he was coming down from his musical buzz and Ben heard him open a can and take a swig.

Rosemary and Ben emerged from their tents and he shrugged at her. 'I'm up for it if you are,' he said and they set off together.

It was a fair way off but it as it turned out the White Room did, in fact, exist. It even had a man in a toga at the door.

'That looks familiar,' Ben said and Rosemary laughed.

'God, were we ever that young?'

'Ten bucks in,' the man said.

'Wow, that's a bit steep,' Ben said, taken aback. 'What do you get beside mangoes?'

'The whole world,' the man said, grinning. Ben looked past him inside and saw trestle tables set up, covered in food with a golden tray of fruit at its centre. Someone was playing guitar and singing and there seemed to be quite a party going on inside. Looking in even further he could see there were cushions everywhere, and it was filled with smoke, but it didn't seem to be pot smoke so Ben relaxed.

'I'm game if you are,' he said, turning to Rosemary.

'You only live once, I suppose.'

Ben paid the man and they entered, taking in what appeared to be a pretty cool scene. One of the guitarists they'd seen on stage that day was singing 'Space Oddity' by David Bowie and people were either listening or lying about murmuring as they drank and smoked.

Ben walked over to the tables, searching through the refreshments but found no sign of mangoes.

'Hey,' said a voice, and Ben turned to see the strange man from before. 'Didn't you want the golden goodness?'

'We did but I can't see any,' Ben said.

'Just give me a minute,' the man said, walking over to talk to someone in the corner.

Ben shrugged, grabbing a sandwich and beer and finding Rosemary a wine while they waited.

'Here,' the man said, beckoning, and they went over to find him holding a plate with a few mango halves lying side by side. 'Only take one.'

'Bit scabby, isn't it?' Ben said.

'Trust me, they do the job.'

Ben was definitely of the opinion the guy was a bit of a weirdo by now but the mangoes did look juicy so he ate anyway, Rosemary doing the same.

'Mmm,' she said. 'So good. They're my favourite fruit, you know.'

'Poppy said that once. "Food of the gods" you used to say, didn't you?'

She laughed, licking her fingers. 'Something like that.'

'Want to sit?' he asked her.

'Hold on,' she said. The man was whispering something to the man in the toga so she took another piece of mango while he wasn't looking.

'Tsk, tsk, greedy guts,' he said and she grinned as they took their drinks and sat to listen to the end of the song.

He was an excellent musician and the set went on for quite some time, then another musician took over, a woman this time, singing Janis Joplin's 'Me and Bobby McGee'.

'Body,' Ben said.

'Huh?' Rosemary said.

'Body loved Janis.'

'My body loves Janis too.'

That's an odd thing to say, he thought, turning to look at her, but she was changing. Her hair was turning brown and curly and she wore glasses now. Shaded ones.

'You are Janis.'

'Am I?'

Ben had to lie down then. Rosemary was Janis – so something was wrong. No, it was right. It was beautiful in this white room. It was heaven.

More and more people were playing music now, or was it a stereo? They were dancing too. It was 'White Room' by Cream.

The music lifted him in swirls and he went with it, flying around the room that was singing about itself now, telling him tales of silver horses and moonbeams. He was an equine spirit on the wind, his human body gone and he was looking down on a train station where a girl sat with a cello case. Then she turned into a woman, all in white like the room, walking out of mud and treacherous warscape and it was raining letters around her.

'Poppy,' he said, the name more treasured than any word in the world. Then she was in his arms, golden hair brushing his skin and they were naked together. So much skin, so soft, or firm. Maybe that was his skin, maybe it was hers. Maybe it was everyone's. Beautiful, beautiful, someone was saying.

Beautiful woman. Beautiful man.

It was dawn. The gold and pink glow of the sky was reflecting across the walls and Ben had to lie for a minute to remember where he was. The Roman tent. The White Room.

Poppy had been here.

He looked across to find her asleep, her breasts bare, then there was another body alongside, a man's. And there were more, strewn about. Half a dozen or so.

'Poppy? Poppy, wake up.'

Only she didn't stir, and as he rolled her over he saw that her golden hair was very, very long.

The fan drifted slowly in circles above them, clicking rhythmically in the sterile waiting room.

'Please God, no, please God, no…'

The doctors were taking a long time, surely that was a good thing.

Angus's eyes were red from sorrow and fear, and Poppy vaguely registered she should probably comfort him but she couldn't seem to move. Ben sat opposite, his face a mask of anguish, but she couldn't look at him anymore. She didn't know if she could ever see him in a normal light again after finding him in the White Room. With Rosemary. The image was burned into her brain. Naked bodies, naked Ben, naked sister. Not moving. Everything was distorted now and it could never be the same.

'Miss Flannery…'

She leapt to her feet, able to move after all.

'Your sister is stable, although there appears to have been some cardiac damage.' Poppy nodded, grabbing onto Angus's arm as he stood alongside, shaking. 'We'll have to run more tests but she's resting comfortably for now.'

'Can I see her?' Angus asked. 'I'm her fiancé.' There'd been no time for introductions when they'd arrived.

'For a minute or two only. She needs to sleep.'

Angus disappeared through the door and Poppy stared at the floor, unwilling to even acknowledge her own fiancé right now.

'I'm…I'm so sorry…' he began.

'No, I can't do this, okay? Just go for now. Just go.'

He stood and she knew he was wrestling with himself as she watched his thonged feet hesitate before he slowly walked away. Then he was gone and she was alone and the ceiling fan clicked.

And Poppy Flannery's heart slowly turned to stone.

Forty-Nine

Sydney, February 1972

She looked better, Angus noted with relief. She was even smiling at something the nurse was saying although that faded when she noticed him at the door.

'Hey,' he said, coming over to take the chair alongside her bed as he'd done the past few days.

'Hey yourself,' Rosemary said, picking up the magazine that had been resting on the blanket and tossing it over to the night-stand. She missed and he picked it up.

'You can take her outside if you like,' said the nurse. 'I've a chair if you want to use it.'

'Want some sunshine?' Angus asked and she shrugged.

'I suppose.'

She stood and walked over to it, still weak from her experience but much improved, and he clicked off the brake, wheeling her out.

It was brilliantly sunny and quite hot so he found a shaded area beneath a large fig tree and sat on a bench next to her, taking her hand. Rosemary stared down at it for a while before she started to speak.

'I've had lots of time to think these past few days.'

'Good thing or bad thing?'

'Bad,' she admitted, 'but necessary.'

'And what conclusions have you come to?' he asked, stroking her fingers with his, tracing the engagement ring with his thumb.

'It's no use, Angus.'

'What's no use?'

'Us, together.'

It was so simple, the way she said it, but the hurt was deep, especially today.

'You know the flowers arrived, no-one thought to cancel them. Poppy said your mother took them down to the church for the nuns…'

'You're not listening.'

'I heard you.'

A bird landed nearby, cocking its head and calling to its flock, and soon half a dozen or so were picking at a bit of sandwich on the grass. They were rainbow lorikeets, 'lovebirds' as Rosemary liked to say.

'We just can't keep doing this to each other. I can't keep hurting you and you can't help hurting me. It's like a horrible roundabout that we can't seem to get off.'

'I don't mean to hurt you.'

'You're just too sad for me to hold it. You're breaking me down, piece by piece…'

'You don't understand…'

'I know Angus, that's been the problem all along. I *don't* understand and I've tried and tried but it's no use. It's just no use.' She said it so sadly and with such finality he knew then that this was the end, too.

'I love you,' he said.

'I know, and I love you; that's been the other problem really, hasn't it?'

'I can't live without you,' he said, tears stinging his eyes.

'Can't live with me though, so where does that leave us?'

He shrugged, staring out at the empty sky for a moment. 'Alone, I guess.'

She nodded. 'I suppose so. It's better for us both, Angus. You know it too, deep down.'

He looked at her eyes, at the damage and the exhaustion, and he knew what she said was true. 'I'll miss you forever,' he said, pulling her into his arms for one last, long hug.

'I'll be around,' she said. 'You'll see.'

They sat for a while, neither wanting it to end, and Angus drank the smell of her hair deep into his lungs.

Then there was a flutter of wings and he finally let her go. And the lovebirds flew away.

Poppy folded the wedding dress back into the box, wondering what she'd hoped to achieve by opening it, but it was such a pretty thing. It deserved to be aired today, even if only to be held up in front of a woman in a mirror. A woman whose tears were still drying after sending the man she was supposed to marry today away.

She didn't suppose he would try again after this. Words had been said that cut to the bone, no mercy given. No forgiveness in her stone heart.

'You knew you were playing with fire when you took her in there.'

'I didn't know Poppy; I swear it to you.'

'How could you possibly not have known?'

'It's true; we just thought it was fruit, but mangoes are her favourite so she had two...'

'I know that. I know how it happened, but don't lie to me.'

'Poppy, on everything I hold sacred…'

'You hold nothing sacred. You had sex with my sister!'

'I thought she was you!'

'How could that be true? How could you do that *to me?'*

'Please don't do this, please my love…'

'Never call me that again. Just go.'

'You need to believe me…'

'I don't believe you. I will never believe you again.'

'I love you, Poppy, with all my heart. Can't you see that?'

'I see a monster.'

There was a terrible silence after those words before he'd left her but Poppy couldn't regret them. She couldn't feel anything beyond her anger.

She folded up the gown, placing it back into the box in the cupboard and closed the door; packing Ben Williamson away for good. Then Poppy picked up her handbag and walked out of the room, to the rest of her lonely life.

Ben picked up the paint brush and ran a bright red line across the canvas. It wasn't working. There was no comfort in his art, no relief to be found in the studio today. He considered smoking a joint but pushed that away too. No more drugs, ever again.

He walked to the window, looking out over the lush grounds of his parents' home, at carpets of emerald-green grass and rows of immaculate flower beds. A world of privilege, picture-perfect in its plenitude and abundance, yet it felt empty to him. Poppy was gone from his life which had stolen away his ability to feel anything but darkness. Everything that was good inside him had left with her, leaving nothing but a vessel of pain.

A colourless man who'd done terrible things. Nothing more than a monster.

A drop of paint fell on the floor and he smeared it with his toe, blood red against the white of the tiles. It clicked at something deep within and he walked back to the easel and picked up a rag, rubbing until nothing was left. Then he opened a bottle of scotch and took a deep swig before starting again. He'd need numbness to paint what was inside him today.

There was a knock at the door and Angus pushed the drawer closed, raising his eyes to the sight of Ben walking in unsteadily, carrying a large package.

'Hey, mate.'

'Hi,' Angus said, downing his beer.

'Cleaning it again?' Ben said, nodding at the drawer and awkwardly putting the package down. He looked three sheets to the wind too.

Angus said nothing, lighting a cigarette instead.

'They'll kill you, you know.'

'Yeah, I know,' Angus said, taking a drag. 'What's in the package?'

'Present.'

Angus wanted to tell him to shove it but they'd already had it out about Rosemary and he believed him that he didn't know it was her that night at Sunbury. That much LSD could make you think you were making love to a unicorn and still enjoy it. Still, it stung, particularly after today.

'Want a beer?' Angus said, ignoring the gift and going to get him one.

'Thanks.'

'Where've you been?'

'In the studio. Went to see Poppy again. Didn't go too well.'

'Still doesn't believe you?'

'No,' Ben said, drinking his beer. 'I'm starting to think she never will.' He looked devastated at the prospect and Angus could relate.

'Rosemary and I broke up today.' It felt strange to say those words out loud.

'Really?' Ben said, sounding shocked. 'That's…that's terrible.'

'It's not because of Sunbury,' Angus said, recognising that guilty look crossing Ben's face; the one he often carried in Vietnam. 'We just…we can't make it work anymore.'

Ben nodded slowly. 'I'm so sorry…'

'Me too.'

'What are you going to do?'

'I don't know…get really drunk and face it tomorrow, I suppose.'

'Sounds like a plan. Mind if I join you?'

'Sure.'

And so they sat, once brothers in arms, almost brothers-in-law, both dumped by twin sisters on the same day. Then Thuy came in and they all watched the cricket until the alcohol eased the pain.

'See you later,' Angus mumbled as Ben headed for home.

'Goodbye mate,' Ben said, and the door closed.

Thuy awoke early to scraping and thuds next door and she dressed quickly to see what was going on.

'Hello?' she said, knocking, then pushing open the door. Angus was there, packing, and she stared at him, surprised.

'You go away?'

'Yep,' Angus said, throwing a jumble of shirts and shorts into a case.

'Where to?'

He sighed, placing in a pair of shoes before answering. 'Home.'

'To parents?' she asked, incredulous now. 'Across red centre, far away?'

Angus paused in his packing and came over to her. 'I need to, Thuy. I've put it off for far too long – I have to see my mother, explain what happened with Spike. She deserves that much.

'What about Rosemary?'

'We're over, Thuy; we're not getting married any more.'

'Not marry?' She was wide eyed and he shook his head, feeling sad.

'No.'

'Why not?'

He shrugged. 'Because we can't make it work. Because she can't handle all my crap, I guess, and it pushes her too far.'

'Because you sad and then she sad. Then she make herself sick.'

Angus frowned then nodded at her simple summary. 'Yes, that's just about it. I guess you've seen it all for a long time.'

'Yes,' she said. 'I see.'

Angus walked back to his suitcase and Thuy picked up a vase. 'Take everything?'

'Yep.'

'You not come back?' She looked frightened and about to cry so he lied.

'Not sure yet. We'll have to see.'

Thuy nodded and picked up some newspaper, wrapping the vase. 'What about gift?' she said, pointing at the package from Ben.

'I forgot about that,' he said, walking over to peel back the sticky tape and slide it out of the box. It was a painting, a bright one of a man in a white room, and angels were flying about above him, laughing and free. One had Spike's face, another had their big friend from the army and there were a few others, mostly Asian, that she didn't recognise.

'It's beautiful,' Thuy said.

'It is,' Angus agreed, then he noticed the title on the back. '*Sự-tự-do.*'

Thuy looked surprised. 'He remember my word.'

'Suits it,' Angus said, then something made him pause. He ran to the drawer and pulled it open and she had a moment of fear but it was empty. 'Shit.'

'What wrong?' Thuy said, as he ran to the phone.

'Look at his hands,' he said, pointing at the man in the painting, and she turned to see that they were very dark red, almost black, but you could still make out the gun.

It felt strange to hold one again after so long, running it through his hands, loading and unloading with practised ease. Ben paused to drink heavily from yet another bottle of scotch, placing the weapon to the side and staring at the paint on his fingers. Blood red. So much violence had been wrought by those ten digits; so much harm to others, but no more.

Ben picked up the brush. Just a few more strokes and he'd be done.

It was painting of a girl, sitting on a red rattler train, not knowing it was the boy near the door's eighteenth birthday, all those years ago. No-one had said anything to him about it at home and he hadn't told anyone at school, so he'd treated himself to some potato scallops that he'd had a sudden urge to share. His own little party, Ben supposed. She had freckles on her nose and a cello case nearby that told you more about her than she probably imagined. A girl who loved the sun and had music in her soul; a girl with messages in her eyes she obviously didn't even know she was sending.

Every stroke of her was clean and brilliant and loving, but the boy was really just a smear of grey. He couldn't really exist now that the girl was no longer a part of his future. Life no longer something of his choosing.

Poppy twirled the flower in her fingers, the only one she'd kept from her wedding bouquet. It was a yellow daisy – simple really, but they'd made sunny partners when teamed with frangipanis. It was sweet even on its own, this humble little piece of nature. Both flowers reminded her of sunshine and sand and Surfers Paradise, the reason she'd chosen them, of course. Pity she'd never shared that small detail with Ben.

It was hard, sitting here on the train and trying not to think of him. The beautiful boy who grew into the beautiful man then ruined everything by turning her heart to stone. Stealing from them both what was supposed to be a beautiful future. She picked up her bag, noticing it felt heavier than it should, and she rummaged inside to find a package. Ben must have snuck it in there when he was waiting for her downstairs today and she refused to see him. She recognised his handwriting on the card attached.

Poppy opened it, unable to resist, and scanned the words.

Dear Poppy,

If you're reading this then you've decided not to give me any more chances so I'm giving you what is left of me now – the parts you never saw. The monster, as you said, that lives within me. Maybe if you see it you'll understand why I've struggled at times and fallen down, there's just so much blood on my hands. So many rules that have always been applied to my life, holding me so tight at times I felt like I was going to suffocate. But then you came, and you waited. Then you gave me everything: love, freedom, choices, happiness. You even gave me back my art which has kept me alive.

And now you're taking it all away because, despite everything we've been through, you don't believe me. I think I could survive this if not for that one sad fact. You don't believe me which means you don't believe <u>*in*</u> *me.*

I can't take that because I believe in you more than anyone on earth. You are the most amazing person I've ever known and I would have got to share my life with you if not for one stupid moment. Please know, once and for all, that I didn't know it wasn't you; that I could never do such a thing in a right mind.

I love you, Poppy Marie. When you think of me think about that. Think of summer nights on the beach and that first time at the snow and the day I returned from war.

I'm sorry not all of me came back,

Yours, forever,
Ben.

Poppy unwrapped the parcel, half-blinded by tears, to see Ben's army journal in her hands and she began to leaf through it, fingers shaking. It was filled with horrors the mind could barely imagine unless you'd been there; mutilated corpses, mass graves, an old lady dead in the street. There were soldiers, shirtless, standing in hell, landmines and machine guns and bodies burning in the napalm. A row of men taking careful steps with 'three, two, one' written across the sky. His art exhibition had barely touched the surface compared to this. Then a photo fell out of the back, of a Vietnamese man, not much more than a boy, and Ben had written on the back of it, over and over, *I'm sorry, I'm sorry, I'm sorry.*

Then the words in the letter replayed in her mind. '*...you don't believe me. I think I could survive this if not for that...*'

Suddenly she didn't need to see any more, stuffing the journal back in her bag and running for the train doors as it drew into the station. Getting to Ben was the only thing that mattered in the world. To tell him her heart was no longer hard, that he wasn't a monster at all. That he was a victim of the cleverness of mankind, just like they all were, creatures who could devise far too many ways to die. That the dark days were gone and the future would be bright.

To hold on to his beautiful life.

It was all finished. The painting, the scotch, the struggle to live. No more rules, no choices to be made. All he had to do was squeeze the trigger, a simple enough task, he'd done it many, many times before. Just one more song, he decided, then he'd send the monster away.

Just one more cigarette then he'd be gone.

She was running as fast as she could make her legs move, every muscle straining, fear pumping hard at her heart. Begging Jesus for one more miracle in life. Let him be alright. Let it just be her imagination – fear gone wild. Just four more houses, three. Two, one.

Crack. The sound of a gunshot ripped the air and Poppy screamed as she reached his gate, hurling it open and beginning to sob.

'Please God, no, please...'

'A Whiter Shade of Pale' was playing on the stereo inside and she made it to the studio door, leaning her hands against it, terrified of what she'd see but pushing anyway.

He was there, slumped in his chair, chin resting on his chest, the smoking gun in his hand.

'Ben,' she wept. 'No, no...'

She knelt in front of him, forcing herself to look at his face.

But she didn't find blood, she didn't find death, she found a miracle instead.

'I heard a shot,' she said. 'There was a shot.'

'I...I missed.'

Poppy stared at the hole in the wall then back into his desolate eyes, glassy and bloodshot. Desperate. Then she looked at his fingers, still clutching the gun, and reached into her bag with shaking hands.

'This is over, you hear me?' she said, holding up the journal, her tears streaming. 'Gone.' Then the daisy from before fell on the floor and she picked it up.

'I do believe in you, I do,' she said, trembling as she placed the flower in the gun hole. 'No more war; not between us.'

Water filled those eyes then and he started to shiver.

'Please Ben, please...put the gun down.'

He lowered it slowly and it fell to the floor and she threw herself into his arms.

'I love you so much,' she said, her heart beating hard against his. 'You never need to doubt that again, I promise. Never, ever again.'

Then the beautiful man dissolved into racking sobs, and she held him as he released all the pain. All the memories, the rules, the hurt and the fears, as Poppy willed it all away.

'I don't know if I would have done it or not,' he told her, wiping at his face.

'We'll never know and we'll never need to think about that now. We're never going to look backwards again.'

'Do you really think I can do that?' he whispered.

She shrugged. 'If not, I can always wait. I'm rather good at that, remember.'

She kissed him softly and earned a shaky smile, only a small one, but it was there, and Ben touched her face with one paint-stained, brown finger. 'Yes you are; you always were,' he said, 'but I think...I think I might have finally made it all the way home.'

Fifty

Sydney, December 1972

The news on the radio was ending, mostly about the new Whitlam government and how the last of the troops were being pulled out, and it was followed by a song: John Lennon singing 'War is Over (if you want it)'. It seemed the world did want it now. A photo of an eight-year-old girl crying as she ran from the liquid fire, clothes literally burning from her skin, had sealed the deal for good.

Angus listened as he stood, taking one more look around before he closed the door to his apartment for the last time. So many memories came to mind of this home. A mad tea party and a surprising cake, rainy days in that bed, the reading of draft papers. Spike making tea and singing along with the radio. Rosemary baking and giving Barrel leftover pizza.

Thuy watching sport just to watch over him. The moment he found an empty drawer.

He'd stayed the rest of the year in the end, to be there for Ben and Rosemary and give Poppy some support. They'd finally got married yesterday, Ben and his girl, and Angus was truly happy for them. Ben seemed a different person since 'the day of the gun', as Angus thought of it, like he'd made his peace with the past, well, as much as any of them could. Angus couldn't say the same for himself but he was better than he was. Ben's experience had taught him not to let things spiral too far. To ask for help if you needed it and so he had been, seeing a counsellor for a while, opening up more, especially to Thuy.

He and Rosemary were somehow transitioning to friendship and he would miss visiting her but she was probably better off with him out of her life. She'd been right about them, of course, and he realised now she'd been the brave one, breaking it off. They couldn't be together, not any more. Still, when she'd walked down the aisle as a bridesmaid Angus couldn't help but be moved to tears by the sight. Healthy again, heart condition notwithstanding, and as beautiful as ever. She looked finally to be on top of things, now that they'd parted ways.

He'd said most of his farewells and the car was all packed, and there was nothing left to do except one final, painful task: to say goodbye to Thuy. She'd become so close to him now that it was part of the reason he needed to go. He couldn't afford to fall in love again so soon, his heart was too sore, and lately there were too many times when he could easily have kissed her, pulling himself back just in time. She was better off with someone less damaged than him, someone who could actually give her what she truly deserved.

Angus closed the door and locked it, which felt strange, then walked over to knock on Thuy's.

'Come in,' she called, and he opened it to find her standing nervously in the centre of a barren room. Everything was gone except the original furniture and Thuy stood next to a large suitcase, waiting.

'You can't come with me, Thuy.'

'You say that when we at river once and I say "okay". You say it when we in battle and I say "okay" again and wait with gun. Then you say it in field when family die and I say "please". Then you say "yes",' she reminded him.

'I can't say "yes" this time. It's complicated.'

'It not.' She walked over and put her hand on his arm, her touch as light as a butterfly. 'I love you, Ang-gus.'

He took a deep breath, fighting his heart that was starting to leap about in his chest. 'I'm not good enough for you; you should be with someone who isn't…who isn't broken like me.'

'I strong enough help you. I come too.'

He looked down at her stubborn, pretty little face and realised it was true. She was strong, and he was stronger when she was around. Then she did something she really shouldn't have done. She kissed him.

'I come too.'

Angus felt his resolve melt away like butter in the sun and suddenly he was kissing her back, drawing her into his arms, pouring all those times of temptation over the last few months into one glorious moment of abandon. Then he pulled back and smiled into her ever-trusting eyes.

'Alright Thuy. You come too.'

Fifty-One

Thanh Long Creek, November 1980

The sound of children's laughter drifted in the air as they walked over together, towards the foot of a giant tree near some dragon fruit bushes and a field of wildflowers.

'Look Mum, I can fit inside,' Spencer called out to Thuy, crawling into a hole at the base.

Thuy nodded but didn't say anything and Poppy saw Angus take her hand and squeeze it tight.

'Annie!' Spencer called. 'Come and see!' Poppy watched as her daughter ran over and sat alongside him like the two little peas in a pod they were, always together and laughing at something the other one said. They were giggling now and Poppy placed her finger on her lips.

'Hush you two, this is a very sacred place.'

They sat in a row, three people's graves, each with a wooden plaque that told of their fate. Poppy had no idea what the Vietnamese epitaphs said but there was a new tribute recently added nearby that was in English, written on an unusual form of marker: a piece of surfboard secured in concrete.

The children came over to investigate.

'Hey, that's my name,' Spencer said, and he tried to read the inscription printed on the fibreglass. 'In loving memory of Spencer "Spike" Turner, one, nine, four…'

'1946–1968,' Angus helped him.

'Killed by brav-er-y in this land, for…'

'Forever in paradise.' Angus finished.

He'd chosen the wording with his parents last year when Angus had told them of this pilgrimage he was making with Thuy and they'd collectively decided to erect this memorial for Spike while he was there. Poppy smiled at the bright yellow cut-off surfboard, loving the idea that Spike's guitar lay beneath it. Music and surfing. So him. She was glad she and Ben had decided to attend this small but very special ceremony.

Poppy looked around at the brilliant countryside, thinking about Spike's last days on earth over here, living life with reckless abandon right till the end. Treating even war like an adventure. It was different to any place she'd ever seen before; lush and peaceful in a thousand shades of green. If it wasn't for the scars on this land it would be hard to imagine the carnage that occurred here. Vietnam seemed too beautiful a place to be the scene of such violence.

Angus and Thuy stood together, arms around each other as they watched and Poppy felt a wave of affection for both, so glad life was kinder now to these dear friends. It had never upset Poppy that they'd ended up together – they made more sense as a couple than Angus and her twin. Besides, Rosemary had found love too, eventually, with her own cardiologist as it turned out. He was a fair bit older and their parents had been scandalised by her wayward sister, yet again, but, as Ben pointed out, she never had been a particularly orthodox individual. Annie adored the doctor which was all the proof Poppy needed that her sister had made a good choice.

Yes, the heart wants what the heart wants, Poppy reflected, looking over at Ben who was sketching the scene in a journal, Annie now on his knee. He lifted his eyes to smile at her and Poppy basked in his sun, knowing that in her case the heart had been proven wise.

Thuy beckoned Spencer over and he helped her plant flowers alongside her family's graves, talking softly to him in Vietnamese.

'Did you want to say anything in English?' Angus asked his son once they'd finished, and Spencer leant against his parents' legs, considering.

'Hi grandfather and grandmother and uncle, I'm Spencer. That's my other uncle's surfboard that Dad broke to stick in the ground next to ya. He can't use it anyway because he's in heaven too but I reckon he still surfs invisa-bab-ly on clouds and stuff which is cool. He was Australian so he can't speak Vietnamese but he was a funny bugger so maybe you should get Jesus or Buddha to translate…'

'Don't say "bugger",' Angus muttered, although everyone was stifling chuckles, including him.

'You say it all the time, you say "Spike was a funny b…"'

'Spencer.'

The seven-year-old rolled his eyes. 'Anyway, I hope you have fun in heaven on your twelve year an-vers-ry and I hope you get cake. The end.'

'Well,' said Ben, trying not to laugh, 'what about you, Annie girl? You want to say something too?'

'He's not my uncle,' she said shyly, her adorable lisp poking through.

'He was a kind of uncle. Dad says soldiers are brothers in arms,' Spencer told her. 'They carry each other around so they must get tired a lot.'

'That kid really has to stop listening to you,' Ben told Angus under his breath.

'Go on, say something,' Spencer urged Annie. 'I wanna eat.'

Annie bit her lip then began, so softly they all had to strain to hear. 'In the name of the Father, and of the Son, and of the Holy Spirit, Amen...'

'Bugger, I forgot that bit.'

'Spencer.'

Annie looked scandalised but giggled before continuing. 'Hello uncles and grandparents of everybody else. I hope you are happy in heaven and don't ever cry anymore because war is sad. Love from Annie. In the name of the Father, and the Son and of the Holy Spirit, Amen.'

'Amen,' everyone said and Poppy kissed her daughter's little fair head.

'Food now?' Spencer said hopefully.

'After the song,' Thuy told him.

Angus had chosen it, one for all the souls who had lost their lives here, and he pressed play on the tape recorder that rested on a branch of the great tree. They stood together as John Lennon's 'Imagine' lifted up through the swaying leaves and strange fruit towards a sky of cloudless blue and Poppy took those words deep into her heart.

Imagine if it had never happened, she thought, sad to consider the cost of a war that meant nothing in the end as she looked out on the southern fields of a united, Communist Vietnam. Surrounded by the cost, weighing old griefs. It had taken the public to end it, to give peace a chance, and it had changed the world, that people power. She could only hope the politicians had learnt their lesson, this time around, that there wouldn't be another large-scale war after three successive ones in a mere sixty years.

Watching the children run off to play she asked God for that one last miracle, to spare them the pain of any more conflict. But it wasn't something He could tell her; they'd all just have to wait and see what humanity would do.

For it would come down to the choices of those too-clever men on earth; whether to reach for the stars or just self-destruct. Poppy liked to believe they'd learnt their lesson now, but perhaps not. Perhaps she was just being a dreamer, but she knew something for certain, after all this.

She wasn't the only one.

Author's Note

War Flower is a work of fiction and although it is based on real events in history, artistic licence has been employed at times to ensure cohesion is maintained.

Acknowledgements

They say it takes a village to raise a child and in many ways that remains true for works of fiction. It isn't just a writer tapping away at the keys that produces a story, numerous others influence it and help it to grow.

For a start, you need publishers, and I have the best at Harlequin: Sue Brockhoff (Publishing Director) and Jo Mackay (Publisher), without whom you wouldn't be reading this book. Their tireless belief and support is an essential part of my village and I am grateful for their presence every day. You also need an editor and I am incredibly fortunate that Annabel Blay took on that role. Thank you for your painstakingly hard work, sense of humour and kindness and for not freaking out when the final manuscript file corrupted. Thank you also to my wonderful agent Helen Breitwieser who carries the torch for me overseas, expanding my book-child's horizons.

Other villagers helped by providing great influence upon its characters. There is much of my sisters Genevieve and Linda in the Flannery twins, much of Theresa, Zoe, Gemma and Carmie in their friendship. And my brothers, brothers-in-law, friends and neighbours flavoured the Aussie humour and mateship.

I hope other undercurrents can be felt too, such as the exuberance of youth, inspired by my sons. My father's great compassion for his fellow man. My mother's understanding. My husband's patience.

Some villagers have provided particular impact and I would like say a special thank you to my next door neighbour, Thuy.

Thuy Simpson is strong; possibly one of the strongest women I have ever met. She is also my very first Vietnamese friend, and what a wonderful, supportive one she is. Traces of Thuy can be found in her namesake character: her determination, her strength, her loyalty to the man she loves (her husband Paul), her great compassion for others, her dignity. Thuy told me the story of her family's migration from Vietnam – made possible by the sale of a ruby necklace, their only possession of value. She gave insights into what would be hard for a refugee coming into Australia, how our country would seem from their eyes: clean, abundant, overwhelming.

She is little but her heart is very big and she's made me understand so much more about Vietnam. I'm very grateful to her for lending her insights to inform my novel and I hope that this book sheds light on, and raises compassion for, the Vietnamese people themselves during the Vietnam War.

Others in my neighbourhood have shed light too, in particular my friend Chaddy who lived through those turbulent years and shared many, many hours with me explaining details about the war and the sixties culture that surrounded it. Thank you for your generosity and friendship during this time.

There was input from the greater village too, brave vets who've shared their stories with the public so freely and who've helped me understand the realities of modern warfare and the depth of struggle they faced back home. I've done my best to be true to your history and share some of your tale with the world. To try to right a little of those many, terrible wrongs.

There was also influence from those wonderful advocates of peace who marched and protested to force an ending, who taught the world the true value of people power. May we continue to uphold the ideology you expounded: that silence is condonement and to always stand up for what is right.

Finally, I'd like to talk about the inspiration behind the character 'Spike': my brother, Matthew John Best.

'Matt', or 'Besty' to those who knew him, was both hilarious and fun, living life at maximum speed and always up for a party or a dare. He taught me so much in the short life he lived, not only about making the most of every second but about not sweating the small stuff. He was wise and ever the peace-maker and perhaps too good for this earth. I wish I didn't know how it felt to lose a brother like Matt but at least I can channel that pain into my work and hopefully raise compassion for others who grieve, especially soldiers who've lost brothers in arms. And the family and friends back home who never got to see them again.

Death is so sudden, so final, and war is designed to wreak it en masse. I suppose that's why I was so determined to write about its influence upon modern Australia across three novels, to reflect on its impact; how it has forced us to grow and evolve as a nation. To reject it now, in these days of unrest, once and for all.

It took a long time for us to learn the true value of peace. Lest we forget that hard-won lesson evermore. I would like to dedicate each and every word of these three books to the Australian soldiers who fought for their country, not for fame and glory but for love. For I do believe they loved our way of life; our beautiful, sunburnt country, our diversity and our character.

And I truly believe they would all say 'no more war'.

The Letter

One

Killaloe, County Clare, Ireland, April 1851

Playing games, whether for opportunity, mischief or seduction, was a pastime Kieran Clancy should have quit long ago. But 'should' was a word he seldom obeyed.

'Check.'

Maeve O'Shannassey frowned at her cornered king.

'However did you manage that?' she muttered, perplexed. Her pretty face suited consternation. Hell, she looked delectable no matter what she was feeling, and Kieran further warmed to the contest at hand.

'You'll find I have many hidden talents, Miss Maeve, games of chase being one of my specialities,' Kieran told her.

'And yet I continue to outrun you, Mr Kieran,' she replied, rather brazenly for her, before moving her queen to block his knight. 'Check, I believe.'

Kieran barely glanced at the table, raising his eyebrows instead and leaning in close to take the queen. 'You may well run, fair maid, but you cannot hide.' The words were spoken in her ear and he could smell her hair, still damp from the outdoors and sweet with the honey-scented soap she favoured. He held the breath in to savour it, momentarily intoxicated, before adding 'checkmate'.

Maeve stood in a rush, almost knocking over the board, and Kieran cursed himself for breaking one of his own rules in life: appear bold but never cocky.

'T…tea?' she suggested, her earlier confidence gone.

Kieran sighed as she made a swift exit to the kitchen where her mother was ostensibly baking but really keeping guard over her daughter. Leaning back against the French settee, he reflected that Maeve was proving far more difficult to court than any of the local girls he'd been interested in over the years. That was probably part of the attraction – but not all of it.

The rain pelted hard against the pane and Kieran looked out, glad to be away from the fields for a change. Green and lush the farmlands near Killaloe may be, but when the wet set in it lost much of its appeal, turning soggy and grey. He studied the parlour window itself instead. Aside from the luxury of glass, it was framed by polished oak and had lace curtains, a step far above most other homes in the area, and the fine furniture and thick carpets herein further emphasised how remote the chances were that he, Kieran Clancy, a poor Irish farmer, stood any real chances with this girl.

Listening to Mrs O'Shannassey's lofty tones drift through the door he knew he should just leave. But of course, he wouldn't.

Kieran stood to pace the room and plot instead. It was simply a matter of evening the scales somehow, offering more than other suitors, more than material wealth and all the trappings her family prized.

Such as? he asked himself.

Well, he could work on his charm; she seemed to enjoy some of his more humorous witticisms and compliments. Hopefully that might lead to delicious stolen moments of shared desire. Noting the nervous knot twisting in his gut at the thought, he acknowledged he could well end up giving her his heart. Then he paused to look across towards town to where Mr O'Shannassey would be working today and he knew that, even if that were enough for Maeve, it would never be enough for her father.

The man was quite a success story, and it wasn't just the impressive house that bespoke the fact. He had a thriving business at his new store, which sold everything from silk stockings to imported perfumes, but by far the greatest attraction to the locals were the apothecary vials that lined the counter, a curious assortment of concoctions, handmade, mostly, by Mr O'Shannassey himself. It seemed people couldn't get enough of the often ill-tasting liquids that promised cures for maladies from ear infections to rheumatism.

It didn't hurt, perhaps, that he had so desperate a clientele. Most had suffered these past few years and ill-health was commonplace. Overworked by English landlords and robbed of much of their crops by Queen Victoria, the final straw for many in the village came when the potato crops had failed a few years previously. Starvation had led to disease; consumption, cholera and smallpox. In the end many lives had been taken, including those of Kieran's own mother and father. Where were Mr O'Shannassey's 'miracle cures' then?

Kieran shoved his hands deep into his pockets, pushing resentment and grief away. It wasn't the man's fault that Ireland suffered so. Perhaps some of his remedies even worked, although Kieran placed far more faith in his sister Eileen's tonics. Still, he supposed O'Shannassey was giving people hope and that was a gift in itself, even if, on their meagre wages, they could ill afford it.

Money. Kieran sighed at the enormity of the word, acknowledging that the odds against him were stacked high in this particular game. Maeve might well fall for Kieran's romantic overtures but her parents would require a man of means, especially if he had any chance of actually marrying her.

Unless his brother Liam could pull off what he had planned.

Maeve returned then and that last glimmering thought evaporated as Kieran turned to watch her move, her creamy skin pushing against her dress as she bent to pour the tea.

'Milk?' she asked.

'Please.'

Kieran returned to the settee and he was pleased when Maeve sat beside him, slightly closer than before. Near enough for him to see the flecks of green in her otherwise brown eyes and smell that hair once more. He closed his own eyes momentarily, memorising the scent, his determination to win her returning with force.

'Are you feeling poorly?' Maeve asked.

'Not with you around,' he told her. Her lovely face flushed and it gave him a heady rush that he could affect her so. A small tip of the scales.

'Perhaps I should fetch you one of father's tonics.'

Kieran smiled at her. 'I'm perfectly fine, I promise.' He was tempted to add that he doubted her father had invented a cure for desire but that was, of course, a flirtation too far.

Maeve looked to her tea and circled her spoon about her cup demurely. 'Father's had some rather wonderful news actually: Lord Whitely has agreed to fund mass production of some of his inventions.'

Kieran swallowed his distaste with his tea at the mention of Lord Whitely's name. Long how he'd ached to tell the owner of their small farm to stick his power over the tenanting Clancy family up his pompous Cambridge arse.

'Is that so?' Kieran said, feigning what he hoped was a mixture of mild curiosity and politeness.

'Yes, there's a factory in Kilrush that will start producing them next month.'

'Truly?' Kieran said, trying to maintain his composure, but all he could envisage were those scales dipping dramatically back against him.

Maeve nodded, her face alight with excitement. 'Lord Whitely has invited us to dine at the family estate this Sunday to celebrate the partnership. His son is returning to Killaloe.'

Those scales weren't only dipping now; they were set to fall over. He'd heard from Eileen that Maeve's mother was distantly related to an earl, rendering her just passably genteel, and, even though it was slightly beneath a gentleman to work in commerce, this fact also seemed forgiven of O'Shannassey now. Such social elevation meant any hope Kieran had with Maeve was fast disappearing. Whitely's rich but unattractive son was known to be looking for a wife and he would surely take an interest in her. And Maeve's parents would never choose the tenant over the lord for their daughter; an aristocratic Englishman would win such a battle without contest.

Kieran had little choice but to seize this rare opportunity to win her affections, right now, while he still had any possible hope.

'Sounds grand,' he said, opting for nonchalance and changing the subject. 'Another game of chess?'

'I do believe you are a better chess player than I, Master Kieran,' she said. 'Perhaps I should challenge you to a game of cards instead. My cousins taught me well as a child and I don't mind telling you I could fair whip you at whist.'

Bold but never cocky, he reminded himself.

'I'm sure you could fair whip me at many games Miss Maeve.'

He was rewarded with another blush. 'Really, Master Kieran, you shouldn't say such things…' She looked to the open kitchen door and he took advantage of her momentary distraction, taking her hand before she could stop him.

'Maeve, I...' He'd been about to declare his feelings but instead he took one look at her shocked face and parted lips and found himself kissing her, a sudden, heated event that took them both by surprise. Passion flooded through him as he poured all that yearning for her into the moment, before pausing to read her expression, knowing her first reaction to him was crucial. *Kiss me back*, he pleaded silently, and his heart leapt as she swayed towards him, but they were interrupted by a distant voice.

'*Kieran!* Kieran, where are you?'

He would have done his best to ignore it but Maeve had pulled away, startled, and Kieran took a deep breath, cursing his brother Liam for his unbelievably confounded timing.

'Excuse me,' he said, sending her what he hoped was his most irresistible smile before standing and walking over to open the front door.

'Here,' he called, stepping out and bracing himself against the unwelcoming day. The rain was still falling and he pulled his coat over his neck, wishing he'd grabbed his cap. Liam turned and spied him, letting out a whoop of excitement as he ran down the cobblestone road, nearly losing his footing as he skidded to a halt.

'It's arrived. We got it!' he panted. 'It's ours, Kieran. All ours!'

Kieran's annoyance with his brother evaporated as he stared back, barely believing the news as he took the outstretched letter from Liam's hands and read it under his coat to shield it from the rain. But there it was, in black and white.

'Land,' Kieran breathed and they looked to one another in a moment of pure joy before embracing right there in the street.

'We have land,' Kieran cried as they danced about now, drenched by the rain but uncaring as passers-by stopped to watch, sensibly beneath umbrellas.

'*Land*, Mrs Flannery, *land*, Mr Leary,' Liam yelled to their neighbours who were smiling with them.

'It came then, lads?' Mr Leary said.

'Aye, it came.' Kieran patted the letter, now safely in his inside pocket, barely able to hold back his tears.

'You're lucky you've got such a way with words there, Liam,' Mr Leary observed. 'They don't give it away like they used to, from what I hear.'

'We'll have to pay some money off over time, but it's nothing we won't be able to handle,' Liam told him, still beaming.

'So they're providing free passage for you to cross the ocean then they'll just hand it over,' Mrs Flannery said, shaking her head in wonderment. 'Imagine that.'

Rainwater poured down upon Kieran as he looked at those old, familiar faces, lined by grief and hardship as so many of the locals were, yet finding it within themselves to rejoice in their neighbour's good fortune. He tried to take in the enormity of what this could mean. He wasn't the only one to leave; the Irish were emigrating in droves, forced to seek whatever work they could find in foreign cities or, worse still, taking to the crowded poorhouses – a wretched existence indeed. But this…this was something else altogether. This was opportunity. A fresh start in a new game. A chance.

'The great southern land,' Liam said, looking at him, then laughing at his own incredible words. 'I'm still trying to believe it.'

'Aye, you can believe it alright,' Kieran said, grinning at his brother before spying Maeve as she stood at her parents' door. 'We're going, the whole lot of us,' he said, more meaningfully now, 'as a family.' He let the emphasis rest on that last word and Maeve sent him a tremulous smile, the scales tipping back with force.

'Your father'd be well proud, lads – and your good mother too, God rest her soul,' Mr Leary said and Kieran felt the tears well and fall now. 'Never forget your roots though, boys. You're Irish first and foremost – make no mistake.'

He watched as Maeve dipped her gaze and closed the door and wondered if her father had a vial that could alter the loyalty to Ireland that ran through all their veins. It had brought them nothing but heartache so what use was it in the end?

'Not for much longer, Mr Leary,' Kieran told him, 'we'll be Australians. Free men…on Clancy land. Clancy owned.'

Far away from the weight of English oppression, no longer mere Irish pawns, pinned in their corner of the chessboard.

The dark clouds rumbled above and Kieran bared his face to the lashing sky, letting the wonderful news wash through and consume him.

'Checkmate,' he told the rain.